Emmie smiled and shook her head. Even though they worked with bands for a living, everyone got all goofy and fawning when the artists came in.

Except Emmie, of course. She'd grown up around musicians. She saw beneath the glitter to their tortured, attention-craving, twisted souls. Everyone wanted a piece of them, to be the one to get in, breach the barrier. To win their hearts. But she knew better. They didn't let anyone in. Not really. They drew people in with their dazzling charisma, and then pushed them back when they got too close.

Loving an artist *hurt*.

YOU REALLY GOT ME

Erika Kelly

BERKLEY SENSATION, NEW YORK

THE BERKLEY PUBLISHING GROUP
Published by the Penguin Group
Penguin Group (USA) LLC
375 Hudson Street, New York, New York 10014

USA • Canada • UK • Ireland • Australia • New Zealand • India • South Africa • China

penguin.com

A Penguin Random House Company

YOU REALLY GOT ME

A Berkley Sensation Book / published by arrangement with EK Publishing LLC

Berkley Sensation Books are published by The Berkley Publishing Group.
BERKLEY SENSATION® is a registered trademark of Penguin Group (USA) LLC.
The "B" design is a trademark of Penguin Group (USA) LLC.

For information, address: The Berkley Publishing Group,
a division of Penguin Group (USA) LLC,
375 Hudson Street, New York, New York 10014.

ISBN: 978-0-425-27728-7

PUBLISHING HISTORY
Berkley Sensation mass-market edition / January 2015

PRINTED IN THE UNITED STATES OF AMERICA

10 9 8 7 6 5 4 3 2 1

Cover art: Man with guitar © Bad Man Productions/Shutterstock.
Cover design by Rita Frangie.
Interior text design by Kelly Lipovich.

This book is dedicated to my grandmother,
who showed me the world through literature

ACKNOWLEDGMENTS

♪ It all started with five simple words: *You should write a book*. Thank you, Laurie.

♪ My best life began when my husband whisked me away from home. He gave me all the room in the world to grow into the woman I've become. I love you with all my heart.

♪ My books would still be shoved under the bed were it not for my critique partner and dearest friend. Thank you, Sharon, for your invaluable help and, most important, for accepting me exactly as I am.

♪ To my first reader, Olivia, thank you for swooning. I needed it more than you know.

♪ For years I studied craft—oh, boy, have I studied craft—but I didn't really hear anything until I met Jenny Crusie. You are the best and most generous teacher in the world. Thank you.

♪ And to Kevan Lyon and Leis Pederson, thank you for taking a chance on me. You've made this whole experience as lovely as it could be.

ONE

"Oh, bollocks, *Emmie*!"

Emmie Valencia's boss hollered so loudly her teeth rattled. And there was a *wall* between them. She pressed the button on her intercom and said, "Be right there." He could be such a baby.

Seconds later, the office came alive with excited voices and laughter. Her coworkers hurried down the hall, heading for the foyer.

Frontierland was back from their tour. Which meant . . .

Alex.

Her gut twisted hard. Briefly, she imagined ducking under her desk, maybe dashing to the mail room. But, of course, she wouldn't do that. She could face him. No big deal.

In fact, that's exactly what she *should* do. Talk to him as casually as she did the rest of the guys. She hated the way people looked at her whenever he came into the office. Besides, they'd ended it months ago.

One of the interns popped breathlessly into her office. "They're here." Her features flushed, she mouthed, "Flash," and pretended to fan herself. Then she darted down the hall.

Emmie smiled and shook her head. Even though they worked with bands for a living, everyone got all goofy and fawning when the artists came in.

Except Emmie, of course. She'd grown up around musicians. She saw beneath the glitter to their tortured, attention-craving, twisted souls. Everyone wanted a piece of them, to be the one to get in, breach the barrier. To win their hearts. But she knew better. They didn't let anyone in. Not really. They drew people in with their dazzling charisma and then pushed them back when they got too close. Loving an artist *hurt*.

Obviously, she'd thought Alex would be different. They'd grown up together. Their parents were best friends. Silly girl. Musicians were musicians. She'd *known* that.

As she pulled papers from the printer, she heard, "Emmie!" in a far more upbeat tone than her boss's. She spun around to find the boys from Frontierland crowding into her office.

Crap, was Alex there?

She'd keep her cool. Treat him exactly the way she treated the other guys. No big deal. Because *he* was no big deal. Not after what he'd done to her. Lifelong friendship be damned.

"Great job, you guys," she said, as the drummer pulled her to him. They played an outrageous mix of rockabilly, country, and country rock, so they dressed like badass banditos in leather, vests, and straw cowboy hats. "Have you read the reviews yet?"

"Brenda doesn't make those fuckin' scrapbooks like you do, man." The keyboardist pushed through the others to give her a hug. He smelled of whiskey and patchouli.

"Why couldn't we score Irwin as our A&R guy?" another one asked.

She winced. Her boss wouldn't sign them because she'd been dating their bass player.

As the next guy leaned in for a hug, Emmie made a quick scan of their faces. No Alex. *Good*. But right when the rhythm guitarist belted his arms around her and lifted her off the floor, Emmie caught sight of him.

Alex Paulson, clad in black leather pants and a stretched-out white T-shirt, flirted with the new receptionist across the hallway. Emmie hated that he'd do it right in front of her, of course, but mostly she couldn't believe he thought so little of their relationship that he actually felt *comfortable* doing it. Like their time together hadn't really counted.

It had to her.

Flash, the lead singer, yanked her out of the other guy's

arms and said, "There's my girl." Gorgeous in a rough way, Flash had gotten his nickname because in the middle of every show he asked the girls in the audience to "flash me your tits" so he could take a photo on his phone and post it on the band's website. Classy. "You gonna marry me yet?"

"I think I'd rather marry your fiancée. She's hot."

Just as his hand skimmed down her back heading for forbidden territory, she jerked her hips and pulled out of his embrace.

"You're no fun, Emmie Valencia."

A sharp pain sliced into her heart. Her gaze flicked over his shoulder to the office where Alex and the receptionist shared a quiet laugh. "So I've heard."

"Hey." Tilting his head, he gave her a concerned look. "I'm just playing with you."

"I know." She smiled, hoping to brush away the uncomfortable moment. God, she had to get ahold of herself.

"But if I can't get you to marry me, then can you at least get me one of those bags you got Irwin's kid?"

"You want me to score you the latest Hermès purse?"

"For my fiancée."

Emmie let out an exaggerated sigh. "What did you do this time?" She whipped her hand up. "Never mind. I don't want to hear. And you don't need me to do it—just get yourself on the list. Make a call like I did."

"Oh, come on. We're stuck with Brenda. She doesn't do shit for us. Besides, I don't have your connections. You make shit happen."

"Yes, for Irwin. And I don't *have* connections. I make them when I need to."

"I could make shit happen for you."

Their gazes caught. Behind his incessantly flirtatious vibe lived a shark of a businessman. "You offering me a job, Flash?"

A slow smile ate up his ruggedly handsome features. "Fuck, yeah."

"What kind of job?"

"What kind of job you want?"

Wasn't that just the question? She didn't want just a *job*. She wanted *inside*. Eight years on the periphery of the music industry as Irwin Ledger's personal assistant was enough. She needed to take that next obvious step to A&R coordinator—discovering bands, working with talent—and Flash couldn't help her with that. Only Irwin could.

"Flash?" his bandmate called. "Leave Em alone and get in here. Bob's waiting."

"We'll finish this convo later." Flash started to go.

"Hey, can you close the door behind you?" She didn't need to watch Alex flirting.

Unfortunately, Flash followed her gaze, got an eyeful of Alex and the receptionist, and then looked back at her with a hint of pity. He pointed a finger at her. "Golden rule, baby. Never get involved with the talent."

She smirked. "So we're *not* getting married?" So much for her resolve not to make people uncomfortable. "You know what? Leave it open. I haven't said hello to Alex yet."

He gave her an appreciative smile before taking off.

"Oh, for fuck's sake," her boss shouted. "Emmie?"

"Coming," she said into the intercom box.

"I can't imagine what's taking you so bloody long. I have a crisis, Emmie. Cri-sis."

She pressed the button. "Crisis as in you scuffed your favorite Bruno Magli chocolate suede loafers and they don't make them anymore so you need me to call the designer himself and get a pair custom-made? Or crisis as in the drummer from Wicked Beast fell off the wagon again and can't make the show tonight so I need to get to the hotel and get him sobered up?"

"You mock me. I count on you, and you mock me."

She smiled. "Two seconds." Grabbing her iPad, she spun around to the door . . . only to catch the receptionist pressing her body against Alex.

Oh, hell.

Memories slammed her. His hard chest, the spicy scent of his soap, the creak of his leather. How many times had she held him just like that?

Alex's hand wrapped around the woman's waist, pulling her tight against him. That moment of intimacy, the way Val conformed her body to his, the way her hands cupped the back of his neck, her features soft—it struck Emmie right in her core.

It was so intimate, so sensual. And it hurt. God, it hurt. Because she wasn't sexy like Val. She just . . . wasn't.

Tucking the iPad to her chest, she leaned back against the

wall, out of sight. Why did she let him affect her? It wasn't like she missed him or even wanted him. He'd cheated on her.

The sex is fine. It's just not . . . you're not wild, you know? You servicc me.

She cringed remembering his words.

A guy wants more than that.

Oh, God. She couldn't bear the memories. She charged out of her office. Just as she turned into the hallway, she saw Alcx capture Val's leg, his hand cupping her thigh, as he murmured against her mouth. Val curled around him, her expression sultry.

God. Emmie had never held him like that. Not with that kind of total abandon.

"Emmie?" Irwin shouted.

"I'm coming." Seeing Val be the woman Alex had wanted *her* to be, the kind of woman who melted around a man, who lost herself in sensation, well, it just made it hard to breathe.

The worst thing was that she'd never felt that kind of passion, that urgency. Not for any guy.

She stood there a moment longer, contemplating barging in and greeting Alex, letting the whole office know she was cool with him. Letting *him* know he didn't affect her anymore.

But then she realized something. She *wasn't* cool with him. She wasn't unaffected at all.

Because he flirted right under her nose with the receptionist.

And that was just a lousy thing to do.

Taking a deep breath, Emmie pushed off the wall and strode out into the hallway. She didn't even spare Alex a glance as she hurried into Irwin's office.

She came to a halt when she saw her boss's expression.

Lips drawn into a taut line, he held the phone to his ear. She walked right up to his ultramodern chair, which hung from the ceiling like a hammock, and he looked at her with utter relief. Immediately, his features turned slack, and he thrust the phone at her.

Placing it to her ear, she had about two seconds to get up to speed, not having the slightest idea who was on the line.

"He wants me to be there, Daddy. I'm, like, his muse. He said he for sure can't do his best work unless I'm there. Do you want this track to suck?"

"Caroline," Emmie said. "Who're we talking about?"

The girl exhaled roughly. "James. He wants me in the studio with him."

Honestly, Emmie did not have time to deal with this nonsense. "James is a drug addict, Caroline. Your dad had to drop him from the label because he couldn't fulfill his contract. Do you see why your dad wouldn't want you hanging out with James while he's out of the country?"

"So, what, I'm supposed to be all locked up because my dad's out of town? I'm an *adult*."

"Not when your dad's paying your bills, including the lawyer he keeps on retainer for your *indiscretions*."

"Oh, my God—"

"Last weekend the sound engineer got you so drunk you blacked out. Your dad and I spent seven hours racing around the city, out of our minds, trying to find you. You can't blame him if he's not comfortable giving you the run of Manhattan when he's not around."

"You don't even know what you're talking about. Rory didn't *get* me drunk. I thought I was drinking iced tea. I didn't know they were *Long Island* Iced Teas. That's not his fault. We were just hanging out. Besides, it's not like I'm going to be *alone*. You'll be here."

Tipping her head back, she blew out a breath. "Caroline. You know I'm going with your dad. Look, hanging out with James the drug addict is obviously out of the question, but let's come up with a few—"

"No, you're not."

"I'm not what?"

"Going with my dad."

"Of course I'm going with him." She glanced to Irwin, found him examining his cell phone, swinging in his chair. He didn't have a formal office, the kind with the big oak desk facing two guest chairs, a potted plant, and a filing cabinet. Why would he need a desk? No, he had a plush couch, a world-class sound system, a pinball machine, a dartboard, and a Picasso hanging on the wall.

Movement from the corner of her eye made her turn to the door. Alex stood in the threshold, a hint of remorse on his face. Her heart pounded, and her nerves tingled. But before he could take one step into the office, Irwin flew out of his chair, stalked to the door, and slammed it in her ex's face.

Emmie smiled.

Irwin stalked back to the chair, gripping the metal arm, and set it off rocking again.

"I'm not talking to either of you anymore," Caroline said. "I'm going into the studio with James because I'm his muse and he needs me. And if my dad doesn't like it, then you can just come with us and hang out in the lounge."

"I won't be able to come with you because I *am going to Australia.*"

Irwin got up, leaving the leather and chrome chair swinging. He went to the built-in media center that took up one wall and got busy shuffling through his CDs.

"You're not going to Australia! Dad said. God, why are you being such a bitch?"

Emmie closed her eyes, taking a moment before responding. "And so ends my efforts to help you. Here's your dad." With that, she handed the phone back to Irwin. "Hold your ground. She shouldn't be anywhere near James Beckman."

He put the phone back to his ear. "What did you say that made your auntie Emmie hand me back the phone?" His gaze kicked up to Emmie's. "Nothing? Are you sure? She's usually so indulgent with us." His brow furrowed. "A bitch? Ah, well, then. I'm afraid you're on your own on this one, darling. Must go, my love. Kiss, kiss." He hung up on her. "Wretched child, isn't she?"

Emmie smiled, knowing how he adored his only kid. But the smile quickly faded. "So, Australia?"

"Yes, right. Slight change of plans." He ran his hand through his messy, floppy hair. Only the silver streaking through his dark hair made him look anything close to his forty-nine years.

"We're not going?"

"That would be a *total* change of plans. Slight means only one of us isn't going."

"Irwin. We leave tomorrow."

"Emmie, darling, I'm sorry, but I can't leave Caroline alone for six weeks. I'm going to need you to stay here."

Okay, wait. For months Emmie had planned this trip. Two weeks ago one of the producers had realized his passport had

expired. She'd had to wave her wand, cast spells, and rub
magic lamps in order to push his renewal through. She'd
planned every detail down to the minute of their time there.
Down to using MapQuest to find the coffee shops closest to
the recording studios. She'd booked reservations, arranged
delivery of industry periodicals to his hotels, and spent
months researching and contacting up-and-coming bands.

Oh, and hang on. She'd spent last night *packing* for her
boss. Yes, that meant handling his black silk boxers.

Not only that, but this trip meant more than assisting
Irwin. She'd gotten him to agree to let her go off and discover
some bands of her own. So she could finally get that promotion. But now, the day before departure, he was telling her she
couldn't go. Because . . .

"Wait a minute. You want me to *babysit*?"

"Don't be ridiculous. Of course not. You're not changing
nappies. You just need to look after her."

"You want me to babysit your daughter." She said it dully,
lowering herself onto the plush leather couch. "I'm twenty-
five years old, I've worked for you for eight years—" She
flashed him a look. "Even as a high school intern I did more
for you than your own secretary. And your best use for me is
babysitting."

"You make it sound so trivial. This is my daughter we're
talking about. And you're more like a mother to her than her
own mother."

"I'm four years older than her. I'm not like her mother."

"No, you're better than her mother. And something's off
with her."

Emmie narrowed her gaze.

"More so than usual. You heard her. She's all screechy."
His phone buzzed, and he quickly answered it.

Coward.

She needed to get a handle on this situation. Heading to the
window, she glanced out, pressing close to look down to the
street twenty-seven floors below. If she focused on the steady
stream of pedestrian traffic, the yellow cabs, the exhaust-spewing
buses, she could tell herself he really was just looking out for his
daughter. But she knew better. It was so much more than that.

Oh, hell, she couldn't hold it back. The unbearable pain of

being shut out again rolled in and threatened to just *crush* her. God, it hurt.

She wanted in so badly. Why was it so elusive? All these feelings . . . God, it was her childhood all over again. Being shut out of her dad's world for not being creative enough, for not really *getting* him, had made her too sensitive to these slights. Because, truthfully? Artists didn't have a lock on creativity. She had it, too, just in other ways. The whole reason Irwin valued her as his assistant was for her ability to think outside the box. She'd proven herself an Amoeba a hundred times over. So why did he hold her back? Sure, he needed her in this role as his assistant. But she could do so much more.

She knew she was lucky to work for the top A&R guy in the business. At the best record company in the world. She didn't take it for granted, but she also knew it was time for more. If she actually stayed behind and babysat Caroline, she'd never break out of this role. At some point, she had to take the initiative and actually say no to one of his demands. She had to force him to see her in a more creative role, or she'd never have the chance to explore that side of herself. To unleash it.

Besides—*hello*?—he couldn't function without her, so how could he get through the next six weeks on the other side of the world?

She spun around, pointing a finger at him. "What are you going to do without me?"

He looked alert then. Most of the time he had a dozen very important ideas going on in his head all at once, so it was nearly impossible to gain his full attention.

Those sharp blue eyes pierced her, and she knew she had it then.

"Right," he said to the caller. "Emmie will get back to you later." He stowed his phone in the back pocket of his jeans. "I'm taking Bax with me."

Had she been standing on a trap door? Because the floor gave way, and she was in free fall. Baxter Reynolds had started as an intern five years ago. When Irwin hadn't shown any interest in promoting him, he'd attached himself to Bob, one of the other A&R guys.

And *now* Irwin was showing an interest in him? Instead of Emmie?

She didn't know what to say. "Bax?" How was *Bax* better than her?

His phone buzzed, but he ignored it as he came right up to her, close enough that she could smell the Christian Dior cologne she kept stocked for him. He brushed his hand down her arm. "I'm sorry, Em. As much as I need you with me, I can't leave Caroline alone."

"Where's her mother?"

"Well, that's the point, isn't it? I can't really count on Claire. But I *can* count on you."

See? When he did that, she caved. Irwin loved his daughter, and who else could he trust to look out for her? His entire family lived in England. Flighty, gorgeous, sexy Claire Murphy flitted around the world on a whim, barely touching down long enough to take care of anything but her most immediate and impulsive needs.

But Emmie needed more. She needed *in*. She couldn't stay his personal assistant forever. So what should she do? Of course, if Caroline were in any danger, Emmie would have to help. But the girl was twenty-one. And, sorry, but Emmie simply wasn't her mother or her big sister.

She didn't want to let Irwin down. But she was continuing to let herself down if she never took the next step—which meant taking charge of her own career.

She needed the promotion. "I'm not going to babysit Caroline, Irwin. You need me in Australia, and I need to go to Australia to see the bands I've been researching."

He let out a deep sigh. "Truth is, you've set everything up perfectly, as you always do. You've got my every moment organized and arranged to the point that I *don't* need you there."

"But you need Bax?"

"You've given me the list of bands to check out, along with the scheduled times to meet them. So, yes, I need Bax."

"I researched those bands."

"From the privacy of your office. Bax *lives* it, Emmie."

"You're saying I'm not good enough to be promoted?" She felt the sting of it, like he'd doused alcohol on a blister. *No, no, no.* That was bullcrap. She *was* good enough.

"I'm saying that I need you right where you are."

"And I need a career. Not just a job."

His phone buzzed again, and this time he checked the caller ID. "I have to take this."

"No. Please, Irwin. Not until we settle this."

"It *is* settled, Em." He said it gently. "I'm taking Bax." He punched the button on his phone. "Yes?"

"Then I quit."

Irwin's eyes flared. His features burned crimson.

She stood there, letting the words settle around her. The only sound was her own breathing, the only movement the wild and erratic beating of her heart.

Had she actually done it? Quit her coveted job?

"Wait, wait, hang on a moment," he said into the phone.

"I'm sorry, Irwin. I can't keep doing this. You have no intention of promoting me." *Standing on the periphery hurts too much.*

"You can't quit." He turned back to the phone. "Let me get back to you." Without waiting for a response, he hung up. "You can't quit." He looked utterly lost and baffled. "Why would you quit?"

"I'll find my replacement." She turned to go.

"Good God, Emmie. You cannot leave me."

"You've given me no choice."

"All right, just stop this. Stop it right now. I can't function without you, and you know that. You're threatening me. That's not a good way to get a promotion."

"It's not a threat. I told you I needed a career, and you told me you needed me right where I am. Fetching your Americanos and cajoling your landlord into letting you keep amphibians in your penthouse apartment isn't a career. I can't be your personal assistant the rest of my life. You get that, right? I've loved working for you, but it's supposed to be a stepping stone. You've just shown me it's a cage. I deserve more."

He had a strange expression, like he was listening to an incoming message from an ethereal source. "It's not right for you."

"What isn't?" He'd punched the accelerator on her pulse, making it rev so fast she went light-headed. *This is not happening.* He was *not* shutting her out of this world.

"A&R."

"I . . ." She found it hard to take a full breath. But he was wrong. Of course it was right for her. She pretty much did the job anyway. Maybe not discovering the bands, but . . . oh, God. She needed to breathe. *Deep breaths.* "That's ridiculous. I've been doing it for eight years."

"Em, look, I have to get to the studio. You simply can't quit. I won't allow it. We'll find a way to compromise, right? I want you to be happy."

"I'm not happy babysitting your daughter."

He winced. "Loud and clear."

"I need to know there's a place for me here other than going through your laundry room and drawers looking for a missing cashmere night sock."

Looking pained, he touched her arm, ignoring his buzzing phone. "Let's both think on it. Come up with a solution."

"Am I going to Australia with you tomorrow?"

"No."

She bit down hard on fear. It was scary as hell, but she had to do this.

"Emmie . . ."

She turned and walked out of the room.

TWO

It's not like Slater Vaughn didn't like lingerie. Hell, the only thing he liked better was peeling it off a woman's body. So, when the panties started flying, he tried to convince himself that catching just one single pair and meeting their manager's expectations was a no-brainer.

Clutching the microphone, taking in the screaming crowd as Ben doubled his beats on the high hat, he knew if he didn't do it this time—if he didn't snatch the underwear midair and pretend to breathe them in—the manager would bail.

And it'd be Slater's fault. He'd drive off yet another one. Which, he was pretty sure, would mean the end of the band. How many could they go through? They were getting too old for this shit.

But hell. Sniffing random underwear?

Fuck it. He couldn't do it. The panties landed like confetti around his feet. He looked toward the bar, across a sea of ecstatic faces, where John, the manager, yanked a bill out of his wallet and tossed it on the counter. He got up to go—just when Slater should've launched into the first verse of the song—and looked him dead in the eye. John shook his head with a bitter frown and strode out of the club.

Shit.

He didn't want to see his bandmates' reactions. He especially didn't want to see Derek's. The guys kept playing, and Slater tried to pick up the beat, find his way back to the opening, but he couldn't. He had to know if he'd just put a bullet through the brains of the band. The other guys would probably forgive him, but while he loved them like brothers, they were just instrumentation. Snatch could carry on without them. Derek, though? He was the CEO of the band. If he'd had enough, if Slater had finally pushed him too far . . .

Derek would walk. He'd have to. He'd kept up his end of things—the bookings, publicity, social media. Christ, he was *Eddie Valencia's* son—success in this industry was his legacy. What the hell was Derek doing with Slater anyway? Whose only legacy was failure?

The melody kept looping back, and each time Slater let it pass. Because he *knew*. It was different tonight—he'd sensed a change in Derek. A growing impatience. Was tonight the breaking point?

Time to find out. Slater turned—just as he sang the opening line, just as the crowd started screaming—and found Derek . . . jamming.

That's it. Head lowered, fully concentrating on the bass. Not a care in the world.

What the hell?

After the set ended, the guys gathered around their usual table near the stage. Slater headed for the bar, grabbed the beer that always waited for him, and let the girls swoop in. Sure, he'd have to face it. But, hey, he could stall a few minutes while the girls rubbed his dick or pressed their tits on him. It's not like the guys expected anything different.

Yeah, okay, no stalling. Not tonight. He hoisted his beer and nodded his thanks to the bartender, pushing a bill his way. As Slater disentangled himself from the girls, one of them slipped her hand into the back pocket of his jeans and cupped his ass, giving it a lusty squeeze. He turned to see which one and wasn't disappointed. The blonde with the huge tits and juicy lips. Perfect. He leaned down, licked the shell of her ear, and said, "Twenty minutes."

"Mmmkay." She breathed it like she was two seconds away from a climax, bringing her other hand to his cock and rubbing it with the heel of her hand.

As Slater approached the table, he watched Derek clear out the groupies. They scattered—all of them except one. Only she didn't look like a groupie. She looked . . . well, Slater didn't know what she looked like, other than maybe a teacher. A kindergarten teacher. She wore her dark hair long and straight—no particular style—and he could actually see her complexion, uncovered as it was by makeup. What was she doing at their table? She glanced up at him and smiled. All sweet and innocent, like he was her date at the movie theater, bringing the popcorn and soda.

Like she didn't want anything from him at all.

It felt like Slater stopped moving. Even though his legs continued toward the table and cold beer slid down his throat, it felt like time just . . . stopped. But it hadn't, because he wound up at the table, standing behind an empty chair. He took her in—the shiny hair that ended in a slight bounce. She was pure, innocent, clean . . . and yet she had a mischievous look in her eyes that made him wonder. She turned back to Ben, the drummer, giving him her attention like she actually cared what he had to say—not like she was trying to get with him.

Slater set his beer bottle down. It was go time. "Come at me, bitches."

Derek tilted his head. "You didn't catch the panties, man."

Slater returned Derek's challenging look.

"John told you if you ignored one more thing he wanted you to do, he'd quit. And you know what?"

"Yeah. I know. He quit." Feigning nonchalance, Slater glanced over his shoulder to the bar, found the blonde watching. He gave her a slow smile, and she nodded with a deliberate lick of her glossy lips.

"The guy was a douche." Cooper drained his beer.

"The *guy* was our fifth manager." Derek scraped his chair back and stood, folding his arms over his chest. "And last."

Get to the fucking point.

"You want to know why I'm not losing my shit right now?" Derek asked.

The woman looked between them, completely unfazed,

like she didn't notice the crackling tension. Slater just cocked his head, pretending like he cared. Well, he did care. He cared a lot. But he wasn't going to let Derek know that.

"Because I have a solution to our problem."

Slater held Derek's gaze, curious but not giving anything away.

"We're done with them. Managers, agents, fuck 'em. We obviously don't play well with others. So why don't we manage ourselves—"

"You mean, *you* manage us," Slater said.

"Are *you* gonna do it?"

"Fuck no."

"Let him finish," Ben said, his arm stretched across the back of the woman's chair. Man, she sat so primly, and yet, there was something about her. Like she had a naughty secret. Who the hell *was* she?

"I'm twenty-seven years old," Derek said. "I don't know about you, but I'm not fucking around. We've got one chance to make a go of this band. I'm too old to start another one. Look, I can manage us, right?" He looked around the table, and everyone nodded in agreement.

He continued. "We don't need anyone telling us what we should look like, how we should act. What kind of music to play. I mean, the hell with John, right? Telling Slater to capitalize on his 'man whore' image? How's that going to get us a record contract?"

"Totally agree," Ben said. "What's that got to do with the music, man?"

"*Snatch*ing panties out of the air?" Cooper snorted. "Fuckin' lame."

Derek got energized. "Exactly. Dude was an idiot. Anyhow, we've already got a following. We just need someone to get us bigger gigs, get us some publicity." Derek waited for a response. Pete's gaze roamed the room, barely hanging on to the conversation. Ben nodded warily, and Cooper rubbed the label off his bottle.

"Slater?" Derek said.

"I guess." To be perfectly honest, Slater was like a lizard, wanting nothing more than to sun himself on a rock. With a good book in one hand and a spectacular pair of tits in the other. He liked singing and writing—well, he *needed* to write. Couldn't stop the lyrics and tunes from coming. But the rest of it? Couldn't give a shit.

Not that he didn't want to be famous. Huge. A mega–rock star. Sure. But Derek would take care of that end of things.

And who was this woman sitting with them? She didn't look like a publicist or someone in the music industry. Plain hair, plain clothes, not much makeup . . .

And why did his brain reject the word *plain* when he took her in?

"Bottom line," Derek continued, "we don't need someone to mold us into some kind of fake image. We don't need anyone *building* us into rock stars. What we need is someone to get us to that next level. Because, guys? We've done all we can here. We might be the biggest college band in Texas, but that's all we are. And we've been that for too long. If we don't take it to the next level, we become just another sad wedding band. I'm not down for that."

Hell, no. "And how do we find this person?" Slater kept his tone snarky.

Derek motioned to the woman, looking pleased with himself. "Emmie."

Slater's gaze slid to her. She smiled sweetly. *Her?* Turning back to Derek, Slater gave him a look that said, *What the fuck?*

Derek scowled. "I told you she was coming out. I've been talking about it for the past couple of days. Haven't you been listening?"

Slater'd been working the last two nights. What had he missed? Cooper tossed a damp, wadded-up napkin at him. "His sister, asswipe."

The woman stood up, and he couldn't help noticing her plain V-neck T-shirt and floral skirt. Shouldn't she be going to class or something? Working at Gap?

"Hi, I'm Emmie."

Did she live on a prairie? Seriously, she looked like she churned her own butter.

Oh. Oh, shit. *Emmie.* Of course. "You work for Irwin Ledger." Biggest A&R guy in the business. Shouldn't she look a little more rock 'n' roll? He'd always had an image in his head of what Derek's sister—not just an A&R chick from New York City, but the daughter of Eddie Valencia, a fucking jazz legend—would look like, and this wasn't it.

"I do," she said. "But I'm taking a leave of absence."

"Here's the deal," Derek said. "Irwin's in Australia right now, so we've got Emmie for six weeks. She's in Austin to check out some bands. So, we give her room and board, and in exchange she'll get us gigs and promote us. Emmie's the shit. Believe me, if anyone can get us to that next level, it's her. So, what do you think?"

"Fucking great." Pete pushed his chair back. "Now, I'm gonna go get laid."

"Wait," Derek said.

"Are you gonna get us a record deal?" Ben asked.

"Hey, hey, that's not what she's here for." Derek sounded a little too protective. If his sister needed protecting from a simple question, how the hell was she going to *live* with them?

"Isn't that the next level?" Cooper asked.

"No," Derek said. "The next level is getting exposure beyond Texas college towns—"

Emmie cut her brother off. "I did play Irwin your demo a while back, but he wasn't interested."

"Why not?" The way her head snapped toward Slater told him he'd sounded too harsh. Well, it was a damn good demo.

"Don't put her on the spot," Derek said. "Let her just get us some gigs, okay?"

"You worried I'm going to drive off your little sister?"

"You've driven everyone else off." Derek gave Slater a hard look.

"Okay, jeez." Emmie touched her brother's arm, giving it a gentle rub. It was a soothing gesture, and Slater felt it on his own skin.

"*Jeez?*" He waited for a wounded look, but she just kept her serene smile. "Really? Is that how they talk in New York City?"

"What's your problem, Vaughn?" Derek said. "Do you want this or not? Because we don't have a lot of options left."

Slater couldn't help filling in the omitted part of the sentence, *because of you.* "I need another beer." He waved the empty bottle to his blonde, and she immediately spun around, flagging down the bartender.

"She says *jeez*, Derek. How the hell is she supposed to live with us?"

The guys all looked to Derek. Legit question.

Slater scrubbed a hand over his chin. "And live where, exactly? The *five* of us can't fit in the house. How do we add a sixth?" He gave Derek a meaningful look, hoping he got the message. Not just another person, but a woman. With all the debauchery that went on, adding a Girl Scout would never work.

"Ben and I are moving into the garage," Derek said. "She can have our room. It's only temporary."

Across the hall from *Slater's* bedroom?

"Why would you want your sister living with us?" If he had a sister, he wouldn't expose her to guys scratching their balls and belching as they stumbled around the house hung-over and sporting hard-ons.

Warm fingers clasped around his upper arm, and the blonde thrust a beer bottle at him. "Thanks, babe," he said.

Derek shot a look to his sister and smiled. "What do you think, Em? Think you can handle us?"

"Oh, come on. I've been around musicians all my life. And you have no idea what I've seen as Irwin's assistant."

"The bigger issue," Ben said, "is, you know, hooking up."

Pete spat out a mouthful of beer. "*Hooking up?* What the fuck? I'm not banging Derek's sister."

"Thank you, Pete," Emmie said, like he'd just defended her honor.

"It's not you I'm worried about." Ben turned to Slater. In fact, all the guys looked at him.

Me? Like he'd get it on with an American Girl doll, prairie edition? She probably wore waist-high cotton underpants. If she'd ever even had sex, which seemed unlikely, she'd been flat on her back looking up at the ceiling, waiting for the guy to finish.

Not sure why he was thinking about her having sex.

Must be that saucy look in her eye. Underneath that whole-some exterior, he suspected she had a whole sideshow going on in there. She had *something* going on. He just couldn't figure out what.

"Slater won't touch my sister," Derek said. "That's a deal breaker. He wouldn't end our friendship or the band over it."

"He fucked the manager before John," Cooper said.

Actually, he *hadn't* fucked her. That had been the problem. But the why never mattered, did it? Just the results.

"Okay, hang on," Emmie said. "I'm here for six weeks. No one's getting naked. Guys, seriously, I'm here to work."

"You'd be surprised what Slater can accomplish in six weeks," Cooper said.

Emmie sighed. "Yeah, yeah, he's hot. I get it. Sorry, just . . . not my thing." She glanced at his blonde, who pressed against him. "Seriously, you guys have nothing to worry about. I don't party. I don't drink, do drugs, or sleep around, and I don't get involved with musicians. Period. So, see? I don't want you, and you certainly don't want me. Perfect match."

"So, are we good?" Derek asked.

The blonde's hand slid down Slater's ass, diving between his legs, and curving around to his junk, her fingernail scraping over his balls. He nearly buckled right then. "Fucking good."

Holy mother of God. She hadn't had a single cup of coffee, and yet her body vibrated like a live wire.

Seriously, what had she done?

She'd taken a gamble, and she had no idea if she could win. Just because she had six weeks in Austin didn't mean she'd discover a band in that time.

Not like she was panicking or anything.

Six weeks.

Her lungs seized. She was totally panicking. Finding a band took total immersion in the music scene—something she'd never been able to do while serving her boss's constant demands—but it also took a degree of luck. Could she find the talent in such a short time period?

Heavy footfalls on the stairs pulled her mind away from the list she'd been working on. "Em?" Derek called.

"In here." Quickly adding the last tip from her friend at Capitol Records, she closed out the document. With all the information she'd gathered from the promotions guys in Austin and her own research, she'd put together a comprehensive list of bands to visit. She had enough acts to fill up her calendar for her whole stay.

"Hey." Her brother leaned in the doorway, hands braced on the frame. Even his Best Buy uniform couldn't contain all that made up Derek Valencia. From the bulging muscles to the tats and leather bands around his wrists and neck, he screamed pure badass. "I'm off. Just making sure you're all settled in."

"Yep. I'm good."

"Uh-huh." One side of his mouth hitched up in a look that said he wasn't buying it.

"No, I mean, sure, I'm a little worried. But I'm mostly excited. This is a great opportunity to, you know, get to the next level. Yeah, I *wanted* to go to Australia—it meant something to me that he was taking me. But this is even better, I think. I get to prove myself on my own."

Dipping his head, he smiled. "You're freaking out."

She let out a shaky breath. "I'm freaking out."

He came into the room, worrying the bands around a wrist. "You know you're awesome, right? I mean, there's nothing you can't do."

"Well, I guess we'll see about that."

She knew that troubled look. He had something to say. "Yeah, but I mean, even if Irwin doesn't promote you, you'll get a job somewhere else. You've got enough connections and—"

"He'll promote me." Of course he would.

"I know. I'm just saying if he's dumb enough not to, you'll get an A&R gig with another label. Irwin's great, sure, but he's not the only game in town."

She got up to face him. "But he's the best game. And I'm this close to getting inside. All I have to do is discover a band, and I'm in. Anyone else will hire me as a secretary. You think I haven't gotten offers? They all want me to do for them what I do for Irwin. But I'm not going to start over with someone else. Not after putting in eight years with Irwin."

"Inside what, Em? You're already in the music industry. You always have been."

"I've always been on the *periphery*. I don't want to book a tour bus. I want to work *with* bands. I want to be in the studio, helping them choose their first single. The important things."

Derek's lips pressed together, his brows pulling in.

Did he not think she could do it? "What? If you have something to say, then just say it."

"No, I just . . . I can relate. We both work so hard, we're both damn good at what we do, and yet we're still on the outside."

"Oh, my God, you're a *musician*. You're in the club. I'm a glorified secretary. I sit on the other side of the closed door. It's not the same thing at all."

"Of course it is. How many years have I been inviting A&R guys to come see us, sending out our demo, and I get nothing but rejection. It sucks."

She'd never thought of it like that. He was right. How funny she'd only ever seen his musical abilities as making him an insider. Well, the fix for him seemed simple enough. "I know you don't want to use Dad's connections, but he said—"

"No. I won't be associated with him, you know that. He's an asshole."

She knew Derek needed to achieve success on his own. The intense need to prove their dad wrong—to become the self-supporting musician her dad said he'd never be—fueled his every move.

Well, she wouldn't give him platitudes or make baseless promises. Of course she'd help him, but she needed to go to more shows, spend time with them to see how they worked as a band, before she could assure him of the success that eluded him.

He rubbed the back of his neck, drawing in a breath. "It's just . . . it's all too familiar, you know? This frustration. This wanting in all the time."

"What do you mean? Familiar how?" She had a sense of something, could feel the energy of it like a hand hovering just over her skin but not making contact.

He tipped his head back, pulling his bottom lip into his mouth. "It's like . . . Dad all over again. He just . . . he never fucking let us in."

Nothing was more vivid to her than sitting on the floor outside the basement studio in her flannel nightgown listening to the laughter, the disjointed music through the walls. She could feel the pressure of her dad's hand on the small of her back—to this day she hated when a guy guided her that way—as he shut the door behind her. *Go see your mom*, he'd say, before shutting her out. "But you were with him all the time. He let you into his studio."

"You're kidding me, right? He fucking tormented me. His

friends would ask me to jam with them, and then my own father would make fun of me. Make those shitty comments about how my music didn't count because it was just noise. That I cared more about my 'costumes' than about learning technique. He always had to tear me down because I'm not some virtuoso like he is."

"Derek, God, I didn't know that. I mean, of course I heard you guys fighting all the time. But I didn't know he did that to you in front of his friends. That's awful." How could she have known? She'd been shut out of the studio.

He lifted his arms, the muscles bunching, like he wanted to hurl something, and then he looked around. Finally, he crossed them over his chest. "He's an asshole, and I never understood how you could've worked for him all those years."

"He's my dad." Other than musicians, her dad had difficult relationships with everyone. His son had moved out the day after high school ended, his wife had divorced him, and his girlfriends came and went like patients in a waiting room.

But he was her *dad*.

"He treated us like shit."

"I know that. But he's an artist. He—"

"Stop." He shook his head. "I can't listen to you defend his asshole behavior. I'm just saying it all feels too familiar. Me wanting to get signed by a label, and you wanting this damn promotion. I just . . . I don't want Irwin jerking the same strings Dad always did, making you feel you're not good enough. You *are* good enough. You're better than good enough. Em, you're amazing. No one gets shit done the way you do."

"He didn't say I wasn't good enough." She drew in a tight breath. "He said it wasn't right for me."

"What isn't?"

"A&R."

"What the fuck does that mean? That's all you've been doing the last eight years."

This was good. She could throw her deepest fears onto the screen and see her brother's reaction. Her brother knew her better than anyone, and he wouldn't lie. She shrugged. "Maybe it means I'm not creative enough. I'm obviously not musically inclined. Maybe to guide an artist's career you have to be one yourself. You know?" She watched him carefully.

"Is Irwin a musician?"

"Not really. He's always in the studio with his bands, and he knows what he's doing." No one could question Irwin's creative genius.

Derek stroked the short patch of whiskers on his chin, looking thoughtful. "I don't know. It makes sense—how else can you relate to the work, you know? How else can you recognize talent in its primitive form if you don't understand music?" He gazed off unseeingly. "Maybe he's right. Maybe A&R isn't right for you."

The arrow pierced her heart, giving a jolt so violent it practically lifted her off the ground.

So her brother agreed. She *wasn't* creative enough.

"But who cares?" he continued. "There're a dozen other jobs you'd be great at. Publicity, management. Christ, Em, you could do anything. Not just because you're smart, resourceful, and fucking tenacious, but because working with Irwin's given you exposure to literally everything. You don't need him or A&R anymore."

No. "I don't want any other job—I only want to work with the artists creatively. Besides, I know this job inside and out. So what if I can't help them in the studio—they don't need me for that. That's what the producer and the sound engineer are for. I'm creative in a different way—a problem-solving way. And you know what? Bax might have a better sense of which producer should work with which band, but I can guarantee you there's no way he'll ever be better than I am at making the decisions that are important to a band's career."

Breathing too quickly, she set her hands on her hips. Her body shook with how right she felt.

Derek's slow smile started before he cocked a finger gun at her. "Amen, Sister. Fucking A. That's the Emmie I know and love."

She smiled. "I feel *so* much better."

He laughed. "I can see that. Listen, I'm out. Can't afford to lose a paycheck."

She followed him out of her room, knowing the fear that chased him. At some point, most bands broke up for economic reasons. The guys got married, had kids, had bills to pay. They grew up. Every day that passed took him one step away from the luxury of being able to wait it out.

At the bottom of the stairs, she rubbed his back. "We'll get you there, Derek."

He gave her a tentative smile, and her heart ached for him. "If anyone can help us, I know you can. I'll see you tonight."

After the door closed behind him, determination set in. She wouldn't just get Snatch some gigs and put together their press kit. No, she'd do more.

In fact, what about that singer her dad had been talking about? Piper Lee not only wrote her own songs, but she was gorgeous and sexy, and had movie-star charisma.

He'd said she was gearing up for her first big tour. She'd need an opening act, wouldn't she? Of course, Emmie'd have to see Snatch live a few more times, get a better feel for their stage presence, but in the meantime, she'd do some research.

Imagine Snatch opening for a rising star like Piper Lee.

Emmie would totally make that happen for her brother.

THREE

Emmie slipped the folded piece of paper in her pocket and headed downstairs. Time to address her second agenda. The secret one.

It felt weird to be alone in this house. Thrift-store furniture, bare walls, bookshelves that held nothing but a basketball and some empty beer bottles . . . the place felt like a well-used fraternity house. Entering the all-white kitchen, she immediately spied the ground beans her brother had left out for her. The aroma, rich and robust, filled the room. She tipped the beans into the filter, set the carafe under the faucet, and thought, *Should I really be doing this?*

Well, she'd already gotten the contact information for Piper's manager, finished compiling her research, filled the dates on her calendar—and it was only eight in the morning—so, yeah, she could spend some time on herself.

She stilled, listening for sounds, before pulling her secret list out of her pocket.

Her brother had made it clear she had the place to herself until at least noon. They'd all arranged their work schedules so they could get off at four, leaving plenty of time for rehearsals and gigs. Slater tended bar at the hottest club in town, so he didn't come home until at least three in the morning. Later, more likely, since she guessed he did his hooking up after that. Derek assured her she wouldn't see him until at least noon.

So, she was good. All the time in the world to address her personal issue. Unfolding the list and smoothing it on the counter, hope unfurled in her chest when she read the words. *My Body Electric.* She'd thought of a dozen titles—Getting Wild, Unleashing the Inner Vixen—but nothing had hit her as hard as the Walt Whitman poem. She loved the whole concept of rejoicing in her sexuality, her femininity. Besides, what if someone found the list in her purse or on her dresser? *Can you imagine?* She would die if one of the guys found it. *Body Electric* wouldn't mean anything to them.

But, honestly, it wasn't like she had sexual hang-ups. She and Alex had done it in bathrooms, the office supply room, even in a utility closet at a gig in Greenwich Village. Hadn't he liked *any* of it? He'd certainly seemed to at the time. But he'd said she wasn't passionate. She wasn't wild.

What did *wild* mean, exactly? No, she hadn't pole danced for him. And she'd never been so carried away she'd screamed when she came. Did anybody really do that?

But, God, to say she'd *serviced* him.

The humiliation burned in her chest, an ember that flared and sparked every time she thought of it. She'd been so secure in her relationship. Talking about him in the office as though they were a solid, happy couple, when all along everyone knew what he was doing on the road . . . everyone but her.

It made her feel so inadequate. Of course she knew *he* was the jerk for cheating on her. But that didn't take away the deep, enduring sense that she just wasn't sexy enough.

He'd struck her where it hurt the most. In her core—her femininity. She'd always suspected she wasn't all that sexy. His behavior—his *words*—had only reinforced it.

She wasn't *hot.*

Okay, okay. *Stop this.* She'd made her checklist, for goodness' sake. She was *working* on it.

She'd get in touch with her sensuality. Ignite that flame that surely glowed deep within. *You can't be sexy if you don't feel sexy.* And then she'd meet the right kind of guy. No more musicians. God, never again. No, a good guy. A solid guy. A guy she could *trust.* She could let herself go with someone like that.

Coffee ready, she poured herself a cup, then looked into the fridge for creamer. Yuck. Crud caked the shelves—probably spilled milk, leaked sauces. Other than some decaying take-out boxes, she found beer bottles . . . and more beer bottles.

Okay, she needed to talk to the guys. While she wasn't going to become the housekeeper, she did need to eat. She wouldn't do their laundry, but she would happily cook for them. Because she needed food. And not crap. She'd talk to them. Maybe they'd all put money in, and she'd do the shopping and cooking. *That* she could live with.

She didn't drink her coffee black, so she dumped it in the sink and opened the sliding glass door. The heat felt wonderful, and the air smelled fragrant, so she stripped off her T-shirt and shorts, setting them on the counter. Then, she stepped outside in her red bikini.

On to the first challenge on her list: skinny dipping.

Checking out the backyard—a concrete patio, a small kidney-shaped swimming pool, a tall wooden fence, and all kinds of weird foliage that looked like elephant ears towering over it—she made very sure no one could see her.

The bathroom window looked out onto the backyard, so if Slater got up to use it, he would definitely see her. But how likely was it that he would wake up this early? Four hours after crashing?

Come on. She was safe. No excuses.

She pulled the tie at the back of her neck, but the cups of her bikini remained stubbornly over her breasts. All she had to do was yank on the bow at her back, and the girls would spring free. Instead, though, she stripped off the bottoms. Okay, so, halfway there . . .

Just do it. She was sick of herself already. She tugged the last tie protecting her modesty, flung the bikini top aside, and dove right into the pool.

The shock of the cold water made her eyelids snap open, and she watched the bubbles swirl around her as she pawed her way to the surface. She broke through, gasping for air. *Oh, God, that's cold.* She clung to the wall, and her legs fluttered. Scraping the hair off her face, she watched the ripples arc across the pool.

When her body got used to the temperature, she started to notice how the water felt as it churned around her. It rumbled between her legs, creating shock waves across her skin. Her nipples hardened, and she pushed off the wall, enjoying the rush of sensation. She kicked, doing a butterfly stroke, loving the cool water gliding across her skin.

Oh, I like this.

Not ten minutes into the set, and Snatch's energy electrified the club. Emmie stood in a sea of moving, shrieking bodies, her gaze fixed on Slater. Holy smokes, the man was hot. Not just his hard, sculpted body, but his whole look. He kept his thick dark hair cut short but stylish. His tight black T-shirt stretched across well-defined muscles and a broad chest, and his worn jeans hugged an extremely tight and perfectly round ass.

But he was more than just an incredibly hot guy. He had presence. He didn't just sing. He sang to *someone*. Well, several someones, since he shifted his attention from one girl to another, holding long enough with each to make her feel singled out. *Noticed.*

Something about Slater just . . . riveted. That man could sing.

She'd watched a couple of bands on Facebook earlier in the day, after her swim. They were all right, she guessed. Hard to say if they had potential or not. Maybe she was too new at looking for talent. But Snatch . . . she *knew*.

Her phone buzzed in her pocket, and she reluctantly took her eyes off the stage. Alex's name lit up the screen.

Alex? What did *he* want? She needed to pay attention to the show, but curiosity compelled her to answer. "Hello?"

"Hey, Em. How's it going?"

Really? Small talk? Since she'd caught him in the act all those months ago, they hadn't talked once. *And now he wants to chat?* "Great."

"You're at a show?"

She had to press the phone to her ear to hear him over the music. "Yep. What's up? What do you need?"

"Ouch. Come on, Em. We've been friends forever."

Friends? Friends didn't . . . She drew in a deep breath. Not the time or place to get into it with him. "Alex, seriously, I can hardly hear you. What do you want?"

"I just, uh . . . Do you want to go outside and talk?"

Just then, Slater lifted the mic, tilting his head back and knocking out a note that had such clarity, such perfect pitch, such *emotion*, she all but stopped breathing to hold on to it and ride it out with him.

"Em?"

"Yeah, I'm here. I'm just . . . God, can he sing."

"Who? What band? Where are you?"

She slid off the stool, making her way to the stage. "Derek's. I'm in Austin. They've got serious potential." Slater could be a superstar. If he wanted it enough, if he focused. But everything she'd heard about him led her to believe he'd just languish at the college level for a few more years before sputtering out and becoming a manager at Best Buy. He was a slacker who cared more about his groupies than his career.

"Em? It's too loud. Should I call you back?"

Bodies knocked into her as the crowd erupted in wild applause at the end of the song.

"Just say what you have to say." Curiosity led her to the red neon Exit sign, though, and she stepped out into the warm September air.

"Yeah, all right. Listen, Flash told me . . ." He paused, and she leaned against the brick wall of the club.

What had Flash told him? That'd she been pining for him? Because that wasn't true. Just because she'd asked Flash to close the door . . . God, she hoped Flash hadn't said anything that would lead Alex to believe she still cared about him. Because she didn't. "What? Flash told you what?"

"Look, I shouldn't have done that. With Val. Right outside your office. I wasn't thinking."

A dozen responses danced across her mind. *No problem. Hey, you can flirt with whoever you like.* But nothing came out of her mouth. It *had* been a rotten thing to do.

"I want us to get along," Alex said.

"In other words, Flash told you not to piss off Irwin's assistant."

"No. Not at all. It's not like that. It's about you. Us. We used to be friends and now . . ."

Now what? *You screwed your brains out on the road.* She didn't think they could ever be friends again.

"I shouldn't have been such a dick, messing around with Val like that right in front of you."

"Whatever. Look, I have to watch the band. Let's—"

"No, not whatever. I'm sorry, Em. And I really want to be friends again."

"I don't see that happening, Alex. You . . . God, you treated me like dirt." She'd never had this conversation with him, and while she didn't want to have it just then, she couldn't keep the words from charging out. "Why didn't you just break up with me before you guys left? It didn't have to be like this."

"I know. But you're not easy to break up with. You took care of me. I miss that." He paused again. "You're good, Em."

"Not good enough, apparently."

"Hey, you're the one who started drifting."

"What?" How could he say something like that?

"Oh, come on. Soon as you got us signed and we started working with Bob, you started pulling away."

Unbelievable. "Whatever you have to say to live with yourself." Blaming her because he couldn't keep it in his pants?

When the door to the club opened, she could hear the intro to the next song. She quickly held it open to peer inside. The audience seemed to know this one because they started screaming, jumping up and down. She thought maybe some girls up front were crying.

Slater had his eyes closed, like the song brought up emotions too powerful to bear. And then his hand flexed on the mic, his mouth opened, and he keened. There was just no other word for it.

She blew out a breath, forcing her attention back on Alex. "Listen, Alex, I appreciate the apology, but I really should go."

"Hey, listen. I've got a friend in a band out there. You should check him out."

"I'll definitely do that. Why don't you text me the information?"

"Will do."

She cut the connection and entered the club.

The whole world narrowed to the haunting sound of pure pain coming out of Slater Vaughn. And then he gasped for a breath, lifted the bottom of his T-shirt to swipe the perspiration off this forehead, and launched into the bridge.

Take it back, take it back,
You don't get to say those words
Take it back, take it back,
They're mine. You left. You lose

Tears streamed down the girls' faces. How did he do that? She could feel her own eyes burning. And, really, she wasn't even susceptible to rock stars. He was good.

A new chord progression started, and the song shifted again. Goodness, the crowd was having seizures. Slater fell to his knees.

Puncture me, again and again, I don't mind

It's the only way I know I'm here
Without the wounds you might never even see me,
So go ahead and puncture me
At least I know I'm alive

Her stomach churned with emotion as she watched Slater's head tip back, his features twisted in agony, as he sang.

Puncture me
Leave a scar
You'll never see me,
But I'll always know you're there

The song came to an abrupt end with a clash of instruments that sounded like a car crash. The audience screamed, stomped their feet, and clapped thunderously.

Slater smiled. *Good God.* Slater clutching a mic, voice soaked in emotion, wrung her heart out. But Slater smiling, his eyes sparkling with mischief, lit her up inside. Standing near the stage, all she could see were arms waving, thrashing, reaching. His voice, his energy, swept her away.

And when had she made it to the stage? She stood dead center, two rows back. Perspiration glistening on his skin, he held the gaze of first one, then another girl in the crowd. The corners of his mouth tipped up in a sexy smile, and it made her want to know what he was thinking, who he was—

His gaze hit hers. Adrenaline punched through her system,

and energy sparked along her spine. He looked at her so intensely, like he knew her intimately. Like if she reached out to him, he'd grab her, yank her onto the stage, and pull her body up hard against his.

Oh.

Heat exploded in her core, radiating out in shimmery waves, making her legs go weak. And then he looked away, leaving her feeling limp and ragged.

Okay, what had just happened? Shaken, she wove through the sea of bodies toward the table with the Reserved sign on it and slumped in a chair to watch the rest of the show.

Body Electric? Who needed a checklist when she could just watch Slater perform and feel all the things she'd never felt before.

The man was *good.*

———

Slater stumbled out of bed and made his way to the bathroom. His head hurt, his throat burned, and his dick was hard enough to break through wallboard.

Standing in front of the toilet, he heard a splashing sound through the open window. They didn't have someone to clean their pool, so . . . ? He stepped around the toilet and gazed outside. Vision still blurry from not nearly enough sleep, it took him a moment to make sense of what he saw.

Luscious pink nipples poked out of the water. Sudden awareness wiped out the haze of exhaustion, and he leaned against the window, full-on staring. Derek's sister did the backstroke, dark hair fanning out, breasts arching out of the water with each lift of an arm. The curve of her waist, the flare of her hips, the splash of water with each stroke of her feet . . . Christ, he hadn't imagined he could get harder than he already was, but he fucking hurt.

But, wait, *Emmie?* The prairie girl?

Skinny dipping?

———

With her eyes closed, the sun burning her back, Emmie sliced her arms through the cool water. Turned out she loved skinny dipping so much, she'd swum every day this week. She loved the water rushing over her bare skin, loved the feeling of wantonness. She couldn't say it aroused her—not, like, on fire, *I have to go have sex right now*—but it did make her feel aware of her body in a way she hadn't been before. The day before she'd tried to touch herself, hoping the awareness would spark into arousal with the stroke of a finger, but she found the water washed away the slickness, so . . . nothing had really ignited.

Today, she thought she might try touching herself on the chaise—if she could get past the uneasy feeling someone might be watching. She'd checked from every angle, and it seemed they had total privacy back here, but did she really want to take the chance? She kind of did.

Flipping over, she pushed off the wall at the far end of the pool and drifted under the water, reveling in the muffled stillness. Maybe she'd wrap a towel around her, cover up a little, do it that way. But, no, that wouldn't be as bold. And wasn't that the whole point? To get wild, she had to be fearless, daring. How could she find her rapture if she held back?

Popping her head out of the water to take a breath, she realized she'd reached the steps in the shallow end. She got out of the pool, pushing the hair off her face and swiping the droplets away from her mouth and nose.

A figure at the edge of her peripheral vision sent fear spiking through her. Slater. He just stood there, like it was totally normal to see her naked. "Oh, my God." In the split second that followed, her brain registered the distance to the towel on the chaise—too far—and without thinking she jumped back into the shallow end, holding her hands over her breasts. "What are you doing here?"

"I live here."

"God, Slater. Go away."

But he just stood there. It was so odd to think of him as a rock star here at home, out of context, because he looked like such a frat boy. No, not just a frat boy. More like the Grand Poobah. He wasn't just good looking. He was big—at least six-three—all sculpted muscles, and stunningly gorgeous. No tats, no piercings, no messy hair, no leather wristbands. He didn't look anything like a rocker.

"You're supposed to be sleeping."

He cocked his head. "I am? Why's that?"

"Stop it. God. Why would you *do* something like this?"

He crouched at the side of the pool, giving her the full force of those penetrating blue-gray eyes. "Why didn't he like the demo?"

"Excuse me?"

He didn't answer, but his gaze bore into hers, insistent.

"Could you please go back in the house?"

"Just answer me. What reason did he give?" His dark hair, cropped close to his head, stuck up, making him look like he'd come from the salon and not from bed.

"Back up, for God's sake. What is your problem?" She held on to the rim of the pool, her body pressed to the wall so he couldn't see anything—well, of course he'd already seen everything. Crap, had she shaved her bikini line? She'd thought she'd be alone. Her eyes squeezed shut. She didn't think she'd shaved there.

Just kill me now.

He leaned slightly forward until his face was too close. Her heart pounded, and her muscles tightened. But then, she had to admit, she didn't see a guy who was leering at her. Didn't see a guy interested in seeing her naked at all.

She just saw a guy who genuinely wanted to know why he'd been rejected. "He said you don't know who you are yet."

Frowning, he gazed out at the elephant ears. Then, he reached for her towel, shook it out, and held it open for her.

"I'm not getting out of the pool with you standing there."

"What does that mean? We 'don't know who we are yet'?" He looked so contemplative, like the comment ate away at him. "What does that mean?" He turned away from her, still holding out the towel, so she hoisted herself out of the pool, water streaming down her naked body, and quickly snatched it out of his hand.

The moment she'd finished wrapping it around her, he turned back and said, "We know exactly who we are. People *like* us. You see them. You see the response we get."

She didn't want to tell him her thoughts yet, so she just lifted the bottom of the towel and wiped her face.

"What did he mean?"

"I can't speak for him. He didn't say anything else, so it wouldn't be fair for me to guess what he meant. He doesn't explain. He's intuitive. He just knows." She shrugged, feeling the water from her hair saturate the back of the towel.

"Do you agree with him?"

She almost smiled. Slater didn't seem like the kind of guy to value her opinion. Or to care what someone thought of his demo. "I have some thoughts, but I'd rather not talk about it until I've seen the show a few more times. Besides, you know how subjective it is. Everyone has his own taste. Just because—"

"Don't bullshit me. I know who Irwin Ledger is. And I know you know what you're doing. Is it my songs? Because I know I have a lot of variation. I thought that was a strength."

"No, it's not the songs. Your songs are great." In fact, she couldn't quite understand how his songs could be so good. That level of songwriting came from years of studying music theory. They didn't just have catchy tunes and hooks, which in themselves made careers. They had polish. Only a very serious musician could arrange songs of that caliber. "Let me see you guys a few more times before I say anything else, okay?"

He nodded curtly, turned, and walked back into the house. The sliding door rolled, and she felt the thud of its closure like an insult.

She stood alone in the backyard, naked under a towel, and she'd never felt so utterly sexless in her life.

It wasn't like she thought he'd ever be attracted to her—obviously—but he hadn't even taken a peek. It was like she wasn't even a woman to him.

How *humiliating.*

FOUR

Emmie set the tamale pie on the table. She hoped the guys liked chili. She didn't know how to feed six people as cheaply as possible. So, other than chicken, pasta, and chili, she didn't have a lot of interesting ideas. But she'd look up recipes online and come up with some good meals.

The guys tore into the corn bread she'd put in the center of the table and then took turns spooning the pie onto their plates. Slater piled salad on his—he was the only one besides her who ate it, so she'd learned to make a small one.

"Okay, so we only made ninety bucks at the merch table last night," Derek said. "And we can't afford to get new T-shirts made until we make another grand. So—"

"Just take some money out of the studio fund." Slater poured dressing on his salad. "We'll pay it back when we sell some shirts."

"Not touching the studio fund."

Slater looked at Derek like he was slow. "Well, you're not going to sell T-shirts if you don't have any to sell."

Emmie couldn't help noticing the way Slater distanced himself by talking about *Derek* selling shirts. She hadn't lived with them all that long, but Slater was unquestionably an essential—if not *the* essential—element of the band. Why did he distance himself like that?

"Nothing's more important than making a new demo," Derek said.

"What about the press kit?" Ben said. "Where do we get the money for that?"

Derek looked at her. "How much will that cost?"

She set her fork down. "Other than the demo itself, the kit's not that expensive. We'll need a great picture of the band, but the rest is stuff I have to write up. I'll need to get your bios—no more than, say, a paragraph or two for each of you. I'll need your fact sheet, you know, where you've performed, who you've toured with. Do you have press clippings?"

Derek nodded. "So when can we have it?"

"The press kit?" *Here we go.* The problem with sharing her opinions with Derek was that—thanks to their dad—he heard any suggestion as criticism. She had to tell him, of course, but she had to do it the right way.

"Em?" her brother said.

"I'm not sure we're ready for that."

Slater set down his fork. She knew he'd been waiting to hear from her.

"What?" Derek said. "We're more than ready. We're beyond ready. That's the whole point of having you here."

"I know that," she began. "But I'd like to throw out some ideas before we go ahead with the press kit. Of course, I'm not here to tell you what to do, so you don't have to listen to any of it. But maybe you could hear me out?"

"Talk." Slater leaned forward, a napkin balled in his fist.

She studied Derek's face. He sat rigidly, chewing the inside of his mouth. "If you don't like any of my ideas, we'll go ahead with the press kit, okay?"

Slater held her brother's gaze. It was weird the way they looked at each other, some big, silent communication going on born out of nine years of working together. After several tense moments, Derek's shoulders slumped, and he exhaled. "What're your ideas."

Not even a question. Just resigned. "Thanks for hearing me out. Okay. Well, let's start with the merchandise table. You guys are great up there. You really are. But as soon as you leave the stage, it's over. You go to your private table and close yourselves off from everyone. Well, except Slater, who goes to the bar and starts hitting on women."

"I don't *hit* on anyone."

Was he really going to argue about who initiated the moves? "That wasn't a judgment. Just a statement of fact. Am I wrong about what happens when you leave the stage?"

Slater's expression gave away nothing. If he let pride keep him from facing the truth, he didn't have a hope in hell of making it in this ridiculously competitive business.

"No." His deadpan response made her smile. He kept surprising her.

"Now, hang on a second," her brother said. "We're the biggest college band in Texas. People love us."

"Okay." *So?* "Mostly, the girls love Slater." She expected a self-satisfied expression, but his jaw tensed. She could practically hear him urging her on, *Talk.*

"That's not true," Ben said. "We've got thousands of fans."

"Fans aren't enough. Especially when the bulk of your fans are girls who want to play Seven Minutes in Heaven with the lead singer. If you want to get signed, if you want to be the next U2, you have to have more than fans. You have to have fanatics."

Cooper barked out a laugh. "I like that." He clapped his hands once. "That's good."

"Have you seen the crowds at our shows?" Derek sounded like he couldn't believe what he was hearing. "They know every lyric. They wear our T-shirts. They're all over our website."

"Posting naked pictures of themselves for Slater."

"Hey," Derek said. "He's not the only reason they like us. We're a good band. We've got a great sound."

"You do. You absolutely do." She held his gaze long and hard, projecting only one thought, *Let's get you to the next level.*

"Hear her out." Slater gave her a chin nod, her cue to continue.

"Let's go back to the merchandise. So, the show ends, and you guys go to your private table." She motioned to the four guys. "And you go to the bar." Slater didn't move a muscle, just listened. "Who's working the merchandise table?"

"I always get some chicks to help out," Derek said. "It's always covered."

"But you want to *sell* the merchandise, right? You need the cash for the recording studio. And not only that, but you want fanatics. So wouldn't you sell more if you guys took turns working it?"

"Valid point," Cooper said.

"We can do that, no problem," Ben said.

"We'd sell a shitload more stuff, for sure." Pete reached for the casserole dish, scraping the bottom for the last of the tamale pie.

"What else?" Slater said.

She cleared her throat and wiped her mouth with a napkin, though she hadn't eaten anything. "So, my boss only said one thing. He said you don't know who you are yet." She watched Slater, how he focused on her every word. "I didn't know what he meant because the songs were fantastic. And you gave a really nice selection of them. I mean, I knew your name and logo wouldn't work, but—"

She felt the guys reel back. The energy in the room grew charged.

"Now you don't like our name," Derek said. "That's just fucking great. We've had that name and logo for eight years."

"Shut the fuck up," Slater said, never raising his voice. Pete's chair legs hit the floor. The room went silent.

She wouldn't budge on this one. "No record label's going to sign a band called Snatch whose logo is a beaver. That's not only low class, it's just plain unacceptable."

"Jesus Christ, you're trying to change us," Derek said. "Just like all the managers. Which is *why we don't have them anymore*. I told you we didn't need somebody to come in and change us. You're only here to promote us, Em. That's it."

"Yes, promote you so you get to the next level." Her brother was so stubborn. She wanted to say, *I'm not Dad*, but that would embarrass him. "It's unlikely there *is* a next level for a band called Snatch whose logo is a beaver." She looked to Slater to see if he wanted her to go on. "Talk?"

He cracked a smile, nodded.

"Let's stay focused. So, back to Irwin's comment. You've got Pete and Cooper with tats and piercings, Derek and Ben with shaved heads and chains dangling off their tuxedo pants, and then you've got Slater, your *GQ* cover boy, as your lead singer. I mean, who are you? And you know what's even harder to understand? You write amazing music. Better quality than anything I've come across in all my time at Amoeba Records. And I started there as an intern in high school."

"Really?" When Slater talked to her, it felt like they were the only two people in the room. How did he do that? No wonder the girls loved him. Who didn't want that kind of attention from a freaking gorgeous man?

"Really. You write great songs." She turned to the rest of the guys. "So, who are you? A grunge band?" She motioned to Pete and Cooper. "Ska? Punk? Emo?" She looked at her brother. "Or what? What are you?"

"We're whoever we want to be," Derek said tersely. "It's all about the music."

"It is if you want to stay right where you are. Unfortunately, if you want to sign with a national label, your band is going to need an identity, an image that fits the quality of the music."

"We're not changing the name," Derek said. "We've got thirty thousand followers."

"Yeah, it's too late to change the name," Ben said.

"Then don't. Guy Ritchie made a movie named *Snatch*. The word has multiple meanings." She shrugged. "Just change the logo."

"To what?" Derek shoved his plate away, tipping his chair back on two legs. "I think we all know what snatch means."

"That's right. We do." She paused. "It's an Olympic weight-lifting event. That's what you meant, right?" She smiled at Slater. "I can just see a Barbie-waisted, big-breasted, stiletto-boot-wearing chick squatting in the weight-lifter pose with a huge barbell over her head. Snatch."

Derek smiled. "Ha."

"I can see her as just a sketch in bold black marker, you know?" she said. "Give her a slash of red for her mouth."

"I'm getting wood," Ben said.

"Hey, you want pretty boy here to get tatted up?" Pete said, elbowing Slater. "Grow out his hair so he looks like a baller." He ruffled Slater's all-American haircut.

"Not at all." How to say the next bit without hurting feelings? "Nobody has to change his physical appearance . . . much. I mean, Pete could trim his hair." She hoped she didn't hurt him, but his big bush of frizzy strawberry-blond hair should probably go. "And you and Ben could probably lose the chains. It wouldn't be that big a deal. The thing is, you don't have to dress the same. You just have to all fit one image. So, if you choose to be, like, alt/indie rockers, which in my opinion is your sound, then you each decide how to dress within that concept. Whatever feels comfortable to you . . . within the image."

"So we all have to look like Slater?" Ben asked, not looking happy about it.

"Well, at least we'll get laid more," Pete said.

"You don't have to look like Slater." They couldn't look like him if they tried. They didn't have his soulful eyes, his insanely sexy mouth . . . No, no, that wasn't it at all. They didn't have his sexuality. Oh, God. It just struck her—he was her polar opposite. She had zero sex appeal, and he was pure sex.

Derek leaned back, opened a drawer, and pulled out a pad of paper and a pencil. "So. Take turns working the merch table. New logo." He pointed the pencil at Slater. "You on that?"

Slater nodded, like he couldn't care less.

"Unified look. What else you got?"

She smiled, so freaking relieved he'd opened up to her ideas. Although she doubted her next comment would be well received. "Maybe that's enough for tonight. I'm starved."

"Emmie," Slater warned.

"Right. Okay, well, the thing is, and again, this is just a recommendation, but you guys might want to consider not drinking on performance nights."

"Okay, time to get laid." Pete got up and brought his dish to the sink.

Well, she hadn't expected that one to go over well.

Ben and Cooper got up, too, but left their plates on the table.

"We're not drunks," Slater said.

"We're totally professional," Derek said.

"I didn't say you weren't."

"You said we have to stop drinking," Slater said.

"Is that what you heard? 'Cause it's not what I said."

"Explain." Slater urged her on, but when she kept looking at the three who'd gotten up, who'd had enough of her ideas, he said, "No one's going anywhere."

They stayed right where they were. Pete leaned against the counter, crossing his arms over his skinny chest.

She really wished she'd kept her mouth shut on this one,

even if she knew she was right. "Your live show is great, tons of energy, well-rehearsed."

"Damn straight," Derek said. "We rehearse four or five times a week. Most bands can't do that."

"So what's the problem?" Slater asked.

"I could be wrong—"

"You're not wrong," Slater said. "What?"

"It's just . . . there're times when you falter. Ben loses the beat, or you guys start one song but quit and start another. Most people won't notice it because you're so charming. You make everything fun. So, I think what you're doing is fine for where you are right now, but if you want to jump to the next level, you've got to be just that much sharper, more professional." She looked to Slater. "You have to know nothing dries out the vocal chords like alcohol."

His mouth flattened into a grim line. "I don't get drunk before a performance."

"Not until after." Oh, she really shouldn't have said that. She actually didn't know what he did after a show. She'd seen the others come home drunk lots of times. But she was always asleep by the time Slater got home.

"What I do after hours is nobody's business."

"Actually, everything you do is the band's business," she said, unwilling to let him intimidate her. They didn't have to take her advice, but they'd asked for it. She believed in it, and she wouldn't back down. "Everything you do reflects back on the band. I'm going to be inviting reviewers to your shows. You think they won't notice when you falter up there? When your voice gets hoarse? They're *looking* for ways to criticize you. Why give them anything that's within your power to control?"

She got up, figuring they ought to have some time alone. "Like I said, these are just my suggestions. Do what you like. I'll stick to my end whether you use them or reject them. Think about it, and get back to me. I'm ready to move on the press kit when you are."

Slater opened the door to the sound of laughter at nine in the morning. *What the hell?* After another mostly sleepless night, he needed to fall into bed, but curiosity got the better of him, so he followed the sounds into the kitchen.

"Oh, come on, just give me a chance," he heard Emmie say, voice bubbling with humor. And then everyone started talking over each other.

"He's gonna look like a girl."

"Shut up."

"Would you let her work?"

Slater found his bandmates sitting around the kitchen table. The plates with leftover scrambled eggs and toast crusts, the glasses of orange juice, and mugs of coffee let him know they'd just finished eating together.

Emmie stood behind Pete, who had a towel draped around his shoulders, his hair wet and long.

"Dude, you're home late," Cooper said.

"Did you go home with that redhead?" Ben asked. "She was smoking hot." Tiana, his girlfriend, cuffed the back of his head. "What? I went home with you."

He caught Emmie's gaze, wondering if she'd made the same assumption about what he'd done last night and if she judged him for it. But she seemed completely unfazed. Squirting some gel into her hands, she rubbed them together and then dragged them slowly through Pete's hair, starting at the top and sliding down to the ends. The gentle slide down the long, wet strands set Slater's body humming.

Interesting. Not long ago some chick had done that same move on his body with cinnamon-flavored lotion, but it hadn't evoked anything like his response just then. Yeah, he'd gotten hard. But he hadn't felt . . . seduced. Gooseflesh hadn't popped out on his skin.

Maybe because that woman had been frantic to please him, where Emmie seemed so quiet inside. Peaceful. And she moved like she had all the time in the world, like she loved the feel of the hair in her hands.

An electrical current traveled down his spine, igniting a flame in his dick.

"What're you doing?" he said.

Everyone shot him a look, but what the hell? Why was Emmie making love to Pete's hair? Her eyebrows lifted in surprise, but she didn't stop working her hands through it.

"She's fixing my hair."

"He's always wanted it straight." Derek tried not to smile,

but then when the other guys burst out laughing, he joined in. "He wants to be a pretty boy like you."

"No, I don't. I just hate having pubic hair on my head. Emmie's gonna fix it."

"I'll show you what it looks like straight, but honestly, your hair is so kinky, I don't think you're going to like it. It's never going to look sleek and polished like you imagine." She picked up the blow dryer and a round brush, and started blowing out a section.

The room went quiet as they watched, waited. She concentrated on the job. Her pink tongue flicked out to wet her lips, and then her teeth bit down into the soft flesh of her lower one. When her head tilted to one side, her long hair spilled over her shoulder, gleaming in the morning light streaming in through the kitchen windows.

She shut the dryer off, held up a mirror to Pete. "So this is what it'll look like straightened."

"You're going to blow your hair dry every day?" Slater couldn't believe it.

"No," Emmie said with a scowl. Like she had to protect Pete. "He'd get a treatment done. It would keep his hair straight for months."

"You'll look like a girl," Cooper said.

"So?" Ben turned to Slater. "The redhead? She must've been really good for you to have an actual sleepover."

Tiana let out a huff of breath and rolled her eyes. She had her thick wavy hair piled on top of her head, like she'd just woken up. Her extremely curvy body was bursting out of her tank top and tiny gym shorts.

"What?" Ben said.

"You make me look like a bad girlfriend," Tiana said.

"Oh, don't worry," Cooper said. "We know better. We can hear everything."

"Why don't you just break up with me—again—if you want a shot at the redhead?" Tiana said. Everyone knew this game they played, so no one thought they were actually fighting. "I mean, if I don't rock your world . . ."

Ben pulled her close, and she fell onto his lap. He immediately started tonguing her neck. "But you do. And I don't want anyone else. I want you."

"Jesus Christ," Slater said. "I got shit to do."

"Rehearsal at one," Derek said.

"What?" Rehearsal never started before four, thanks to his bartending schedule.

"New schedule," Derek said. "I emailed it to you."

Slater cut his gaze to Emmie. "I've been kind of busy." He gave a half smile, still looking to provoke her, but she just smiled pleasantly back, as if he hadn't just suggested he'd been busy fucking. But it wasn't like he'd tell them why he'd avoided being home.

She turned her attention to Pete. "You know what I think is best?"

"Shave it off?"

"Dreads. Really neat, clean, polished dreads." She pulled her laptop off the little built-in kitchen desk, set it on the table, and leaned over, tapping the keys. "Hang on a second."

She had curves, too, nice ones, but she didn't display them the way Tiana did. Everything about Emmie was . . . suppressed. Made him want to tug that tank top down and expose those plump mounds she kept hidden. Underneath that prairie-girl persona rumbled something else . . . something just waiting to burst out of her. He'd like to see that. The bursting.

"What happened to our *image*?" Derek asked. "We're not a reggae band."

"Here. Look. Not reggae at all."

All the guys gathered around her, looking at the screen.

"Fucking A," Ben said.

"Oh, I like that a lot," Tiana said. "But how do you keep them from getting all nasty and smelly?"

"Wax. And keeping them dry." She motioned to the screen. "This guy's one of our artists, and he's had these dreads for years. Don't they look great?"

Slater watched them together, talking and laughing. The warm kitchen smelled like cinnamon and butter. The coffee cake on the counter looked good, browned with sticky nuts on top, and he realized what she'd done for them. Just by cooking, she'd brought them together in a wholly different way. Like a family.

He thought about joining them, having a look at the picture, maybe grabbing a piece of cake.

Instead, he turned and headed for bed.

FIVE

The next morning when Slater looked out the bathroom window, he was disappointed to find the pool empty. A few leaves floated on the surface. It looked like she hadn't been swimming at all. Had he put an end to that?

Guess he hadn't needed to stay away after all. He wouldn't be perving on Derek's sister today.

Well, hell. He shouldn't have gone out there when she was naked. She'd been enjoying herself. He headed out of the bathroom, listened outside her door—right across the hall from his bedroom—and heard the sound of clacking on a keyboard.

Should he knock? He wanted to give her the sketch of the new logo, but he knew he didn't like to be interrupted when he worked, so he dropped it outside her door and went downstairs to make a pot of coffee. According to Derek, nothing drew her out like a fresh pot.

Just as expected, she came downstairs a few minutes later holding his drawing.

"Hey, what are you doing up at this hour?" she asked. She stood there in her white tank top and cotton pajama shorts, no makeup—she hadn't even brushed her hair. Her breasts bounced with her every movement, and he got all stirred up just looking at her.

And there he went. Perving.

He'd said no yet again to the bevy of little lovelies last night just to spend this morning with her. His curiosity had gotten the better of him. Who was she, exactly? "Hoped I'd catch you skinny dipping again."

She ignored his comment, instead waving the sketch. "I love this. It's just what I pictured. Only better."

He lifted the pot to her.

"Sure, thanks. Now that we've got milk and sugar, I'd love some coffee." She pulled out a chair and sat down. "Show this logo to the guys at rehearsal tonight. It'd be great to get new merchandise made in time for the new gigs."

"You've booked us already?"

"Not yet. But, I mean, once I send out the press kit, it'll happen fast. I'm trying to get you into the Austin City Lights Festival at the end of October."

His heart slammed into his ribcage. "What?" She could do that?

"Yeah, I know the promoter. We've booked a bunch of bands with them over the years."

He couldn't form a single coherent thought.

She smiled. "It's not that big a deal. Bands cancel all the time. We can always score a spot."

He poured the coffee into his Steve Earle mug and set it in front of her. When she made to get up, he stilled her with a press of his palm on her shoulder and got the milk out of the refrigerator. "You think we're ready for that?"

Her expression changed, and he liked that he could read her emotions. She didn't try to impress or manipulate. She was true.

He sat down. "Tell me."

Pouring some milk into the mug, she stirred it slowly, thoughtfully. "Again, this is just my opinion—"

"Emmie."

"Yeah, okay. I know. It's just most artists don't take feedback well."

His skin prickled, warmth saturating deep into his bones. She'd called him an artist. He was used to being called a man whore, a slacker. But who considered him an *artist*? Other than his mom, and she just thought he was wasting his talents with rock music, so it didn't count.

Emmie drew in a breath. "You've got some great material. I told you that. It's just . . ." She stirred her coffee, looking lost in thought. She inhaled, straightening. "To play a gig like this, you have to have the right set list, obviously. And you've got to know how to play to a huge crowd."

"We've played big crowds before."

"Sure, but you mostly play in clubs. On stage, you act like you're playing for the groupies in the front row."

"What are you saying?"

"I've been listening to your songs. You've got some rock anthem material. Some of your songs—like "Fiona"? If you just changed the chord progression leading up to the bridge, make it build to this huge breaking climax, you'd have a rock anthem good enough to rival anything by U2. But you just have to sing it like a rock god. Not like a guy who wants to get laid."

"I don't sing to get laid."

"It seems like you do. That's what it looks like."

"Maybe it only looks that way for people who want to get laid?"

Again, she didn't bite. No reaction whatsoever. "I just think it might be time to stop thinking about seducing your groupies and start thinking about wooing an entire stadium full of fanatics."

He got up, finding it difficult to process her words.

"Are you angry?" she asked.

"I don't have an ego here. It's a waste of my time if I'm just going to play local venues the rest of my life."

"Go big or go home?"

"Yeah."

"I heard you sold out at the merch table last night."

He nodded, still thinking about the way he sang. *Did* he do that? And more importantly, was he undermining himself? Man, that would piss him off. All the time and effort devoted to making a go of this career . . . believing his dad's crap that he had some special talent . . . only to languish on the bottom rung. God, he owed his dad better than that.

"You should work it all the time. You'll have your money for the studio session in no time."

He gazed out the window. The early-morning sunlight sparkled on the surface of the pool. He felt her come up beside him, felt her heat. She smelled of coffee and something sweetly fragrant.

"What're you thinking?" Her voice washed over him, cool and soft as a clean sheet.

"I don't want to fuck this up." He wished he'd met her sooner. He wished he—and the band—had made these changes long ago.

"You won't. Slater, you're incredibly talented. I screen all of Irwin's demos. I know what's out there. You've got a gift. And it's not just your look, though, believe me, being the gorgeous, swoon-worthy lead singer matters a lot in this business. But it's your songwriting. That's the real ticket for you."

She paused, giving him a mischievous smile. "You do know you could make way more publishing your songs than fronting a band, right?"

"But then how would the chicks find me?"

"True. Just a thought. Anyhow, the tiniest shift will turn your hard-driving songs into rock anthems, and your lyrical melodies into ballads that'll make girls cry." She frowned. "Well, they cry now, actually. But I can't tell if they're frenzied because you lifted your shirt and showed them the most amazing abs in God's kingdom or if they're really listening to the lyrics."

"How come I don't make you swoon?"

The skin between her eyes puckered in disappointment—but only fleetingly. "It's so tired, isn't it? The whole rock star/player thing? I don't know. It just doesn't do anything for me."

He knew he should be insulted, but oddly, he wasn't. Because what she said rang true. So true, it was like gears locking together. He *was* trite. And it *had* gotten old. He'd known that for a long time. It's just . . . the girls were there . . . it was easy. What guy didn't want to get laid?

"What does do something for you?" he asked.

"I wish I knew." She leaned across him—her smooth, warm skin brushing across his arm—turned on the faucet, and rinsed out her mug.

And then she lowered the dishwasher door and her plump, soft breast bumped into the back of his hand, and it sent a shock wave rippling through him straight to his dick.

"I'd sure like to find out." She let out the sweetest little sigh.

He couldn't even begin to make himself calm down because,

yeah, he'd just felt the fullness of her breast, but he'd already had a look at them, so he had the double whammy of a visual along with the actual touch, giving him a semi right there in the kitchen.

Jesus, he had to get a hold of himself. What were they talking about? Oh, what turned her on. Christ. Great conversation for a guy with a semi. "Any more coffee cake left?"

"No, but I got bagels. You know that deli right up on Pleasant Valley? They're not bad."

Bagels. Excellent. He could think about bagels. "If you don't like musicians, who do you like?"

She leaned back against the counter and crossed her arms, lifting those lovely breasts. They bounced when she pulled her hair up into a ponytail, using an elastic from her wrist. "I guess I'd really like a guy I can trust." She glanced at him. "But that's not a type is it?" Her soft laugh breezed around his heart.

He watched her pull a bagel out of a paper bag on the counter, watched her hips sway as she headed for the stairs, and he felt something he'd never felt before.

He wanted more.

———————

Across the table Emmie watched a gorgeous brunette drag her hands across Derek's scalp, her breasts undulating against his chest. When one of those hands lowered to his lap, her brother's lazy smile froze, and he hitched up in his seat. Beside them, a girl straddled Pete as they made out, and he cupped and squeezed her breast. Glimpses of pink tongue had Emmie looking away.

She felt strangely hurt. Usually, she felt pretty close to the guys. But just then, in the club, they made her feel invisible. She forced her attention back to the stage, back to the band she'd come to see.

She checked her notes. Clever Jimmy was the seventh band she'd seen so far. Those slash marks through the previous six made her nervous, especially since she had a feeling she'd be making another tonight. Seven bands rejected. None she could pass along to Irwin.

God. She knew from listening to demo tapes how hard it was to find talent. Why had she thought she could discover the next Guns N' Roses in six weeks in Austin?

Maybe she should reconsider some of them. She should probably see them a second or third time before striking them from her list.

Except that Irwin never gave a band a second chance. He knew right away if they had talent or not. But she wasn't hearing any potential. Which brought back her brother's comment about recognizing talent from primitive sounds. She only now understood what he meant. And how it was possible that maybe she *couldn't* do it.

Four and a half weeks left.

A bump had her turning to find yet another fangirl jamming herself between her and Slater, lowering her ass to his lap. His large hands came up, cupped her sculpted globes, and pushed her away. Emmie couldn't hear the conversation, but she did catch the look in his eyes—he wasn't playing.

She couldn't help wondering why Slater was the only one not indulging in a little groupie action. From the moment the band had arrived, he'd blocked the women's advances. Why?

Yikes. Listen to me, trying to analyze his behavior. She really had to stop noticing him so much. It was just . . . she didn't react to him the way she reacted to the other guys. Her pulse kicked up when she saw him, and her stomach flipped when they brushed against each other or when he looked at her a certain way.

Okay. God. She was attracted to him.

But she wasn't going to act on it. She wasn't stupid. Emmie focused on the stage, on her reason for being there. She would find something good to say about Clever Jimmy. The singer had a growly voice—not unappealing—and the lead guitarist's jangly, arpeggiated licks reminded her of Johnny Marr of the Smiths. Other than that . . . oh, the drummer wore a kilt. With nothing under it. So, there was that.

What would Irwin think?

"Hey, can I have this chair?" she heard someone ask.

Emmie glanced up to find a very beautiful woman with long dark hair and artfully applied makeup eyeing her eagerly. She looked around, not understanding the question. There were clearly no extra chairs at the table. "I'm sorry, what chair?"

"Yours." The woman motioned to Emmie's chair.

"Mine?"

"You're not using it." The woman tipped her head toward

Slater and gave Emmie a look that said, *You're not going after him, let me get in there.* And then she mouthed, *Please?*

Emmie could not believe this. "Are you serious?"

Slater gripped the woman's hips, shifting her aside. "You want her chair?" he asked the woman. He seemed *delighted*.

And just like that the woman's posture relaxed. Her eyes softened, and her back arched, thrusting her bodacious bosom into Slater's face. "Yeah. Is that all right?"

"Absolutely." Slater got up, grabbed Emmie's arm and started to lift her. "Come on, babe. Up."

"Are you out of your mind?"

"Come on. Give the pretty lady your chair."

Heat spiked, racing up Emmie's spine and burning to the tips of her ears. "I am not giving her my chair." She planted her ass more firmly in the seat. So much for Slater being a good guy who wouldn't throw her over for some groupie action. She jerked out of his hold.

But he held firm. "Let's go. Give . . . ?"

"Hilary," the woman said breathlessly.

"*Hilary* the chair." He gave the woman a devastating smile. Wrapping an arm firmly under Emmie's breasts, he pulled her from the table. With his other hand, he motioned to the chair she'd just vacated. "All yours," he said to Hilary, then grabbed Emmie's hand, leading her through the packed club.

Emmie glanced over her shoulder to see Hilary stunned, jaw hanging open, as she watched them walk away. She burst out laughing. What a ridiculous woman, trying to kick Emmie out of her chair so she could hook up with Slater. And, yeah, Emmie was kind of digging him a whole lot just then.

They stopped at the hostess's podium. His arm went around Emmie's shoulder, pulling her close, as he whispered in the young woman's ear. He smelled so good, and his body was so freaking hard. Emmie wanted to touch his chest, feel those muscles, curl her fingers into his hair.

Stop it.

The hostess smiled brightly and then led them to a table for two in the far back corner. Slater discreetly handed her some cash as she whisked the Reserved sign off and disappeared into the crowd.

He held Emmie's chair out for her, leaning down to her

ear. She could feel his heat, smell his masculine scent. Her body lit up with excitement. She waited, but he didn't say anything. He just stood there, his cheek touching her hair, and she tensed, not sure what he was doing or what he expected from her. Excitement exploded across her skin in chill bumps.

"Is this too far from the stage?" he finally asked, mouth practically nuzzling her ear.

She shook her head, wishing he'd move away. *Baloney.* That wasn't what she wished at all. She wanted to turn into him and feel the smooth skin of his freshly shaved cheek on hers. *God.* "No, this is fine." Her heart pounded so fast it hurt. She felt uncomfortably warm and just wanted to go home, but without a car in this huge, sprawling city, she was out of luck. "I don't think I'm interested, though."

"Not at all?" he asked softly.

Wait, what were they talking about? The band she'd come to see? Or was it something else? Jittery nerves had her feet shifting restlessly under the table. She shook her head.

Finally, he stepped away, taking the seat across from her. While her pulse thudded in her ears, he looked calm and comfortable. Perfectly at ease.

Of course he did. She was so stupid. Getting worked up over a guy like Slater, who would never see her as anything but Derek's sister. He was being *polite.*

Determined to shake it off, get her focus back, she reached for the clear glass candleholder in the middle of the table. The glass warmed her fingers. "So, thanks for that . . . back there. I can't believe she wanted to take my chair." Gazing into the yellow flame, she said, "Why, um, why *did* you do it?"

"Hey, nobody puts Emmie in a corner." He gave her a devilish smile.

"The rock god knows a line from *Dirty Dancing*?"

"Emmie. I'm hurt. There's so much more to me than you realize."

"Yeah? Well, you might consider showing me more than the rock god if you don't want to keep getting your feelings hurt."

He sat back, regarding her with a blank expression.

She had no idea what he was thinking, but for the first time she saw his vulnerability.

And that was not good. Because that meant there *was* more to him than she'd suspected.

———————

Slater didn't normally get turned on by conversation. Nice tits, a firm touch, the flick of a tongue, sure. But something about Emmie's honesty, her directness . . . it shouldn't, but it turned him on. Placing his elbows on the table, he leaned forward. "So, you want to get to know me?"

"Well, yeah. We're home alone together most days. Might as well have actual conversations. If, you know, you can handle it."

He smiled. "Let's just see if I can." He picked up his chair and moved it a quarter of the way around the table, toward her. "So, tell me something. I hear you typing away in your room every day. What're you working on?"

Her head dipped, her shiny hair spilling forward. "Oh, I'm writing an article for *Rolling Stone*."

He leaned closer to hear her better over the shrieking guitars. He watched her fingers gently stroke the candleholder. An image of those fingers on his dick flashed in his mind, making his skin tighten.

What the fuck? Emmie's fingers weren't going anywhere near his dick.

Focus. *Rolling Stone*.

But then she shifted, and a ripple of awareness rushed over him when he got a whiff of her fresh floral scent. She licked her lips, drawing all his senses to that juicy pink mouth.

He was *not* thinking about Derek's sister that way, obviously. Just that . . . she had thick eyelashes framing gold-brown eyes that sparkled with intelligence and humor. And that was the thing about her. Living with five raunchy guys, her future up in the air, she still maintained her sense of humor.

He dragged his chair even closer. So he could hear her better. "You're published?"

She nodded, setting the candle down. "Yeah, they've printed a few of my articles. I don't have much time to write. But sometimes an idea comes to me, and I just knock it out."

"Published in *Rolling Stone*? That's fucking impressive."

"Well, I'm Irwin's assistant. It gives me certain advantages."

"I didn't know you were a writer. Derek never said anything."

"Oh, no. No, no. I just write articles because . . . well, I have certain insights that *Rolling Stone* readers appreciate." She looked away, cocking her head as though she was just realizing something. "Well, yeah, I kind of am a writer. I mean, I don't write very often because I don't have time. But I keep a journal, I write articles . . . so, you know what? I am a writer. It's how I work out my thoughts, my issues. It's how I express myself. So, yes. I'm a writer." She looked so happy, so triumphant, he had to smile. Her features turned pink.

He shook his head, too aware of her. Every time her tongue came out to lick her lips, he felt a jolt of desire. Every time she used her hands to gesture, she unknowingly pressed her breasts together, causing them to plump at the V of her T-shirt.

"Of course, I'm not a *creative* writer like you. Your lyrics are unusual. Really emotional and powerful. How do they come to you?" She leaned closer, and now their shoulders touched.

She had the warmest, kindest eyes. And she always seemed so interested in what he had to say. "As a kid, they came as stories. Like the kind my mom read to me. Sometimes she'd be reading, but I wouldn't hear her because I'd be changing the direction of the story line. And then, after she'd turn out the light and leave me alone, I'd continue imagining the story. But I learned to focus on one . . ." He was about to say *emotion* but stopped himself from getting too intense. "One aspect of the story. Concentrate on it and turn it into a song."

"What were you going to say? You weren't going to say 'aspect of the story.'"

He smiled, a little uncomfortable. He didn't usually get so real with people. They saw him one way, and he delivered. "I learned that a song is about one emotion, one feeling. So, I had to keep narrowing the story down, trying to figure out what I was trying to say."

"Like finding one core moment and then writing a song about it."

"Exactly. Because behind every story is that one core moment. That emotion that's fueling it."

"You're absolutely right. I never thought of it like that."

She looked at him so attentively, like she was interested in what he had to say. "It's hard work, huh?"

"It's fucking hard."

She laughed, leaning back in her chair. "Why is everything in life so hard?"

"Your life is pretty sweet."

"Ha. You think because I work for Irwin Ledger my life is easy? I'm a personal assistant, Slater. Other than writing a few articles for *Rolling Stone*, which I never even considered a huge achievement until you just pointed it out, I've done nothing on my own. Ever. Before I left for college, I was basically my dad's personal assistant. I work for people. I don't have a talent of my own."

"You're great at figuring out what we're doing wrong. That's a talent."

She looked at him, and slowly, surely, a smile bloomed across her features. "Maybe it is." And then she sighed. "I don't know why we picked such a mean, tough business."

He looked away, his chest tightening. He wanted to say it had obviously picked them, but he'd exposed enough of himself. "I don't know about you, but I want to get laid."

She eyed him skeptically, sadly even.

"Sorry. Old habits."

She leaned just a tiny bit toward him, so close now he could feel her cranberry-scented breath on his skin. "What do you really want? For real?"

His pulse kicked up, making him feel a little panicky. His impulse was to crack a joke, be crude, but the way she held his gaze . . . it skewered him to the spot. And then, without really thinking, he said, "I don't want to be a failure. Like my dad was." And where the hell had *that* come from? Christ, he didn't even want to see her reaction. Then again, she probably knew all about his fuckup dad from Derek.

Why wasn't she saying anything? Finally, curiosity got the better of him—he *wanted* to know her reaction—so he looked at her. The moment he did, she gave a gentle smile.

"I don't think that's possible. I've heard your songs. You're really talented. Was your dad?"

He shook his head. "My dad was all over the place. He

wanted to be a rock star, but he never stuck with anything
long enough to actually be good at it."

"Does he have any songs lying around that you could, I
don't know, finish for him? That'd be kind of sweet, right?
Maybe he failed during his life, but his son, the one he devoted his entire life to helping, turns one of his songs into a
hit. Kind of a tribute to all he did do right in raising you."

Slater swallowed. He felt like he'd taken a blow to the chest.
He couldn't take a full breath. Could she see how he was struggling here? Did she know the impact her idea had on him? He
chanced another look at her. Still with that gentle smile.

"Just an idea." And then she turned back to the stage to
watch the shitty band.

He didn't move, he was still holding on to the idea she'd
planted in him. All the things *his dad had done right* in raising him.

He'd always resented his dad—had lived with a tight knot
of rancor in his chest. Like a tumor growing close to a joint,
making him wince with every move he made. Yet, oddly, in
spite of the anger, he'd held on to a bold and vibrant love for
him. Yeah, his dad had embarrassed the shit out of him, but
he was . . . well, he was Slater's dad.

And, frankly, he owed it to him to become a rock star.
Because, seriously, no matter what Slater thought of him, his
dad had devoted his entire life to making his son successful.
Even if he'd gone about it the wrong way. Even if Slater had
hated every moment of it.

It would suck if his dad's life's efforts amounted to nothing.

But, man, what a fucking compliment. That Slater's talent
was *proof* of something—Jesus. It blew him away. Not just
that someone like Emmie thought he was talented enough to
write hits—although that idea alone made him feel a degree
of success that had always seemed elusive to him.

But that his dad had done right by him.

Jesus, the power in those words. It just floored him.

What the hell did Emmie see in him?

He took in her profile, her attention now fixed on the band.
Closing him out.

And, *fuck*, he wanted her back.

SIX

Slater heard the front door slam. He opened his bedroom door and heard Emmie sigh. Quickly setting his book aside, he headed down to the living room to find a pile of stuffed recyclable grocery bags by the front door. Lifting them, he brought them into the kitchen where he found her sweaty and flushed.

And then it struck him. "You *carry* the groceries?"

"Of course. How else would I get them home?"

"I don't know." He hadn't even thought about it. "Why don't you drive your brother to work so you can have the van on days like today?"

"He needs it. He does errands during his breaks. Like today, he's picking up the new T-shirts."

Slater couldn't believe it. For two weeks, she'd done the grocery shopping by herself. He pulled a receipt out of the bag. "Safeway? What the hell, Emmie, I thought you were going to Desi's."

"Why would I go to Desi's? It's way more expensive." She drew the back of her hand across her damp forehead. "Seriously, I don't mind. In New York I walk all the time. I'm not used to being so sedentary."

Could Derek be that much of a dick that he'd let his sister

walk a mile and a half to buy groceries for the six of them? He opened the refrigerator, pulled out the pitcher Emmie used to make lemonade, and poured her a glass. "Here."

"Oh, that's okay. You don't have to—"

He gave her a stern look.

"Okay, thank you."

He got busy unloading the bags. "I'm here all day. I'll take you to the store, for Christ's sake. Why didn't you ask me?"

She didn't answer, so he turned around to find her smirking.

"What? You can ask me for a ride."

"Seriously, Slater? I wouldn't ask you to drive me around on my errands."

"I'm telling you I don't mind." He shoved a gallon of milk into the refrigerator, filled with actual food for the first time in—ever. Yogurt, butter, cheeses, mustard, ketchup, lunch meat. Actual food.

He felt like an ass. All this time—two weeks—she'd been without a car in a sprawling city. They lived on the outskirts of Austin, practically in the country, in a crappy little development. Without a car she could only go to the strip malls along Pleasant Valley Boulevard.

He wished she'd been comfortable enough with him to ask for a ride . . . but . . . his thoughts went back to the skinny dipping incident. And all the cracks he made to get a rise out of her. He wished he hadn't done that with her, and he didn't know how to fix it.

He straightened, stalling, not sure where to begin. *I'm sorry* wasn't going to come out of his mouth. "You stopped swimming."

Her thumb rubbed the condensation on the glass. "Yeah. Not much of a swimmer."

"I fucked it up for you." He took a step closer to the table, hands resting on the back of a chair.

"Yeah. You did."

He rubbed the wood with his thumbs. "You left me hanging, not saying why Irwin didn't like our demo."

"That's not why you did it."

No, it wasn't. But what could he say? *You got under my skin?* Not likely.

"You're so used to the game. I can't tell whether it's the

only way you know of interacting with women or if you're testing me to see if I secretly harbor fantasies about you."

"Do you?" He tried to play with her, get his leer on, but since she'd just called him out on it, he couldn't find the energy. He felt like a tool.

"Oh, I think you're safe with me."

Something was going on with her. Some kind of internal crisis that went beyond wanting a promotion. She didn't give away much at all, but the occasional reference to her love—or sex?—life made him wonder.

See, this was why he didn't like to be around her so much. Sitting here, talking to her, he wanted to know more about her. She *interested* him.

And, of course, he couldn't help noticing her mouth, her delicate wrists, the tiny little constellation of freckles on her right shoulder. Seriously, how cute was that? No freckles anywhere else but the little constellation on her shoulder.

"I can hear you composing in your room."

Well, that ripped him out of his dangerous thoughts. He turned back to the counter, reaching into a bag and pulling out boxes of cereal. She joined him. They worked quietly, side by side.

"You practice every day." She looked at him, but he concentrated on shoving the boxes into the cabinet over the refrigerator.

"I guess I have my answer as to why your songs are so good."

"No idea what you're talking about." He handed her some boxes of pasta, since she stood in front of the pantry.

She took them, lining them up on a shelf. "Oh, please. You like when I talk straight to you, but you don't want to be straight with me? Stop hiding behind this clichéd bad-boy persona. There's more to you than a singer in a rock band who likes to get laid." She leaned in close and fake whispered. "I saw the book you're reading."

"You've been in my room?"

"Down, boy. You left your laundry in the dryer. I simply put your basket inside your room. Your copy of *The Jazz Theory Book* was lying on your bed. I won't tell anybody that not only do you work on your songwriting every day, but you study across genres, which would explain the depth and breadth of your material. Self-taught man, huh?"

Reaching down to the bottom of a bag, he pulled out some boxes of butter. "I went to UT with your brother."

"But you dropped out. You both did."

"Halfway through junior year. The band took off. Gotta hit it while it's hot." He handed her jars of pasta sauce and watched her slide them onto a shelf.

She turned to him, hands reaching, but he had nothing more to give. Their gazes caught. Her expression changed. Her features softened. Her lips parted. Slater's pulse quickened, and he felt panicky. He needed to get away, but he couldn't move. His feet wouldn't move.

And then she smiled. Soft, warm, sweet. A slow spread that filled him with heat and happiness because it said, *I like you.*

And that got him moving. She definitely shouldn't be liking him. Not Derek's sister. Not this nice girl who wouldn't like anything about his life. He headed out of the kitchen, pausing only to say, "Let me know next time you need a ride." He took the stairs three at a time, shutting himself in his room.

———

Emmie pressed her ear to Slater's door. Not a sound. Too bad. She loved hearing him work on melodies. Everyone joked about his lifestyle, but she couldn't figure out when he did all this "banging." The bar where he worked closed at two AM, and for the last several weeks he'd come home well before three. He got up early—completely contrary to what Derek had promised—and spent most of the day reading, writing, or composing.

So, what gives? Why did he let everyone think he was such a player? She knocked, hoping he wasn't napping. Lord knew he needed his sleep. If he wasn't performing, he was bartending. The guy worked all the time. How he thought he could turn out to be a loser like his dad she didn't know. The missing ingredient in most artists was discipline. Slater had it in spades.

"Yeah?"

Oh, he *was* in there. "Are you busy?"

"Come in." He sounded sleepy. She cringed.

She opened the door and peered in to find him sprawled on his bed. He was a big guy, but the way he took up the bed, his feet almost hanging off the mattress, made him look like a conquering warrior. A pillow bunched under his head, a book lying on his chest, he rubbed his eyes.

"What's up?" he asked.

"Did I wake you?"

He lifted the jazz theory book. "Can't imagine how I dozed off."

She smiled, coming in a little further. A breeze from his open window ruffled a shirt slung over the back of a chair and brought in the lovely scent of honeysuckle. "I have a favor to ask. If you're too tired, I totally understand. But I'd like to pick up some supplies, and I just found out the bus schedule I've been using is out of date as of yesterday."

He swung his feet off the bed, jammed a bookmark in the open page, and got up. "Not a problem. I need to run an errand myself." Scooping keys and coins off his dresser, he shoved them into his jeans' pocket and motioned for her to lead the way. "Where we going?"

"The Staples on South Lamar."

"You need office supplies? Can't you get them at CVS?"

"You're such a boy. Of course I can get them at CVS. I can even get them at Safeway. But I want the cute stuff." She rolled her eyes. "Boys."

He smiled, shaking his head.

She got into his big, ancient Land Cruiser. It smelled of coffee and . . . candy? She leaned down to scoop up the empty Bit-O-Honey wrappers. As he jammed the key into the ignition, she shook a fistful at him. "Didn't your mamma ever tell you candy'll rot your teeth?"

"My mama wrote the book on the subject."

"What's she like, your mom? I've only ever heard about your dad."

"My mom's great."

"Is she a rocker like your dad was? Should I be picturing tattoos, nose rings, bright orange hair?"

He cracked up. "Dr. Vaughn? She teaches at UT. Not only doesn't she dye her hair, she wears it in a sensible bob. She's never worn makeup a day in her life and chooses her shoes based on arch support." He gestured to the candy wrappers. "As for these . . ." He smiled, and for the first time ever, he wasn't the jaded, womanizing rock star. He looked boyish. "I like the little bits of nuts in them."

He leaned over her, opening the glove compartment, and wrapped candies spilled out. "Help yourself."

Oooh, she liked the way he smelled, all clean and masculine, and loved the thick, corded muscles in his arm. Would it be so awful to touch them, run her hand along the smooth skin? "Thanks." She unwrapped one and popped it in her mouth. It took a few moments for the honey-flavored candy to dissolve enough that the little pieces of peanuts stuck out. "Mm. Nice."

"Tunes are in back."

"Actually, do you think we could listen to this instead?" She pulled a Piper Lee CD out of her bag.

He glanced at it. "I don't care."

"She's playing at Austin City Lights. That's why I want you guys to play there. Just have a feeling you guys will fit well together."

"Why do we need to fit well together?"

She shrugged. She'd found out Piper already had an opening act, but Devil's Den had a reputation for being unreliable. Not to mention they had flaky management. She'd push to get Snatch in. If not to replace them, then to be an additional opener. But she wouldn't mention it yet—just in case it didn't work out. "Just thinking."

"You do that a lot. Hey, speaking of my old neighborhood. My mom's got a list of things she needs me to do. I'd like to stop by. Do you have somewhere to be this afternoon?"

She'd *love* to see where he grew up. "I was supposed to meet with the Pugs. Have you heard of them?"

He nodded. "They're pretty cool. We play some of the same venues. Why, you interested in signing them?"

"Well, I don't know."

He cut her a quick look, obviously hearing the frustration in her voice.

She glanced at his profile, wondering if she could confide in him. A week ago, she wouldn't have dared. He'd been so stand-offish. But now? "How do I know? I mean, how can you tell if there's potential? I just . . . sometimes I'm completely befuddled."

He grinned. "Befuddled?"

"Yeah. I've watched Irwin. He gets this expression when he's hearing something good. It's how I know he's into a band. And I try hard to listen, but, I swear, I don't know what he hears."

"Stop trying to hear what he hears and just listen for yourself. It's about you responding to something in the music. Not Irwin. And that's the good news. *Because* it's so subjective, it means there's a band for you to discover that Irwin never would."

She smiled. "I like that. A lot." And, wow, the more she thought about it, the more significant it became. She let the idea sit with her, letting it expand and push out the doubts. "You know something? You just did something huge for me. You took the focus off Irwin, off trying to please *him*, and onto the bands. Onto *me*." She wanted to touch his arm, let him know how much she appreciated what he'd said, but she squeezed her hands together instead. "That's really cool."

"Good." He muttered a curse as a pickup cut in front of him, forcing him to brake hard. Once he'd resumed his normal speed, he said, "So, you were supposed to meet the Pugs this afternoon?"

"Yeah, I was going to meet them for a band practice, but they cancelled. They don't seem like the most together band."

"Most aren't."

"You guys are." Wait—

It hit her all at once. The realization so obvious, so clear, she felt it pulse under her skin.

Oh, my God. So what if Irwin had passed on Snatch's demo? He hadn't seen them live, hadn't seen them since they'd made some changes. She let out a huff of breath, overwhelmed with the joy of it, and he glanced at her.

"What?"

"Nothing." She shook her head. "I'm such a knucklehead."

"A knucklehead?"

Snatch would be the band she discovered. But she wouldn't say anything yet. Not until she'd made a little more progress—particularly with Piper. If Snatch scored this tour, Irwin would absolutely pay attention to them.

"You okay?"

"Better than okay." She reached for his knee, but he grimaced before she even made contact, so she withdrew. She couldn't help the sting of hurt from his reaction. God, did she have man hands or something?

"So, if you're into fancy office supplies, there's a place called Go to Work out in Riverdale, which just happens to be right by my mom's house."

Okay, she knew she didn't have man hands. Maybe he just didn't want to encourage her—what else did he know but women coming on to him? "Way better than Staples?"

"Beyond your wildest imagination."

"Like you have the slightest idea what's in my imagination."

"True. And the mystery keeps me up at night."

She turned away from him, hiding her smile, because to be perfectly honest? The only thing firing up her imagination these days was *him*.

Not that he'd ever know.

———

As Slater turned into the Riverdale Country Shopping Plaza, he noticed Emmie leaning forward to get a look at Go to Work. Yeah, they went all out with their window displays, but, man, she sure liked her office supplies.

Only, as he pulled into a spot, he realized her gaze was fixed on the shop next door.

Bella Donna sold high-end, elegant lingerie. And Emmie practically drooled at the fancy shit in the window.

Interesting.

He cut the engine, pocketed his keys, and met her in front of the car. They stepped onto the walkway, and as she cut right for Go to Work, he started left.

"Where are you going?" she said.

"I'm following your heart."

"What?" She glanced nervously at the Bella Donna sign.

"Come on. You know you want to."

"Yeah, right." She laughed it off, but he saw the interest in her eyes.

"We can just look around."

"Right. You go ahead and look around. They should have *something* in your size. I'll be in here." She pointed to the office supply store.

"That's fine. You can work up to it."

She shook her head as she went inside for her supplies.

After grabbing a basket, Emmie's gaze roamed the aisles and displays, a look of reverence overtaking her features. "This place is amazing."

She started filling her basket with crap he was sure she'd never use in a lifetime.

"Didn't you bring any supplies with you?"

"I left everything at my apartment. Six weeks, remember?"

How could he forget? He was keenly aware of everything about her. From the changes she'd made to the band and the way she'd brought them together beyond rehearsals or gigs, to the fact she was only there temporarily.

She had three and a half weeks left.

"Oh, my God," Emmie said, her attention turning to a clipboard. "Look at this. Is this the prettiest thing you've ever seen?"

Yeah, a *clipboard*. So it had a light blue background and bright yellow daisies all over it. And . . . it was still a clipboard.

She clutched it to her chest. "I have to have it." Spotting another one—this one with orange dots on a hot pink background—she grabbed it, held them both out to him. "Which one?"

He looked at her, dumbfounded.

"I should get both." She started to put them both in the cart, then stopped. "But what do I need them for?" She gazed up, lost in thought. "I don't. I don't need them at all. What would I use a clipboard for?"

"Inventory."

"I don't do inventory."

"Exactly." As adorable as she was being, this whole shopping experience was lost on him. Couldn't she have chosen the lingerie shop instead? He'd have lots of opinions there.

"You know what?" She set them back on the shelf. "I don't need them. You have to stop me from impulse buys. I can't just randomly spend money."

"I'm in charge?"

"Do you want to be?" She trained those warm brown eyes on him with her mischievous smile, and suddenly she no longer wore the simple pink T-shirt and khaki shorts. He imagined her standing before him in the purple chemise he'd seen in Bella Donna's window.

What the hell? "Let's get a move on." But, Christ, did she fill it out nicely. He strode off.

In the next aisle, she agonized over how many and which sizes of multicolored Post-its she needed.

"You're looking to sign bands. Other than a pen and a cocktail napkin, what do you need?"

"Buzzkill." She turned back to examine the ridiculous array of choices.

"Funny how you need all this color in your office supplies but not in other areas."

She swung around to him. "What does that mean? You think I'm boring?"

"You wear white underpants and bras."

Color rushed to her cheeks. "How do you know what my undergarments look like?"

Undergarments? He chuckled. "We share a bathroom and a laundry room."

"I don't just wear white." She turned and snatched random packages off the shelves, tossing them in her basket.

He tugged the back of her shorts, peered inside.

"Hey." Whacking his hand away, she stumbled into the display bin of highlighters.

"You're right." He reached out and grabbed it before it toppled over. "My bad."

She cocked her head.

"You've got beige, too."

"They're comfortable. I shouldn't *feel* my underwear." She frowned, heading down the aisle. "What does it matter what I wear?" But then she hesitated and turned back to look at him with turmoil in her eyes. Waiting for a woman to pass by with her cart, Emmie grabbed his shirt, pulling him close. He could feel the heat of her, her intense energy. "*Does* it matter? I mean, is it a total turnoff to see a woman in boring underwear?"

He could see how much it mattered to her. "If a guy wants to get off, then, yeah, sexy underwear on a hot body'll do the trick. But if a guy's into you, then he doesn't need you wearing sexy lingerie to get it up. If he does, then he doesn't want you enough or for the right reasons."

Her features relaxed, and she was just so damn pretty. Her

complexion so clear and smooth, the shape of her mouth so sexy.

"I like that."

Oh, she shouldn't have smiled. Not when he could see the sparkle in her eyes and the little dimple under her eye, right at the top of her cheek. "I'm more interested in taking it off, anyway," he said. "I want what's underneath."

Her gaze drifted from him, looking dreamy and contemplative.

The girl took all the fun out of trying to rattle her.

She drew in a slow, deep breath, her chest rising. "But I wonder how it would make *me* feel, you know? I wonder if it would make me feel sexy."

"Only one way to find out."

And he'd said that out loud *why*? Should he really be encouraging Derek's sister to wear naughty lingerie?

And why the hell was she sharing this shit with *him* anyway?

The realization hit him like a telephone pole. She could talk like this, walk around the house braless, only if she didn't see him like that, like a guy. He was just a player who banged groupies. She'd never take a guy like him seriously.

It wasn't just a line she'd used. She actually wasn't susceptible to him at all.

Holy fuck. Why did that realization drop him to his knees?

After she'd paid for the few items she'd wound up buying, they headed out into the hot sun. Slater watched her toss her bag in the backseat, then head to the passenger side of the car. "Last chance," he said, nodding toward the lingerie shop.

She looked past him to Bella Donna, and he knew the moment hesitation turned to commitment. "Maybe I'll just take a quick look."

"Good idea." He met her on the walkway, then reached for the door to open it for her.

She turned to him, her hand resting lightly on his chest. "You want to get us some coffees?" She tipped her head toward the coffeehouse a couple of stores down. "I won't be long."

"Yeah, sure. I'll be right back with them."

"Or, you know, maybe just wait for me there?"

He smiled. "Sure thing."

Not a fucking chance.

Ten minutes later, Slater peered through the window holding their two coffees. He didn't see her, so he went inside and was immediately overwhelmed with scented vanilla candles and Debussy's "Clair de Lune." Pink wallpaper with black bows made the shop feel cozy. An older, well-heeled saleswoman stood behind a table folding a satin peignoir.

She smiled. "You looking for Emmie?"

Of course she knew Emmie's name. He nodded with an indulgent smile. Emmie'd probably revolutionized her folding system by now. The girl got shit done, and she did it in the sweetest, nicest way possible.

"In there." She pointed toward the dressing rooms. "You're going to love her choices."

Yeah. Like he'd go into the dressing room to see Derek's sister trying on teddies. When the woman's features fell in confusion, he lifted the coffees as an excuse.

She nodded in understanding. "You go in. A girl always appreciates her man's opinion. More so than an old lady's."

"Thanks." *Still not going in.* He headed to the dressing room as the woman turned to hang a scrap of silky material on a mannequin. A row of four curtained rooms gave way to a small sitting area. Champagne-colored walls with a crystal chandelier gave the area an elegant feel. He peered in to find a round dais facing a three-way mirror. Emmie stood on it, wearing an indecent nightgown.

Lace formed the cups of the top, revealing the fullness of her breasts, the dark pink of her nipples. A yellow satin band fit snugly just underneath them, and the skirt floated over her hips, stopping just below the incredibly sexy curve of her ass.

Head tilted, all that dark hair shifting to one side and revealing the deep V of the back, she examined herself. He couldn't tell if she liked what she saw. She seemed unsure until she brought her hands up to her breasts, touching her nipples as if to see how they felt through the thin material.

She hissed in a breath, her whole face transforming, tightening with a rush of desire, and then her hands cupped those lush, round breasts. She gave them a gentle squeeze, eyelids fluttering closed.

Holy shit. Desire exploded inside him, rushing through his dick, making him instantly hard. The door chime jangled, and as he jerked away from the wall, hot coffee spilled onto his hand. He could hear the saleswoman talking quietly to whomever had just entered.

Fuck. He set one of the coffees down on a shelf, then dragged his wet hand on his jeans. His heart pounded, and he couldn't for the life of him get the image of Emmie touching herself out of his head. It just kept repeating like a GIF.

He had to get out of there.

SEVEN

She'd taken too long shopping. She could tell because the moment they got in the car, Slater cranked the stereo and tore out of the parking lot.

"Sorry about that." Well, sorry she'd wasted his time. But thrilled she'd taken care of number seven on her list: Wear sexy lingerie.

"No problem." His hands gripped the steering wheel.

Emmie loved her new bras. Loved them with a passion normally reserved for dessert and pretty office supplies. She sipped her coffee, which he'd prepared perfectly for her, and then set it between her legs, since the old car didn't have cup holders.

Opening the pretty pink and black bag, she withdrew one of the bras, quickly sliding it out of the tissue paper. She could not believe a bra could be so beautiful and sexy. The teal satin demi cups with black lace overlay had hoisted the girls into the most delectable mounds she'd ever seen.

She held it up by the straps. "Is this to die for?"

He barely spared her a glance.

"I love it," she said more to herself, since he obviously didn't care about bras. "How far is your mom's?"

He didn't answer, just kept his gaze trained on the road, jaw set tightly.

Okay, he was pissed. She flicked off the stereo. "I thought you wanted me to go in there."

He frowned, giving her a dismissive shrug like, *Whatever.*

"I didn't take that long, did I? I mean, come on. Less than twenty minutes."

He ignored her and turned the music back up.

Taking another sip of her coffee, she balled up the tissue paper, put the bra back inside, and pulled out another one. Tearing off the paper, she brought this one to her chest and clutched it. This one she *adored*. Super-sheer black lace covered in tiny yellow and white daisies, it had nice lift from the underwire but plunged deeply across her cleavage, exposing lots of skin and making her breasts really bouncy. She'd never felt sexier in her life than when she'd tried it on.

She flicked off the stereo. "This one's my favorite. Isn't it pretty?"

He sighed, all long and drawn out, letting her know his exasperation. "Sure."

He hadn't even looked at it. "Okay, what's the matter?"

"Nothing."

"We're adults, not middle schoolers. We don't say, *Nothing.* If I took too long in the store, just say so."

"You're fine."

If he wanted to sulk, let him. "Oh, I'm fine. Very, very fine. And I'm not letting you lick off my frosting."

"Excuse me?" His eyes practically bulged out of his head. Now, he looked at her. She held up her bra and let it dance before him. He glanced back at the road before squeezing his eyes shut and actually groaning.

"The best part of cake is the frosting. Derek used to lick mine off—every single time, my birthday, his birthday, anywhere—and it used to make me so angry. Until I decided not to let him get to me anymore. And guess what?"

"He stopped licking off your frosting." He shifted uncomfortably, narrowing his gaze out the windshield.

"Bingo. God, I can't believe I never bought bras like these before."

He groaned again.

"I didn't bother with the nighties. I mean, do women actually sleep in those scratchy things?" She lowered her voice, leaning closer to him. "Some of them had thongs. Imagine that crawling up your butt in the middle of the night?"

"Emmie, I'm a man. You do know that, right?"

"Uh, yeah." Was she boring him? "Fine. We'll talk football stats." She smiled at him. "I can do that, too."

Mouth a grim line, he turned the stereo up loud enough to make conversation impossible.

His mom lived only a few minutes from the shopping plaza, so she didn't have to endure his foul mood for long. Growing up in Westchester County, she was used to grand colonials, rolling green lawns, and stone walls. But these homes looked newer, all browns and beiges, and the landscaping more rustic. Lots of terra-cotta and dusty-looking trees and shrubs, unlike her White Plains neighborhood, which was vibrant with flowering trees and red maples.

As the streets grew narrower, the houses became closer together, less formal. A few more turns and the homes grew even smaller. This area made more sense for a music professor's salary.

A quick flash of water appeared between houses. "You live on a lake?"

He nodded. When he turned onto his street and began to slow, a feeling bloomed inside her and made her . . . happy. The band's house in the suburbs seemed so artificial, so bland. But where he'd grown up? Lovely.

"I always had this fantasy about living in a cottage on a lake, a swath of green lawn canopied by towering trees. My private little fairy forest."

He pulled into a driveway. "That was my childhood all right. A real fairy tale."

Bougainvillea spilled off the terra-cotta roof of the stucco one-story house, and a stone walkway bracketed with rose-bushes led to an antique oak door.

"This is gorgeous." She got out, breathing in the rose-scented air. In their development, the air smelled dusty and dry, and the landscape was stark and desert-like. "You grew up here?"

"Hey, Mom." His flat, guarded voice had Emmie swinging around to find him at the front door.

"Jonny." A petite woman in loose linen pants and a sleeveless tunic gazed up at him with so much love and admiration, Emmie's breath hitched in her throat. Her parents had *never* looked at her like that. She was so similar to her super-efficient mom that everything good she did was just expected. And her dad? Well, unless she suddenly tapped into her inner virtuoso, Emmie didn't think she'd ever get more than a vague sense of appreciation from him—when she did something he wanted.

But wait a minute. What had she called him? *Jonny?* His mom called him *Jonny?*

Slater angled back. "Mom, this is Emmie. Derek's sister."

"Emmie Valencia. How wonderful to meet you. Come in, come in." Her warm smile drew Emmie up the walkway.

"So nice to meet you, Dr. Vaughn."

"Please call me Elizabeth. I wish I'd known you were coming sooner. I would have rearranged my schedule." His mom clasped Emmie's hand in her dry, cool ones. "You look so much like Derek."

"Well, except I have hair and he has tattoos." She stepped into the tiled foyer. The house smelled of old paper and something extremely familiar—the valve oil for brass instruments.

"Yes, except for that." His mom laughed, eyes sparkling. "I'd love to make some tea and sit with you awhile, but I've got to leave for a meeting in a few minutes." She gave her son a playfully admonishing look.

"I didn't know I was coming until a few hours ago. Emmie hit up Go to Work."

Pleasure lit up his mom's features. "I love that store. Have you seen the new clipboards they just got in?"

"Are you serious?" Emmie said. "I wanted one of each. They were gorgeous."

His mom smiled almost shyly, cupping a hand around one side of her mouth. "I did get one of each."

Emmie laughed. "Totally jealous."

"Do you have the list?" Slater asked, all business.

Emmie noticed the disappointment pull across his mom's features. This was his home, his mom. He couldn't chat for a few minutes?

Reaching for the chain dangling off her neck, she lifted her eyeglasses, then patted her pockets. "Now what did I do with it? I was sitting at the kitchen table, writing it up after you called, but I got distracted." She peered at him over the top of her glasses. "I'm reviewing a student's dissertation. She's got some interesting ideas on modal jazz theory." Her brow lifted, and she gave Slater a probing look. Right then, Emmie could see the professor in her. "I'd really love to get your input."

Slater's eyes narrowed. His posture slumped—barely, but still. Emmie noticed. "Mom . . ." He gave her a disbelieving look.

But she never wavered. "I would appreciate your insights."

He exhaled, looked down at his big black boots and rubbed his chin between his thumb and forefinger. "Yeah, sure. Okay. Leave it on the table. I'll take it with me."

Okay, so, wow. First, his professor mom needed *Slater's* help with jazz modal theory? And, secondly, sure, Slater was guarded—even around the guys—but he was always so laid-back, so . . . nonchalant. Around his mom, though, he just bristled. What had she done to hurt him?

"Wonderful. Okay, let me check the kitchen for that list." As she strode off, she called back to him. "I'll be so relieved to have the use of that powder room again. You can imagine the inconvenience when I've got a full house."

Slater started after her, but then he turned to Emmie. "This won't take long. Do you want to come with me or hang out here for a few minutes?"

Figuring he could use the time alone with his mom, she said, "I'm good. Take your time." Plus, come on, she was in Slater's childhood home. She was dying to look around. She gestured to the living area, her gaze fixed on the wall of bookshelves. "Can I look around?"

For the first time since she'd met him, color infused his cheeks. He hesitated. Was he *embarrassed*? "Have at it." With a resigned expression, he turned and went into the kitchen.

What could possibly embarrass him about his home? It looked warm and inviting. She could hear them talking quietly as she took in the living room. The low ceilings and bloodred walls gave the house a cozy feel. The furnishings were old and funky. A pink chandelier hung over a bar in one corner of the room. A deep purple chaise with gold fringe caught her eye—it looked so pretty but was completely impractical in a living room. Clusters of tables and chairs were set up around the room. Actually, it kind of looked like an old-fashioned pub. A gathering of small sitting areas instead of a traditional living room arrangement of a couch and coffee table facing a couple of chairs.

But then she started to notice details. Weird-looking instruments hung on the walls, rested on the tables, stood in corners. Not a bar, then, but a place to jam. She recognized the harp, of course, and the balalaika. Leaning against the wall sat something that looked like a guitar, but with a bloated middle section and a squat but wide fingering band. But, really, other than some tambourines and a xylophone, she didn't recognize the other unusual-looking instruments.

She could imagine the room filled with the scents of a Moroccan stew and burning candles as people jammed, talked, laughed, and sang together. What a great childhood he must've had.

And so similar to her own. Only, no one touched the instruments lying around her house but her dad and his friends. Even Derek, who'd played guitar and piano from the time he could walk, wasn't allowed near them because he would just "abuse" them. This home seemed so welcoming. Why would Slater be embarrassed?

Wandering to the built-in bookcase, she found it stuffed with framed photos, books, vases, and figurines. The longer she looked, the more she noticed the photos basically chronicled Slater's life.

"Got it," she heard his mom call and then laugh. "It was on the washing machine."

One photograph snagged her attention. A wild-haired man, loads of necklaces and chokers around his neck, tattoos all over his arms, stood beside a slightly younger version of Slater's mom. With her salt-and-pepper hair, probing eyes, and serene smile, she looked like a pottery teacher or a woman who owned a healing arts store. What an odd pair. The man had his arm slung around her shoulders, his purple-framed round glasses askew on his nose.

"I'll see how much of this I can get done today." Slater came out of the laundry room with a tool box in one hand. He watched Emmie for a moment, and she thought he might say something, but he just scowled and turned into the powder room.

"Well, I'm off." His mom breezed past her but stopped to look at the photograph. Her head came to Emmie's shoulder. "That was taken on Jonny's first day of college. We'd just dropped him off in his dorm."

Emmie wished she could see *that* picture, of Slater in his dorm room. She wondered if he'd been the stud on campus. Had he joined a frat? But she wouldn't ask about Slater, not when he was a few feet away. "How did you and your husband meet?"

Her smile seemed a little tight. "I know we look like quite the mismatched couple, but we worked. We lived down the street from one another. His parents hired me as his music tutor." She reached for the frame, her thumb gently rubbing the glass. So much conflicting emotion in her eyes. "He was full of energy, full of life. Couldn't sit still. And I was very serious, very thoughtful. He needed my clarity of thought, and I needed his passion."

Emmie's heart wrenched open. *I love that.* "That's so nice." She wished so badly her parents had thought about their differences that way. Instead, her dad had accused his organized, efficient wife of being uptight and cold. As much as he'd obviously needed her, he'd never appreciated her. He'd shut her out for not understanding the temperament of an artist.

"That's such a beautiful way to look at it." Emmie turned back to the shelves. So many photos of the wild-haired man with a boy—a teen—who was clearly Slater. In most of the pictures Slater looked angry, which didn't quite fit the whole mini-me look he had going on with his dad. He almost looked embarrassed, but then weren't most teenagers when forced to pose with their parents?

Funny to see how much Slater had changed his look from hard rocker to frat boy. Then again, he didn't wear khakis and Ralph Lauren. He favored jeans, black T-shirts, and boots. So maybe he had some rocker in him. Just without all the accessories.

"Jonny and his dad." His mom tapped the glass frame of a picture.

"Looks like they were close." Emmie could feel the hurt all the way down to her bones, that need to be with her dad, hang out with him just like Slater and his dad. But he'd always pushed her away.

"Two peas in a pod." A note of envy wound through his mom's wistful tone.

A jarring sound came from the powder room, like a toilet seat slamming down. They looked at each other, eyes wide.

"Everything all right?" his mom called.

"Peachy," he said, voice tight.

His mom rolled her eyes, smiling, then looked back to the photo. "They did everything together. Honestly, I don't think there was another person on this earth Jonny enjoyed being with more than his dad."

A tool clattered to the tile floor. "I thought you had a meeting?" Slater stood in the doorway of the powder room, looking like a gunslinger in a saloon.

"Oh, goodness, yes. Yes, I do. And I can't be late." She reached for Emmie's hand again. "Really, it was so lovely to meet you. Please come by one evening with Jonny. We'll have supper, and you can hear him play. Wouldn't that be fun, Jonny? Playing for your friend?"

"Mom." Emmie had never seen him so agitated, and she couldn't imagine why. His mom was kind and so obviously admired her son's talent. But instead of reveling in it, Slater just stood there, grinding his teeth. He drew in a breath, shook his head, and went back into the bathroom.

His mom gave Emmie an uncomfortable smile. "I'd hoped after his father passed that he'd come back to us, but . . ." Looking terribly sad, Elizabeth grabbed a large cloth bag from the dining-room table and headed to the door. "Let's make plans soon, dear."

Emmie stood there, awash in the strange sadness that had a grip on this family. Slater had a mom who clearly loved him, yet he held himself back from her. He'd had a dad who'd obviously adored him, and yet he was filled with such anger. Emmie found herself drawn to the powder room to check on him.

"You okay?" she asked softly.

"Yeah, just need to replace the flapper valve assembly."

Not exactly what she'd meant. She watched him put the lid back on the tank, then wash his hands at the glass bowl-shaped sink. "Your mom's so nice."

"She is."

He grabbed the tool box, and they headed out. Pulling the list out of his pocket, he scanned it.

With his mom gone, he seemed more relaxed. "She's really proud of you."

He nodded. "Hey, can you do me a favor? Can you grab that trumpet over there and stick it in the freezer?"

Nice subject change. "The freezer?" Was he messing with her?

"Yeah, she can't get the mouthpiece off." He went over to a side table, picking up the instrument. "I hope she didn't use pliers. It's soft metal." He set the tool box down and examined the area around the mouthpiece. His fingers gently skimmed it, and a tingle shimmied along her spine at his careful touch.

His phone rang, and he checked the caller ID. Frowning, he handed the trumpet to her. "Hey, Mom." He listened for a moment, then grimaced. "Yeah, thanks, but I think we're all set. We've got plenty of food. Emmie takes good care of us."

She smiled, liking that he'd put it that way—that she took care of them. She liked taking care of them. With her roommates in Manhattan she'd felt completely alone. They'd never shared a meal or borrowed each other's clothes. Living with the guys, as crazy as it got, was fun. She liked it. It felt almost like family.

"Okay, later," he said, disconnecting and shoving the phone in his back pocket. "My mom's got something going in the Crock-Pot. She wants me to take some home, but . . ." He shuddered.

"What is it?"

"Something with lentils and kale."

"Ah. A vegetarian?"

"That doesn't begin to describe her food philosophy."

"What does she teach?"

"Music theory." He headed down a dark hall.

She followed, noting the walls lined with more framed photos. "Was she your teacher?"

"Nope." He flipped a light on in a bathroom and set his tool box down in front of the vanity. "Not at UT anyway."

"This trumpet's beautiful." A pretty pinkish gold, it looked old with beautiful, elaborate etchings on it.

"It's from the twenties." He pulled a wrench from the tool box and got down on his back, pushing himself underneath the counter until she could only see him from the neck down. His broad shoulders spanned the width of the cupboard, and she loved the way his thigh muscles pulled against the denim of his jeans. When her gaze landed on the slight bulge between his legs, a bolt of pure lust shot through her.

Oh, God, really? Looking at Slater Vaughn's junk? She smoothed a hand on the trumpet, forcing her mind off Slater's incredibly hard, masculine body. "It's pink." Um, the trumpet. Not his skin. His skin was more like caramel.

"Yeah, pink gold was popular back then." The muscles in his long legs clenched and flexed as he worked on the pipe inside the vanity.

The trumpet, Emmie. Focus.

"I love the engraving. It's so intricate. Do you play?"

He slid out, the back of his shirt riding up, revealing the skin of his torso.

Seriously, she was only human. And he was the hottest man she'd ever seen in her life. It wasn't her fault she wanted to crouch beside him, touch that warm skin, and slide her hands up his chest to feel each ridge and slope.

Watch him grow hard from her touch. Oh, she'd *love* to see that.

This is ridiculous. She absolutely couldn't allow herself to think about Slater this way. She had to live with the guy. Even if he had any interest in her, she'd never do anything about it. She'd never be more than a hookup to a guy like him.

Tossing the wrench back in the tool box, he got up. "The mouthpiece is stuck. She tried using *pliers . . .*" He looked incredulous, and she loved his appreciation for the antique instrument. "Could you do me a favor and put it in the freezer?"

"You were serious?"

"Metal contracts when it's frozen, and the mouthpiece isn't made of brass, like the rest of the trumpet, so it'll contract a little bit more. Once it's as cold as it's gonna get, the mouthpiece should come right off."

She held his gaze for the longest time. Why did she find that so hot? That he knew something like that? She slowly broke into a smile.

His head tilted, as though he didn't understand what she found amusing. "Would you mind sticking it in there for me? I'll leave my mom a note to take it out when she gets home."

"Sure."

When she came back, the bathroom light was off. "Slater?"

"Last room on the right."

She found him in what had to be his mom's bedroom. Compared to Emmie's mom's, decorated to within an inch of its life by a pricey designer, this one was plain. It had little more than a neatly made bed with a plain navy duvet, an adorable fringed lamp on the nightstand, and a huge sliding glass door that led to a lush backyard.

"Can I open the door?"

"Sure."

"Alarms won't go off?"

"No alarms, New Yorker."

As soon as she opened the door, the sound of wind chimes filled the air like a symphony. They hung from the gutter, tree branches, awnings, just about everywhere. A patio with moss growing between the stone panels gave way to a sloping green lawn. Trees bordered the property, their limbs spilling forward into the yard, making them look like graceful dancers.

"This is beautiful." An idea struck her, and she went back inside. "Hey, your mom mentioned something about having me over for dinner. What if we had the guys over, too?"

His features tightened. "No."

She could picture them all outside, playing Frisbee, maybe heading down to the lake to kayak. "We'd keep it simple, maybe grill some burgers. I'd do all the other cooking."

"No." He lifted a portrait off the wall and set it down in front of a dresser.

"I get the feeling your mom—"

Before she could finish her sentence, he whacked the wall with a hammer. The sound of wallboard breaking made her jump, and she gaped at the hole he'd just made. "What're you doing?"

"She's got a leak." He pulled at the damp pieces, widening the hole.

"I just think your mom would really love it if you had your friends over here."

"Yes, Emmie. She would."

"Then why—"

"Fuck." His brow furrowed as he peered inside.

As she stepped closer to him, she saw the copper pipe had

turned green from a steady stream of water. He whipped out his old-style cell phone, punched a number.

"Jonny?" she heard his mom ask.

"Yeah, you're going to have to call the plumber. Looks like you hammered a nail into the pipe." He paused to listen. "I'll stop it up temporarily, but you've got to get a plumber in here. Make sure you let the wallboard dry out. Yep, okay." He hung up, stowed his phone in his pocket, and said, "I hope she's got some electrical tape." Watching the pipe, he ran his finger idly over the leak.

She could see the steady pulses of water through the small hole, indicating a good bit of water pressure. "Not sure tape will hold it."

"You're right. I'll wrap a piece of rubber around it. Be right back."

"Can I help?"

He stopped, turned to her. "Yeah, you can stop trying to fix me and my mom."

"I'm not—" Well, she was. "But she loves you so much, and it's obvious she doesn't know how to reach you."

"Reach me? My mom doesn't want to *reach* me. She wants me to drink red wine, and play music with her students and colleagues, and talk modal jazz theory."

"She wants you in her life." How could he not see that? How could he not want it, too?

"That's exactly right."

"What does that mean?"

"She wants me in *her* life."

"I'm sorry. I'm not seeing the problem."

"That's because there is no problem. It is what it is." He dropped the hammer on the carpeted floor. "Now let me get this pipe fixed up so we can go, okay? I'll be right back. Maybe I can find something in the garage."

She watched him go, surprised at how well she understood his pain. This visit had shone a light through the screen surrounding the super-cool, über-confident ladies' man to reveal the lonely boy within. Sad, really, that he had two parents who'd loved him so much yet had failed him somehow, leaving him feeling just as alienated in his family as Emmie had in hers.

Placing a finger over the water pulsing out of the hole, she thought of him all alone in that cool, dark garage, and just like that an idea came to her. She hurried to the sliding glass doors and stepped outside. "Slater?"

He poked his head out of the garage. "Yeah?"

"Do you have an old bike? You can use the inner tube from the wheel."

He broke out in a devastating smile, sunbeams piercing through cloud cover. "Good one."

She shrugged, looking away from the approval beaming in his eyes. "My dad wasn't exactly Mr. Fix It. We had to be pretty resourceful."

"First you're all wide-eyed over Post-its, then you're turning into sex on a stick in a lingerie dressing room, and now you've got a fix for a leaky pipe? Are you for real?" He laughed as he headed back into the garage. "Be right back with an inner tube."

She watched him go, so caught up in the happiness of his approval that it took a few moments for the meaning of his words to register.

"Wait, you saw me in the dressing room?"

EIGHT

"**What happened?**" Emmie asked, stepping back so the guys could get a wounded Slater into the house. Glistening blood caked a gash over his eye, and his black T-shirt, torn at the neck, was soaked in dark patches. "Oh, my God. Is he all right?"

"Bar fight." Derek edged past her, Slater's arm slung over his shoulder.

"Let's get him upstairs." At the foot of the staircase the guys tried to make a seat for him with their joined hands, but Slater shrugged them off.

"Jesus Christ, I wasn't shot in the spine." Gripping the handrail, he climbed up himself. She could see the bulging muscles, the white knuckles, and she hated the painful effort it caused him to get upstairs.

"Slater got into a fight?" she asked Derek quietly. That hadn't happened before.

He shook his head. "Some assholes had a bet over the Rangers game. Loser wouldn't pay up. Fists were flying. Some chick got in the middle, so Slater jumped the bar to get her out of the way."

"Where were the bouncers?"

"Too many guys involved. Someone called the cops."

Emmie heard a grunt, and she raced up the stairs to check on Slater. She found him in the bathroom, bent over the sink. Everyone crammed in, trying to help.

"You should go to the ER, man," Ben said.

"He probably doesn't need the ER." Derek looked under the sink and pulled out Band-Aids. "We've got these butterfly things."

Cooper opened the medicine cabinet just at the moment Slater straightened and wound up clocking Slater in the head.

"Shit." His hands went up to cover the wound. "What the fuck?"

"Okay, out, everybody." Emmie pushed them, and they all filed out.

"You got this, Em?" Ben asked.

"She's our house mom," Cooper said, striding down the hall. "Of course she does."

"Good, 'cause I haven't gotten laid yet," Pete said. "Anyone coming back to the bar with me?"

"I'm in," Cooper said.

Derek paused at the top of the stairs. "You might want to watch him tonight. He got hit pretty hard."

"Concussion?"

He shrugged. "Could be."

"I don't have a fucking concussion. Jesus." Slater swiped a wet hand towel over his wound, sucking in a breath.

She didn't say a word, just pried the towel out of his hand and nudged him over with her hip. Rinsing the towel out with warm water, she cleaned the blood off his face around the wound. "Let's see how bad it is," she murmured.

After a few moments of her ministrations, his breathing slowed, and his shoulders dropped. He sighed.

"Okay, this is going to sting a little," she said as she gently dabbed the heart of the wound. "But I have to see how deep it is."

She could feel his breath on top of her head, feel the waves of heat rolling off his body. "You know, it looks okay." Reaching for the medicine cabinet door, she smiled and said, "Now's a good time to duck." She took out the antibacterial cream and smeared some onto the gash with one of her cotton swabs.

"I'm going to put the strips on now." She said it quietly,

softly, glancing up to see if he minded. Good God, their faces were so close she could see the stubble on his chin, the black flecks in his blue-gray eyes. His lids were hooded, his lips slightly parted, and if she didn't know him better, she'd think he was totally turned-on.

But he was hurt, so the last thing on his mind was sex. "Can you sit on the toilet seat so I can reach it better?"

As soon as he sat down, she almost regretted her request. It put his mouth about two inches away from her breasts. *Oh, dear God.* Her nipples hardened, and in her thin tank no way did that go unnoticed. Involuntarily, her thighs squeezed together against the rush of arousal. God, she had to remember he didn't see her that way. And not just because of Derek, but because she was so far from his type it was almost sad. Not that she wanted to be a groupie, but she wouldn't mind being ridiculously sexy. The kind of girl that drove a guy like Slater wild. *Yes.* That's what she would love.

"I think we're good." She smoothed the second strip in place. Leaning back, she smiled at him, only to find him staring at her breasts—mesmerized. *Oh.* Not what she expected at all. "Let's get you to bed."

If she were a different kind of girl, she'd thrust her chest out, lick her lips—act like a sexual woman. But, of course, she wasn't like that, so she just turned and hurried out of the bathroom.

She got to his room first, straightened his sheets, and put his pillow back in place. He collapsed onto the bed, immediately curling up.

"Okay, hang on." Emmie cradled his head with her hand as she eased him back onto his pillow. "Let's take off your boots."

"I can do it myself," he said. "Let me just get some sleep." But his eyes started to close, his body going limp.

Emmie untied his big black boots and pulled them off his feet. She started to lift his legs, to draw the blanket over him, but then wondered about his pants. Would it be okay to take them off? Who could sleep comfortably in jeans?

She reached for the top button, and he jerked.

"Enough, Em. Thanks, but seriously, get out."

"Oh, cool your jets. I just want to make sure you're comfortable." She pushed him gently back so she could unbutton the rest. As she tugged them down, the boxers came down with them, exposing a birthmark. Or . . . wait a minute. She looked more closely. It wasn't— Oh, it was a tattoo. A tribal star in bold black ink.

Her body thrilled at the sight of it. He had this rock-hard plane of ripped stomach, smooth, caramel skin with just a scattering of dark hair. And then, beneath the navel, a thin line of hair led to the thicker thatch below the waistband of his boxers. Just above that thatch sat this tantalizing tattoo. Something about the placement—God, it was just so naughty. It begged to be touched. To be licked. And thinking about licking it made her think of licking his erection, that smooth, hard, hot column of flesh, and oh, God, desire swept through her like a brush fire.

"Jesus, Em, I need to sleep."

"You have a tattoo."

He stiffened. His eyes opened, narrowing on her warily.

"It's so unbelievably hot." It was the most erotic thing she'd ever seen in her life. She ran her finger over it, leaning closer to make out the pattern.

"Em," he said with clear warning.

"God, I'll bet everyone just has to lick it."

He growled, lifting his hips and kicking off his jeans. His face twisted in agony.

"Oh, shoot. I'm sorry. I'm so sorry." She got to the end of the bed and pulled the jeans off.

He tugged up his boxers, one arm slung over his eyes.

"I'll be right back."

"No." He didn't sound so tired anymore. "You won't."

"Uh-huh." She'd get him some more Ibuprofen, leave it on the nightstand. He might be hurting in a few hours. Turning off the light, she headed to the bathroom, shook out some pills, and filled a glass with water. The whole time, her body hummed and tingled. She couldn't get the image of that tattoo out of her head—how close it was to his private parts.

Letting out a slow breath, she returned to his room, nudged him over, and got in beside him.

"You're not sleeping in my bed."

She stiffened. Oh, God, he thought she was going to put the moves on him. Again. She remembered how he'd responded to the *idea* of her hand on his knee in the car that day.

He wasn't attracted to her.

Yeah, well, she wasn't there to seduce him. "I'm not sleeping on the floor. And Derek said to keep an eye on you." So what choice did she have? No, she had to be there. "Good night, Slater."

She went quiet, her body on alert for any sound of discomfort from him. She hoped he'd fall asleep quickly, escape from the pain for a few hours. Closing her eyes, the tattoo popped into her mind, unleashing a whole new wave of arousal. She'd never gotten turned on thinking about an erection. Had never imagined licking one. Obviously, she'd given blow jobs before, but come on, of course her mind had wandered. She was giving the guy pleasure, not herself.

But just then? The thought of taking Slater into her mouth lit her up with rampant desire. Pressing her legs together, she pushed her face into the pillow to make a silent scream. What was happening to her?

"You're not gettin' any."

She burst out laughing, amazed he still had a sense of humor. She patted his arm, aware of the thick knot of muscle. "Hey, I can do whatever I want to you tonight, and you won't even remember it in the morning. This should be fun. Now go to sleep. I've dealt with concussions before. I'm supposed to check on you in two hours."

Staring up at the ceiling, she listened for his breathing to even out. It didn't.

"Is there anything I can do?" she whispered.

He didn't answer. Maybe he'd fallen asleep? But then he let out a breath, sounding exasperated, and his arm belted around her waist, and he tugged her against him.

Happiness gushed through her. She wanted to relax into him, but all she could think about was that tattoo. And his erection. It was too much. She was on sensory overload.

Within seconds, his breathing slowed, and he was out.

At least one of them would sleep tonight.

Arousal streaked through her. Emmie's breasts tingled, and she felt swollen between her legs. Mindlessly, her hips thrust back, and she heard a sharp intake of breath as she made contact with a very hard, big erection.

Slater. She was in his bed, his chest plastered to her back, and she could feel his thick length nestled between her thighs. And, oh, holy mother of God, did it feel good. Not just good, but . . . God, wildly delicious.

Reflexively, her hips pitched back again, lodging his hard-on firmly up against her seam.

"Jesus, Emmie." He withdrew.

She couldn't move. Couldn't even breathe. How did she get out of this situation? Someone had to say something. She couldn't just throw off the covers and breezily head to the bathroom, could she? She'd felt his boner, for God's sake. She'd *welcomed* it.

"Sorry. Morning wood." He sounded all casual, no big deal.

Which made her flush with embarrassment, because it had been a huge deal to her. To feel these sensations . . . that was the *whole point* of her list.

This attraction she felt to Slater was becoming dangerous. She had to meet other guys. Had to.

She couldn't put it off any longer.

She came downstairs to find the guys sitting around the table.

Ben's girlfriend, Tiana, got off his lap, her scrubs pulling tightly around her generous hips. "How is he? Thought I'd come by before work and check on him."

Emmie hadn't even asked. "He's coming down in a minute." Was he? She'd been too embroiled in her spectacular embarrassment to even think about his condition.

"Hey," he said, entering the kitchen. Tousled hair, bandaged forehead, puffy circles under his eyes—it only made him look hotter and rougher. "Any coffee left?"

Emmie jumped into action. "I'll get it." When everyone looked at her, she said, "I was going to pour myself a cup anyway."

Derek stood up. "You okay?"

"I'm better," Slater said gruffly. "I just needed sleep."

After pouring his coffee, she handed the mug to him without making eye contact. Then, she poured herself a cup, dousing it with cream and sugar, and turned to lean against the counter.

"Let me have a look at you." Tiana tipped his chin and examined his eyes.

He batted her hand away. "I'm fine."

"Let me at least look at the cut."

"Too late for stitches. Besides, no one touches this body but Emmie."

The guys snorted, and Tiana rolled her eyes, perching on Ben's thighs.

"Hey, thanks for bandaging me up." He sidled up beside her. "That was scary."

"I hadn't slept in two nights. I was more tired than concussed."

Now was her chance to ask him where he'd been. He hadn't missed a night at home in a while, so she'd been worried. She'd wanted to text him, find out if he was all right, but she didn't want to get too pushy. It's not like she had a right to know where he slept. And besides, she could imagine how he'd feel if some groupie was going down on him and he had to interrupt things to let his *house mom* know where he was.

She hoped she hadn't jeopardized anything by staying with him last night. Her relationship with the guys mattered to her. She just felt confused because he'd brought out all these erotic feelings in her. "Tiana," she blurted.

Tiana stopped playing with Ben's earlobes to face her.

"Where can I meet nice guys?"

"Hey," Ben said. "I'm a nice guy."

"You're *my* nice guy," Tiana said, kissing him on the mouth.

How had *she* managed to tame a rocker? Wait, why did Emmie care? She didn't want a rocker.

"I'm assuming you mean a guy you don't meet through these man whores?" Tiana asked. "A guy you don't meet in a bar or a club?"

"Exactly." She wouldn't look at Slater.

"You're leaving soon," Slater said. "Why bother meeting someone now?"

"I'm talking about a *date*."

"With a *nice* guy," Slater said. "A nice guy's going to want a relationship. Which you can't give him because you're leaving."

"Eager to get me out of your hair?" She watched him, wondering. Did she mean anything to him?

As always his features remained impassive, but his eyes

told a different story. And it made her wonder. Could he possibly feel this attraction?

"Not at all. Just wondering why you'd waste your time dating."

"You could stay." Everyone turned to look at Derek. "Stay and be our manager. We can't pay you anything yet, but hell. You're the best thing that ever happened to us."

"True story," Ben said.

She'd love to stay. And it wasn't like she'd discovered a band yet. Of course she'd keep looking, but she'd already gone through half the bands on her list and not one of them could compare to Snatch. She knew Irwin would sign them. But she wasn't ready to approach him. She'd wait until she heard back from Piper's people, after they'd had a chance to listen to the demo.

The way Slater looked at her made everything in her clench. Need burned in her veins. She wasn't ready to leave him.

"Could you?" When Slater studied her with that intensity, the whole world disappeared. It was just the two of them. Emotion rushed her so hard and fast it brought a fluttering sensation to her chest.

She looked away. What was the matter with her? "No." Slater wasn't attracted to *her*. A female body, sure. But not her. Besides, even if he was attracted to her, he didn't do relationships. And she wasn't about to have a meaningless hookup with her brother's best friend.

She had to stop investing so much . . . want in him. "I was lucky to get the six-week leave of absence. No way would Irwin tolerate longer."

"Describe your perfect man," Tiana said, breaking the mood.

"I'm going to work out." Derek looked to the others. "You want to come?"

Ben and Cooper shook their heads no, and Pete said, "Yeah, sure."

When Slater opened his mouth to speak, she stepped in and said, "You're not going anywhere. You're hurt."

Everyone looked at her and burst out laughing. "House mom," Pete said. He and Derek left the room. "Don't leave us, Em," Pete called from the hallway.

"Okay, Pete," she called back.

"Seriously, Em," Cooper said. "You can stay here as long as you want."

Her heart filled. "Thank you." That was a lovely thing to hear.

"So," Tiana said, "dream date. Go."

Emmie wrapped both hands around her mug, letting the heat infuse her. "Well, I like them clean-cut, you know, the all-American boy next door."

Tiana's gaze shifted to Slater. "Close your ears, *GQ*, she's not talking about you."

He smirked. "Pretty sure no one's gonna mistake me for a dream date."

"I wasn't finished," Emmie said. "Quiet, thoughtful. Creative, kind, generous. Funny."

"Likes to spend quiet nights around a fire reading poetry." Cooper fluttered his eyelashes and then burst out laughing.

"Loves dogs and long walks around the lake," Ben said.

"Hey," Emmie said. "I don't know where you guys get these crazy ideas about me. I hate poetry." She enjoyed their laughter. They looked like little boys when they cracked up like this.

Tiana looked to Ben with an incredulous expression, then back to Emmie. "You just described my brother."

"She's not going out with your brother," Slater said.

"Why not?" Tiana popped off Ben's lap and grabbed a bagel off a platter on the counter. "He's exactly what she described. He graduated from UT in 2004 with a degree in math. He's an actuary."

Slater made a rude sound.

"What's wrong with an actuary?" Tiana said. "He makes a good living. He's a provider."

"She said thoughtful, creative, funny. Is he all that?"

"Why are you being so nasty about my brother? You've never met him."

"I met him."

"He came to one of our shows," Ben said. "He and Slater talked for a while."

"And he wasn't funny."

"Is he cute?" Emmie said.

"Totally. Want to see his picture?" Tiana pulled her smartphone out of the pocket of her scrubs and started fiddling with it.

"You don't need a blind date."

She cut Slater a look. "I'm a little isolated out here, and if it's her brother, it's not exactly blind. It's just a little blurry."

He leaned over and whispered into her ear, "He's boring."

"Here," Tiana said. "Hector."

Emmie leaned over Tiana's shoulder. Totally clean-cut, the guy had twin dimples bracketing his mouth and very warm dark-brown eyes. A guy she could trust. "I'm in."

The bus should've come seventeen minutes ago. Perspiration trickled down her back as she waited on a bench under the blazing sun. A familiar tune blasted out of car speakers, and Emmie turned to see the dark-blue Land Cruiser ease over two lanes to pull alongside the curb. The Stevie Ray Vaughan song cut off and a shockingly good-looking singer leaned across the passenger seat.

"Where you headed?"

Oh, God. She would not—could not—tell him. "I'm just going shopping." She said it smoothly.

"Cool. Get in. I'll take you."

He hadn't slept at the house in three nights. She looked away, mortification burning through her.

He'd told her not to sleep in his bed, but she hadn't listened. And now things were weird between them. So weird he hadn't slept at home since.

"No, thanks. Bus'll be here any minute." Her attraction to him was getting out of hand. *I mean, God, you rubbed the guy's tattoo.* Given the location, contact with it was meant for girls he was having sex with. Girls he wanted.

"It's on my way."

She rolled her eyes. "You don't even know where I'm going." And she sure wouldn't tell him.

He held up a hot pink Post-it. "It's 869 South—"

"Slater!" She shot off the bench, lunging through the window for the paper, but he whipped it out of her reach.

"What?" He grinned wickedly.

Reluctantly, she got into the car. Could she be any more humiliated? Of all the roommates to come across her note, did it have to be this one? She belted herself in. "Where did you find it?" Please, please, let the Post-it have fallen off her checklist. *Please.*

"Your pocket."

"What were you doing looking through my pockets?"

"Laundry. I needed a few more things to make a full load." She sighed. "Take me home."

"Oh, no. No way. We're doing this." He paused. "I've always wanted to go to Pillow Talk."

She closed her eyes, wanting to dig her fingernails into her thighs until she drew blood. "No. We're not."

"We absolutely are." He drove on. "There's nothing to be ashamed of. We're adults. We like sex." She could feel his gaze on her and hated the way his voice dropped a few bars. "Right?"

She closed her eyes. "I wasn't lucky enough that you found the Post-it all by itself, was I?" Please, God, spare her. Please let this man suffer a serious brain injury in the next five minutes to wipe out any memory of what he'd seen.

He dug into his pocket and pulled out . . . What else? Her list. "My Body Electric."

"I hate you."

"Well, I feel very differently about you. In fact, I like you."

"So that explains Sunday morning."

His cheeks turned pink. "That was morning wood."

"Oh, believe me. No confusion there. I know it had nothing to do with me. You'd have had it if you'd woken up next to Mary." She wondered if he'd bring up the tattoo, the way she'd touched it, come in so close to inspect it.

Please don't.

Ever.

He got on the freeway. "Mary?"

"Your neighbor? The mom with the mullet?"

"I have a neighbor with a mullet?" He shook his head, as if to shake the image out of his head. "So. Body Electric?"

She groaned. "It's a Walt Whitman poem. "I Sing the Body Electric." It means—"

"Oh, I have a good idea what it means."

"Slater . . ." *Don't torture me.*

"Who's Alex?"

She sighed in utter resignation. "My ex."

"When did you break up?"

"Six months ago." She looked out the window, watching the strip malls whiz by.

"Why?"

"Excuse me?" She couldn't believe he would ask such a question.

"Why'd you break up with him?"

"He cheated on me." She shot him a look that said, *Are you happy now?*

His brows shot up. "Really? He cheated on *you*?"

Why did he emphasize the *you*? Like he couldn't believe someone would cheat on her? "Uh-huh."

"The rat bastard."

"Did you ever listen to that Piper Lee CD?" She pushed the Eject button, and Stevie Ray Vaughan popped out. She slid the CD back into the case but didn't see the Piper Lee one anywhere. "Hey, what did you do with that CD? I need it."

"How'd you find out?"

The look she gave him begged him to drop it. She couldn't bear telling the sex god her sad story. On the other hand, she had a date with a great guy this weekend, so her sad story would soon end, and she'd lead a healthy, fulfilling life, satisfying in all ways. Besides, everyone had a sad story. At least she was fixing hers.

Fine. Where to begin? "He's the bass player for Frontierland. They went on tour." She shrugged. Need she say more?

"He went on tour . . . ?"

She exhaled loudly enough to send the message she didn't want to talk about it.

"If I ask you a third time, there will be a consequence."

"Really. A consequence?"

"I live with four guys. I'm just saying." One side of his mouth hitched up in an adorable grin as he held up her list. "This could wind up on the refrigerator with one of those cowboy magnets you bought."

She growled. "Why do you care?"

"Trying to figure out why a woman like you would bother with a checklist like this. Only reason I can see is if you had some pussy boyfriend who made you feel like something was wrong with you instead of owning his own shit."

Every bone in her body softened. Her blood slowed, her muscles relaxed, and she sank into the upholstered seat. That might have been the nicest thing he'd ever said to her. "He said I wasn't wild enough. He said I *serviced* him, and he needed more." She could not believe she'd said those words out loud. To *Slater.* "You may have noticed. I'm very efficient and organized."

"So, how'd you find out?"

"First, it was Facebook."

"Pictures? Someone tagged him?"

She guessed he was looking to see if Alex had been careful about his behavior. And, yes, he had. "No. I read his messages."

"How did you see his Facebook messages?" he asked with a scowl.

"Whenever we were at each other's apartment, we shared a computer. If he left his email or Facebook account open, I could see what he was up to." She flicked a piece of lint off her shorts. "I snooped, okay?"

"You didn't trust him." He made an impatient gesture with his hand to get her back to the story.

"He'd gotten friendly with several girls. They were very grateful to him for spending such *quality* time with them."

She closed her eyes, remembering the icy sensation coursing through her when she'd read those messages. Four of them. She could still see the girls' profile pictures—so slutty. So unlike Emmie.

And then she felt the warmth of Slater's hand over hers. The unexpected gesture made her feel . . . better. Because it was a reminder. She was here now. What happened with Alex was in the past.

"And the second way?"

Must she, really? "I surprised him on tour. Yeah, that was fun. They were playing in Chicago. We'd done nothing but fight because I kept accusing him of cheating and he kept denying it, and it was just so exhausting. It's not like I didn't know he was cheating. Come on, I read the messages. I guess I just wanted to believe him. I'd known him most of my life, you know?"

"Are we getting to the good part yet?"

"Fine. So, Irwin and I were headed to LA for some party— one of our artist's songs was used in a movie, and we were invited to the premiere—but at the airport, *after* we'd gone through security, he decided to go to London instead because his mom was going to have a garage sale, and he was worried she'd sell his record collection. So, I thought about how Alex said I wasn't spontaneous or passionate enough, and I switched my ticket to Chicago. To surprise him."

"Is there any naughty sex in this story at all?"

"Literally in the next sentence. So, I get to the venue, and I'm asking around for him, but no one knows where he is, so I go to the tour bus and hear these sounds . . . I mean, right out of a porn movie . . . and I find him upstairs in the hall-way . . . with two naked women." She paused. "Twins."

"That's so fucking hot."

"It was horrifying. I don't know why he didn't just tell me and break up with me."

He looked disappointed. "So what did you do? And this better be good. I want some hair pulling, a nice right hook. Actually, you're a lefty, so make that a left hook. Better yet, how about when you picked up his guitar to brain him, the twins came at you like spider monkeys and ripped off your clothing so then there were three naked women?"

"I ran out. He followed me. I told him I couldn't believe he'd betray me like that. We'd talked about our relationship right before the tour. I *know* the temptations. But he insisted we were solid. I think he just wanted to make sure I kept pay-ing his bills and watering his plants."

"There's no more naughty sex, is there?"

"Nope." She flexed her hands, then curled them into fists and dug her fingernails into her palm. "There never was."

"You never had naughty sex with him?"

"You mean like threesomes and spankings?" She stuttered out a laugh. "Uh, no. But it's not like we didn't do fun stuff."

"*Fun* stuff?" He snorted.

"What?"

"So he got the wild stuff, the *passion* that was missing from your relationship, on the road. From other girls."

"Obviously."

"Man, did he do a number on you." He shook his head, frowning. "You really think that was passion, what he got from groupies?"

He was confusing her. "Of course. He wanted wild."

"Wild and passionate are two different things."

"You know what? Bottom line? He didn't need me anymore. That's all it boils down to." And there it was all over again. All the negative, horrible feelings rising, churning in her gut. "It was great when I could help him with his career. But once he got signed, his needs changed." He no longer needed a woman to help him with his career. He needed a woman who went wild for him. And to think Alex had told her *she'd* drifted once the band had signed with Bob. Please. "I wasn't enough for him." And, God, she had no idea why she couldn't let herself go when it came to sex. Just lose herself in the moment.

"Chicks."

"What's that supposed to mean?"

"Em. *He* wasn't enough for *you*."

"I already told you. He said I *serviced* him. He wanted more."

He shook his head. "When he touched you, Em, did you burn? Did he drive you crazy?"

She thought of all the times he'd come up behind her and press his erection to the small of her back. Or when she'd be working at her computer and he'd cup her breasts—his way of saying he wanted to get naked. No, she hadn't felt aroused. She'd felt irritated.

"We were together three years. It wasn't like that."

"What did he do to turn you on? To make you go wild?"

"I don't know. He let me know when he wanted to have sex."

"And how did he do that?"

"Well, how does any guy do it?" An elbow on the window, her hand shielding her eyes from the glaring sun, she stared unseeing at the rush of traffic. What a mortifying conversation. And yet . . . she was curious. *Had* Alex been in some way at fault?

"The thing is, Em, we want a girl to *want* to have sex with us. It's not a warm body that turns us on. It's a responsive woman. So if a guy just gets himself off, it's unlikely she's going to be all that excited to do it again with him."

He flicked on the turn indicator, glancing over his shoulder before changing lanes. "Did he do that? Just get himself off?"

Definitely. "In bed, yeah, he just got himself off. But he did other things, romantic things. He bought me flowers sometimes. Ran me a bath when I'd had a hard day. Those are the little things women like that *you* don't take into consideration because you've never been in a long-term relationship."

"I'm talking about *fucking.* Not dropping bath bombs in your tub. Did he ever get you so worked up that you rubbed your foot on his dick under the table in the restaurant, rammed your ass against his junk in the stairwell, and banged him against the wall as soon as you got into your apartment? Because you just had to have him? Did he ever turn you on that much?"

She squeezed her eyes shut, knowing how much Alex would have loved her to do any of those things with him. "No." She would love to feel that much desire. She just didn't think she was capable of it. "That's why the checklist. I'm working on it."

"Jesus Christ, Em, don't let this asshole do a number on you. He wanted to bang groupies on the road, and he didn't have the balls to break up with you beforehand. He's a shit." He crumpled her list in one hand. "Problem solved."

"Why did you do that? Give it back. You don't even know me."

He gave her a look that called her out. Because they *did* know each other. In their time alone together in the house they didn't make small talk. They *talked.*

"I know that he didn't turn you on."

"Well, guess what, Slater? No one ever has."

"None of your other boyfriends?"

"He's the only one I've slept with."

"That's a startling answer to an entirely different question. But you've dated other guys. Did you feel attracted to them? Or just other guys in general? You *can* feel attracted to someone else even when you're in a relationship. You just don't have to act on it. There *are* other options. Hey, maybe you could make one of your lists and send it to him. A list of possible alternatives to fucking other women when you're in a committed relationship."

He brought up a good point.

"So, *have* you felt sexual attraction for other guys?"

"Sure, I guess." She guessed? Like she hadn't been lusting after *him* just the other night?

"So, see? You don't need to get in touch with your saucy

side. You just need to find the right guy." Awareness lit his features. "Unless you're trying to win him back. Is that the plan? Trying to get yourself all hot and bothered for the guy who cheated on you?"

"You're not very nice."

"Did someone tell you I was?"

"Okay, stop. You're twisting me up."

"Hearing the truth after blaming yourself for someone else's bad behavior only *feels* twisted. Until it sinks in. Listen, while I'm all for sex toys, they won't release your inner vixen. It's chemistry, Em. It's carnal. It's raw, unadulterated attraction. Forget the list. Get the right guy."

Her head tipped back, hitting the headrest. So much of what he said sounded true. And yet, if she felt attracted to Slater, another musician, maybe something was—

"Emmie," he said, cutting into her thoughts. "Nothing's wrong with you."

She rolled her head to look out the window, watching the blur of highway traffic.

"You are sexual."

"How do you know that?"

"Because you want to lick my tattoo."

NINE

Bells tinkled as Slater pulled open the door. Red and black polka-dotted wallpaper and the strong scent of vanilla overwhelmed him as he entered after Emmie. On the stereo, Teddy Pendergrass sang, "Let's take a shower, shower together," from "Turn Off the Lights."

And just like that Slater's imagination carried him to their shared shower stall. How many times had he stepped in only moments after she'd gotten out, his senses filled with the sweet scent of her body wash? How many times had he soaped up imagining her gorgeous breasts filling his hands? How many times had he fisted himself, jerking off so that he could handle being around her in the kitchen as she walked around without a bra?

"So, um, where should I start?" Emmie stood there, taking in the various display tables. Her eyes widened at the lingerie hanging on well-endowed mannequins in back.

Nothing like the elegant chemises she'd seen at Bella Donna. This stuff was *dirty*.

Oh, hell. How had coming after her today been a good idea? "You don't need to be here at all. This isn't going to make you feel attracted to your ex."

"What?" She turned fiery, gazing up at him, and he understood for the first time her true frustration. "I told you. It isn't about him. It's about me."

"Yeah? And you still don't get it. It's about *chemistry*. Not skinny dipping, not crotchless panties, and definitely not blind dates with boring guys." Why was he pushing her? This wasn't any of his business. And what would Derek think if he knew Slater had taken his sister to a sex toy shop?

"Right. From the expert. Like you've ever felt true passion. I'm not looking to rut."

He snickered. "Rut." She cracked him up.

"All the books say to get in touch with yourself first. So, I'm doing that. I'm getting in touch with my sexuality." She looked up at him, and there it was, that compelling intimacy he felt every time he looked into her eyes. The world narrowed to her, as if he'd known her all his life, and yet she wasn't familiar to him at all. She was a mystery he was only beginning to figure out.

Why did he want to know her so damn much?

"What is it you want, Emmie?" He tugged on her arm, pulling them off to the side.

A sales girl spotted them and, with a huge smile, came steaming over. Slater gave her a hard look. She did an about-face and returned to the counter.

"You want to swing from chandeliers? Have a threesome? Because you're at a sex toy shop, okay? You can get nipple clamps here. Is that how you want to get in touch with your sexuality?"

She shook her head. He couldn't bear the pleading look in her eyes. "I just want to feel something."

But you do feel something. Something for me. He stepped back from her. He'd had a head injury. His brain had been rattled by the force of several blows to his skull. "Let's just start with some simple things, okay?"

He ventured forward, but she grabbed the back of his shirt.

"That's exactly what I want. Simple. Nothing kinky."

"Right. *Fun* stuff." He headed for the massage oils, lifting one and uncapping it so she could smell it. He thrust it in front of her nose. "Chocolate."

She turned her face away from the smell. "Why do you say it like that? You make me sound so naïve, so . . . childish."

"Say what?"

"Like in the car, when I said Alex and I did *fun* stuff. You made out like I just didn't get it at all."

"Because you don't." He shouldn't feel so angry. She wasn't doing anything wrong. But he couldn't stop the anger from charging through him. He shouldn't be there. He should be home, coming up with a hook for his song.

"I don't know why you say that. Alex and I did it in parking lots and restaurant bathrooms."

He stalked off. He didn't want to hear about her sexcapades.

But she followed him. "What's the matter with you? Now, suddenly, you don't want to talk about sex? All you've done since I moved in is try to make me uncomfortable with your sexual references. You, the guy who has sex with a different woman every night."

"I don't have sex every night. What a stupid thing to say."

"Uh, you haven't been home in three days."

"And so you assume I've been having a sex marathon?"

She thought about it. "I guess so. Maybe."

He headed down an aisle—the wrong aisle, since he didn't think handcuffs and sex swings would be a good place for Emmie to start. But she followed on his heels.

"If you're not having sex, then where are you going? Why don't you come home?"

Come *home*? She was playing house with him now?

Did she *like* having him around? Because he liked coming downstairs for lunch and finding her at the kitchen table—in fact, he tried to time it so they could eat together. He liked going to the grocery store with her—making her laugh by tossing tins of Spam into the cart or watching her feel up a cantaloupe. He'd taken to leaving his door open so he could get a glimpse of her working across the hall from him. He *liked* to see her in a tank top with a big aluminum water bottle on her desk and a neon-colored straw sticking out of it as she clacked away on her keyboard.

"What do you care what I do with my time?" he said, and not very nicely.

"Well, I was worried about you. I wanted to make sure the wound was healing properly."

"It's healing fine. Thank you, Nurse Valencia." He strode into the lingerie section and right into the sales clerk with a customer. The woman wore a lace body stocking, and the clerk seemed to be adjusting the straps for her. Emmie bumped into him, her hand fisting in his shirt. Both women looked up. The woman seemed annoyed, but the clerk smiled.

"I'll be with you in a moment, okay?" the clerk said.

"We're just looking, but thank you." Emmie pulled him away.

She dragged him down the aisle, back toward the front of the store. Clutching his shirt again, she looked up at him, fear in her eyes. "Oh, my God. This is not what I wanted at all."

He knew what she wanted. "Yes, I know. You want to lose yourself. You want to feel passion." He leaned down to her ear, breathing in her sweet scent, feeling her silky hair brush across his cheek. "Passion isn't something you find in a sex store, Emmie."

"I wanted this to be fun. I want sex to be fun."

"If you're having fun, you're not doing it right." He picked up some Ben Wa balls. "Get a basket."

"What does that mean?" She grabbed a red wicker basket with black ribbon woven through it. "Tell me what you mean."

"Here." He dropped a bottle of cherry-flavored lubricant into it. "Sex is naughty, Emmie. It's hot and filthy, and it drives you wild. It makes you literally lose your mind. There's nothing *fun* about it. Sex is raw, sweaty, and dirty."

She contemplated his words. "Then I've never had sex at all."

He dropped in some candles. "That's it. Let's go."

Looking into her basket, she frowned. "I have three things."

"If you want to pleasure yourself, light a candle, lube yourself up, and figure out what gets you off." He leaned closer. "And then shove those Ben Wa balls in your pussy and walk around with them in there."

She started to speak, but he put a finger over her mouth. He did not want to talk about this anymore.

He shrugged, like none of this mattered to him. "Or not. Your call."

———

"Great news, guys," Emmie said, cheeks red as apples.

Something was going on with her. Slater ignored his growling stomach, uninterested in eating until he figured out what.

She'd loaded the table with cold cuts, condiments, pickles,

potato salad, and a pitcher of iced tea. On the counter she had freshly baked chocolate chip cookies cooling on a rack.

Her flushed features, sparkling eyes, and breathlessness made him wonder if she'd tried the Ben Wa balls. Were they inside her right then?

The guys quieted down but continued building their sandwiches.

"You're in Austin City Lights." Her smile turned into laughter as she clapped her hands over her mouth. "Sunday of the second weekend. The last day."

Holy shit. That was fucking great news. But as quickly as the euphoria hit, it fled, replaced with a strange sense of hollowness. He should be thrilled to play a gig as big and important as ACL. And he was, it was just . . . it sucked that his dad wouldn't be in the audience hollering and clapping like a lunatic. A crazy, proud lunatic.

The old bastard had worked so hard for this moment. And he'd never get to see it. What a damn shame.

The guys cheered and shouted. Derek jumped out of his chair and lifted Emmie off the ground, swinging her around in a bear hug. The yellow sundress bunched around her waist, revealing the backs of her creamy thighs.

"You're awesome," Pete said.

"I can't believe it," Ben said. "How?"

Emmie shrugged. "I sent in your demo."

"The demo's all right," Derek said. "But, come on, your connections? Don't tell me they didn't help get us into ACL."

"Everything helps," she said. "But they wouldn't add you to the lineup if they didn't like you. And they did." She looked at Slater. "They really like your songs . . ." And then to the whole group, "And your image."

They had done a pretty good job of unifying their look. When Ben had come home with a leather top hat, nose ring, and tight leather pants, Emmie had kindly suggested he take a little more time to figure out who he was. The guys had made fun of him for trying to look like Slash, which had really pissed him off. So he'd come back a few days later with a whole new look. His hair hadn't grown out long enough to rock a real pompadour, but it was getting there. And with a preppy wardrobe a frat boy would kill for, he actually looked more like himself than he ever had before. And, more importantly, he felt comfortable in it.

"And that picture." Ben gestured to the eight-by-ten shot of the band Emmie had framed and hung on the kitchen wall.

"Yeah, that's a great one of you guys," Tiana said.

They continued to talk excitedly about the gig, and Emmie turned back to the counter. Slater couldn't stop thinking about the Ben Wa balls, so he got up and stood beside her. As she sliced an avocado, he leaned over and said, "Are they inside you?"

She nodded, rolling her eyes with the lustiest expression he'd ever seen. She blew out a slow breath. A rush of desire tore through him, powering through his dick, making his legs go weak and his mind bob in a sea of lust. Right then, right beside him, she was slick and aroused, practically squirming against the counter, and he could imagine what it would feel like to slide inside of her.

"Oh, my God," she whispered, opening her mouth wide, her eyes rolling back in her head.

And that was it. He threw open the sliding glass door and stepped out into the backyard. "Jesus fucking Christ," he shouted.

The guys hooted, chairs scraping back. They thought he was flipping out over the festival, about the future she'd made possible for them. They all flew out of the house. Great. He couldn't just stand there with his huge, jutting hard-on, so he let out a warrior cry and threw himself into the pool.

Slater got out of the pool to grab some towels from the laundry room and found the girls had left the kitchen. Had Emmie gone to her room to get herself off? Was she touching herself right then? He wished he'd never seen her in that dressing room, never seen her expression when she was aroused, because the image of her on her bed, legs spread, finger rubbing her juicy clit, back arched in ecstasy, came alive so vividly in his mind, he had to rub the heel of his palm on himself right then and there.

Drawn by a force beyond his control, he stripped out of his soaking wet clothes, tossed them into the washing machine, and wrapped a towel around his waist, making a beeline for the stairs.

"Hey, where's Em?" he heard Derek ask.

"Tiana's taking her shopping," Ben said.

Slater thunked his head against the wall. No, she wasn't up there pleasuring herself. But, worse? She was checking off number five on her list. *Dress to feel sexy.*

He wished he'd never seen her damn list.

———

In two hours Emmie had powered through four stores, slammed back two iced coffees, and relieved her checking account of a couple hundred dollars. She and Tiana had such different taste, and nothing Tiana had chosen had suited Emmie at all. But she'd decided to go with her friend's judgment, just to try something new. *Why not, right?*

As Tiana turned onto her street, Emmie sat up at the sight of her driveway filled with big, sweaty, shirtless guys playing basketball.

Slater.

Good God, did he stand out from the others. His skin gleamed with perspiration. Not only was he taller, but he was so cut. Hard, well-defined muscles on his arms, thighs, chest. And that perfectly round ass. She knew he worked out regularly, so he'd earned it, but still. A lot of guys worked out, but they didn't look like Slater. The sight of his powerful body made a rush of desire stream through her.

As Tiana pulled to the curb, Emmie's gaze narrowed to the waistband of his black gym shorts. She thought she could detect a few black lines from the tribal tattoo, but his torso twisted away.

He played fiercely. No doubt about it, Slater dominated the court. She loved his commanding presence, his confidence. She thought about Alex's body—fit, certainly, but less defined, less muscular—and wondered why just looking at Slater made her body hum, while she hadn't really gotten all hot and bothered over Alex.

"You going to get out of the car?" Tiana asked, a smile in her voice.

"Of course."

"Please tell me you won't be fantasizing about Slater Vaughn when you're making out with my brother?"

"Ew, no. I'm not . . ." But then she laughed because it wasn't like she could lie about it. "I mean, how can you not look at him?"

"Oh, I know. Believe me."

Emmie rolled up the window of the old Toyota and got out of the car. "And I'm definitely not making out with your brother. It's a blind date."

"Yeah, but he doesn't stand a chance if you're lusting after that guy." She nodded toward Slater, who stood at the side of the driveway, lining up his shot. The ball arced over the guys' raised hands and dropped neatly into the basket.

"Is there anything he can't do?" Emmie had seen his fans crying as they listened to him sing and watched him fix all kinds of random things at his mom's house as well as theirs. He wrote songs that she knew without a doubt could sell to the biggest artists in the world. He was gorgeous, smart, athletic . . . Seriously, what couldn't he do?

"He can't give you what you want."

Emmie felt a jolt to her heart. "I know that. I'm not interested in him that way."

"Yeah, but that's your head talking. Look, I'm not trying to get into your business, but I've seen the way you look at him." Tiana stepped in front of Emmie, blocking out the guys. "I'm not saying you want to get with him. I believe you when you tell me what kind of guy would make you happy. But the way you look at him and . . ." She looked away, clearly troubled. "I don't want to say this because you're a girl and you'll take it wrong, but I know the way he looks at you, too. It's obvious to anyone. That boy tracks your every move. He gets this really intense expression as he watches you. It's actually kind of hot. I wish Ben looked at me like that."

"No, it's not like that. He just appreciates that I'm helping him out with the band. And we're both home during the day, so we just, you know, spend a lot of time together." Who was she kidding? They did have this crackling, sparking energy between them. She could admit it. It wasn't like they'd do anything about it. They just seemed to really enjoy each other. "Hey, come on, not all musicians are bad. You're with one."

"They haven't gone on tour yet. Besides, Ben and I are off and on so much, and he gets plenty of action in the off time. But he's different anyway. I think he gets so sick of all the groupie action that he comes running back to me. He's torn. He wants to want it, but ultimately, it's not who he is." She turned to watch the guys. Just then Slater jumped, both hands cupping the ball. His shoulders lifted, the muscles bunching and flexing, as he made his shot. "But it *is* who Slater is."

The guys shouted and whooped as the game ended. Slater's team had obviously won, since his teammates were circling and high-fiving him. Slater grabbed his towel off the ground, glanced in Emmie's direction, and did a double take. His gaze thrilled her, made her body burn with arousal. And then a wicked smile curled his delectable mouth as he tugged the waistband of his shorts down just a tiny bit, revealing his tattoo.

The pulsing between her legs turned into a throb.

"Shit," Tiana said in a whisper. "There isn't a woman in Texas who wouldn't run down her own grandma to get that man to look at her like that."

Emmie's heart raced so fast she could barely breathe.

"You sure you want to go out with my brother tonight?"

"Oh, God, yes." The sooner she found a good guy to date, the better off she'd be.

———————

Once again, Slater found himself hiding in his mom's backyard. As if sleeping here brought him any respite from the constant ache of wanting the one woman he couldn't have.

Well, he probably could have her. For a night or two. But her time in Austin was almost up, and his boys, well, good things were coming for Snatch. Emmie would make sure of that. They'd get signed, get a tour, something that would take him away from the quiet house in the suburbs and put him into the decadent world she so despised.

And one night? Giving in to the call of the wild, when she was looking for a real relationship with a solid guy? No, it'd be the worst thing they could do. First, it would ruin their friendship, and he actually *liked* her. Looked forward to spending time with her.

If he fucked her, she'd hate him. But worse? She'd hate herself. And that was the last thing he wanted. So, yeah. No Emmie.

No matter how he burned for her. How attuned his senses were to her every sound, scent, and touch. All night he'd rouse at the slightest noise coming from her room across the hall, his body on constant vigil for a sign, a piece, a hint of her. He'd hear the sheets rustling, hear her sigh, a whispered moan, and he'd light up, waiting for what she'd do next, wondering what she was dreaming or thinking about. All day he'd listen to her moving around the house, and hope to see her, to be near her, even if it meant just the slightest brush of her skin against his.

Christ.

Tapping his pen on his notebook, Slater listened to the conversation, the occasional bursts of laughter, and the sounds of various instruments being played inside his mom's house. He couldn't concentrate, couldn't hear the melody, and the lyrics wouldn't come.

Probably because the only sound in his head was Emmie's and Tiana's laughter from earlier this afternoon as they'd gotten her ready for her date. Which explained why he was sitting in his mom's backyard yet again.

He didn't want to see Emmie dressed in her new outfit designed to woo Hector, the actuary. A steady job, nice manners, a tidy haircut . . . How did that translate to attraction? It obviously didn't.

But he couldn't find peace here any more than he could find it at his own house. Hadn't all his previous attempts taught him that?

The screen door opened, and his mom came out with a plate and a glass of red wine. He got up to take them from her, setting them on the table beside him. "Thanks."

"You've been working so hard on these songs all week. Why don't you come in and workshop them with us?"

He cracked a smile for the first time that day—only not a happy one. They played this game all the time. She tried to entice him to jam with her students and colleagues, and he turned her down. As a teen, he'd told her to piss off, winning his dad's approval, but as an adult, he had to admit he liked her perseverance. She'd never given up on him. No matter how much harder his dad's pull, his mom had never given up on him.

"I'll pass."

"How did I know you were going to say that?" Her fingers tapped on her knees. Her facial wrinkles mapped out the hard years of her marriage to an impossible man. Her hair had gone completely gray. She looked like a woman in her seventies instead of a fifty-seven-year-old. "You know, your father's been gone a long time."

Where the hell had that come from? "Yeah."

"So maybe it's okay for you to come play with us."

"I came out here to work. That's all." *Too many distractions at home.*

"Do you remember when you were a little boy, how you'd be right in the thick of it?" She had a look of awe. "You took my breath away. You could pick up any instrument and play it like you'd studied it all your life. And nothing held you back—nothing intimidated you. It was marvelous to watch you, so uninhibited, so free, so immersed in the music."

Oh, Christ. Here we go. "Mom." She could just stop now.

"I used to say you were a prodigy. But your dad didn't like that. Of course, he associated it with my world. I couldn't get him to understand the actual meaning of the word. He kept thinking it meant you'd be a violinist in the Austin Symphony, with baggy slacks, greasy glasses, and a plastic pocket protector." She smiled, but he knew her well enough to see the bitterness underneath. "That's not, of course, what I meant. But you have always been prodigiously talented."

His mom didn't nurture. Not physically anyway. On sick days she'd leave cans of chicken soup and boxes of crackers on the kitchen counter. But she always went to work, and she never ran her fingers through his hair the way Emmie had. She rarely touched him.

But Slater didn't doubt his mom's love. It was as fierce as his dad's. Just better because of its reliability.

"Your father had a profound influence on you. That's not news, certainly. But he has been gone quite some time."

Nine years, actually, since the police had shown up at the door with the bad news. "What are you trying to say, Mom?" Slater was exhausted. Staying away from the house hadn't brought the peace he'd anticipated. He didn't need one more puzzle to figure out.

"Well, it just seems you're old enough now to figure out who *you* are. He's not directing your life anymore."

Anger flared. "So you think the real me is just dying to get in there and play music with your buddies? That the only thing holding me back is my need to please my dead father? Is that it?"

"I do wonder, yes."

"So, we're still there." He sighed. He was so sick of this game they played. "Did you really think I wanted to spend my time playing with your students and colleagues? Did it occur to you that I might have become bored by your little collection of instruments by the time I was eight? Did it occur to you to ask me what *I* wanted to do?"

His mom reeled back, a mix of shock, embarrassment, and hurt in her eyes. She looked down at her hands, clasping them in her lap. She drew in a shuddery breath. "I don't know how to answer that." She paused, lifting her chin in an almost haughty manner. "I . . . Where did *that* come from?" And then she sighed. "You obviously think I didn't."

"Not once. Not one damn time."

Her gaze wandered out to the lawn. She looked deeply lost in thought, one eyebrow cocked, as though sorting through images and memories, looking for clues. Anything to support her own vision of his childhood.

But she wouldn't find any supporting evidence. They hadn't asked—neither of them. Not once. They'd always tugged him in one direction or the other. His dad had been stronger because he played to win. Not to nurture, not to guide. But to get what he wanted for himself. It wasn't about anyone but Slater's dad.

Finally, she let out a shaky breath. "Well, if I didn't . . ." She paused, making a slow, rolling gesture with her hands to indicate she would allow the possibility that she hadn't. But then she just slumped forward. "Well, hell. I thought I *knew* what you wanted." Her head tilted toward the house. "I started this for you. I thought if I surrounded you with it, in your own home, you could feel free to be yourself. I've kept it up all these years in the hopes it would draw you back out. Back to the person I thought you wanted to be." It took a moment for her to pull herself together. She shook her head, frowning.

And then, looking uncharacteristically rattled, she said, "What . . . what did you want to do?"

He thought of Emmie encouraging him to talk to his mom. But she didn't get it. It was way too late for this discussion, so he didn't bother answering.

"Jonny, I . . . I don't know what to say. I thought . . . well, I thought I *knew*."

He glanced up at her, all his anger gone. He felt like shit for hurting her. She hadn't been a bad mom at all.

"So, I'm asking you now. What did you want to do?"

"I wanted friends." How could they not have known something so obvious? What kid didn't want friends? "I didn't want to hang out with your people. I felt like you were showing me off to them."

She let out a stifled sound, looking like she might cry. "Wonderful. So, ultimately, I was no better than your father who dragged you across the country making you perform for anyone who would listen." She shook her head, focusing on her hands. "I honestly thought I was offering you a refuge, a chance to immerse yourself in the world you belonged in."

"Yeah, well. I just wanted friends."

His mom gave him a funny look, like the concept was so foreign.

"What?" He sounded petulant, but he couldn't hold back.

"If you wanted friends . . . well, for heaven's sake, why didn't you make them?"

"Are you kidding me? Who would be friends with me? Dad dressed me like a freak. Did he really think I wanted to look like Axl Rose when I was eleven? And if I did bring someone over, they didn't think he was cool, like he thought. They thought he was scary. He was wired all the time. He was embarrassing." He drove everyone away.

His mom looked stricken. "I thought it was your choice. That maybe you were more mature or . . . I don't know." She looked away. "Preferred your dad's company."

"My only *choice* was to keep to myself. Just let them think whatever they wanted of me. It didn't matter anyway." He'd always wanted his mom to step in and do something. Make his dad back off.

She looked deeply troubled. "I had no idea. None. I feel so . . . How could I not have seen any of that? I thought you loved your dad so much, you wanted to look and act like him."

"Are you f—" He stopped himself. "All those photographs you've got in there? The bookcase full of pictures chronicling my childhood in ridiculous costumes Dad made me wear? Every time I see them, I want to smash them. A constant reminder of what a freak I was."

"But why didn't you say anything? Why didn't you fight back?" Her imploring tone only fueled his anger. How did she not get it? She was the man's wife, and she'd never stood up to him.

"Like you? Because you were such a great example of fighting him?" His mom flinched, and Slater regretted taking out his anger on her. And, yet, he couldn't help it. He *felt* anger toward her. Because she hadn't defended him, hadn't helped him at all. "I think you know what fighting him accomplished. After being bullied and then ignored . . ." Slater snapped his fingers. "Just like that, he'd forget about it and whisk me off to the next audition or whatever his next brilliant idea was. I didn't exist. He just used me."

"Your father loved you," she said quickly, her voice filled with emotion. "You were his whole life."

"Literally." He held her gaze. "As you can imagine, that sucked."

She let out a shuddery breath. "He was a difficult man."

Slater hated that telling her all this made her feel bad. Made her think she'd failed him. His childhood . . . it was an impossible situation.

She blew out a breath between pursed lips. "I really should get back in there." But she didn't get up. "I just . . . I'm a little at a loss here. I'm glad we've started talking, Jonny. I am. It's what I've wanted for so long. I just need to . . . to sort through everything you've said."

She got up, reached for him, but stopped short of making contact. At the sliding glass door, she said, "I am truly sorry for not asking what *you* wanted."

Hearing her say those words took the piss right out of him. He'd resented her for so long. How could she not have intervened? Tried to save him? But he understood her better now. All three of them had lived parallel lives, never really connecting.

What if he had told her what he'd wanted? Years ago. He may never have gotten through to his dad, but his mom . . . well, he could've tried. Just like Emmie had suggested.

And suddenly he didn't want to be there anymore. He wanted to be around the one person in this world who made him happy.

TEN

When the doorbell rang, Emmie turned to the mirror one last time. She'd never have chosen this outfit, but she hoped it made her look younger and sexier. The navy miniskirt hugged her hips and flared around her upper thighs. The silky shirt had an unstructured, plunging neckline that drew attention to her breasts like a curtain bracketing a stage.

Her new teal and black lace bra lifted them, creating plump mounds that wobbled with her every move. Not a look she'd intended, so she tugged the top at the shoulders to raise the neckline.

"Uh-uh." Tiana yanked the top down, lowering it again. "You wanted sexy? You got sexy. Don't chicken out."

"You sure my makeup's not too much?"

"First of all, I'm Latino. That's how we roll. Second, my brother's Latino, so that's what he's used to. And third? You wanted sexy." She shrugged. "I gave you sexy."

"But it's not me."

"*You* is a quick swipe of mascara and lip gloss. And Gap shorts."

"True." Emmie leaned in to give Tiana a hug. "Thank you. You've been a good friend to me."

"Hey, it was fun. Now get down there and—"

"Emmie," Slater bellowed from downstairs.

Their gazes caught in the mirror, Tiana's eyebrows hitching up. "Damn."

Mostly, Emmie was surprised he'd come home. She thought he'd left for the night. She opened her door. "Be right down."

"All right, I'm off," Tiana said, picking up her purse and tossing her makeup back into it. "You have fun. And don't let my brother get in your pants."

Alarms went off in her head. Did he expect sex on a first date?

"Look at your face. Damn, girl." Tiana laughed. "I'm kidding. Hector ain't no playa. He'll treat you right, I promise. You two are the perfect fit. You'll see." She left, leaving the door open.

Emmie opened her messenger bag, putting in the new berry lip gloss she'd bought, her wallet, and her cell phone.

"That's what you're wearing?"

She spun around to find Slater in the doorway. Smoothing a hand down the skirt, she said, "You don't like it?"

He came into the room, all wild energy and heat, his gaze dropping to her cleavage. His expression turned feral, and his nostrils flared. He brought both hands close to her breasts, made a squeezing motion. "Are you trying to drive me out of my mind?"

"No," she whispered. "Am I?"

He stood so close, his look so dangerous, so purely sexual, she found it hard to breathe. But that only made her breasts wobble more. Her nipples tightened, and she felt an insistent throbbing between her legs. Was it just him that did this to her? Or had she just spent too much time focused on her stupid list? She ached with want.

His jaw hardened, his fingers went rigid, and then he lowered his arms, exhaling slowly and deliberately. "You don't look like you."

And the moment passed. "Well, that's kind of the point, isn't it? If I look different, maybe I'll feel different."

"*Dress to feel sexy* isn't the same as *look like someone different.*"

"Well, how I looked wasn't really working for me."

"Where did you ever get that idea?"

She swallowed, her mouth dry. "It's not like . . . I'm not exactly a sexpot."

"You're not looking to get laid, are you? You're looking to date a decent guy. Or do I have it wrong?" He yanked her top up. "Jesus, Em. You don't need to show your tits to get the kind of guy you want."

"It's not to get a guy. It's to make *me* feel more sexual. That's the point."

"And is it working? Are you feeling more sexual?"

"God, yes." Arousal slammed into her. If she wasn't careful, she'd throw herself into his arms, drag her tongue all the way down his chest, and lick his tattoo. She thought about it all the time, that tribal symbol . . . so enticingly close to his penis. Well, it wasn't just a penis when she thought about it. It was his erection—him being thick and hard, fully aroused. *For me.* God, every time she imagined it, she got the same electrical response charging through her body.

"The *point* is for you to feel arousal when you're with a guy. You want to go wild, right? You think you're going to go wild over Hector, the actuary?"

"You think you know everything, but you don't. I'm . . . I'm . . . I don't know what else to do. I'm *trying.*"

His features softened as he took her in. "There's nothing wrong with you."

She held her breath, lust coursing through her with such intensity she felt dizzy.

Those soulful blue-gray eyes caressed her features, settling on her mouth. "Don't go out with him."

How swiftly lust flashed into anger. "Why, Slater? Are *you* going to date me?"

He took a step back, looking wounded and a little scared.

"Then get out of my way and let me find a guy who will."

Her blisters had popped, making her heels burn. She'd grown sick of tugging the hem of her skirt down. Miniskirts were not for her. She hated how they rode up her thighs in the car and in the restaurant. But she'd had a nice time. Hector was a really nice guy.

Nice. God. Why did that make her yawn?

The moment he turned onto her street, she saw cars parked everywhere. Every light in her house blared.

"Looks like you've got company." Hector double-parked in front of her driveway. "Does this happen a lot?"

"Not really. They're pretty good about not partying at home much. It's not too bad."

"Well, I had a nice time, Emmie."

Something was wrong with her because who wouldn't be happy with nice? Nice could last a lifetime. But, no. She had to be attracted to a rocker. Why? Why couldn't a sweetie like Hector do it for her?

"Me, too. Thank you for dinner." She supposed she should invite him in, but she just didn't feel like it. Was that rude? No, it was a first date.

"It was my pleasure." He killed the ignition and got out of his car to open her door.

At about five-ten or so, he stood shoulder to shoulder with her in her painful three-inch wedges. With his short-cropped hair and lean frame, he was handsome. He had a degree from UT in business, a master's in accounting—all in all, he was perfect. Perfectly nice.

When he started to walk her to the door, she automatically pulled back. He seemed hurt, so she smiled and said, "Sounds pretty crazy in there. Probably best to say good night out here."

He smiled and kissed her cheek. "Can I see you again?"

"That'd be great. Good night."

He waited until she opened the door, then turned back to his car.

The moment she stepped into the house her gaze landed on Slater, drink in one hand, a girl's butt cheek in the other. He faced the door and looked up the moment she walked in, almost as though waiting for her. Unfortunately, instead of smiling or nodding at her like a normal guy would do, his mouth swooped down and burrowed into the woman's neck. *Real mature.* The girl's fingers slid sensuously into his hair, her hips tilting into him and swaying.

Emmie shouldn't have any reaction. He wasn't doing anything wrong. Well, other than the fact he wasn't doing it to *her.* Not that she wanted that kind of attention from him. This side of him, the guy who flirted, that wasn't the guy she spent her days with.

Pushing her way through the bodies, she couldn't help noticing how the women around her were dressed. Their skintight bandeaux dresses made her skirt look like something a middle-aged woman on a walking trip of Europe would wear. The blouse she'd tugged up all night to cover her chest looked like a tarp compared to the slinky tank tops these women wore. Her face felt greasy, and the last time she'd caught a glimpse of herself in a mirror in the restaurant bathroom, she'd felt garish and cheap.

"Emmie." Derek caught her around the waist. "How was your date?" She hated to be around him when he was drunk. She couldn't stand the glazed look in his eyes.

"Great, thanks."

"This is Jezzie." He grabbed a blonde and jerked her over.

"Hi, Jezzie." Emmie offered her hand and then felt like an idiot because the girl didn't even look her way.

"It's Jessie. Hi." The girl seemed completely out of place, like she'd meant to follow her family into Cracker Barrel but had somehow gotten shanghaied into this party instead.

"We're celebrating," Derek said. "I can't believe you did this for us. We're going to be fucking rock stars. You"—he stabbed a finger at her collarbone—"are making my dreams come true."

"Fucking rock stars," Pete shouted. The guys nearby attempted to whoop their support, but they were totally wasted.

"Aw, baby, where you been all my life?" Ben plastered a wet kiss to her cheek. She'd never seen him so drunk. He could barely stand. When his hand slid from her back to her ass, she jerked away from him.

"Well, I spent the first part of the evening with your *girlfriend,* and the second part with your *girlfriend's* brother. Where *is* Tiana?"

"We broke up."

"What? What're you talking about? You were together three hours ago."

"Our lives are changing, man," Pete said. "No girlfriends. Everyone's got to commit to the band, free and clear. We can't have distractions right now."

"Tiana's not a distraction." She couldn't believe how disgusting they were all being. Was this how they were going to handle fame?

"Girlfriends are distractions," Pete said. "Period."

Cooper came up, a girl hanging off each arm. "Emmie, you rock."

She ignored him, focusing on Ben. "Did you guys have a fight?"

He shook his head, looking miserable.

"So, you broke up with Tiana because you're going to play the music festival? That's it? How does that make sense?"

"Whoa, whoa, whoa," Cooper said. "Come on, we've been waiting for this a long time. We can't be weighed down by baggage. Girlfriends want shit. They want your time and energy."

"They're energy suckers," Ben said, rallying.

"You have got to be kidding me. Tiana's the coolest girlfriend in the world. She gives you all the space you need."

"She doesn't let him fuck other girls," Pete said. "What's the point of being rock stars if we don't get pussy?"

"I hope in the morning you all sound more intelligent." She gave Ben a shove. "You're a jerk. You're not on the road, you're not a rock star, and you're damn lucky to have a girl like her."

Emmie wished so badly she had the strength to head up the stairs without sparing Slater a glance, but damn her weakness. And what a punishment she got for it. Leaning back on the couch, he had one girl on his lap and another beside him pressed close, and both of them had their hands all over him.

She'd had enough. As she climbed the stairs, she thought that while her date hadn't lit any sparklers in her panties, he was at least a good man who didn't want to score as much "pussy" as humanly possible. So maybe she needed to compromise. She wouldn't necessarily get passion and lust, but she could have a satisfying sexual relationship with a stable, decent, and intelligent man.

She felt sick and wanted nothing more than to take off this stupid bra and forget all about her mission to feel lust. Why was she so obsessed with relationships anyhow? Shouldn't she be focusing on her career? She'd come out here to discover bands. More than halfway through her leave of absence, the only thing she should be thinking about was presenting

Snatch to Irwin—and hoping to God he signed them. Because she sure hadn't found any other bands yet.

She shut her door, barely dulling the music, and stripped out of her clothes. Stepping into her sleep shorts, she threw on a tank top, her breasts relieved to be freed from the tight demi-cup bra she'd worn, which had dug into her skin, causing deep red indentations. She couldn't get to the bathroom fast enough to wash off the greasy, unflattering makeup.

With her face over the sink and warm water splashing over her skin, she felt a presence. A big black hole sucking all the energy out of the small room. She jerked up to find Slater looming behind her. She grabbed a towel, wiping the water off her face. "What do you want?" The image of the girl's ass in his hand blew up like a billboard in her mind.

"How was your *date*?" Great, he was drunk, too.

"My date was terrific. Thanks for asking. I'll be out of here in second, so if you'll excuse me . . . ?"

"You're pissy."

"I'm tired, and I'm going to bed."

"You're not supposed to go to bed angry."

"That's for spouses, Slater. It doesn't apply to roommates. Can you please get out of my way?" She skimmed around him, but he didn't move. So she looked up at him. "Please?"

"Afraid you might touch me?"

"Oh, I think you've been touched enough for one night." She sounded as disgusted as she felt.

"You're pissed because I touched other women?"

"Of course not." Was that her voice, all shrill? On the verge of hysteria? "Isn't that what you do?"

"Yes, it is. So why're you pissed?"

Excellent question. Because he'd groped three women in the five minutes she'd been downstairs? Yeah, *so* none of her business. "I'm not. I'm sorry. Just . . . I hate that Ben broke up with Tiana because of this festival. And seeing you all drunk and whoring it up, it just . . ."

"Do we disappoint you?"

Right. Again, none of her business what they did. She forced a smile. "No, I'm not disappointed. I'm happy for you. This is what you want. This is why you're doing it."

"*What* is why we're doing it?"

"As Pete succinctly put it, for the pussy. And I promise, when you do score a tour, you'll get enough to satisfy even you guys."

"Why do you keep saying that? You know me better than that. Better than anyone. You know I don't do this for the *pussy*."

She looked away, paying too much attention to draping her damp towel over the rod.

"I don't need to stand up on stage to get *pussy*."

"Yes, Slater, I'm well aware of that. I told you that's what *Pete* said."

"But you said that's why we all do it. For the pussy. And that's not true."

"Then why do you do it, Slater?" She turned to face him, regretting it instantly. Everything she'd hoped to feel with Hector crashed over her at that moment. Her breasts felt heavy, her nipples tight. And a deep, compelling yearning twisted her heart. "Why?" She heard the plea in her own voice. Knew what she was really asking him. Why did he have to be the kind of guy who needed fame and groupie adulation? Why couldn't he be happy with one woman? Why didn't he want more out of his life?

Why didn't he want her?

But he was who he was. He was an incredibly hard-bodied, gorgeous sex god. He wasn't a guy who wanted true love, who wanted to work with his soul mate by his side as they strolled hand in hand through life. He wasn't who she wanted him to be. And that wasn't his fault or his problem.

So she gave him a smile, letting him know she didn't judge him. Because the other artists she'd worked with over the years? She certainly hadn't judged them. She hadn't cared what they'd done. As long as they'd kept their hands to themselves, she was cool.

She reached for him, thinking to pat his arm, and head off to bed. But he caught her hand before it reached him.

"Are they still inside you?" His voice had grown husky, and he pulled her so close she could feel his beer-scented breath wash over her cheeks.

"Are what still inside me?" A tremor shot down her spine, and she had to whip her hand back. And then she knew what he meant, and her inner walls clenched against the remembered sensation of the Ben Wa balls. She shook her head. "I took them out."

"Why?"

"I don't need them."

His finger stroked down her cheek, and her heart leaped into her throat. "Why is that? Because of *Hector*? Did he turn you on?"

Her mouth felt dry, and she struggled to take in a breath. She licked her lips. "No."

"No? So you're not going to see him again?"

"I . . . I don't know." She tried to step around him. "Maybe." She couldn't take all his badass energy and heat a second longer. "I should give him a chance."

"Bullshit."

"God, just back off, Slater. I don't . . . I don't know what you want me to do. I've been attracted to exactly one guy in my entire life, and he's not exactly the kind of guy a girl grows old with. He doesn't want to snuggle on the couch with me on Sunday mornings, hold my hair back when I puke, and come with me to Christmas with my family. So what do you want me to do? Have random sex with a guy who'd be happy to bang me once or twice and then dump me? Is that what you think I should do?"

He stared at her for too long. Long enough for every emotion to play out across his gorgeous features.

"That's what I thought. Good night, Slater." She stepped out of the bathroom. "Just . . . just leave me alone, okay? I don't want to do this anymore."

———————

As he scraped the razor over his cheek, Slater's hair kept flopping into his eyes. "Dammit." He tossed the razor down, aware he'd left his soapy beard foam in the sink like Emmie hated, and blasted out of the bathroom. "Emmie?" he hollered. Her bedroom door was ajar, and he leaned in, saw the rumpled sheets, heard the whir of her laptop's motor, and took in the crumpled heap of clothing she'd worn last night.

He hoped she never wore that ugly shit again. It didn't look anything like her.

"Em?" he shouted, trampling down the stairs. He found

her in the living room, headphones on, shaking her ass to a Piper Lee song. At the sight of her bare legs, the feminine curve of her shoulders, and the sweep of her long hair, his impatience snapped into agitation. "Emmie."

She jumped, one hand covering her heart. Seeing him standing there, she tore off the headphones. "What?"

"It's three in the afternoon. Why aren't you dressed?" If he didn't know her better, he'd think going without a bra and wearing those thin little pajama shorts were a ploy to get him to throw her down and fuck her senseless.

"What do you care what I wear? Besides, I've been writing all day. I'm on a roll."

See? She didn't have it in her to manipulate a guy. And he totally understood staying in his boxers all day when he worked. "I need a haircut. I'm playing tonight."

"I like it a little longer. It's sexy."

"Yeah, well, it pisses me off. Keeps getting in my eyes."

"Women love that." She looked so sweet and innocent, standing there in her tank top and bare feet, her face scrubbed free of last night's nasty makeup.

"Can you just cut it?"

"Of course." She turned back to the sponge she'd left on the coffee table, continued wiping off the potato chip and pretzel crumbs.

"Now?"

She snapped around to him. "I'm cleaning up *your* mess. And not because I have to but because I can't live with the filth. If I leave it to you guys, it won't be cleaned up for a week."

"I'll personally clean it up tomorrow."

She smirked, gesturing to the mostly clean living room. "Thanks." Tossing the sponge on the coffee table, she grabbed a garbage bag that clanked with beer bottles. He snatched it out of her hand and slung it over his shoulder. He'd toss it in the garbage can while she set up in the kitchen.

Only when he returned did he realize he was wearing gym shorts and nothing else. He smiled. "I think we're becoming too comfortable with each other."

She cocked her head. She didn't get it. Way to hit him where it hurt. Did she not notice he wore no shirt? Onstage, the chicks loved it.

"Oh. Right. Well, don't put a shirt on now. I'm only going to get hair all over you."

Hadn't she indicated last night that *he'd* been the one to get her hot? That's what he'd thought she'd meant. That's what had prevented him from getting laid last night. He couldn't even go back down to the party after that bathroom conversation had left him painfully hard, out of his mind with wanting her. He had no solution to this lust he couldn't satisfy.

She turned on the faucet, fingers flicking under the flow. "Come over here." She motioned for him to get his hair wet.

Leaning over the sink, he shifted until the stream of warm water hit the top of his head. She pulled out the side spray faucet, gently moving it around, saturating his scalp. Their bare thighs brushed together, hers were so smooth, and he could imagine grasping them, spreading them, gaining access to her slick heat. When her fingers slowly scraped along his scalp, desire shot through him with such potency he jerked his head up, banging it into the faucet.

"Shit." Heat flooded him, and the moment she handed him the towel, he draped it over his head so she wouldn't see his reaction to her.

Her hands landed on his head, as if to help dry his hair. He pushed her away. "I got it."

"Okay, but don't dry it too much. We need it wet."

He whipped the towel off, and she led him to the chair. Once he was settled, she draped the damp towel around his shoulders.

Softly, gently, she ran a comb through his hair, smoothing it, straightening it. Desire spread, a slow burn, making his dick harden and his balls ache. Her fingers gathered small sections of his hair, and he could hear the quiet snick of the scissors. She hummed the Piper Lee tune.

He wanted to make a joke, ask why she wasn't humming one of his songs, but he couldn't speak. Couldn't move. He was totally and completely caught up in *her*.

When she came around to stand in front of him, he spread his legs so she could step closer to his head. And there were her breasts again, gently bouncing with each short, quick motion. No barber in his life had ever made cutting his hair so erotic.

Each time she finished a cut, she scraped the comb through his hair, then sifted her fingers back into it and lifted a small section. All the while she hummed and swayed her hips.

He wanted to sweep his hands across her abdomen, trace the soft undersides of her breasts with his thumbs. If he didn't get to feel the weight of those breasts in his hands, he might go mad. His mouth watered to taste her neck and his hands flexed to keep from cupping her ass. He wanted to bring her down onto his lap so he could finally, finally grind his aching, throbbing cock against her.

Slater snapped. Abruptly, he grabbed her ass, sliding his hands between her legs. His thighs snapped together, and he set her down so she straddled him. She exhaled, looking startled and a little scared. His hands dug into the delicious flesh of her ass, holding her tightly in place.

It took everything he had not to suck those pretty pink lips into his mouth, slide his tongue inside, and relieve all this want. He wanted to feel her fingers clutching him, her arms pulling him closer.

He closed his eyes and breathed her in. And then he leaned toward her, his mouth at her ear. "I can smell you."

She sucked in a breath, her muscles tightening, her body pulling away. But he held her firmly.

"I think it wouldn't take much to show you how wild you can be. I think if I slipped my hand underneath your little cotton shorts, I'd find you wet for me. I bet your juicy pussy would like my fingers inside you, and you'd be squirming on my lap, and in about a minute your body would go off like a rocket."

Her breathing sounded labored. She arched her back, bringing those sweet nipples right up to his bare chest. Close, but not touching.

"But I'm not going to be the man that makes you go wild. And not because you're Derek's sister. And not because Derek's right about me. He's not. It's because while I do, on some level, like your vision of sharing my life with a girl in a cottage on the lake, it's not something I would even contemplate for years. Because I'm going to become the rock legend my dad groomed me to be. I'm going to play stadiums, tour the world, make acceptance speeches, and give interviews. And nothing—not even a pretty, sexy girl who tempts me like no one else ever has—is going to sway me."

She stilled. Her breathing erratic.

He was glad he'd finally put it out there. No doubt he'd put an end to the whole braless thing every day. He'd probably hurt her, but it had to be done. They couldn't keep torturing each other. He'd done the right thing.

But instead of getting off his lap, she leaned forward, mimicking what he'd just done by whispering into *his* ear. "I can see your arousal."

Desire raged so fast and hard, his whole body tightened, blood surging into his cock. He shifted his shorts to better conceal the hard-on tenting them.

She licked her lips. "I can see how badly you need to release all that pent-up lust. But I'm not going to be the woman who gives you the release you so desperately need. And it's not because I'm not attracted to you. You know I am." Her hips tilted forward, rolling on his thighs.

He could feel the heat of her, and he didn't think he could stand one more second of this intimacy without being inside her. Her expression, more sultry than any of the seductive women he'd ever met in his life, nearly gave him a heart attack.

Her breath at his ear singed his skin. "You know I can't sleep at night for wanting you so badly. And you can probably guess what I do to make myself fall asleep. I have to kick off the covers, close my eyes, and pretend you're there while I touch myself, imagining it's your mouth, your hands on me." She sighed. "But I'm not going to give you that release because, while I *do* want to know what it would feel like to have you in my bed, it's not something I would even consider. I would never risk my heart to a virgin."

He pulled back to look at her. Was she joking? What could she possibly mean?

"You may have screwed a hundred different women, come thousands of times in your life, but you've never once made love. You don't know what it feels like to come inside the body of the woman you are madly . . ."

She brushed her lips over his cheek, rocking her hips gently on his thighs.

"Desperately." She said it all breathy and seductive.

Her mouth brushed his ear, making him harder than he'd ever been in his life.

"In love with. So you'll only ever skim the surface of your sexuality, much the same way you'll only ever skim the surface of your life since you're so set on living your dad's idea of happiness and not your own. Why would I ever waste my love, my desire, my *longing*, on a man who's only living a half life? I want a man who knows himself, knows what he wants, and lives a life that's completely and utterly authentic. Not some guy chasing someone else's dream."

She leaned back. "Now, do you want the haircut or not?"

Three hours later, Emmie stood at the kitchen counter pouring spicy mole sauce into a casserole dish, spooning it over the cheese and chicken enchiladas.

"We don't have time to eat," Slater said, as he came into the room, keys jangling.

"This isn't for you."

She didn't want to see him. She'd hoped he'd go right out the door. As ballsy as she'd sounded on his lap—and as truthful as she'd been—she felt awful. What game were they playing with each other? He wanted her—he'd told her so. That should make her feel good, but it didn't. It just . . . rattled her. She didn't know how much more she could take.

When she turned, she found him shoving handfuls of shredded cheese into his mouth. "Hey, that's for my enchiladas."

"I love enchiladas." He peered over her shoulder. "Those look great. Who're you making them for?"

She heard the accusation, *If not for me?* "Not everything revolves around you."

He lifted a lock of her hair, tucking it behind her ear. "Maybe I'm the one revolving around you."

She froze. Her body hollowed out, turning her into a tin can with nothing but a huge, beating heart in it.

"I need to get going. Sound check starts in half an hour." And just like that, the moment of intimacy passed. Again.

Killing her.

He snagged another handful of cheese, and she whacked his hand.

"Make yourself something to eat."

"Don't have time." His finger took a swipe of the sauce. "Oh, that's good."

"You have three minutes to make a sandwich. You can eat in the car."

"I'll grab something on the way." He tapped his fingers impatiently, looking at the mess. "What can I do? We have to go now."

"I'm not going to your show."

He stilled, all emotion wiped from his features. "Why not?"

"Because Tiana's coming over."

"So you can both come."

"Ben broke up with her. She's not going to his show. We're having a girls' night in."

He just stood there, keychain dangling off his finger. He didn't say anything for the longest time. She didn't know if he expected her to say something. She didn't know what he was thinking or feeling.

Then again, it was Slater. He was probably deciding whether he wanted a sandwich or a Big Mac on the way to the club. Or wondering which woman he'd take home tonight. Based on what? Hair color? Maybe he alternated, brunettes on Mondays, blondes on Tuesdays, redheads on Wednesdays, and then back to brunettes on Thursdays. He—

"But I want you to come."

Heat swept over her, and the breath left her lungs in a whoosh. Slater wanted her to come to his show. He was *telling* her he wanted her to come.

"I like when you're there."

She didn't know what to say. She didn't even know what it meant that he would say something like that to her. She seriously wanted to drop what she was doing, leave the enchiladas on the counter, and jump into the car with him.

But, of course, she couldn't. Because Tiana was destroyed and needed a friend. And that came first. But, man, he *liked* when she was there. She had no idea how to respond. If she softened, he'd harden. Crack a joke. If she said something snarky, she'd hurt his feelings and possibly close this door he'd just opened.

And she did not want to close this door. She wanted to

walk right through it to a whole new level of . . . *something* with him.

But before she could respond, he said, "I'll make a sandwich, sure."

Flustered, she finished pouring the sauce over the enchiladas and carried the dish to the hot oven. Then, she watched him lean into the refrigerator and move things around. At this rate, he'd never get a sandwich made. She got the bread out of the pantry. "Turkey's in the top drawer, cheese is in the middle."

She could hear the drawers opening and closing. "Got 'em. Hey, can you do that thing you did last time? That vinaigrette you put on it? That was good."

She smiled at how quickly they'd fallen back into their routine. They got so intense, so emotional, sometimes she thought he'd wash his hands of her. But he always came back, as though nothing had happened. Except . . . each time they seemed to go deeper. Like just then, telling her he liked when she came to his shows.

He shut the fridge, set the turkey and cheese on the counter, and started opening the packages. "Tiana's fine, you know. They do this all the time."

"Have *you* talked to her? Because I have." She let out a breath, hating how upset Tiana was. "She's devastated. They didn't break up because of a fight. They broke up because of the festival. Because of this big change that *might* come. Ben wants to be free to 'bang' as many 'chicks' as he can."

"He was drunk."

"You all were, but you all said the same thing. *Girlfriends are a burden. We need to be free.* I mean, what the hell? Why do you treat women that way?"

"Now, hang on. I've never misled anyone. The women I get involved with know exactly what they're getting. And I'm pretty damn sure Ben's never misled Tiana, either. He has fun with her, sure, but he's not ready to get serious. And he shouldn't. We're not in any position right now to offer promises." The way he looked at her caused her to do a double take, wondering if she saw particular meaning in his gaze. But she must've been mistaken because he wore his usual stoic mask.

"Oh, please." She didn't know why she was talking to him about this. She turned away. "You don't get it at all."

"What don't I get?"

"Forget it."

"No, tell me. What don't I get?"

"It isn't about the timing." Did she really have to explain it? "It's about doing whatever the hell you guys feel like doing. When he wants Tiana, he's with her. When he wants groupies, he dumps her. It's as simple as that."

"You're acting like Tiana's being played. She's not. Ben's straight up with her. She makes her own choices."

"Yes, Slater, because obviously she wants the whole package from him. And, I'm sorry, but it *is* misleading to a woman. When he's with her, he acts like he's wildly in love. And then you guys get a gig out of town, and he dumps her because . . . because what? He wants his freedom? You guys don't get to use the 'Hey, I Told You Upfront I Wasn't Ready to Commit' card every time you want to get some play."

"I agree."

"So, then, why, when he has this great girl, a girl he's obviously crazy about, does he discard her so easily? How many meaningless encounters will it take to satisfy you?" Oops. Crap. "*Him.* I meant him."

He gave her a look that asked, *Did you?*

She looked away, ignoring him. "Women are wired differently. Well, *I'm* wired differently anyway. I want enduring, all-consuming, heart-and-soul commitment. I need to know I can count on someone's love." Embarrassed, she turned away from him, shoving the cheese toward him. "And I just don't know if that's even possible."

She could feel him studying her for a long moment, and it made her uncomfortable. She didn't know what he was thinking. Why had she brought the subject up?

"We're talking about two different things," he said carefully. "Love, marriage, all that is fine. Just not right now. And to ignore the reality of where we are in our careers . . . Well, it's just setting yourself up for failure."

God, she was an idiot. Talking to him about this. He needed to get going. She tried to hand him a knife to cut his sandwich in half, but he just looked at it like he didn't know what to do with it. "Cut it. It'll make it easier to eat in the car."

"Is this about Alex?" he asked softly.

When he didn't take the knife, she cut the sandwich herself. She grew increasingly uncomfortable at the truth he was digging toward. "No. Well, obviously yes, but it's not just him. I'm sure you know about my dad."

Stuffing the remaining turkey back into the plastic bag, she reached for a sponge to wipe away the crumbs.

"*You* tell me."

She didn't think he realized the effect he had on her when he was like this, all caring and interested. It just made her feel so close to him. "You know he cheated, right? I mean, like, all the time. But my mom said it wasn't always like that. In the beginning, they were a team. My dad had all this talent but no interest in the business side of things. So my mom took charge. She's the one who got him gigs, handled tours and managers, all that stuff. And then, as soon as he gained some traction, started building a name for himself, he started treating her like crap. He'd be gone for days at a time, always with some transparent excuse. He was jamming or the commute was too far to come home or he'd had too much to drink. It was awful. We all knew what he was doing. I don't know why my mom stuck it out—well, I do. She did it for us. She wanted us to be a family." She swallowed, willing herself not to cry. "Anyhow, the point is my dad didn't need her anymore, so he dumped her."

She turned away from him. "It was devastating. Everything changed after that. Derek moved to Texas, and I . . . well, I became the best little helper my dad could ever hope for." She'd been so afraid he'd dump her, too. And he would have. He didn't keep in touch with people he didn't need.

When she forced a smile, Slater didn't return it. He came toward her, cupping her chin, brushing his thumb over her cheek. "All this for a prick."

"What? My dad's not . . ." Well, yeah, he actually *was* a jerk.

"It's so fucked-up. You've got Derek driving himself so hard just to prove to your dad that he really is a great musician. And then here you are killing yourself to show him you're worthy of his love."

She turned away, not wanting him to see her as that weak. "I'm not killing myself. And I want my dad in my life, Slater. That's pretty normal."

"Yeah, but the thing is, you're never going to get what you want. Neither of you. He's a narcissist. Em, you gotta know, even if you became bigger than Irwin Ledger, if Derek became the next John Paul Jones, your dad wouldn't give a shit. It's all about *him*." He shrugged. Like it was all so simple. "He's got nothing to give."

The truth of it slammed into her. Her dad gave nothing. He never had. He just took. She'd known that—intellectually. But just then, for the first time, she actually got it on a gut level.

He'd *never* have anything to give her. Not friendship, not companionship, not love. And not respect. Because he didn't care about anyone but himself. He *was* a narcissist.

Slater leaned close enough for Emmie to see the tiny red line in the curve of his chin where he'd nicked himself shaving. "It's not you, Em. Your dad's just an asshole."

Then, he grabbed an apple out of the fruit basket, rubbed it on his shirt, and gave her a sweet smile. "Thanks. I have to go."

She stood there, after he left, wishing she hadn't burdened him with her story, wondering if he was relieved to have escaped the kitchen. She heard his feet on the stairs, charging up and then moments later trampling back down. The front door slammed, and then his car engine rumbled to life.

Her phone buzzed. She grabbed it from the kitchen table. A text from Slater.

Hold out for it. You deserve that kind of love. You deserve everything.

Emmie smiled, but then fear stabbed through her happiness. She was falling for him. It wasn't just lust. It was . . . come on.

It was so much more.

ELEVEN

"Uh, Em? You might want to come up here," Tiana called from upstairs.

Emmie shut off the faucet, leaving the casserole dish to soak, and went to find her friend. As she climbed the stairs, she saw Tiana leaning out of her bedroom with a mischievous smile. "What?" But Tiana had already slipped back inside.

Emmie found her friend standing beside the bed, hip jutting, pointing questioningly toward her pillow.

Where she saw a scrap of paper and some bills.

Cab fare. In case you have time to come to the show.

Emmie held the note in her hands, holding her breath, as electricity sped along her nerves. He surprised her all the time. Why did it matter so much to him?

"I'm guessing it's from Slater?" Tiana leaned over Emmie's shoulder.

Emmie nodded, trying to play it off like it was no big deal. "I'm going to get all these critics and record people to come see them at ACL, so they want to work on their performance."

"Uh-huh."

"What?" She couldn't keep from smiling. It was just so . . . so sweet of him to want her there.

"What's going on between you two? Have you slept with him?"

"Of course not." She stepped back and headed out of the room.

"Yeah, so you say, but now he's leaving money for you to take a cab to his show?"

"I just told you why."

"And you're super great at coming up with brilliant excuses, but you suck at lying. No offense, but I can read every emotion on your face."

"What you're reading is a tiny bit of infatuation. You said it yourself, who wouldn't have a crush on him? But he'd never see me that way—not when he's got his choice of the entire Hooter's lineup every night of the week."

"Well, something's going on. But you don't need the cab fare. I'll drive you."

Emmie swung around at the top of the stairs. "That's the last place you want to go."

"Actually, I have to."

"You've just spent the last two hours telling me how glad you are to be free of the 'stupid bastard.' "

"Yeah, but I always say that after we break up. And then time passes, and we miss each other, and we're tearing up the sheets again. This time I want it over for good. I want to see him in action."

Emmie shook her head slowly. "That's going to hurt."

"Exactly. And I'll carry that hurt around so that the next time he sends me a text or shows up at the office, I'll be able to ignore him. Let's go."

She'd never seen the club more crowded, and Snatch had played there plenty of times.

"I'm not even going to attempt to go out there," Emmie shouted to Tiana, indicating the dance floor. "Let's get a table back here." Tonight she'd videotape them, send it to Irwin. She knew if he saw Slater onstage, he'd see the magic.

And, really, she was running out of time. She had two weeks until Irwin came back from Australia and expected to see her in the office. She wouldn't go back without a promotion, and her greatest shot was Snatch. Sending him the video with the press kit? No way could he say no.

They skimmed the perimeter of the dance floor and found an empty table at the very back of the room. A waitress came over and set down cocktail napkins.

"What can I get you ladies?"

"Gin and tonic," Tiana said. "To hell with the tonic. Just give me gin, straight up."

Emmie squeezed Tiana's knee under the table. "Cranberry and seltzer for me."

"Got it. Be right back."

Emmie wondered why Tiana sat with her back to the stage. "The action's over there."

"That's not the action I need to see. Watching him play drums gets my panties wet. I want to see him with the girls. He's a total jackass when he's trying to get some."

"This should be a fun night." Emmie brought herself up on a knee on her bar stool and focused the camera on the stage. Then she turned it on and sat back down, keeping her hand high over her head.

When the waitress brought the drinks, Emmie used one of Slater's twenties to pay for them. She'd pay him back tomorrow after she hit the ATM.

The song came to an end, and the crowd went crazy.

"Thank you," Slater said. "Thank you so much. You guys are fucking great."

The girls screamed like he was Mick Jagger or something. It was insane.

"I want to thank you guys for coming out tonight and for all the support you give us. You make it fun to play here."

The crowd quieted down, and Tiana drew in a breath before turning to face the stage.

"Got some pretty cool news for you. You know that little show Austin puts on each year? What do they call it, boys?"

"The Turkey Trot?" Derek shouted.

"Naw, that doesn't sound right," Slater said, his smile so utterly disarming, Emmie's heart fluttered. He acted like he had no idea that he was gorgeous and sexy, that every woman in the room wanted to strip him out of his clothes and lick his extremely hard body. His charm was in his total ignorance of how very impressive he was.

"Oh, I know," Cooper said. "The Celtic Festival. We playin' that?"

Slater laughed, dipping his head, making him seem a little shy, a little embarrassed. "Hm, can we pull that off, boys?"

Oh, God, Irwin would love his stage presence. She was so glad she'd brought the camera.

All at once the band started riffing, sounding nothing like Celtic music, until Pete found a beat on his synthesizer, and the others backed off to let him run with it.

"There we go," Slater said. "Pete, we're just gonna sit down and have a drink. Get to know some of the pretty ladies out here, and let you handle the whole Celtic thing."

"Why don't you come down here and handle me, Slater Fucking Vaughn?" a woman called from the audience. The whole place went up in laughter.

"He's amazing." Tiana leaned across the table. "If I didn't think he was half in love with you, I'd offer up my skanky self."

Emmie held a finger over her mouth, hoping her friend's voice hadn't been picked up by the video camera.

"Okay, okay," Slater said, quieting the audience. "Screw the fucking Celts. Let them do their thing. While they're fucking around with their bagpipes, we're going to be shredding it at Austin City Limits."

Screams, catcalls, and clapping exploded in the club. Feet stomped, creating a thunderous rumble.

Slater gave them a few moments before quieting them down. "So make sure you get tickets for the second weekend. We're playing on Sunday. More info to follow. Okay, back to the music. I promised you 'Get it, Boy,' so . . ."

But then his brow furrowed, and he looked down at his feet. It was such an intimate moment, like he needed to make a confession. And then he looked up and shook his head, like he couldn't go through with it.

Emmie knew everything they did up there was calculated, so she knew this little diversion for what it was. A way to get the crowd to feel like they were part of something special. She was so glad she'd brought the recorder tonight. Her arm started to tingle, but she knew she was capturing pure gold.

He turned to the boys, murmuring to them. They looked genuinely surprised. She knew her brother well enough to see his concern about messing with the set they'd crafted with such intention. The guys looked at each other, waiting for someone to make a decision. But they always listened to Slater. They trusted him implicitly. Yeah, her brother ran the business end. He also created a lot of the chord progressions, but the music was all Slater's. Finally, Derek nodded, and the band cleared the stage. A few seconds later someone brought out Slater's guitar and a chair.

Slater sat down, lowered the mic, and started tuning his guitar. "We're going to do something a little different. I don't know about you guys, but I work my shit out through songs. And let me tell you, I've got some shit on my mind. It's really turning me inside out. So I'm going to try and work it out right here, right now. You up for that?"

"I'd like to get *you* up, Slater, baby," a woman shouted.

He laughed into the mic. "Hey, now. There's a time and a place. And I'll text it to you after the song."

Again, the crowd blew up with laughter and catcalls.

And then he started strumming, the lights cut out on the stage, and a spotlight focused on him. His broad shoulders hunched, and his face pulled in concentration.

Up all night, up all day,
Baby, you got me in the worst way
Try to run, try to hide,
Too late, you're already inside

Get out of my head and out of my heart,
Because this thing we got, it ain't gonna start

Under my skin, not in my bed,
This magic you weave's messin' with my head
Leave me in peace, leave me be,
Aw, fuck it, too late, you're all I see

You, you're all over me, inside me, around me
You, you've sunk in, wound around, and pulled tight
You, you gut me, destroy me, sink in
You, you'll never, you'll always, you are,

Get out of my head and out of my heart,
Because this thing we got ain't gonna start

Tiana spun around, her jaw hanging open. She mouthed, *Is this about you?*

Emmie shook her head hard. It couldn't be. But, God, it was freaking amazing. Intense, powerful. And she'd captured it on tape. She couldn't wait to hear Irwin's reaction.

Slater finished the song, and the silence in the room held a pulsing energy. Scraping the hair off his forehead, he gazed out at the crowd expectantly.

And then applause shattered the silence. The band came out, Pete kneeling before Slater and pretending to fan him. Derek shook his head, grabbed the mic out of the stand, and said, "Show-off," but he could barely be heard over the clapping and stomping.

The roadie came back out, whisking the chair and guitar away, and Cooper and Derek started wailing on their axes. A few seconds later, Slater raised the mic stand, gripped the mic with both hands, and launched into "Get it, Boy," one of their most popular songs.

"You know what?" Emmie shouted to her friend. "Let's get out of here." Tiana didn't need to witness Ben's behavior after the show, and Emmie really needed to process the song Slater had just sung. Because part of her believed he *had* written it for her. The other part wondered if that was just part of his game. All he knew how to do was flirt.

Then again, come on, that song was not flirtatious. At all.

Tiana turned to watch the band, clearly reluctant to leave.

"You don't really want to see him in action," Emmie said. "And I want to go home."

"Oh, we're not going home. Hell, no."

"Where do you want to go?"

"Zephyr."

The club the guys usually went after a show to blow off steam. "Uh—" Emmie shut off the camera as Tiana slammed her bag over her shoulder.

"Oh, hell, yes." She strode toward the exit. "I'm not gonna sit around on my sorry ass. Not when I can show him what he just gave up."

————————

Slater knocked back another shot. Was she *trying* to piss him off? She'd heard his song tonight. Didn't it mean anything to her?

Emmie's arms were waving over her head, her hips bucking, breasts bouncing wildly like she was in the throes of fast, hard sex. It made him angry. It made his blood burn and boil. It made him hard as a fucking baseball bat.

It made him *want* like he'd never wanted anything before in his fucking life.

Did she even know which guy moved in sync with her? She couldn't because she hadn't looked around once. She hadn't stopped dancing since she and Tiana had pushed their way onto the crowded dance floor an hour ago.

"Hey, baby," a voice purred in his ear, fingernails dragging across his scalp. "I got you another one."

He took the shot, downed it, but kept his gaze trained on his Girl Gone Wild.

When the cat woman stepped in front of him, placing her bony ass on his lap, he finally snapped out of it. He focused on her, her straight blond hair, blue eyes, and bright red lips. She had a barbed wire necklace tattooed just above her collarbone.

His gaze flicked to the dance floor just in time to see Emmie spin around, bucking her hips like she wanted it harder, faster. Only this time she faced the guy, so her breasts pressed into his chest.

Slater tightened, blood screaming in his ears, and he got up so fast, the woman nearly fell to the floor.

"Hey," she said. He caught her under her arms and held her until she regained her balance on those fuck-me heels. "What was that for?"

But Emmie had already moved on to another guy. She was completely lost in her own world.

"Sorry," he said. "You okay?" He smiled at the woman, her features undefined. All he really noticed was the tat and the big tits. Did he want to fuck her?

"Yeah, sure. So, you want to go somewhere quieter?"

Did he? As he'd been doing for weeks now, he waited for

desire, temptation, anything to stir. But, as usual, he felt nothing but restless and edgy. He really wanted to want to fuck her.

But he didn't.

Because of *Emmie*. She consumed his thoughts, his dreams . . . his shower time.

What was he *doing*? She was leaving in two weeks. Her career was in New York City.

He ran a hand through his hair. He couldn't believe he was thinking like this. Getting involved with Emmie? Forget her moving back to the city, what about him? *His* career? He couldn't even think about a relationship for the next fucking *decade*.

It could never happen between them.

Unless they were just fuck buddies. But he didn't want to just fuck her. He wanted . . . Oh, dammit all to hell. He wanted *her*.

He glanced back out to the dance floor. Fear shot through him. No Emmie. He pushed through the bodies mingling in front of him to get a better view. Where the hell had she gone? With her new lingerie, Ben Wa balls, and her fucking *list*, she could very well have left with some guy.

Why did that send him into a panic?

Because she was his. He knew that in his bones. He just knew it. And he was goddamn tired of fighting it.

The woman sidled up to him, lacing her fingers through his and—oh, surprise—rubbing her tits against his arm. He could feel her nipples, but he couldn't feel an ounce of want.

Not for her.

Emmie came into view, bumping hips with the shorter, curvier Tiana. If he didn't know Emmie better, he'd think she was wasted. Who danced like that sober? He cracked a smile.

Everything she did surprised him. The woman dancing like she was in a street dance-off didn't look like she'd just come in off the prairie. She looked uninhibited, free, and wild. He loved that she couldn't be labeled. That she had so many layers and contradictions.

The woman squeezed his hand, reminding him of her offer. "Wanna do a shot in my tits?"

For the first time all night, Slater started laughing. He wasn't sure what set him off. It wasn't her language, although he'd never heard a body shot sound so unappealing. It wasn't even her lack of seduction skills. It was more what his life had become. Instead of focusing on what he could readily have, right here, right now, his whole being was focused on what he couldn't have.

But he was starting to think the obstacles no longer mattered.

She was his. Plain and simple.

————————

Bass pounded in rhythm with her heartbeat, the tempo pulsed in her veins, and Emmie lost herself in the driving vibrations of the music. Her body took over, shutting down her mind, giving her free rein to thrust, spin, jerk, sway—whatever it needed to express itself. She felt nothing but the movement of her body and the sweat on her skin.

A guy came up from behind, clamped his hand on her stomach, brought her hard up against him, and started thrusting in a purely sexual act. Icy fear snapped her out of her trance, and she tried to break out of his hold. His hands clutched her hips, holding her in place, as he rhythmically thrust into her. She could feel his hard-on against her bottom, and she twisted away from him. He wouldn't let go. What was his problem? Where was Tiana? Nobody seemed to notice what this guy was doing to her.

And then the guy was gone, hands ripped off her. Emmie swung around to find Slater with his elbow cocked, sweat gleaming on his hard, furious features. He swung, connected, and the guy dropped to the floor. People scattered, and a couple of guys bent down to help the jerk. A spot of blood bloomed at the corner of his mouth.

Red-faced, Slater lunged for the guy, but Emmie pushed in front of him. "Slater," she snapped, trying to get his attention. He cut her a harsh look, breathing hard. "Don't. Just don't."

The muscles in his jaw flexed. His eyes flashed, watching the guy move to get up. Emmie pressed her hands on Slater's chest. "I'm okay."

Quickly, the guy scrambled to his feet and glared at Slater before taking off.

Slater started after him, but Emmie pressed harder, putting her body fully in his path. "He's not worth it." She cupped his chin, forcing him to look at her. "I'm okay."

She could see the difficult transition as he slowly climbed

down off the tower of rage. Finally, he let out a rough breath, squeezed his eyes shut, and dragged a hand through his hair. "Fuck."

As bodies slammed into them, jostling them, she picked up his hand and ran a thumb over his raw knuckles. "Thank you." They stood there unmoving among the chaos, the press and push of dancers. Adrenaline still pulsed through her veins. "I can't believe you saw me." In a packed club, how *had* he seen her?

He drew her up hard against him and held her to his damp chest. For a long moment he looked into her eyes. Her blood heated from the look she saw there. She couldn't believe he was looking at *her* like that.

With her hands pressed to his chest, she could feel the moment the tension left his muscles.

He tipped his forehead to hers. "Enough, all right?"

What did that mean? The moment was so strange and confusing, she didn't say anything. A tremor shuddered through her. Her heart pounded. She should probably walk away and let him go back to his flock of girls, but she really needed him to hold her. She wasn't ready for him to let go.

They stood in the middle of the dance floor, holding each other, and she wanted to sink into him. It felt so good. Yes, it felt exciting to be in his arms, not to have him resisting or taunting or teasing, but it also felt so . . . peaceful. So right.

She didn't want him to get all weirded out, so she started to pull away. But the moment she relaxed her hold on him, he tightened his. "Dance with me."

Emmie looked up, overwhelmed by the emotion pouring off him. For her. He wanted to be with her. Without thinking, she let her head fall to his chest and just . . . surrendered.

He reached for her hands, brought them to his chest, and held them there tightly. She could feel his heart pounding. His feet shuffled closer to her, his chin lowered to her shoulder, and his nose nuzzled into her neck. She thought he'd possibly inhaled. Sensation bloomed on her skin.

They barely moved, just held each other, as though slow dancing at the prom. The frenetic beat of the music, the flashing strobe lights, the thrashing bodies all around them made no sense against the slow roar of blood in her veins, the thick swirl of desire churning deep inside of her.

She let out a sigh of relief, pulling her hands out of his grip and wrapping them around his neck. Slowly, she moved closer to him, their hips connecting, bound like magnets, moving together in a slow, gentle sway. His arms came around her, pulling tighter, until their dance turned more into an embrace. Was this happening? This sweet, intimate moment with him? He was allowing himself to get close to her? His gentleness stole the breath from her lungs.

When his hands flattened on her back, when his hips surged into her, when she felt the shock of his hardness against her stomach, she pulled away from him. What . . . what was *that*?

She fled into the crowd, not even knowing if he followed. Why had he done that? That deliberate gesture announcing his interest in wanting to have sex with her? After sharing an intimate moment, he'd turned to sex. No, no, it hadn't been intimacy at all. It had been the precursor to sex.

Because that was all he knew. God, she was so stupid. Thinking he wanted something different from her. That somehow she was special. She pushed her way off the dance floor.

God, she was only human. She couldn't take much more of this . . . this teasing from him.

He shouldn't treat her like all the other girls he could screw and discard, pressing his boner into her like it was hers for the taking.

She hurried into the bathroom, locked herself in a stall, and just stood there, unable to catch her breath, to calm down her jittery nerves.

Hers for the taking. He had been. He'd made that perfectly clear. She closed her eyes. God, the feel of his erection had ignited a flash flood of desire.

She wanted him between her legs, pushing inside of her. She'd never wanted a man so desperately before. Had never felt it between her legs, the throbbing, the pulsing, the *need*.

She'd never felt things like this. And she loved it. She did. It didn't make her feel slutty or depraved or anything. It made her feel sexy.

She *loved* the way it made her feel.

She loved the way *Slater* made her feel. But not for one night. God, no. That just wasn't her at all.

She had to get out of there. She fished her cell phone out of her bag and texted Tiana.

Can we go? Please?

Not a minute later, Tiana texted back. Meet me at the bar. Emmie'd had enough for one night.

She found Tiana waiting for her, looking wrecked. All Emmie's problems dropped away, and she reached out for her friend. "Are you okay?"

"Let's just go."

"Did you talk to him?"

Tiana shook her head. "He just sat there watching me the whole night. The way Slater watched you."

"Slater watched me?" Was that how he'd seen the guy mauling her?

"The whole night." Tiana's brow furrowed. "You didn't notice?"

"I'm not the one obsessively staring at their table trying to make my boyfriend jealous. Besides, Slater's preoccupied with his nightly task of choosing which groupie to go home with."

Tiana cocked her head, looking confused. "He hasn't gone home with anyone in weeks."

Emmie'd suspected that, but she had wanted to hear it confirmed. "Oh, please. Just last week he didn't come home for three nights."

"According to Ben, Slater hasn't been hooking up at all. They think it's because of something you told them—something about how their success is based on girls wanting to get with him and not with their sound. I don't know." Tiana's gaze narrowed, her shoulders shifted back. "See? Look at that jerk. Look at him."

Emmie followed her gaze, found Ben staring right at Tiana. Some girl on his lap ran her fingers through his short pompadour, breaking through the wax, making it hang off his head like ferns. He seemed oblivious to the attention.

"What does he want?" Emmie asked. "Does he want you to go over there and claim him?"

"Oooh, I like the sound of that." Tiana's body practically

undulated with need, but then she abruptly turned away. "Oh, my God. Forget it. Just forget the whole damn thing. He obviously wants *me*—not some brainless bimbo. But he won't let go of this stupid idea in his head. Well, screw him." She glanced back at the table. "How come I'm not enough?"

Emmie's heart broke for her friend. "It's not you, Tiana. It's him. You know that. He's immature."

"He pursues *me*. Every time we break up, *he* comes after *me*. I mean, I'm not stupid. Ben's no Slater. I'm not stupid enough to go after a guy like Slater." Her eyes widened and she cringed. "I'm sorry. I don't mean—"

"No, stop. I know exactly what you mean. I'm not stupid enough to fall for him, either." Even if she shot up in flames every time he looked at her . . . touched her. God. She felt it all over again. His erection, how it made heat burst from her core.

"It's just . . . Slater's in a whole different category. I mean, girls *know* they can't get him. They feel lucky to get a piece of him, so they'll take whatever they can get. He's larger than life, you know? I mean, Ben breaks my heart all the time, but I'll bet Slater's *never* broken a girl's heart. We just know not to put our hearts on the line for a guy like him." She blew out a breath, giving her head a little shake, as if to snap herself out of her mood. "Let's get out of here."

Emmie trailed Tiana toward the exit, unable to keep herself from scanning the dance floor, searching for him. She'd interrupted his selection process, so he'd chosen her for the night. That's all. Nothing more. Now that she'd gone, who was he pressing himself against in his super-suave invitation for one hour in nirvana? But she didn't need to look at all. He stood right there, leaning against the door, those big, muscled arms folded, watching her.

"Oh, damn." Tiana slowed. "What is going on with you two?"

"Nothing. I swear."

"Whatever you say, girl. You must be made of stronger stuff than I am because if that boy looked at me the way he looks at you, my legs would be strapped around his hips right now. I don't care where we are or who's watching."

Emmie couldn't get to the door fast enough. She ignored him, pushing outside, breathing in the warm night air, which was way better than the suffocating club air.

"Emmie," he said.

"I'll meet you at the car," Tiana said quietly.

Hesitantly, Emmie turned to him. "What? What do you want, Slater?" She felt frantic. She wanted to run from him as badly as she wanted to throw herself into his arms and grind against him. God, to relieve this constant ache . . . there was just no relief.

"I thought that was obvious."

"You want to have *sex* with me?" Was he that drunk? He didn't seem drunk. But why else would he talk to her like this? Since when did he expect sex from her?

He seemed amused. "I wanted to dance with you."

She held his gaze, wondering. He sounded so sincere, but then she couldn't think straight. Fear had a good grip on her nerves. "Yeah, well, something got between us."

He laughed. That look on his face? He seemed so vulnerable. He didn't behave like this, ever. Oh. Oh, oh, oh. Was this how he made girls fall madly in love with him? Was that his secret? His charm? Pretending to be vulnerable?

"Tiana's waiting for me." Without looking back, she struck off for the parking lot.

He kept pace beside her. "You're angry with me for being attracted to you?"

Heat rushed up her neck. She did not want to remember how his hard-on had made her sizzle and ache. No, no. Not when just the mention of it right then set her juices flowing. "Me, Slater? Or would any girl do right about now?"

His hand closed around her arm, and he jerked her to him. They gazed into each other's eyes. Heat blazing in his. What was this force field around them? Why did her heart have to be so tangled up in his? It no longer mattered how she kept reminding herself that every woman had this same physical reaction to him. It didn't diminish it. Didn't cheapen it at all. She was drawn to him. And she knew he was drawn to her.

Just then, the look in his eyes, maybe she was naïve, maybe hopeful, but she saw her own want mirrored there. With two fingers, he held her chin, his gaze drifting down to her mouth. Sensation skittered across her skin and fluttered in her chest like a trapped bird.

His thumb stroked across her lips. "Go home."

TWELVE

After washing the sweat and grime off her body in a steaming hot shower, Emmie got into bed. Number six on her list was sleeping naked, but with a house full of guys, she hadn't felt comfortable doing it. What if they had a fire? She could just imagine leaping out of bed, racing downstairs, and facing the guys buck nekkid. Yeah, not going to happen.

She got back out of bed and put on her underpants and a tank top. Not the same feeling at all, but still. Better than the pajamas she wore in her apartment with the three roommates and all their guests.

Curling onto her side, she tucked her hand under the pillow and willed herself to fall asleep. No thoughts of Slater tonight. Just sleep.

The skin at the back of her neck tingled, and her whole body tensed in awareness. Someone had entered her room. Well, *Slater.* Who else could she sense before she saw him? Who else made her body light up at just the thought of him?

The covers pulled back, the mattress depressed, and Slater got in beside her.

"Wrong room," she said.

He slung an arm around her waist, scooted closer. "You."

He shifted around on the pillow, and his knees bumped into the back of hers. "Only you."

Wide awake, body wired and alert, Emmie held perfectly still, not even breathing. *Only you?* Oh, holy moly. What did that mean?

He snuggled closer, his hand tucking under her waist, his breath hot on her neck. He smelled of toothpaste and only a hint of alcohol.

What, what, what does he want?

If only her body would calm down. If only she could relax into his warmth and sleep the night away in his arms. She would love that. Love it so much.

But she just ached for him, felt swollen and hot and desperate to feel his hands on her breasts, his mouth on her skin, oh, God, *everywhere.* Liquid heat gushed between her legs at the very thought of his tongue licking into her, stroking over her clit.

Fire swept across her skin, and he flinched. He'd felt it.

"Emmie?" he whispered.

She stiffened. "Yes."

"Did you like the song?" This softness, this . . . vulnerability, it was a whole other side of him. A side she loved. So unlike what he showed the rest of the world.

"Very much." She held her breath, waiting. He couldn't have written it for her, but at the same time, her gut told her it couldn't have been for anybody else. There *was* nobody else. She was with him all the time.

She would die if it were for her, but she would be destroyed if he'd written it for someone else.

"I can't fight this anymore." He searched for her hands, found them, tucked them in against her stomach.

Fight what? He might as well have poked her with a branding iron the way the shock of his words tore through her. She had to calm down. Something was happening, changing, but she didn't know what exactly. It was too complicated between them. She couldn't respond until she got ahold of herself. This was Slater. The man she wanted so badly she couldn't sleep at night. But he was her friend first. Whatever she said or did, she couldn't ruin the friendship.

And, God, she was leaving. This wasn't her real life. She

absolutely couldn't start anything. She had to find the strength to keep herself from giving in. It would only break her heart.

Forcing herself to slow her breathing, she rested her hand on his arm. Just let it sit there until it felt normal to touch him that way. Then, when the anxiety subsided and she felt like she was back in her own skin, she turned in his arms. The slightest tilt of her chin and they'd be kissing. One stroke of her hand down his chest, and he'd be hers.

But for how long? Twenty minutes? How would he handle the morning after?

She couldn't help but believe that whatever happened, whichever path she chose right then, she'd lose him. If she turned him away, he'd go back to his random hookups. If she gave in to this intense connection, it'd be worse. He'd run. The first scenario she could recover from, the second? She couldn't bear it.

"What do I have to do?" he asked. "Quit the band? Not tour with them? Because I don't think I could do that."

"I would never ask you to do that."

"Is it enough to not sleep with anyone else? Because I can do that."

He could? He wanted her enough to stop screwing around with all the groupies? "Now's probably not a good time to commit to something like that. I've got some things in the works for you guys." She wouldn't share her plans. Not yet.

"I haven't slept with anybody since the day I saw you skinny dipping."

A slow smile spread across her face. "Are you serious?"

He smiled, but he still looked pained and unsure. "It's not something I have a hard time keeping track of."

They laughed softly, their breaths mingling. Her hand shifted to the back of his neck, her fingers sifting through all that thick, soft hair. "Why?"

"I want you." Again, that look of sadness and frustration. "But I know you don't want me. Well, I think you want *part* of me. But you'd have to take the whole thing—the singer and the songwriter, you know?" He let out a frustrated breath. "I think you only want the songwriter."

She shook her head. "I'm attracted to both, but you're right. I don't think I could give myself to the singer."

"Come on, you get hot watching me perform." His teasing smile cut through the tension. "You looked pretty worked up tonight."

"Please. You can't see me when you're onstage with all the lights in your eyes."

"I only see you." He breathed the words, his gaze stroking over her cheek, her eyes, her nose, and then finally, finally, settling blazing hot on her mouth. "You walked in ahead of Tiana, taking charge like you always do. You found the table and went right to it, not waiting for anybody to seat you. You faced the stage. Tiana had her back to it. You paid with cash. You recorded us."

"You did not see all that."

He gave her a look that said, *Really? After all that detail?* "But I can't look at you. If I do, I'll lose my place in the show."

She didn't think she could stand hearing this. He noticed her? He wanted her? He actually *wanted* her. And, God, she wanted him so badly, beyond what she could bear. But . . . "I don't think I can." *Be with you.*

He gave a curt nod, swallowing. He looked so pained. "Because you're leaving?"

"Because I'm afraid."

"Of what?"

"I'm afraid if we do anything . . . physical, you'll run. I couldn't bear to lose you. You've become so important to me. Slater, I—"

She felt the tremor wrack his body as his forehead pressed against hers. The restraint in his powerful muscles thrilled and terrified her. He wanted her so badly—it would have been unbelievable except that she felt the answering call in her own body. How could this intensity be one-sided? *Of course* he felt it, too. She'd known it for a while. Just hadn't been able to deal with it.

Because it would change everything. A risk she wasn't willing to take.

"I want you, I do. And I know I can have this . . . this part of you right now. But it's the only part of you that you give away so freely." She searched his eyes, wondering if he could ever understand. "I want the part you don't want to give."

He swallowed and closed his eyes like he was in pain.

She rubbed her thumb across his cheek, and he opened his

eyes. "As much as I want you physically—and you know I do—I can't lose you, okay?"

Stupid words. She'd turned him down. He'd go now. Of course he would. She hadn't given him sex—the only connection he knew how to make with a woman.

She knew when she woke up, he'd be gone. And tomorrow night? He'd be back to his partying ways. And they'd pass each other occasionally in the hallway or in their shared bathroom. And it would hurt like hell, because while his life rolled on seamlessly, hers would have this gaping hole. When had he become so important to her?

She rolled onto her other side, letting him leave with the least amount of embarrassment. Eyes open, she listened with her whole body, waited to feel the weight of the mattress lift, to hear the tread of his feet across the floor.

Instead, she heard the rough exhalation of a man not nearly satisfied. Then, she felt his arm wrap around her waist, a little less delicately this time, his body hot against hers, and the warmth of his breath at her neck.

A rush of emotion brought tears to her eyes.

He'd stayed.

Tonight, he would have her.

He still couldn't believe what she'd said the night before. She didn't want to lose him. She thought he'd fuck her and dump her, just like the others, and she didn't want to lose him.

He almost couldn't stand the emotion rising up in him at the idea that she liked him that much, needed him in her life enough that she wasn't willing to risk losing him. Even when she wanted him as much as he wanted her.

That was so fucking hot.

He turned onto his street, surprised to see all four cars parked at the house. Disappointment rammed into him, but he knocked it aside. He'd take her upstairs. They'd be quiet. His dick surged at the thought of being alone with her, in his bed, finally sinking into her slick heat.

Parking, he jammed his keys in his pocket. He wanted both hands free to grab her, kiss that mouth he'd been fantasizing about for so long. He fucking *had* to kiss her.

He didn't want to see her around the others, so he pulled out his phone and texted her.

I'm home. Meet me in my room?

She didn't answer. That was okay. He'd see her in a moment. Anticipation made him feel light, almost giddy. Nothing he'd ever experienced before.

He opened the door, heard laughter in the kitchen. "Em?" he shouted, too loud, too full of energy. His hands itched to touch her, to grab a handful of that silky hair. His erection pressed uncomfortably against his jeans.

She came out, eyeing him warily. "Oh, good. You're here." Her strained smile cut into him. "We've been waiting for you."

He charged toward her, but she held her hands out as if to block him.

"I've got great news. Come on."

His excitement died as he followed her into the kitchen.

"Dude," Cooper said. "Where you been?"

"Were you at the gym?" Pete asked. "You're all sweaty and shit."

"Dude. You are sexy as *fuck*," Ben said, and everyone laughed.

"Hey," Emmie cut in. "Guys. Listen. Piper Lee, her manager, and her A&R guy are coming to see you tonight."

Derek's chair shot back, falling backward to the floor in a great crash. "Holy shit, Em. Are you serious? You got them to come?"

Ben banged out a beat on the table with his hands, and Cooper whooped it up.

Emmie had her gaze on Slater, as if checking his reaction. He didn't smile. He couldn't. It was, obviously, great news, but he knew what it meant to her.

She thought he'd forget this little thing between them and go running off on tour, never looking back. Just like her ex. But she didn't understand. She wasn't dispensable. Not to him. And he couldn't wait to tell her.

"That's great, Em." He spoke loudly enough that everyone paid attention. "So they're interested in us as her opening act?"

"They're very interested. They love the demo—"

"You sent the old one?" Pete asked.

"What choice did she have?" Slater said, in her defense.

"Irwin Ledger didn't like it," Ben said. "We should've waited."

"We didn't have time to wait," she said. "Piper's got a national tour. Their opening act fell apart. They were about to go with another band out of Minneapolis, but I overnighted them a video I made of you guys live. And they're interested enough to put the other act on hold and fly out here to see you."

"Holy shit," Cooper said.

"No fuckups tonight," Pete said.

"We never fuck up," Derek said.

"You're awesome, Em." Pete got up and wrapped his arms around her. He hugged her tightly, an unusual display of emotion for him. "I'm gonna catch some z's before the show."

"Yeah, good idea." Ben followed after him. "Thanks, Emmie."

"You're the best," Derek said, hugging his sister. "Thank you so much."

"You're welcome." She closed her eyes, holding him tightly, and in that moment Slater wanted her even more. Because she was so in the moment with her brother. She wasn't worrying about Slater or the fact she hadn't discovered a band yet or anything but just being there with Derek. And he liked that about her.

The guys left the kitchen, and Emmie headed for her laptop on the counter.

He reached for her, his hand clasping her wrist, not letting go, and he drew her toward him. Her expression grew more anxious, and all he wanted was to kiss it away. "Emmie," he whispered, as he brought her full up against him.

Her reserve kicked his need into overdrive. He had to break down her walls. His hands cupped her face. "What's wrong? Why are you so upset?"

She withdrew. "I'm not. I'm happy for you guys." She went back to her computer.

He reached for her again, desperate for her touch. "Can you stop for a second? Please?"

"I can't. I'm late." She clicked on a link, and a band's website filled the screen. Music started playing. "Can you do me a favor and listen to this band? It's just one song." She started to go. "I'll be down in a few minutes."

"Wait, I want to talk to you. Where are you going?"

"I have to get ready."

"For the show?" It was way too early. And what was this music she'd put on? Jesus.

"No, I've got a date."

His muscles clenched, and anger roared through him. "With *Hector*?"

She gave a sad smile. "No, he doesn't want to see me anymore. He told Tiana I seemed a little distant, and she told him that you and I"—she gestured between them—"had something weird going on, but not to worry because it would pass. Slater would never commit to a woman, and Emmie would never screw a man whore. Still, he said he doesn't want the complications." Again, she gave a soft smile. "Too bad. I think Hector might just have been my soul mate."

The screeching guitar riffs hurt his ears. "No. He's not." He grabbed her hips and jerked her to him. "You're not going on a date."

She pulled away from him. "Of course I am. He's a pediatrician in Tiana's office. He could be perfect for me."

"Bullshit. He can't be." *Because I am.* "And you know it. You're running scared."

She stilled. "Maybe I am. But I have a right to be. It's all starting for you now. If they loved your demo and your band photo, imagine how they're going to feel when they see you live."

"But how do *you* feel? That's all I care about. How do you feel?" He held her gaze, knowing he could always count on her for the absolute truth. And, *fuck*, if that music wasn't making him crazy.

"I feel a lot of things, as you know," she said slowly. "But given that we're humans and not animals, we don't have to act on every feeling we have. If I seem a little off, it's because I feel like I've been on a roller coaster with you. But now I'm getting off. Because I'm pretty sure tonight's going to change your life. And I'm going to stand back and watch you go."

"Bullshit. I'm here with you every day, Em. I know how we are together, and this doesn't happen very often, does it? What we have . . ." He had to take a moment, gather his thoughts, because his brain was revving too quickly. "Can you please turn that shit off?"

She looked worried. "Is it that bad?"

"It's for shit."

Reaching for the keypad, she hit a button, and the room quieted. He remembered what she'd said about Alex. Once he'd gotten signed, he hadn't needed her anymore. Now that she'd scored Piper Lee, maybe she'd think the same thing about him. *Wrong.* And he'd just have to prove it to her. He touched her hips. "Emmie. A while ago you asked me what I wanted, and now I know. I want you."

She reared back, cocking her head. "Who are you, and what have you done with my roommate? Because Slater Vaughn would never say those words."

"Jonny, actually. That's my real name."

"I know."

"Do you?" Did she understand what he was saying? Because he'd never been more real in his life.

"I have to get ready. He's going to be here in fifteen minutes, and I haven't even put on my makeup." She turned away from him.

"Emmie, don't go. We need to talk."

She stood there, watching him, her fingertips mindlessly rubbing the tile counter. He could see her struggle—watched her fingers curl into fists.

He closed a hand over them. "Em."

As he held her gaze, hoping his expression could say what his words couldn't, her features finally relaxed, her demeanor softened. His heart couldn't take the whip-snap reversal from fear to happiness. But, hell, he'd gotten through. He hadn't lost her after all.

She started to back away from him but stopped a few feet away. "We will talk. We will. But tomorrow. Right now, I have to get ready. I'm not canceling on him. That wouldn't be right. Okay?"

"No. It's not okay." He had to stand there and watch her go. "You're coming to the show, though, right?"

"Of course. It's your big night. Piper Lee'll be there." She headed up the stairs.

Slater paced in his bedroom, listening for her door to open. The moment it did, he shot across the hall.

She startled at the sight of him, then her features fell in disappointment. "Not now. He's waiting."

Yeah, he knew. He was the one who'd answered the door. "Don't go out with that uptight dick."

She skimmed past him, heading down the stairs. He wrapped his hand around her waist, stopping her. Her sweet, feminine scent whirled around him, filling him with so much want he thought he might throw her down right then and there, lift up her dress, and press his mouth on her stomach. God, he needed her.

He pulled her to him, coming down until he was on the same step. With her back against him, his hands on her stomach, he said, "Be with *me*. We're—"

"Stop this. He's waiting for me."

"He's not who you want."

"And *you* are? I mean, come *on*, Slater. We're just . . . we've spent too much time together."

"Don't. Don't reduce us to some physical convenience."

"It's not like it takes much to get your interest."

His fingers curled into her flesh. "Don't fucking insult me. You think I don't know the difference between getting off and actual feelings?"

She stilled, turning in his arms to look up at him with wonder and, possibly, hope. Finally. His skin tightened. "Slater, what if it's just . . . attraction?"

"Is that all you feel?" He practically shook her, trying to get her to see what they had. How deep it went. "Tell me, Emmie. Because I know the difference between getting hard over a pair of tits and getting hard because of you. What about you?"

"You don't get hard looking at my tits?" She said it with a teasing smile, but he knew how important this answer was to her.

He touched his forehead to hers. "I get hard at the sound of your voice. I get hard when you turn our stupid beaver logo into a smoking-hot female weight lifter. I get hard when you say you don't want to have sex with me because you're afraid you'll lose me."

"Why would that turn you on?"

"Because it means you feel more for me than just checking off a box on your list."

"But it might not be real. It might just be lust."

"Have you ever felt *anything* even close to this? Jesus, Em, did you ever think you would? Because I sure as hell didn't." Slowly, he lowered his mouth to hers. Slowly, so he could watch her reaction, see her eyelids flutter closed, feel the breath shudder out of her throat. He kissed her, and thank the baby Jesus, she kissed him back.

The rush of sensation—the heat of her mouth, the pressure of her fingers digging into his sides—nearly buckled his knees.

Immediately, she pushed him away. "God, let me just . . . He's waiting for me. I have to go."

"No, you don't. If he had feelings for another woman, would you want him to go out with you?"

She shook her head, pushed him away, and hurried down the stairs.

He followed right behind, watching the guy look up from his phone. He lit up at the sight of Emmie in a pretty pink sundress and tan sandals. She wore her hair up in a high ponytail, exposing her sexy neck.

"You look great," the guy said.

"Thank you, Charles. Sorry I kept you waiting."

The dick checked his watch. "That's okay, but we better get a move on. La Maison d'Etre doesn't take reservations."

"Oh, I've always wanted to try that place."

Slater stood in the foyer with them, arms folded across his chest, keeping his gaze on Emmie.

"Charles, you've met Slater. One of my many roommates." She smiled at Slater.

The guy nodded, all business, and pulled his keys out of his pressed khakis. As he opened the door for her, he said, "You should probably bring an umbrella. It's supposed to really come down tonight. I'm sure I've got one in my trunk, but you should probably have one of your own."

"We'll be fine. We're just going from the car to the restaurant, right?"

"Well, I don't want to get this shirt wet. It's got silk in it."

Emmie glanced up at Slater, humor in her eyes. "Okay, then. I'll—" But the challenging look he gave her silenced her, and the humor dropped away. "You know what?" She tore her gaze from him. "I really don't care about a little rain. Let's just go." She turned her back on Slater, reaching for the door handle.

Slater's hand reached out and gripped hers. "Emmie." His sharp tone caused the guy to jerk to a stop and look behind him, his gaze going from Emmie to Slater.

"It's fine," the douchebag said. "I can drop her off in front of the restaurant."

Slater's gaze bore into her, and he shook his head. "Don't go," he said, voice a low growl.

But she just turned and left him.

"Dude, what the fuck are you doing? We're loading up right now." Ben stood in the garage, completely drenched, watching Slater beat the shit out of the punching bag.

"Go on without me."

"What? Why?"

"I'm not ready." He continued pummeling the bag.

"Well, get ready. Get in the shower. We're leaving in half an hour."

Ben turned to go, and Slater tossed a boxing glove at his bandmate's head. It clipped him, and he swung around. "What was that for?"

"I *said* I'll meet you there."

"It's pouring. Everybody's gotta help unload the van."

Slater gave him a dull look.

"You're seriously not going to help us?"

"Not this time. Not this one time out of the five thousand other times I've helped. This one time, I'm not going to. Got it?"

"Whatever. I don't know what your problem is. Maybe you need to get laid."

Slater tossed the other glove. Ben ducked, then picked up both gloves and chucked them at Slater like a girl. He finally cracked a smile, and the tension broke.

"You want to talk about it?" Ben asked, looking worried.

"Nah. Just give me some time. I have to get my head on right to perform tonight."

"Yeah, okay. See you there."

Ben left, and Slater collapsed on Derek's bed. How could he get his head on right when Emmie still doubted him? It wasn't like he felt threatened by her date. Emmie would never be interested in a guy who wouldn't share a fucking umbrella.

But what if she didn't want him enough to get over her fears? Because *he* did. He wanted her enough.

Shit. What was he doing? Tonight he was playing for Piper Lee, her manager, and her A&R guy. He had to focus. This was it, man. Their ticket to the big time. He couldn't fail. He owed it to the guys, and he owed it to his dad.

Jesus Christ. He had to get Emmie out of his mind. Worry about her tomorrow.

He rocked forward, lowering his head into his hands, anxiety rushing through him. He'd run, he'd lifted weights, he'd punched the shit out of the bag . . . and he still had enough energy to lift a car.

Screw tomorrow. He couldn't concentrate until he talked to her. Saw her.

Fucking devoured her.

Showered and dressed for the show, Slater jumped into his car and started the engine. Rain pounded the roof, completely obscuring his view out the windshield. He pulled out his phone and texted her.

Tell umbrella man your boyfriend's coming to get you.

And then he carefully backed out of the driveway and headed to the restaurant. She buzzed back quickly.

Save the theatrics for your show.

He smiled, heading out of their subdivision and toward the main shopping district. At the stop sign, he responded to her.

Four minutes away. Just a heads-up.

Stop it.

You're mine. He sent that one, and then at the light on

Pleasant Valley he wrote another. Two minutes. You should probably meet me outside the restaurant, unless you want to give the patrons a show.

She didn't text him back. He didn't know if that meant she'd blown him off or if she was sending the jerk-off packing. Didn't matter. He'd find her. He'd claim her. Game over.

La Maison d'Etre occupied its own property at the front of a big mall. It had a three-hundred-and-sixty-degree parking lot, the back of which was completely empty. He abandoned his car in the middle of it.

Just before getting out, he texted her once more. Here. I'm coming for you. Heart in his throat, he hopped out of the car and ran through puddles under a deluge of rain around to the front of the restaurant. Would she be there?

He felt too much, more than he'd ever felt in his life, and he didn't think he could take it if she wasn't in this with him. Rounding the corner, his heart slammed against his ribs.

She stood in her pretty pink dress under the blue-and-white-striped awning, her arms hugging herself. The look in her eyes told him she was with him all the way.

He walked toward her, swiping the hair out of his eyes, the moisture off his face. As he neared, her arms fell to her sides, and her lips parted.

"Fuck, Emmie." He grabbed her, holding her so tightly against him she let out a huff of breath. And then he was kissing her, finally gorging on the feast that was her mouth.

She threw her arms around his neck and pushed up against him, their bodies touching from mouth to toes. And when she opened to him, when he felt the welcoming pull of her tongue, he went up in flames. Her hips squirmed against him, making him thrust into her so hard, her back hit the plate glass window.

He grabbed her bare thigh, lifting it, so he could fit more easily against her. Their tongues tangled, hands groped, and hips rocked into each other's. Cupping the back of her head, he said, "I fucking need you, Emmie."

She smiled against his mouth, her body trembling, and gripped a handful of his hair at the back of his neck. "I fucking need you, too."

"Come on." He bent and lifted her, her arms and legs wrapping around him, and dashed out into the drenching rain. She tucked her head into his neck. He moved as carefully but as quickly as he could. At the car, he set her down, one arm still around her waist, not letting her go, and he opened the back door to let her inside.

She hesitated, her hair as wet as if she'd just stepped out of the shower. Water droplets beaded on her lips, and he couldn't stop himself from licking them, tasting every drop. He leaned into her, and she just melted around him, stroking the sides of his head, kissing, kissing, kissing, in complete surrender. They stood in the pouring rain, his car door open, her hands stroking him, her tongue swirling inside his mouth, and he thought he would die from so much pleasure.

And then she pulled away, struggling for breath. "God." Quickly, she turned and crawled into the backseat. He followed, shutting the door and reaching for her. She went right back into his arms and climbed onto his lap. Her scent, sweet flowers fresh with rain, filled the car.

His hand slid underneath her dress, drawing her closer to him, clutching her ass in desperation to get more of her. He wanted it all, everything. She straddled him, her open mouth trailing down to his neck, sucking and kissing, as she unbuttoned his shirt, spreading it wide. Her hands stroked his bare skin, and her tongue licked a path to his nipple.

His back arched, and his hips lifted. "Fuck, Emmie." Gripping her hands, he pushed them away. He couldn't take it. Had to see her. Needed her. All of her.

Unzipping the back of her dress, he peeled the straps off her wet shoulders, and his mouth closed over that smooth, soft skin. He turned into her neck, breathing her in, licking the shell of her ear. She shuddered. Her hands skimmed under his shirt, and her mouth found its way back to his.

Holy shit, she set him on fire. Her hands fumbled with the buttons of his jeans, but she couldn't gain traction. They were too frantic, their hips rocking hard, grinding . . . too much, too fast.

"Christ," he cried out. His dick ached with need and he couldn't stand it anymore. He lifted her, ripped open the buttons, and jerked his jeans and boxers down his hips. Immediately, her sweet hand closed around him. His hips bucked so hard he nearly knocked her off his lap. But his girl just laughed softly at his mouth and reclaimed her grip on him. She held him firmly, her thumb tracing the vein underneath, circling the head.

"I can't . . . Emmie, shit . . ." He tore her hand away, grabbed a condom from the pocket of his jeans, and sheathed himself. Pushing aside her panties, he guided himself into her wet heat.

"Oh," she breathed into his ear, as he brought her down on him.

Holy mother of God. Slick heat gloved him, gripped him, and sensation exploded on his skin, rippling across his body. She moaned, sinking down on him, barely moving, like she was just getting the feel of him inside her. He wanted—oh, God, he needed to move—but those moans she made, the look of pure bliss, made him hold back. His hips made tight, rhythmic thrusts, as she ground down on him with a deeply satisfied sigh, taking him fully and completely inside of her.

And then she started moving, hips rocking. Her fingers curled into his shoulders, her head tilted forward, her wet hair dripped onto his chest, and her lips parted.

She was moaning, sighing, making the sexiest fucking sounds he'd ever heard in his life. He was going to come, but he didn't . . . he needed . . . ah, Christ. Not yet. Jesus, not fucking yet. Too good. Too— "Ah," he cried out as she ground down on him, hips circling, rocking at an angle that, from her gasps, meant she'd hit her sweet spot.

His fingers left her hips to unclasp her bra, peel it off her, and release those beautiful, bouncing breasts. All the air caught in his chest, and he couldn't breathe. Little white lights sparked across his vision, the pleasure so intense he thought he might pass out. He'd waited so long to fill his hands with her lushness that when he did, he nearly came from their softness, their full-ness, and the erotic jolt of pleasure that came from the feel of her hard nipples in his palms. He flicked his thumbs over the hard beads, and she arched into him, head tipping back, all that hair spilling off her shoulders and onto his lap.

Jesus, look at her, so wanton, so purely sexual. His girl. *Mine.*

She was so goddamn slick, so tight, so hot. He couldn't breathe, couldn't quite catch his rhythm. He wanted too much of her too fast. She tilted forward, her hands gripping the seat behind him, and she rode him like she was out of her mind with lust, with need, like her relief was close, so fucking close, but just not hitting. Oh, holy hell, she was the most beautiful thing he'd ever seen.

He couldn't take it anymore. He gripped her hips, slid lower on the seat, and pistonned up into her. His mouth closed over her nipple, taking a hard, hungry pull.

"Oh, God," she gasped. "Oh, God, oh, my God." And then she held her breath, her features frozen in shock. Her eyelids fluttered closed as her back arched with her release.

He was out of his mind, desperate. He rammed up into her, thrusting hard and relentlessly. The tension wound him up so high he had to shut his eyes and just fucking let go before he lost his mind. His body coiled tightly, like the ocean drawing back before surging forward in a monstrous wave, and then he felt the roar of it through him as he came violently. His shouts reverberated throughout the car.

He rocked up into her a few more times, but Jesus, he was so fucking exhausted. His head fell back, and she collapsed against him.

Completely depleted, he couldn't move. Just sat there listening to the rain pummel the roof of his car, feeling the sweet weight of her body on his.

It hadn't been perfect. It'd been frantic and rushed and awkward, but it had finally happened.

When his senses returned, he realized he was missing sound check. *Hell.* "Come on, Em. Get dressed." He held her shoulders, pushing her back off his chest. "I've got to get to the club."

THIRTEEN

She got off him, covering her breasts with her arms.
That was it? He was dismissing her? Oh, God, she *knew* this
would happen. How had she let herself get so carried away?

Popping the lid off an old fast food soda cup, he tossed the
condom inside. Then, holding on to her thigh, he reached
down for her bra and handed it to her. She wouldn't look at
him. Turning away, she quickly put on her bra, but her hands
shook too badly to clasp it.

She stiffened when she felt his warm hands touching her
back, fitting the hooks. Nothing came out of her mouth, no
thanks, no . . . nothing. She couldn't believe he'd just push her
off him. Tell her it was time to go. Of course she understood
he had to get to the club. Piper Lee was coming to see them.
But if he cared for her, if the sex had meant to him what it'd
meant to her, he'd take a moment to just hold her. She was still
shaking, for crying out loud.

Lifting the bodice of the dress, she drew her arms through
the straps. Again, his hands were there to zip her up. Not passionate hands, not a lover's hands. Just hurried hands.

Within seconds, he'd buttoned his shirt, pulled up his wet
jeans. And then he sat there, eyes closed, head leaned back
against the seat.

He wanted out. She *knew* it. Why had she given in? Why had she let him literally charm her dress off? She was the one girl who hadn't thrown herself at him, so he'd been intrigued. He reached for her, patting her leg. But she jerked away. "Ready." At least her voice sounded strong, true. She climbed over the seat and buckled herself in.

He got out of the car and came around to the driver's side. Within minutes they were on the boulevard, heading for the club in downtown Austin. She wouldn't cry. Wouldn't give him anything at all. She stared dully out the window. The rain came down in sheets so thick she couldn't see anything but a blur of color.

Her heart ached. She'd believed him. Well, that wasn't true. She hadn't entirely given herself over to him. Doubt had weighed firmly in her heart. But she'd . . . hoped. He'd sounded so convincing.

Bitterness made her feel ugly, cheap, and she didn't like it at all. She drew in a breath. She had to table the internal conversation for later, when she didn't feel so shattered.

His hand reached out, closed over hers. If she withdrew it, he'd say all kinds of things charmers said to smooth over an awkward moment. So, she let him pretend. He pulled her hand onto his lap, pressing it to his thigh.

She turned to look at him, curious about the current of energy running under his skin. From the exertion? He looked intense. Of course, the hazardous driving conditions would make anyone stressed out. But he looked wrecked. What did that mean?

She pulled her hand away, not wanting any connection to him at the moment.

He parked at the back of the club, by the band's van. She made sure to open her door before he could get to her, hoping to dash inside so she could avoid him completely. But he was too fast.

He blocked her from getting out of the car. Leaning in close, he rested his hands on her thighs—high up on them, high enough to send her pulse skittering. His mouth brushed against her ear, and she had no strength whatsoever to push him away.

"Don't mistake my quiet for regret. That was . . ." He released a shaky exhalation. "Intense." He cupped her face in his hands, forced her to look at him. "Okay?"

Stupid girl that she was, she melted right there. She did believe him. The energy coursing through him? The rasp in his voice? Come on, he was affected, too. He just handled it differently. She could give him that.

He kissed her mouth. "I have to get in there."

Of course he did. He had to shift all his focus to tonight's performance. Not think about *them*. He took her hand. As she climbed out of the car, he shut the door behind her, and they dashed to the back entrance.

The door flew open, and she yanked her hand out of his. It was just a kitchen worker dumping a box into the Dumpster. Not anyone they knew, thank God.

"What the fuck was that?" His voice startled her, and she turned to find him standing there, a wall of hard muscle and bad attitude.

"What?" She wanted to get out of the rain, but he clearly wasn't budging.

He stood there with all that intensity. "You don't want them to know about us?"

"Of course not. It . . ." She gestured to the car. "God, it just happened."

"It's been happening for a long time. We just sealed the deal."

"We're not walking in there like a couple."

"Like a couple? We *are* a couple." He took her hands in his, brought them to his chest, looking like he was trying to calm down. "I can't do this right now. I'm supposed to be onstage in a few minutes. I've missed sound check." He pulled her under the gutter, which gave slight relief from the rain. "Em. We're . . . Come *on*, it's us."

She gazed into those determined eyes, saw nothing but certainty, and then something else took over as his features softened into desire. He kissed her. Oh, did he kiss her, pressing his hips into her, cupping her bottom in his big, strong hands. His tongue teased hers into play, and she sighed into his mouth.

"Yes?" he said again, lips pressed over hers.

"Oh, yes."

He reached for her hand and started to go into the club.

Oh, he was good. She gently pulled her hand out. "Not tonight."

He gave her a hard look. "I'm not lying to my friends. I'm not sneaking around."

"I know." She didn't know anything. She hadn't even thought about it. "But tonight it's about Piper Lee. We can't have any distractions."

"Then you shouldn't have fucked me in the back of my car." His wicked smile, his husky voice, made desire spill through her all over again.

"God, Slater." She practically climbed him, hitching a leg over his hip, gripping the hair at the back of his neck, and kissed him with all her heart and soul.

She could feel him flare up, feel him harden, and she couldn't help but rub him through his jeans. He groaned into her mouth. "Okay, stop, stop, stop." He set her back from him. "Fuck."

They laughed, foreheads touching, rain splattering her legs. "All right. I have to go in. But thank you for pumping me up."

"Great. I've primed you. Now you're ready to make love to your screaming fans."

Fingers closing around the doorknob, he stopped, turned to her. The look in his eye told her not to make light of what they'd just done.

He'd taken it very seriously.

And, God, what was she supposed to do with *that*?

Emmie leaned against the wall. No empty seats tonight. She'd made sure of that by getting the club to agree to one free drink for every customer until nine o'clock. Had to have a full house with Piper watching.

She had to stop thinking about Slater. Slater and sex. But, oh, that was some sex they'd had. She'd never let herself go like that. She'd actually lost her mind. Moments came flying back at her, the awkward ones when he'd almost slipped out of her, when their arms had collided in their haste to touch each other everywhere. He had seemed completely into her. A guy couldn't pretend like that.

It was when he'd held her breasts in his big hands, when he'd taken her nipple into his mouth, that everything had just clicked into place. Everything had turned into *them*. Not sex, not awkwardness, just total, crackling *connection*. Mind-body fusion. She'd come so suddenly, so explosively, her brain had shorted out.

She'd never felt anything like that before.

The sound died down in the room, drawing Emmie's attention to the band. Slater picked up his guitar and adjusted the mic. The stage went dark, a spotlight lit him up, and oh, God, she could hear the collective intake of breath at his beauty, his dynamic presence. He didn't even try to charm the crowd, didn't say a word. Just launched right into a song.

> *Look at me,*
> *I want to see your heart race,*
> *See your mouth fall open,*
> *Watch your hair spill down your back,*
> *And pool on my thighs*
> *Look at me,*
> *So I know you're in it with me,*
> *Opening up to me,*
> *Falling as hard as I am*
> *I want you to look at me, look at me, look at me*
> *I want you and only you*
> *I want you to come and come and come*
> *You.*

He was singing about her. About what they'd just done. Her heart filled to bursting with emotion, and her throat knotted painfully. It was too much for one night. Too intense. She watched his face as he sang, so fierce, so utterly sincere.

Good God, the man knew how to woo a girl.

Right then, Piper Lee entered the club. Just as Emmie could have predicted, the diva came with an entourage that surrounded her. The manager approached the hostess stand, and Piper's chin lifted, her gaze narrowing to the stage.

This was the moment, wasn't it? The moment Emmie'd so carefully orchestrated, when Slater and Piper found each other. Her heart twisted hard, and she thought she'd remember this moment as long as she lived. There was something feral about Piper's expression, the hunter sighting its prey. Her long, lanky body pushed through her entourage, moved closer to the stage. Bodies parted for her, not even knowing who she was—but knowing she was definitely *somebody*. She just had that aura about her. One of her people pointed toward the reserved table, and someone else pulled out Piper's chair. She sat down, never once taking her eyes off Slater.

As if he felt the pull, he looked right at Piper, and he gave her his most devastating grin, as if to tell her exactly what he was going to do to her the moment he got her alone.

Satisfaction shone on Piper's features. Her whole body seemed to inflate with it. Like she *knew*.

Emmie'd had enough. She headed outside, right back into the downpour. Protected from the deluge by the club's awning, she still felt the spray as sheets of rain hit the pavement and sprung back up, dousing her. Tires spun through puddles, shooting out giant waves that drenched the sidewalk. *Breathe, Emmie, breathe.*

Piper was even more gorgeous in person. All that long dark hair, straight and shiny. Her kohl-rimmed eyes, her slender figure. The way she moved—like she'd just had sex, was just about to have sex, could only ever think about having sex. She was the female version of Slater.

They fit perfectly together.

They would lounge in bed all day, party all night. They'd huddle together, sharing private jokes—because only musicians could truly understand each other, of course. Tortured souls finding each other.

Why should Emmie be so upset? She'd brought them together. She'd known in her gut it was a perfect match. She'd had no business sleeping with Slater anyhow.

God, it wasn't like she had a future with him. A guy like Slater would get bored with one woman. He'd want more. He'd always be on the prowl, nothing satisfying him. Even Piper wouldn't satisfy him. Neither one could take intimacy for long, so they'd go their separate ways but then come back together, because nothing would ever feel as right as the two of them together.

Emmie dropped her head in her hands. She was totally

making this stuff up. She really *should* be a writer. Maybe she'd write about Piper and Slater.

Ha. No, thanks. She'd stick to her *Rolling Stone* articles. Those didn't make her physically ill to contemplate.

Her mind cleared, and she shoved her insecurities aside. She had no idea what Slater would think of Piper. Emmie only knew what she and Slater had together. She had him tonight, so she would enjoy him. Because . . . *why not?* She'd never experienced these feelings before. Maybe she never would again.

Smiling to herself, she recalled her list. She'd wanted to lose herself. She'd wanted a wild, uninhibited sexual encounter. Well, she'd gotten it.

And with Slater Fucking Vaughan.

The moment the set ended, Emmie got up from the table. "I'll go get them for you," she said to Piper and her entourage.

"That's okay." Piper's lithe form rose out of the chair. "I've got it from here."

Those simple words made the blood wail like a siren in Emmie's ears. Like she could even compete with this woman? No doubt, Piper would choose Snatch to open for her. That meant she'd be around Slater every day—and night. And where would Emmie be?

Where *would* Emmie be?

Piper graced Emmie with a beatific smile. "I'm so glad you brought me this band, Emily. We're going to be brilliant together."

Emily. Yeah, yeah. She'd been around dozens of catty artists just like Piper. She didn't let it get to her. Piper slinked through the packed crowd, never taking her gaze off Slater.

Slater. He played his role perfectly, shaking hands, signing autographs, listening to excited fans. But he seemed impatient. Normally, he lived in the moment, and the fans loved that about him. Tonight, he looked like he had somewhere to be.

And then Piper appeared before him, and her demeanor changed. She'd been quiet at the table, eerily focused. Not now. Her beautiful face lit up, as she tossed the long hair off her shoulders, arched her chest toward him.

Nice body language. *Could she be more obvious?*

Slater smiled, shook her hand, but she pushed his hand

aside and hugged him—two soul mates dispensing with formalities. And right then, the moment his arms wrapped around Piper's back, his gaze zeroed in on Emmie's.

He didn't smile. His gaze turned hot, filled with carnal intentions. Just like he'd looked at her outside the restaurant as he'd come at her with pure lust in his eyes. And then he pulled away from Piper, all smiles and sexy charm again. He continued talking to Piper, appearing interested, as he led her back to the table, his gaze fixed on Emmie the whole time.

Her body burned for him. Her heart pounded furiously, painfully. If he didn't stop looking at her like that, her knees would give out, and she'd be a puddle of molten desire. She licked her dry lips, forcing herself to pull in a breath. Holy mother of God did she want this man.

The band came trampling down the stairs, shaking hands with Piper's people. Derek zeroed in on Flow Records' A&R guy, and Cooper and Ben talked animatedly to the others. Pete, as usual, got waylaid by a pack of groupies.

A current flashed down Emmie's spine, making the hairs on her arm stand up. *Slater.* He came up behind her. A hand cupped her hip, and Slater's mouth nestled near her ear. "Let's go."

She felt flushed, feverish. It took a moment to compose herself. "We can't." She cleared her throat. "You have to work."

"Work later. Home now."

"That's Piper Lee," she said as quietly as she could, trying not to move her lips much in case the woman could read them. The woman stared openly at Slater, obviously wondering what Emmie meant to him. So, Emmie stepped away and approached her. "So, did you like the set?"

"Loved it." Piper reached out for Slater's arm, wrapping a hand around his biceps like they'd been together for years. She turned to Emmie. "Can you order us some shots?"

Was this chick for real? Before Emmie could respond, Slater motioned for the waitress, the one who'd hovered around him since he'd shown up at the table. She'd ignored the other band members and just stood there waiting for the lead singer to pay attention to her. How many cocktail napkins with phone numbers scribbled on them would wind up in his pocket tonight?

The waitress smiled at him eagerly, and he made a circular motion to include the whole table. "Shots, please. Don Eduardo Silver."

"You bet."

Piper smacked him on the arm. "All right." She looked super pleased.

That smile could launch a thousand hard-ons for sure.

But Slater wasn't looking at Piper. His hand stroked lower, hovering at the top of Emmie's ass, his fingers teasing her through the thin cotton dress. He edged away from Piper, his body forcing Emmie to move with him.

"What are you doing?" she whispered harshly.

"I'm taking you home."

"You have Piper Lee right here."

"So?"

"So? That's your ticket to a national tour. You know, with the big buses? The exposure? The *record company*?"

"Emmie, if you don't come with me right now, your brother—and everyone in this club—is going to find out we're together. Do you know why? Because my tongue is going to curl around your sexy little earlobe. And my hands? They're going to rip that pretty dress off you so that I can hold those fucking spectacular breasts up to my mouth and suck them. And I'm pretty sure you know where that's going to lead. I'm going to be on my knees, my face between your legs—"

"God, Slater. Stop." Beads of perspiration popped out at her hairline. Her scalp burned. "You can wait an hour."

"No, I can't."

"You make no sense. This is your dream, right? This is what you want more than anything?"

He looked at her challengingly. "I think I've just told you what I want more than anything."

"Why are you doing this?" *You have Piper Lee right here.*

"Because I want you, and I'm going to have you right now."

"Are you serious? You'd blow your chance with Piper just to get me naked?"

"I'll have both. But you come first."

Emmie smiled. Piper and her people had already seen Slater perform. Derek would take it from here, make sure the band opened for Piper. "Some big, bad rocker you are. I'm not even sure I'm attracted to you anymore." She felt for his hand, giving it a squeeze. "One hour, okay?"

He growled. "Fifteen minutes."

"Thirty. Nonnegotiable."

"You're so fucking hot."

———————

Every time his girl laughed, she'd lean forward, and that soft, silky hair would brush over his arm. The heat of her body so close to his kept his hard-on straining. He ached.

So while Piper kept trying to create a web of privacy around them with their shared experiences as singers and songwriters, his body yearned only for Emmie. Emmie, who talked business with the manager and record company people. Who smelled like sweet flowers and whose legs opened a little wider for him each time his hand inched up her thigh.

A bunch of fans came over to the table and asked Piper for autographs. The opportunity he'd waited for. "Listen, I've got to get Emmie home. She hasn't been feeling well."

Derek stopped his conversation, his brow furrowing in concern. "What's the matter?"

"She hit her head."

Emmie gave him a disbelieving look.

"How the hell'd you do that?" Derek asked.

"She slipped." Emmie squeezed his thigh. "She was on her date. It was raining . . ." Oh, Christ, could he please get her out of here?

"How'd *you* find out?" Derek asked, looking between them.

Emmie's brow arched, waiting for his answer.

"She'd asked the douche to bring her home, and I was just leaving the house. That's why I missed sound check. I didn't want to leave her alone—"

"So you brought her to a rock concert?" one of the record company guys asked.

"Figured it was better than leaving her alone."

"You all right?" Derek asked her.

She shrugged. "I should get home."

Derek got up. "I'll take her."

"No." Slater gave Derek a look to remind him he was the business guy in the band, and he needed to stay and work

Piper's people. Or whatever. Slater hoped Derek just sat the fuck back down so Slater could get his girl home and naked. Derek nodded. Thank fucking Christ.

Slater reached under her arm and practically dragged her up. "Great to meet you all. Look forward to seeing you at the end of October." He shook hands with the manager and A&R guy. Thanks to the fans, Piper didn't even notice as Slater ushered Emmie out the back of the club.

"That was smooth," she said, as soon as they got outside.

Gripping her arm, he hurried her to the car, opened her door, and practically tossed her into the front seat.

"Slater," she said, laughing.

He slammed her door and cut around to his side of the car, shoved the key in the ignition, and quickly checked his mirrors before peeling out.

"What is your problem?" she asked.

"Getting you home."

"Yes, I know. But we've got all night."

He turned to her, letting her know the ridiculousness of her statement. His dick hurt, and he shifted his jeans to give himself some room. She looked down at his lap, and her eyes flared with desire.

She blew out a soft breath. "Wow."

He wanted her so badly, he couldn't see straight.

Running a yellow light, he accelerated to get on the freeway on-ramp. "Where did you go tonight?"

"What? Oh, when I went outside?"

"It's raining. Why would you go outside?"

"I needed some air." Her brow furrowed. "How did you even see me? The place was packed tonight."

Did he need to answer that? "You left right after Piper came in."

"The way she looked at you. She was like a lion spotting a gazelle."

"You're worried about me and Piper?" He knew he sounded incredulous, but come on, *Piper*? Versus Emmie Valencia? *Seriously*?

"Of course I am. She's beautiful."

"So?"

"So, she's . . . beautiful. And sexy."

"Is she? Well, you're that and so much more."

She smirked, but he could see a hint of pleasure in her eyes.

He sighed. "Okay, here's my list of things to worry about before Piper Lee. Ready?"

Her smile was tentative, wary.

"One, a zombie apocalypse. Two, a land shark attack. And, three, incurable boils." He reached for her hand. "Do I need to go on? Because I can. And I still won't get to Piper Lee. Now, get over here." All he wanted was to feel her, to have her close.

She smiled, undoing her seatbelt and sliding to the center. She buckled herself in and leaned against him, all her heat and fragrance filling him up inside. He wrapped an arm around her, and she burrowed into him.

"Finally."

"What does that mean?" She looked up at him.

"You've been resisting me since we left the restaurant."

"Well, you got all weird. Right after we did it."

"You rocked my world, Em. I needed a moment." She started to pull away, but his hand slid down her arm, holding her to him.

"Did you freak out? Even a little?"

"What? No. Just the opposite. It was so fucking good, it blew out half the grid. I needed to come back to earth."

"You seriously didn't have any doubts?"

"I waited a long damn time for this, Em. I waited until I was sure."

"Sure of what?"

"My feelings. I wasn't going to mess with you. First, you were Derek's sister to me. Then, you were my Emmie. And I wouldn't hurt you with casual sex. You'd hate yourself. So, I waited. And then, tonight, I just couldn't fucking take it anymore."

"I know. I drive men wild."

"You're still being distant."

She turned to him, one hand curling in his shirt. "God, Slater, what do you want me to say? I'm a mess right now."

"*That's* what I want you to say. I want you to be Emmie. I want us to be the way we are together, where we tell each other the truth. That's what I need."

"I can't talk when I don't know what I'm feeling." She worried her hands.

"Start anywhere."

"I'm scared to death."

"Because you think I want Piper?"

"Well, yeah, I do think it's pretty inevitable. At some point you and Piper Lee are going to happen. But it's not just that. It's everything. You have to know it's all going to change for you. Starting with the festival."

"So, you didn't hear anything I said tonight?"

She closed her eyes. "I heard what you said when you were extremely . . . aroused."

"Right. And I get boners for any woman with a pulse. I'm a man whore, right?"

The tension broke when she smiled. "Yes."

"I'm a single guy, enjoying what's offered. No, I've never been in a relationship before. But that's because I've never met anybody I wanted the way I want you." His voice broke, probably from singing tonight. "I'm fucking crazy about you."

"You are?"

"I am."

She drew in a deep breath, turned her face into his chest. She inhaled.

"Do I stink?" He needed a shower.

"You smell delicious. Like your soap and rain and Slater."

His arm tightened around her. "You smell good, too."

Leaning up, she kissed his cheek. Then, kissed it again, only her mouth had opened a little so he felt the hint of moisture. Her fingers started unbuttoning his shirt as her tongue traced the fine cartilage of his ear. He shifted, his erection roaring back, hard and throbbing.

Pushing aside the shirt, her hand skimmed his chest. "I love your body."

"I love yours." He could barely speak.

"Just, um, just tell me why. Why me? I mean, isn't Piper kind of perfect for you? She's like the male version of you."

"Why would I want to hang out with me? Besides, I like who I am around you." He hoped she understood what that meant to him. "You're real, Emmie. I can see all of you." His hand closed over hers. "And I like everything I see."

She nuzzled his neck, giving it a lick. "Slater?" Her whispery voice gave him goose bumps. "I really like you." Her mouth slid down his collarbone, and her hand cupped him firmly through his jeans.

His hips bucked, and he withdrew her arm so he could put two hands on the steering wheel. "Stop. Seriously, Em. I've been hurting all night. We're almost home."

"Can't wait." She licked his nipple, and then her whole mouth covered it and she sucked.

"Ah. Fuck." Desire exploded in his veins, coursing through him, turning him into a fireball of lust. "Emmie, please, wait."

"Nuh-uh." Her tongue traced down his chest, as she reached for the button on his jeans. Slowly, she popped the first one. Her mouth and tongue sucked and licked down his abdomen to the top of his boxers. "You have no idea what this tattoo does to me." Holding his cock through his boxers, she shifted it aside and kissed his tattoo.

And then, looking up at him, her tongue swirled around the ink.

"Aw, fuck, Em."

She popped the next button and then the next, her mouth kissing his erection through the slit in his boxers.

"Jesus, fuck." His ass lifted off the seat, and his foot pushed too hard on the accelerator. "Stop. I mean it—fuck."

He could feel her breath on his dick, as she popped the last button. And then she lowered his boxers with her teeth, turning her head to look up at him with the sexiest eyes he'd ever seen.

"We're going to have an accident," he bit out.

Holding his boxers down, she licked his cock from the base to the tip, and then, holy mother of God, her hand closed around him and she pulled him away from his stomach. But she didn't take him in her mouth. No, she broke out in a slow, seductive smile, and then she let out a contented sigh as she rubbed the head of his dick over her smooth cheeks, across those pink lips. It was too much. Too fucking much. He thought he might come right then.

And then, slowly, she sucked him all the way to the back of her throat. He couldn't see straight. He couldn't drive. Getting off at the next exit, one hand on her head to still her—but not remove her from his raging cock—he pulled off to the side of the deserted country road and jerked the gear into park.

Groping for the lever, he pushed the seat back, making more room for her. She got up on her hands and knees, started pumping him in and out of her deliciously wet, hot mouth, her tongue running zigzags and swirls, licking him, and sucking him in hard.

"Fuck. Oh, fuck. Oh, fuck." His hips bucked off the seat as desire swept across his skin, his balls tightened, and he came violently in her mouth. She kept up the suction as he continued to spurt into her. It just kept coming until he felt completely and utterly spent. He sank into the seat, his fingers sifting into her soft, silky hair.

She sat up beside him, wiping her mouth with a satisfied grin. "That was really good."

He stuttered out a laugh. His body shook with the aftermath of his explosive release. "Jesus. What you do to me."

She came up to him, leaning across his lap and wrapping her arms around his neck. "Take me home."

FOURTEEN

Following her up the stairs, he pulled down the zipper of her dress and pushed the straps off her shoulders. Just before the dress pooled at her feet, he caught it, swept it up over her head. She brought her hands around and unclasped her bra, peeling it off, freeing her breasts. He wanted to see them, touch them, and suck them into his mouth.

His hands pushed underneath her panties and fanned out across her ass. He squeezed her luscious cheeks, and she gasped. Fingers curling in the cotton, he slowly dragged the fabric down her legs.

She stopped, stepping out of them, and he pocketed her panties, then gently bit into the flesh of her ass. When he came up on the step beneath her, he cupped her flushed face in his hands and kissed her. "Shower."

Her lips parted, a look coming over her that made him wonder if she'd fantasized just as fervently as he about showering together. She balled up all her clothing and tossed the pile into her bedroom before dashing into the bathroom. He stripped as she turned on the faucet. She went in before him, and he yanked the curtain open so he could watch her step under the spray. Watching her tilt her head back, water streaming down her lush curves, his body tightened with need.

"You are so fucking beautiful." *Mine*. She was finally his. He climbed into the stall, hot water sluiced down his body, and he cupped her breasts, gathering them, lowering his face into them. Greedily, he sucked on her nipple, taking a deep, long pull.

"Oh, my God," she said, her fingers gripping handfuls of his hair.

He couldn't get enough of her, couldn't touch enough of her flesh at once. He kneaded her ass as his tongue swirled over her nipple.

"Slater, oh." Her hips rocked restlessly, and he slid a hand between her legs.

Needing to watch her reaction, he pulled back as he slowly, gently slid one finger into her curls, parting them until he found the swollen nub of her clit. He took his time, letting his finger circle languorously around it, watching as her mouth opened, her eyelids fluttered closed, and she started panting, moaning, rocking into his hand, those big, round breasts undulating with her every move.

"Beautiful." He sucked her bottom lip into his mouth, running his tongue along the sensitive flesh inside, while his finger slid along her slick length, curving to slip inside her silky heat. She arched into him, her head rolling forward onto his shoulder.

"God, Slater." Her legs parted, her body trembling, as she rested one hand on his arm. He wanted her so badly he couldn't think beyond this moment, the steam, the hot spray, her slick heat, and the intense closeness he felt to her, his Emmie.

He sank to his knees, pushing her legs apart, and licked into her. A rush of moisture flowed over his tongue, and he felt the tremors in her legs.

"Slater." She thrust herself against him, moaning, her fingers digging into his hair, nails scraping along his scalp. "Yes, yes, oh, my God, yes. I'm . . . oh, oh, oh, I—" Her body seized up, her hips frantically jerking with the flicking of his tongue in her slippery, hot folds, and then she cried out, her fingers clamping down hard on his hair. "God." Her back hit the wall, and she closed her eyes, breathing hard. *"Oh, my God."* Slowly, she lowered herself to the tub floor. Drawing her knees to chest, she rested her head on them.

"Em?"

"Hang on."

He sat beside her scooping her into his arms.

She trembled. "Oh, yes. Yes, yes, yes."

"Are you still coming?"

"It's like little aftershocks. Shh. Let me finish."

He laughed, a feeling of perfect contentment washing over him. "You make me happy."

Her chin lifted, a look of utter vulnerability on her beautiful, flushed features. "I can't believe this is happening. I swear, I've wanted to feel this way my entire life. I just can't . . ."

"You can't believe it's with me?"

"I can't believe I get to live it."

"You're immune to guys like me." A shadow crossed his mind—was this a sexual thing for her? Something to do with her checklist?

"I'm desperate for you."

A weight dropped off him, and he tilted her face to kiss that pretty pink mouth.

They heard a door slam downstairs, and Emmie sat up. "They can't be home. Why would they be home?"

Voices, laughter, carried up the stairs. "Em? Emmie?"

A knock at the door. "Emmie?" Derek called.

"Yes." She pushed out of Slater's arms, scrambled to her feet. "Yes?"

"Get out here. You won't fucking believe this."

"Give me a few minutes, okay?" she called. "I'll be right there."

"Where's Slater? He's not answering his cell."

Slater slowly got up, watching her.

"How should I know?"

Anger rushed him, hot and mean. He rammed his hand against the faucet to shut it off.

"Well, hurry up and come downstairs." Derek's boots thundered down the stairs.

Water dripped off her, and she looked so young with her face free of makeup and her wet hair streaming down her back.

"Don't be angry, Slater."

"Don't be angry? Are you fucking kidding me? After all this?" He held her gaze, letting her know he wasn't fucking around. "I'm not lying to him. He's my best friend. Why would you want to anyway? What does it matter if we tell him now or tomorrow or the next day?"

He searched her eyes for an answer. What was the issue? He saw fear, caution, a hint of sadness. "Tell me. Because I'm not playing games here, Em."

She drew the curtain back, reached for a towel. He grabbed her arm, swung her to him.

"You still think I'm going to move on, don't you? You don't want to tell your brother because, in the next day or two or three or four, I'm going to dump you, is that it?"

"Why can't you give me time? This *just* happened. Can you give me a few minutes here? I'm not an impulsive person. When I get flustered, I need to step back and let my mind calm down so I can think straight."

"That's fine, Em. You take all the time you want. In the meantime, I don't want to be around you and your brother. Because I'm not going to hide in the closet or pretend I wasn't just in the shower with you." He leaned closer. "Fucking you with my mouth." Without even toweling off, he threw open the door and stalked to his room.

———

By the time Emmie came downstairs, a party was in full swing. Music blasted and guests filled the house, spilling into the back and front yards. She found her brother in the kitchen, making drinks. She didn't see Slater anywhere.

Derek's face lit up when he saw her. He shouted for the guys to gather around. When they did, he handed each of them a shot glass. He filled a glass of water from the sink for her.

"What's going on?" She found herself unable to keep the smile off her face.

Everyone lifted their glasses. "Em, I love you," Cooper said. "I seriously love you."

"Oh, my God, will you tell me what happened?"

"Snatch is the official opening act for Piper Lee," Derek said. "We leave the day after Austin City Lights."

The guys started hooting and hollering. She showed how happy she was for them with smiles and hugs, but inside she was dying. She felt shattered. She'd finally gotten to be with

Slater, and it had been a thousand times more incredible than she'd imagined. And now he was leaving.

Just as she'd orchestrated.

Derek whisked her up into his arms. "You did it, Em. Thank you so much."

"You're welcome. You deserve this. You've *earned* this."

He set her down, and Cooper poured more shots. "To Emmie!"

"To Emmie!" the guys shouted.

Pulling on his arm, she turned Derek away from the others. "It's happening."

His smile broadened. "It is." But concern flickered in his eyes, dulling his happiness.

She touched his arm. "What's the matter? What is it?"

He turned his back to the room. "Em, shit. Is this . . . is all this about Slater?"

Fear jolted through her. Did he know? Oh, God, she—

"His songs, his voice, his looks. Is this all happening because of him?"

"Oh, God, no, Derek." It broke her heart to see the impact their dad still had on him, making him doubt himself when he should feel nothing but pride in his accomplishments. "*No*. You're the backbone of all his songs. Your rhythms are the foundation. Yeah, he writes them, but you get his grooves on track and keep them there. You know that, right?"

He didn't answer, just held her gaze like she was the shore he was swimming toward. But she had to make him understand.

"You guys are a team," she said. "He couldn't do this without you any more than you could do it without him. It's a partnership. And while you have different strengths, you're *equally* talented."

She remembered Slater's comment about her dad, about the power he had over both of them. "Slater said something to me once that really hit home. He said we both have this driving need to prove to Dad we're good enough. You want to prove you're the musician he said you'd never be—and I want to prove that I'm worthy of his love. But we're wasting all our energy on something we'll never have because—bottom line—Dad's a narcissist. And that pretty much means it's not about us at all. It's never been about us. And it never will be. Did Dad ever really listen to you play? No, because he needed it all to be about him, so he shut you down with his cruel comments." She reached for her brother's hand. "So let it go. Stop trying to prove something to someone who just isn't worth it. Forget about dad, and go out there and kick some ass." Just like she was trying to do.

His smile returned, a look of satisfaction spreading across his handsome face. "A narcissist, huh? Pretty good assessment." He nodded. "So, Slater's more than just a pretty face?"

"It takes a minute to figure that out, but yeah. I think so."

Some girl jumped on Derek's back, squealing, as more strangers streamed into the kitchen. The volume grew louder and louder, until her ears hurt almost as badly as her heart. She watched Derek get sucked into the heart of the celebration.

She was happy for them, dammit. Of course she was. Her gaze landed on the calendar she'd tacked to the wall. Ten days until ACL.

Slater'd leave her in eleven.

Emmie slipped out of the kitchen, climbing the stairs and closing herself in her room. She quickly texted Slater.

Where r u?

She wanted to apologize for hiding their relationship, but how could she? Of course she had to protect herself. But she hated hurting him.

Getting ready for bed, she tried to override the pain by thinking only about the band, all the good things coming their way. All the dreams about to come true.

For her, too. Because no way could Irwin ignore Snatch any longer. Of course he'd sign them now. And then Emmie would get her promotion. Yay. If only she could focus on *that* instead of on Slater leaving.

In fact . . . she picked her phone up off the nightstand and quickly shot off a text to Irwin.

Good news. Just got Snatch on Piper Lee's tour.

She needed some good news for herself. Drawing a leg underneath her, she sat on the bed, waiting for his response.

It didn't take long. She stared at the screen heralding

Irwin's text, holding her breath. Hope warred with fear.
Would he finally promote her? Come on, he had to. Look
what she'd done with her brother's band. One hand over her
pounding heart, she opened his text.

Well done.

She waited. What, hoping he'd come right out and offer
her a promotion? She smiled. Irwin didn't roll like that. Piper's A&R guy came to the show. Think he might want to
sign them.

He'll want to see how they do on tour.

He was right, of course. He was right about everything.
What about you? You could sign them. ☺ And then she
could get her promotion, move back to New York so she
wouldn't be alone in this house while the guys toured. And
Slater? Could she still have him?

Because they're good or because you want the
promotion?

Obvs I want the promotion, but Snatch is good.
Really good. You watched the video I sent you,
right? Slater Vaughn's a star, and you know it.

Could be. But, Em, Snatch doesn't count. It's your
brother's band. You live with them. Not a
discovery.

The hair on the back of her neck snapped to attention. He
was playing her. She'd known it all along, in her gut, but she
hadn't wanted to believe it. He'd never promote her. He
needed her as his personal assistant. You're never going to
promote me, are you?

She waited for his response, each moment that passed
ticked up her anxiety. And then she knew what she had to do.
With shaking fingers, she typed: You know I like working
with you, but I'm not coming back without a promotion.

You can't possibly mean to stay in Texas. They
squeeze their feet into pointy-toed shoes. Is that
the future you see for yourself? Marrying an elf
who spits a stream of saliva into a red Solo cup?

Irwin.

We agreed to 6 weeks. Time is almost up. I need
you back here. As they say in Texas, we have a
shit ton of work to do.

It would never change. She could see that. He'd never take
her seriously unless she took her own life seriously.

I want you to sign Snatch, and I want to be A&R
Coordinator.

Too soon to sign them.

Not too soon to promote me. 8 years. No one
knows this biz like I do.

He didn't respond, so she tossed the phone aside and
slammed her head back on the pillow. If she quit her job,
she'd have no income. Worse, she had no job possibilities.
And, no, she'd never go back to work for her dad. Not that he
needed her help. His flavor of the moment did that kind of
work for him. Flash might hire her, but in what capacity? All
he wanted was for her to make scrapbooks and score swag.
Working for Irwin was cool. It had panache. Working for
Flash of Frontierland would kill her credibility.

If she quit, her chance of getting a real job anywhere else
would diminish. Always better to get a job while employed.
God, she felt sick to her stomach. Her life, once so clear and
focused, now felt out of control.

Quitting was stupid. It was rash. She didn't throw temper
tantrums. Best to go back to work and continue to prove herself. Say no when he asked her to go to Barney's to determine
the difference between cadet blue, cornflower blue, and dark
cyan in shirt colors.

If she went back to New York, she could *live the job*, just like Bax. Earn the promotion not by being Irwin's *personal* assistant, but by being an assistant in A&R.

If she went back to work . . . she squeezed her eyes shut as the pain spread wide, burning through her soft tissue. If she went back to work, she'd lose Snatch—and she truly believed in them. They'd likely get signed by Flow Records, which wasn't nearly as good as Amoeba. Eric, the A&R guy, had no big acts other than Piper to his credit. Not what she wanted for her guys.

She pried open her heart enough to face the truth. It also meant giving up Slater. With her ridiculous schedule and his tour, a relationship wasn't possible. They'd never see each other.

Why was she even thinking about Slater? He was leaving, hitting the road. She knew what that meant.

Okay. *Breathe*. She had to take Slater out of the equation and focus on the job. On Irwin. On *her*. Putting fear aside, what was the best decision for her?

She already knew the answer. She couldn't go back. She had to move forward.

Her hand closed over her phone.

I'm sorry, Irwin. But I quit.

Weight pressed on the mattress, awakening Emmie with a start. "Slater?"

Before she could fully rouse herself, she felt his big, warm palm press flat to her stomach. God, how she loved his hands on her.

"I'm here."

She turned over, so filled with relief she flung herself into his arms. "I'm sorry."

"Oof." He fell back with her on top. His arms went around her, and he rolled her onto her side. They lay facing each other.

"I'm so sorry. I shouldn't have freaked out like that." She ran her fingers through his hair. He looked so tired and worn out.

"Naw. I was a dick."

"No, you weren't." He'd been crazy with emotion, and she'd shut him down. Slater didn't show emotion, so she hated that

the one time he let himself go, she'd hurt him. "I got scared."
She was *still* scared. But he didn't need to hear that. Not
tonight. "You got the news?"

"Yeah." He didn't look happy. And that just killed her
because this was his moment, what he'd worked so hard for,
and he couldn't be happy because of her insecurities.

"It's good," she said. "It's really good for you."

He barely nodded.

"It's your dream, Slater. And it's coming true."

"Yeah, it's great, Em." He sounded testy.

"Were you celebrating with the guys?"

"No," he snapped. "I wasn't celebrating. I was driving
around, wondering what the fuck to do."

"About me? You don't have to worry—"

"Fuck. Are you kidding me? We're still there? Look, get it
out of your head that I'm gonna bolt because we had sex. I
want to be with you, Em. The timing sucks. I have to go on
this tour, but I want *us*."

"Of course you have to go. It's the beginning of everything."

"Yeah, but it's also the beginning of us."

In a million years, she'd never thought she'd hear words
like that coming from Slater Vaughn. "I . . ." But he was right.
The timing sucked.

"You don't trust me." He shrugged. "Why would you? I get
that."

"God, Slater, everything's happening all at once. I can't
think."

"I don't want you to think."

Oh, boy. The way he looked at her, so serious, so intense,
it set her heart racing. He leaned toward her, his gaze drifting
to her mouth, his eyelids lowering. She stopped him with a
hand to his chest. "So, um, I have big news, too."

He stiffened, features tightening.

"I quit my job."

She whispered it, so it took a moment for the impact to hit
his features. "You quit your job? Tonight?" Emotion played
across his features—surprise turning to concern. And then
happiness flashed. "You'd come on tour with us?"

"What? No. I . . . you're touring with Piper and her band."
Go on tour with them? Where had that come from?

He stroked a lock of hair off her shoulder, his fingers brushing across her skin. "So, what happened? Why'd you quit?"

"I talked to Irwin. I was so sure once I got you on Piper's tour, he'd promote me. But he won't. And I finally realized he's been gaming me all along." Fear dug in, squeezing her stomach. She'd never been unemployed in her life. Since graduating high school, she'd never been without a paycheck.

Not only was she unemployed, but she'd have to give up her apartment. Which meant she had nowhere to live. Well, sure, the guys would let her live in the house. But still. She had nothing.

She seized up. *What had she done?*

"Hey, hey." Slater's fingers stroked her shoulder. The warm, sure look in his eyes soothed. "You're Emmie Valencia. You make things happen. This will open the door for even better opportunities." He brushed his lips over the corner of her mouth. "How'd he take it?"

She blew out a slow breath. "He's not happy. But I told him I'm not coming back without a promotion. Do you think I could stay here a little longer, you know, until I find a band he wants to sign?"

His hand pressed harder into her hip. "Yes, of course." He swallowed. "You okay?"

"I mean, I'm freaking out. But I did what I had to do. And it's done, and I don't want to think about it. I want . . ." She drew in a breath.

"What do you want, Emmie?"

"I want . . ." *Oh, just say it.* "I just want my eleven days with you."

He lunged for her, kissing her with a hunger that stole the breath from her lungs and sent her heart beating so fast she could feel it ticking in her neck. His hands held her face, drawing her closer so he could kiss her more deeply, more urgently.

"I want way more than that, Em." His mouth moved down to her neck, her collarbone, her breast. His tongue swirled around her nipple while his other hand rode the curve of her waist, the rise of her hip. He slipped a finger between her legs, and her hips rocked into him at the first fiery wash of sensation. "I want more, but I'll take my eleven days."

"Slater," she moaned.

He gently pushed her onto her back, pressing hot kisses along her stomach. His shoulders nudged her legs apart as he kissed the top of her curls, his tongue licking inside, making one slow, luxurious swipe across her clit. She arched off the bed, crying out, as the heat traveled along her limbs, curling around her heart, igniting her with pure erotic sensation.

And then his hands slid under her ass, lifting her, and he licked her with such passion and urgency that she lost herself in the feel of his tongue, his big hands, the delirium that swept her away. As the tension coiled to inexorable heights, she planted both feet on the mattress, raised her hips off the bed, and thrust against his mouth, needing more, faster, harder. She was out of her mind with pleasure, and she had to cry out for some kind of release. And then her body seized in a climax so intense stars exploded behind her eyelids.

He kissed his way back up her stomach, those big hands touching her everywhere, caressing her skin, charting the territory he owned. His mouth covered her nipple, making love to it, sucking so sensuously she felt the pull between her legs. She couldn't take it anymore. She needed him inside her so badly. She reached between them, closed her hand around his hard, thick length, and guided him to her core. "I'm on birth control," she whispered.

"Oh, thank Christ. I'm tested and clean." He held himself over her, a hand at either side of her head, and took possession of her mouth before pushing inside.

His head reared back as he plunged into her, lighting up every nerve ending inside her sensitive channel. Yearning flared deep within, a driving need heightened and intensified with each forceful stroke. "Oh, fuck, Emmie. So good."

Her hips slammed up to meet his, her body wild to reach satisfaction from this screaming demand for release that kept rising, twisting her, making her strain for something just out of reach.

In a frenzy, he hooked a hand under her knee and lifted her leg up to his shoulder, tilting her hips so that he stroked her clit with every thrust—and God, she cried out from the acute sensations that wouldn't break but kept rising, making her cry out in frustration. She'd never felt so out of control in her life.

His grunts turned to moans, and then he was shouting as he clutched her hips and hammered into her.

Oh, God, finally, her body tightened as desire tore through her. Her eyes shut tightly as her climax hit, held, and wrung her out.

Harsh pants escaped his throat as he arched back, his hips grinding into her, swiveling. The muscles in his arms tightened, flexed. A few more slow, languid pumps, like he was savoring every last bit of pleasure, and then he collapsed on top of her. He breathed heavily, and his damp body covered hers. She wrapped her arms around his back, holding him close.

He exhaled roughly, then rolled to her side, reaching for her and drawing her in tight against him. "Give me a chance." He kissed her cheek. "My Emmie." And then his breathing evened out, and he fell asleep.

Emmie's body thrummed, her nerves tingling all the way to her fingertips.

God, she loved his passion, his intensity. Believed, in this moment, he meant every word.

It was just . . . she knew something he couldn't possibly know. Absence didn't make the heart grow fonder. No, it weakened the bonds, lessened the intensity. It made lovers forget.

She knew what it felt like to wait at home while her man was on the road. It was excruciating. Never knowing what he did with his time, wondering at each voice she heard in the background over the phone. Anxiety driving her to do things she didn't think herself capable of—like checking his Facebook messages, his jeans pockets.

Awful. It was just awful. No way to live.

She couldn't go through that again, not for anything. She already knew how it ended.

But she had her eleven days. And she'd enjoy every minute of them.

FIFTEEN

The guys had trashed the house. Slater picked up a
lamp and grabbed a few beer bottles on his way into the
kitchen. He dumped them in the recycling bin before heading
to the coffeemaker.

He was glad he'd missed the party. He'd needed the time
to drive, to get his head on right. What goddamn timing. He
wanted Emmie—wanted her so damn much—but he *had* to
go on tour, obviously. But no way—no fucking way—would
she wait for him. Not after what her pussy ex had done. Not
with what she'd seen in this business.

So what was he supposed to do? He'd just gotten her—he
couldn't let her go. He had to prove himself to her—if she'd
let him.

Would she?

At least she'd given him the next ten days. He'd have to
show her what she meant to him in that time. How much he
wanted her—for real. Not just for sex or a good time.

For real.

Damn. He thought of the way they'd kissed, the intensity
of their fucking, and it made him hot and hard all over again.
As the coffee machine popped and sputtered, he lowered his
head, letting himself fall back into her touch.

And then he felt her hands slide around his waist, her soft breasts press against his back, and need jacked him up. But they were in the kitchen. Sure, the guys had partied hard and late, but he couldn't take her here. Not with the chance someone could stumble in. So he held on to her hands, pressed them to his body.

She kissed his back, her hands lifting his shirt, gliding up his stomach to his chest. Pressing harder, she let her hands roam down his stomach, slide beneath his gym shorts, and clasp his cock. She murmured into his back, but he couldn't hear anything past the roar of blood in his ears.

He spun around, grabbed her ass, and lifted her off the ground. His foot dragged out a kitchen chair and he sat down, placed her on his lap, and devoured that sexy mouth. She ground on him, her hips making little circles as she rocked against his raging erection.

"Fuck, not here, Em."

"Here. Now."

He was powerless when her tongue was in his mouth, her hands gripped his shoulders, and her pussy rode his cock through their clothes. His hand went up her shirt, the feel of her soft, round breasts filling him with out-of-control lust. He had to have her. Now.

"What the fuck?" roared Derek.

Emmie's body jerked, and she scrambled off Slater. Before he knew what was happening, Derek rushed him. Emmie screamed, "No!" and threw herself in front of Slater. Slater caught her around the waist, taking Derek's fist to the side of his head.

"You fucking scumbag motherfucker, I will kill you. I will fucking kill you."

Ben stumbled into the kitchen, Cooper following close behind.

"Derek, Jesus Christ." Ben threw himself at Derek to hold him back.

"Are you okay?" Slater asked Emmie.

She looked shaken, her gaze trained on her brother, who struggled to get out of the hold Cooper and Ben had on him.

"Stop it, Derek. Just stop it." She stood, straightened her T-shirt.

But Derek pulled at his restraints. "You touched my goddamn

sister? I warned you, man. I fucking told you to stay away from her."

"No, Derek," Emmie said. "You don't understand. Let me talk to you privately."

"No, *you* don't understand. He fucks girls. That's all he does."

"Derek." She reached for Slater's hand. "It's not like that. We're together."

Derek's eyes widened, his face bright red. "You son of a bitch." He tore out of Ben's grip, then yanked himself away from Cooper and flew across the room. Emmie stepped in front of Slater again, and Derek barked, "Move. I'm going to kill you, motherfucker."

"No," Emmie shouted.

Slater's girl was not going to get hurt, so he lifted her, set her aside, and let Derek come at him. Using Derek's own momentum, Slater stepped back, grabbed his friend's shirt in one hand and his arm with the other, and rammed him into the counter. Derek grunted before going down.

"Fuck." He rolled onto his back, cradling his shoulder.

"Oh, my God, Derek." Emmie rushed to her brother, kneeling beside him. "Are you hurt?" She set her hands on his arm.

"Fuck you, Slater."

"Not gonna let you hurt my girl."

Emmie cut Slater a look, her features going all soft and melty, before turning back to her brother. "Just tell me if you're hurt."

"I'm fine." She helped him to his feet. Ben walked him over to a chair.

"What happened?" Ben asked.

"He had his hands all over my sister."

Cooper sucked in a breath, looking at Slater for confirmation.

Ben looked at Slater like he'd known all along Slater would fuck things up.

Yeah, well, fuck him. He wouldn't. Not this time.

"I warned you." Derek slowly got to his feet.

"You warned me about hurting her. I don't plan on hurting her."

"Why her? You can have any girl you want. Why my *sister*?"

A heavy tension filled the room, pressing in on him. Everyone stared at him, waiting.

So he told the truth. "Because I want her." And then emotion got him in a clench, and he said even harder, "I want *her*."

Emmie's eyes flared, and he knew that sultry look. Happiness suffused him.

"Em?" Derek said, grimacing in pain.

She shrugged. "I want him, too, Derek. I do." Her eyes glimmered with tears.

"We're *leaving*, Em," Derek said. "We're going on tour. Thirty-six cities in fifteen states. He's not going to keep it in his pants."

"You think I don't know that? You think there's anything else on my mind *but* that?" She gave him a pleading look. "I can't help it, Derek. I want him. And I can't walk away. I just can't. Not yet. Let me just have my time with him, okay?" She put her hand on her brother's shoulder. "Do you need an ice pack?"

Derek shook his head.

Her time with him. Slater hated that she wouldn't think past their few days together.

"Well, I need a shower." She gave Derek a meaningful look. "Don't hurt him. This is between me and him. I love you for looking out for me, but stay out of it."

She went upstairs.

Slater gave Ben and Cooper a look, and they quietly left the room. Pulling out a chair next to Derek, Slater sat down, keeping his mouth shut so Derek could wrap his head around what had just happened. He'd let Derek go first.

"What're you doing, man?" Derek finally asked. "You don't do relationships."

"I've never met anyone I wanted one with."

"Why my sister? I mean, shit. I'm serious, you've got a thousand chicks to choose from. You didn't have to choose her."

Slater knew he had to pick his words carefully. So he took his time. Derek rubbed his shoulder, grimacing in pain. "You want some ice?"

"What I want is for you to leave my sister alone." Derek set his elbows on his knees, hands coming together. "She's a really good person."

"I know it. And I'm the lucky bastard she wants. You think I should walk away from that? What, because I'm not good enough for her? Bullshit. If I'm lucky enough to be the guy

she wants, you can bet your fucking life I'm going to take it."
And prove to her he wanted more than ten damn days.

Derek didn't look angry. He just looked . . . confused.

Slater got up and poured himself some coffee. "I know you
don't see it right now, but when you calm down, you'll see.
Emmie and I . . . we fit. And I'm not going to fuck it up. You don't
have to like her with me, but you do have to stay out of it. She's
made her choice, and now all you can do is be there for her. Just
like she's always been there for you, whether she agreed with
your choices or not." He poured a second cup for his girl, filled it
with cream and sugar, and followed the scent of her up the stairs.

Nudging the door open with his knee, Slater came in and
put her mug on the nightstand. He sat beside her on the bed,
wanting nothing more than to ease those worry lines around
her eyes. He took a fortifying drink of his coffee, then set the
mug down.

"Come here." As he stretched out on the bed, he pulled her
to him, and they curled up together.

"That was awful." She caressed his arm. "I should've told
him, like you wanted."

"I'm glad it happened."

She gave him a reprimanding look.

"I am. It showed me something. Your brother put it right in
your face—your worst fear. And you came right back at him.
You told him you knew the risk but were going for it anyway."

She lowered her head onto the pillow, relaxing a little. "For
ten days."

The fear in her eyes told him she wasn't in this with him.
Not yet. "Hey. I'm not your pussy ex."

Irritation crossed her pretty features.

"You can't lump all musicians together."

"Slater—" She started to object, getting all worked up again.

He lifted up on an elbow. "Christ, give me a break. I know
what it feels like to be with groupies, Em. I've done it enough
to know exactly what it's like. If I wanted more of it, I
wouldn't be fucking with you."

"What does it feel like?"

He hadn't given it much thought before, but he knew he

needed to now. He had to nail it. So he looked away to find the words, the feelings. "It's reckless. It's titillating. It's fast and hot and raunchy. And then, thirty seconds later, it's done. The high is gone. And she's no longer this sexy object of lust. She's a girl. A little drunk, a little disheveled. And, worst of all, a total stranger."

He leaned toward her. "It's empty. And when I'm done, all I want is to get away." Did she get it? He could still see the apprehension, the doubt. So he dug deeper. "The thing is, I've been alone all my life. Even when I was with my parents, I was completely alone. Because my dad didn't want to know me. He just wanted me to do what he wanted, when he wanted, and how he wanted. Same with the women. So there's nothing more familiar to me than that feeling of a one-night stand. And now I know what it's like to be with *you*. This connection we have, this . . . I mean, you get it, right? You feel it?"

Her features softened, and she nodded.

"So, then, why would I ever trade *this* for my old life? Ever?"

"You'll forget. You'll get lonely."

"Not if we *try*. If we Skype and text and email and Facebook and phone each other, how can I get lonely?"

"You sure you can handle all that technology?"

He smiled. "Testament to how badly I want you is my willingness to learn all that shit." Leaning toward her, he sifted his hands through that silky hair. "I'll take my ten days if that's all I can get. But dammit, Emmie, I want more. I need more. Don't you? Can you really walk away from this?"

She surged into him, kissing him, her hand wrapping around his back. "I don't want to." She pressed into him, her tongue slipping into his mouth, coaxing his out. Desire burned through him, and he couldn't help grinding against her thigh. "Oh, God, Slater."

Her hand stroked down his stomach until she reached his hard cock. She closed her hand around him.

He inhaled sharply when she tightened her hold, running her hand slowly up his length. "Emmie."

She kissed him, her tongue stroking into his mouth, her hand pumping his cock, making his hips move in rhythm . . . his spine tingle . . . his body burn.

"Ah." Prying her hand off him, he sat up. Reaching for her shirt, he said, "Off."

She tugged it off, skimmed out of pajama shorts and panties, tossed them off the bed. He smiled at her, emotion rushing in.

"What?" she said breathlessly.

"I'm happy."

He leaned over her, kneed her legs open. Grabbing hold of his cock, he rubbed it along her slick seam. Her neck arched off the pillow, and she let out a soft, slow moan. God, she was so wet, so fucking hot. Her hips lifted, rubbing herself against him, wedging his cock deeper inside. That scorching heat, the clenching, satiny flesh. Christ, he couldn't take it anymore. He thrust inside her, and her back came off the mattress.

She twisted, eyes closing in ecstasy, as he pushed all the way inside her slick, tight pussy. Gasping, she reached down, grabbed his ass, and pulled him even deeper, squeezing his flesh and holding him tight to her body.

Oh, fuck, he'd never felt so much. His heart couldn't take all this . . . this happiness. How could he go from such an empty life to this—this fullness? It was like he'd been living in shadows, and now suddenly his world exploded in color, heat, laughter . . . She made him so damn happy.

He needed to see her, all of her. Gripping her ass, he rolled them over so she was on top. Damn, those eyes, hooded with lust. She rolled her hips, and her hands stroked over his chest. She moved slowly, like she was getting the feel of him. But he didn't have time. He seriously couldn't take the sight of her looking so wanton and sexy. Just as her head tipped back, her hair cascading behind her, he grabbed her hips, thrust up into her. She swung forward and had to grip his shoulders, dig her fingernails into his skin as he rammed up hard inside her.

She cried out, draping her body across his chest. He could feel her nipples rub over him with each thrust of his hips. He pounded into her so hard, perspiration dampened his skin. She was slick, tight, and so fucking wet. He knew she needed it slow, but he couldn't for the life of him control this ferocious need to have her.

"Em, fuck. I—"

But she wouldn't let him go wild. No, she just rose lazily, giving him a seductress's smile as she dragged her fingers down his chest. Leaning back, her hands gripped his thighs as she continued to ride him in the hottest way he'd ever seen. Her breasts bounced, and her long hair softly whipped his legs. Desire rushed him so hard he stuttered out awkward, pained sounds.

"Oh, fuck, Em. Jesus fucking Christ." His mind gave over completely to this wild, driving demand for release. He couldn't stop the frantic bucking of his hips, couldn't ease the tight, commanding grip on her skin as he guided her.

"Please come, Emmie. Oh, fuck, fuck, fuck, please come." He found her clit, circled it with his finger.

She lurched forward, her hair spilling over her chest, covering her breasts. "Oh, God, oh . . . oh, my God."

Slater sat up, shoving her hair over her shoulders with one hand and thrusting his tongue into her mouth. Her arms banded around him as their bodies frantically mated. Her hips pushed back, and he knew he'd hit the sweet spot when she gasped, started crying out and moaning, and then threw her head back, mouth open, as her inner muscles tightened around him.

His cock erupted, a blinding, scalding release that had him shouting her name.

Holy mother of God. His heart hammered, and tremors wracked his body.

Never. Anything. Like. It.

He lay back down, still holding her to him, remaining sheathed inside her. She slumped over him, her breathing harsh, erratic.

Ten days? Who were they kidding?

Throughout the park, on dozens of stages, bands played under a warm October sun and cloudless blue sky. Emmie breathed in the mingling scents of popcorn, grilled meat, and beer. In the vast stretches of green between the stages, groups of people tossed Frisbees, tanned, and wandered among the vendor booths.

After two weekends of watching dozens of bands, she had no doubt Snatch was the best in the entire Austin City Lights lineup. Not one of them had a lead singer as captivating, as charismatic, or as plain *hot* as Slater Vaughn.

Irwin would sign them, she had no doubt. But why wouldn't he give her the promotion? Maybe he just needed to get that she wasn't coming back. Hopefully, he liked her replacement—and, frankly, shifting the über-efficient office manager into her place had been a brilliant idea. It had to have made the transition seamless—making him see he didn't need her specifically in that role.

As Snatch came to the end of its set, Emmie took in the huge crowd that'd come to see them perform. Hundreds of fans—screaming, jumping, waving—looked utterly enraptured with Slater, as he clutched his mic, knees bent, leaning back, stretching that final note out until his features flushed. He was magnificent.

And he was leaving. Tomorrow. Her chest seized up. He kept saying he didn't want them to end, but come on. *Look at him up there*.

"Hey, girl," a familiar voice called.

Emmie turned to find Tiana strutting toward her. "Tiana." She pulled her friend in for a hug. "You're here."

"Yeah, well, guess who invited me?" She tilted her head toward the stage.

"You're kidding? I thought you hadn't heard from him?"

She shrugged. "I didn't tell you because I didn't know what to make of it, but as soon as he found out about the tour, he told me. I mean, he was standing there with Piper and everybody, and he thought about me? I was the one he wanted to tell?"

"He loves you. He really does. I see him, T. He just looks . . . sad."

Tiana looked wistfully toward the drummer. "Yeah. I'm not sure that's enough, you know?"

"I do know." Emmie turned back to the stage, to watch the man who'd worshipped her body only hours ago. The man who'd held her all night long, his hands moving over her body like he couldn't get enough. "I really know."

"Don't you dare do this."

Her head snapped back to Tiana, and Emmie saw the look of warning.

"Don't you give up on him. It's not the same thing as me and Ben. Not even close."

"Tiana . . ." She gestured to Slater. "Look at him. He's . . . come on. He's meant for this life. He shouldn't be tied down." If she stayed with him, he would break her heart—and it was going to hurt a thousand times worse than with Alex. Because she hadn't felt anything close to this with her ex.

"You're talking yourself out of it. Un-fricking-believable. Any other girl on this planet would grab hold of that man with all her might. And you're not all in? What is the matter with you?"

"How can you even ask that? You said it yourself. He's never broken anyone's heart because women know not to give theirs to him."

Tiana reached for Emmie's chin, forced eye contact. "Yes, I said that. Because he'd never been with anybody before. But he chose you. Anyone can see it by the way he looks at you. Uh, by the fact he hasn't been with anybody else since you moved out here. Forget what I said. It's not true anymore."

"No, it's . . ." Emmie wanted to say it was an aberration. That a man like Slater couldn't possibly want her so desperately. But reality proved otherwise. Their time together proved otherwise. Still, it couldn't last. It just couldn't.

Besides, pursuing a relationship was the last thing she should be thinking about. As wonderful as her time with Slater had been, the tension of unemployment pulsed with each beat of her heart.

"Emmie, you caught the hottest, most uncatchable man in the world. You better grab hold of him and hang on with your life."

Tears blurred her vision. Tiana didn't understand. "We just got together. Five minutes before he goes on a national tour. Don't you think two weeks down the road he's going to forget what it felt like to be alone with me in the house all day?" Under the covers, in the shower, in the backseat of his car? That intensity, that passion, existed only there. "How long is he going to turn down all that's offered to him night after night, day after day? I've seen it, Tiana. I've seen the girls in hotel lobbies, outside hotel rooms, inside hotel rooms. They get on the tour bus and wait outside the doors of the venue. They're everywhere, and they don't take no for an answer." Just ask Alex. Her dad. How long before Slater succumbed to the temptation?

"Okay. So? You fell for a musician. Deal with it. God, do you think if Ben said he wanted to be with me—in spite of everything you just said—that I'd turn him away? Hell, no. If he said he wanted to be with me, I'd give him everything I've got. Why wouldn't I? If you don't put your whole heart in, what do you expect to get back? Besides, are you really going to let him go that easily? He wants *you*. He chooses *you*."

Emmie's heart cracked open, expanded. God, how she needed to hear this. "I know that, Tiana. I do. And when I'm alone with him, I'm right there with you. I believe him. I believe in us. But when I see him onstage . . . God, he's just . . ."

Tiana scowled. "Every woman's fantasy. You're right. So, how lucky are you? That man up there rocking the house? Wants you. You're crazy to let him go." Her features softened and then she smiled, gave Emmie a hug. "If it doesn't work out . . . that'll suck. But isn't it worse spending the rest of your life wondering what might have happened if you'd had the guts to try?"

Ouch. Emmie didn't like to hear that she was a coward.

"Listen, I've got to get back to my friends, but Emmie, seriously? Go all in. You'd be a fool to do anything less."

They hugged, and Tiana disappeared into the screaming crowd.

Emmie looked up to find the band just leaving the stage. Good, she didn't want to think about it anymore. Time to meet the reporters and critics she'd invited to the show.

Heading for the cordoned-off area behind the stage, she flashed her backstage pass to the polo-wearing bouncer. The guys hadn't arrived yet, so she made her way through the crowd, gathering the press and critics. As soon as she caught sight of Derek, she led them over to him, letting him work his magic.

Then, she excused herself, wondering if she could find Slater in the crush. He was probably surrounded by his fans. She'd give him time to do his thing.

But then she saw him. Impossible to miss, of course, thanks to his height and presence, not to mention the people gathering around him. He looked like a rock star. She smiled. If only his dad could see him right then. He'd be proud. She'd have to be sure to tell Slater, so he'd feel the impact of what he'd achieved.

While he moved through the crowd giving everyone the individual attention they craved, she knew him well enough to sense his tension. He kept scanning the crowd.

Looking for her. Happiness rushed her, hard and fast. She had to get to him.

Just then a rustle of activity drew her attention. Piper Lee and her entourage cut through the crowd, heading straight for Slater. The look on Piper's face—good God—it was filled with such focus, such purpose.

Piper got to him first, threw her arms around his neck like a girlfriend would do. She swayed with him side to side, building up speed until they rocked hard enough to throw them both off balance. The people around them laughed.

They looked great together. They looked like a couple, no doubt about it.

Reporters gathered around, photographers elbowing in for the right shot.

Jealousy started to dig its talons into Emmie's heart, until a stronger, clearer voice rang through. And it said, *Hell, no.* Slater wanted *her*, not Piper.

At that very moment Slater's gaze shifted, locking with Emmie's. And the look on his face? It was nothing like the practiced look he'd given Piper. That was the look he gave his fans.

The look he was giving Emmie? God, it set firecrackers off in her chest.

Her heart pounded fast and hard, and her face felt like it would split from smiling so widely. He pushed away from Piper, and then he was right there before Emmie. She flung herself at him. His knees bent as he cupped her ass and lifted her.

Her arms and legs banded around him, her hands clasped behind his damp neck, and their mouths found each other. She kissed him with all the joy and desire in her heart. When the kiss turned carnal, she pulled away. "You were fantastic. Amazing. I'm so proud of you."

"Words later. Kisses now."

His tongue licked into her mouth, and he kissed her like nothing else mattered on this earth but fusing his body with hers. She melted into him, her body throbbing with need and want.

"Let's go home." His mouth pressed against her cheek.

She laughed, resting her head on his shoulder. "You have work to do."

"The guys can do it. We have to go home."

She loosened her hold on him, lowered her legs, and he set her down. Touching his cheek, she said, "You're amazing."

"I can amaze you better at home. Let's go." He reached for her hand, and she felt the urgency, the energy coursing through him.

"*After* you do your thing. Now come and meet everyone I had to convince to come see you today."

He cupped her ass and gave it a squeeze. "Fine. Twenty minutes, and that's it. Then we go home."

"You're a rock star. Get used to it."

"Emily?" Piper came up beside them.

Oh, come *on*. Enough already. "Hey, Piper. It's *Emmie*, actually. So, what did you think of the show?"

"Fantastic." Piper rubbed Slater's arm. "Our guy's got it going *on*."

Our guy? Really?

Derek and the others joined them, and Piper gave them all hearty hugs. "You guys rocked the park."

Emmie watched them, loving their excitement, smiling as they all talked over each other, reliving highlights. She loved them. Loved them like family. Slater's arm around her waist tightened. Her signal to move things along.

She turned to Piper. "All right, I'm going to steal these guys away for a little bit. They've got some press to do."

"Absolutely." Piper gazed up at Slater. "Get out there and make me look good." She tilted her head toward Emmie. "The more press they get, the better I look. So thank you for arranging it for them today." She leaned in, scrunching her nose. "You're just a little spitfire, aren't you?"

The smile on Emmie's face froze. Had she just been belittled? But, no, not possible. Piper was complimenting her. But . . . *spitfire*?

"Emmie's the best," Derek said.

Okay, yeah, Piper *had* belittled her. Or Derek wouldn't have jumped to her defense.

"She's our girl." Ben threw an arm around her shoulder and tugged her close.

"And our house mom," Pete said. "She feeds us."

"True story," Cooper said. "Never had it better in my life."

"Yeah, and she raised our street cred when she got rid of the pubic hair on Pete's head," Ben said.

Pete punched him.

"Hey." Ben rubbed his arm.

Tugging on Pete's dreads, Derek said, "Em's our stylist, too."

Emmie couldn't have felt closer to the guys than she did just then, as they rallied around to make her shine in front of Piper. She felt all warm and fuzzy inside. But a quick glance to Piper had Emmie's breath catching in her throat. Gone was the sexy smile and carefree expression. The hard look in Piper's eyes made Emmie's stomach clench.

The look vanished in a flash, and just like that Piper's breezy demeanor returned. "Well, aren't you the shit? What are these boys going to do without you? I can't say I've ever seen a bunch of hard-ass rockers eating out of someone's hand before." She gave Emmie a fist bump. "You're so good I should steal you away. What do you say, want to come work for me?"

Wow. Okay. She wasn't going to react to Piper's attempts to make her look like the hired help. Too much was at stake. This tour had the power to make Snatch a household name. Keeping her smile in place, she said, "Let's get you guys in front of the press."

Piper stepped in front of her. "I'll take them." Her arm slid through Slater's. "It'll pack more punch if I'm there."

Emmie wouldn't look at the guys. Didn't want to see their reaction—their pity. Her face hurt with the strain of holding on to her smile. "Lead the way."

Slater clutched her hand, giving it a squeeze, but Emmie pulled away from him, taking a few steps back. The whole situation annoyed her. Not only wasn't she used to being treated with such disrespect, but she hated that she had to put up with it for the sake of the band. They needed this tour to go well. It was the start of everything for them.

Piper glanced over her shoulder, her dark hair spilling all over Slater's arm. "Oh, hey, Em."

Em. Now she was Em. 'Cause they were so close now. What a manipulator.

"Since we added them so late to the tour, we couldn't book them into all our same hotels." Her brow lifted encouragingly.

"Maybe you can look into that? I like to keep my guys nice and close."

Was that a threat? Did Piper just insinuate Slater was hers and she'd keep him close? Hot burning rage churned in Emmie's gut.

No, no, no. She would not let this bitch get the better of her. "You bet."

But Piper had already turned back, arms linked with Slater on one side and Derek on the other as they headed toward the press area. Emmie walked several paces behind.

Her chest hurt as she stewed over Piper's behavior. Because no matter what the guys thought of Emmie, they'd leave her at midnight. They'd be alone on a bus with Piper Lee for two and a half months. And Piper was charming and gorgeous.

She was also the "Next Big Thing," the wildly talented songwriter and singer, and Emmie was—as the bitch had so nastily pointed out—a personal assistant. A damn good one, but still. She worked on the sidelines.

Oh, dammit all to hell. She hated feeling like an outsider. Hated it.

Slater glanced over his shoulder, gave her a look that reminded her exactly what he wanted to do to her, and the ache in her chest eased a little.

No, she wasn't a musician. She'd never be an artist, but she was damn good at getting shit done. Maybe that would go on her headstone: Emmie Valencia. Got shit done.

Slater turned fully around, giving her his full attention. "Hey, is that Chase Lansford?" he asked, gesturing at someone in the crowd.

Emmie's heart expanded, appreciating the way he put her back in control. "It is. He's waiting for an interview."

"Let's do it," Derek said.

The guys headed off, but Slater held back. Leaning close to her ear, he said, "She only thinks she can play us 'cause she doesn't know us yet." He kissed her neck. "But she will."

SIXTEEN

Twenty minutes turned into hours as Slater and the guys had to endure interview after interview and then listen to other bands throughout the park at the insistence of Piper's A&R guy. Then, they had to have a business dinner with all of Piper's people to discuss more tour details. Slater'd kept Emmie by his side, kept a hand on her the whole time, but really, all he wanted was to get her alone.

By the time they finally pulled up to the house, a whole crew had gathered to celebrate their success at ACL and their departure. As the band piled out of the van, Slater held on to Emmie's hand, not letting her out. He dug into his pocket and slapped the car keys in her hand. "Enjoy your wheels."

Where she should've thrown herself at him, she held back, looking worried. "I'll only use it to get groceries—"

He shut her up with a quick, hard kiss. "Em, it's a car. I want you to use it. What's mine is yours. Do you understand?"

Her features softened, her lips tipped up at the corners, and she scraped her fingers into his hair "Slater."

Car doors slammed around them, laughter and voices filled the air, and he brought her hand to his mouth, kissing her palm. "Slater's the guy onstage. Right here, right now, with you, I'm Jonny. Okay?"

"Okay." She breathed it into his mouth, right before she tilted her head and kissed him. And just like that he was gone, lost in the soft, wet heat of her mouth, the tangle of her tongue, and the press of her fingers into the muscles at the back of his neck.

"Keep it in your pants, asshole." Derek leaned into the window. "That's my sister."

She laughed, holding Slater close.

"Come on." He slid out, caught her hand in his when she met him in front of the car, and rushed her into the house. Somebody had turned the stereo on too loudly, so he went to lower the volume. Emmie broke away and headed toward the kitchen. He yanked her back to him. "What're you doing?"

"Shouldn't we put out some food? Drinks? I mean, they want to be with you on your last night."

He drew her in close, wrapped his arms around her. "It's my last few hours with *you*. That's all that matters. Now either get up those stairs of your own free will, or I'm carrying you."

She let out an exaggerated sigh, rolling her eyes. "Fine. I suppose I could be alone with you." She looked wistfully at the crowd already spilling into the kitchen, already with drinks in their hands, already dancing and rubbing up against each other. "I was hoping to rub against some sexy rockers, get my ass groped, but—"

Was she referring to the night she'd come home from her date with Hector? Grasping her ass, he pressed her to him. He didn't stop there, letting his hands inch lower. "I was drunk, Em. I was jealous and angry." He tongued her earlobe. "But I've got you now, and I'm taking you upstairs."

Her knees buckled, and she leaned against him. "Mm. You should probably carry me."

He lunged for her, leaning in and tossing her over his shoulder in a fireman's hold.

"I was kidding. Let me down."

Not a chance in hell he'd put her down, not when he could take full advantage of her position and fondle her gorgeous ass.

At her bedroom she started to set her legs down, but he shook his head. "Shower first."

"What is it with you and showers?"

"Do you have any idea how many chicks touched me today?" He made out like it was just exhausting.

"Oh, that's nice." She swatted him, pretending to look offended.

"Hey. Hot sun, ninety-minute set. I'm showering." He set her down, kicking the bathroom door shut and locking it. "Naked. Now." Reaching in, he turned the water on, making it hot, just as she liked it. He toed off his boots, ripped off his socks, then stripped out of his jeans and T-shirt.

"No underpants?"

He shrugged. "I just did my laundry. Everything was clean, so I didn't want to use any of it."

"I wish I'd known that."

He smiled, painfully aroused. It only got worse when her breasts jiggled as she pulled off her blouse. "So you could fantasize about my package?"

She didn't even crack a smile. "So I could've reached down your pants and touched you." She gripped him in her hand, and electricity raced along his nerves. "I would've liked that."

He couldn't take it anymore. He unbuttoned the top of her jeans, unzipped them, and then tore them off her body. He pulled back, taking in her black-lace thong. "What the fuck is this?"

"A going-away present."

"But you hate these things."

"Yeah, but you don't."

Hooking a finger in either side, he knelt as he eased them down her legs, licking her inner thighs. She shuddered, her legs trembling. He balled the thong in his fist and stuffed it in the wastebasket. "I don't need to see you in shit like that unless they make *you* feel good. I just want you."

Hands on her hips, he buried his face between her legs and kissed her, his tongue licking into the curls, delving into her juicy folds. He fucking loved the way her hips bucked wildly. The sounds she made drove him out of his mind.

He stood up in a rush, crushing her to him, taking her in a bone-melting kiss, as steam swirled around them and her hands moved restlessly down his arms and around to his back.

"Get in." He backed her into the shower stall, walking them

both under the hot spray. He loved when she tipped her head back, closed her eyes, and let the water cascade down her beautiful body. He loved the water coursing over her breasts, and he couldn't stop himself from filling his hands with all that plump, soft flesh. Her eyes popped open, blazing with need.

He sucked a nipple into his mouth, came alive when her hands grabbed his hair, pulling him closer. His mouth moved from one breast to the other, knowing exactly how wild it made her. His fingers rubbed over one nipple while his tongue licked the other.

He moved them out of the spray, backed her to the corner, and then got to his knees. He licked into her, felt her juices on his face, heard her soft moans. His fingers curled inside her, stroking her harder, faster, in tandem with his tongue, which licked in silky swirls around her clit.

"God, Slater. I . . . oh . . . God." Her fingers fisted in his hair, her back arched away from the wall, and her hips rocked. Her cries grew louder, more desperate, and a rush of moisture spilled into her pussy. Holy fuck, he had to fist his cock, had to start pumping, because he couldn't take the building pressure anymore.

And then her hips bucked, her body went rigid, and she held tight against his mouth.

He barely gave her a chance to calm down before he got up, spun her around, clamped his hands on her hips, and jerked her back to him. Holding her firmly in place, he thrust into her incredibly slick heat. She cried out, rearing back.

"Fuck." Oh, holy hell, he wanted this woman like nothing he'd ever wanted in his life. One hand took its fill of her breast, his fingers reaching across to touch the other nipple at the same time. He rubbed his palm across them both, making her grind against him. She swiveled her hips, pushing back hard. He pinched each nipple in turn, back and forth, faster and faster, while his hand dug into her hip, holding her tighter against him.

Blood roared in his veins, and desire raced through him, making his heart beat painfully. Tension coiled tighter and tighter, and he was going to come too soon, way too soon. Oh, fuck, why couldn't this last forever? Please, not yet. But, God, her nipples scraped against his palms; her tight, wet heat pulsed and clenched around him. Her wild cries sounded like she was completely out of control . . .

And then she threw her head back with a cry of release so intense it just undid him, and he came in a soul-gripping, thunderous roar. It just kept coming, the sensations so ferocious he had to keep pumping into her.

And then she collapsed against the wall, breathing erratically. He didn't want to let go, so he belted his arms around her waist, rested his chin on her shoulder. Both of them continued to pant, bodies glued together, the thick steam making it hard to breathe.

Or maybe knowing he was about to leave her made it hard to breathe.

Pussy.

He'd wanted their time together to be what convinced her to stay with him, so he hadn't pressed, hadn't brought it up at all. But time had run out. And he didn't know what she was thinking.

All he wanted was to get into bed with her. "Come here." He reached for the soap, lathered up his hands, and ran them over her back. He loved the feel of her slender shoulders, the delicate bumps of her spine, the incredibly sexy curve of her waist, and the flare of her hips.

His hands slid around to her breasts, and desire stirred yet again at the feel of her nipples hardening in his palms. He growled, not wanting to get worked up again, just wanting to get her into bed.

"What are you doing to me?" she asked breathlessly.

"I'm . . ." he said, his mouth at her ear, his hands gently lathering her breasts, fingers running over her nipples, around the slightly bumpy skin around them. "Memorizing . . ."

She sucked in a breath as his hands stroked slowly down her ribcage, tracing every rib in a swirl of suds, then over her stomach, his pinky dipping into her navel, fingering its shape.

"Every line, every bump, and every"—his hands dipped between her legs, rubbing slow circles—"curve of your body."

"Oh, my God."

He ran his hand along the seam of her ass, and he could feel the gooseflesh pebble her skin. Her head tipped back, resting on his shoulder. Tilting her chin, he brought her mouth toward him and kissed her, plunging his tongue into her wet heat. When she wrapped her arms around his neck, locking them closer, her breasts swayed, and his erection pulsed and throbbed. He pressed between her legs, and she squeezed them tightly together.

Filling his hands with the soapy, firm globes of her ass, he was ready to take her all over again. But not here, not now. He wanted her in bed.

He walked them under the stream of water, rinsing off the soap, then smacked the faucet with the heel of his hand. Snatching a towel off the rod, he wrapped her up. "Bed."

"You have to be at the bus in a little over an hour. Don't you want to make sure you're all packed?"

"I want to get into bed with you. That's all I want."

Because he just didn't know if he'd still have her once that bus took off.

———————

The smell of diesel exhaust filled the air. Cars with their lights on, engines idling, were parked haphazardly around the parking lot. Emmie watched the guys toss their duffel bags and suitcases into the bay of the forty-five-foot tour bus, while the bus driver tried to stop them and make some order out of the chaos.

A finger tapping her shoulder had her spinning around. Tiana stood there, eyes glittering with tears. They fell into each other's arms. "I'm so glad you're here," Emmie said. "I'm about to lose it."

"I know." Tiana pulled away, running her fingers under her eyes. "Smudges?"

"No, you're good. So, I saw you guys 'talking' at the show." Actually, they'd been making out and rubbing up against each other. Emmie gave a hopeful smile. "What happened?"

"Nothing's changed. We love each other, but he's going to go out there and do his thing, and I'm going to stay here and do mine. God, I'm an idiot, but I love him, so . . . it'll be what it'll be."

A whoosh of air had the doors closing. Emmie's stomach plummeted. She hadn't known what to expect, but she certainly hadn't thought he'd take off without saying good-bye. Of course, they'd had a pretty intense good-bye in the shower and then again in bed just a half an hour ago.

Tiana bumped shoulders with Emmie. "So, you're here. Does that mean you've decided to go for it?"

Had she? She couldn't imagine ending things with him. She'd never felt closer to anyone in her life. But they couldn't sustain it. It just wasn't possible given the directions their lives were taking. Once she got promoted, she'd be busy 24-7. She'd be totally immersed in her bands. And him? It'd already started for him.

She pulled in a shallow breath. Funny how she could physically feel the tug-of-war between her heart and her head. Which would win? "I . . . I don't know."

Tiana frowned. "Hey, let's get out of here. You want to get a drink?"

Emmie wanted to go home and crawl under the covers. But that would be the worst thing she could do. "Sure. Meet you at Empire?"

Tiana nodded. She got into her car, tapped the horn, and then took off.

Emmie turned back one last time to watch the bus go, but it wasn't moving. Should she just leave? Or wait for her heart to take off into the night? Only a few cars remained in the lot, but no one else stood there like a lovesick high school girl. And, yeah, she realized they could all see her through the window. She was making a fool of herself.

So what? She didn't care. She wanted to watch him go. She brought her hand over her mouth as she whispered, "Thank you." No matter what happened, she'd always, always have these last eleven days.

She pulled her keys out of her pocket, walking backward to his car. "Bye."

And then the whooshing sound filled the air, and the doors pulled open. Two long legs swung out, arms braced on the handrails, and boots hit the asphalt. Slater sauntered over to her, his gaze locked with hers, looking fierce and pissed.

"Fucker wouldn't let me off the bus."

Emmie hid her big smile behind her hands.

"Actually thought he'd take off without me saying good-bye to my girl."

Emmie broke into a run, throwing herself into his arms. He caught her, lifting her off the ground and holding her tightly as he swayed back and forth. "I'm going to miss you so much," she whispered into his neck.

He tightened his hold, and she burrowed into his neck. Then, he set her down. "You don't have to miss me. I'll talk to you every day."

Emotion rose, gathered in her chest. She couldn't think, couldn't speak.

"Don't let your past make your decision. Let *us* make it."

"Hey," the driver called.

"I have to go." He kissed her, and she started to pull away, but he tugged her closer and deepened the kiss until she sagged in his arms. He smiled against her mouth. "You're my girl."

And then he was gone.

———

"Get your showers now," Slater said as they headed off the stage toward catering. They were always starving after a show. But where Slater grabbed a shower—their only chance to shower on the road—the others didn't want to miss a moment of partying time. If they waited until Piper's show ended, they had to fight for shower time with her band plus all the crew.

Showers were also Slater's only chance to relieve himself. He'd done just as he'd promised, sending his girl pictures from his phone, daily emails and Facebook messages, and so far it had worked. They'd remained close.

But it wasn't enough. Because he wanted her all the time. He missed touching her. He fucking loved his hands on her.

Pushing into the men's bathroom, he dropped his clothes and turned on the faucet.

Stepping into the hot spray, he soaped up, his mind going immediately to her. Her mouth on his, her hands clutching his ass. He wanted her. He wanted her now, always, all day long. When she touched him, she had this expression on her face. Like she loved his body, couldn't get enough of him.

He gripped his cock, lathering it up in long, tight strokes. Desire got ahold of him, and heat burned along his limbs. He pictured Emmie on her knees, one hand around the base of his cock, her tongue swirling around the head, licking down in her exploration of him. Every time they were together, it seemed she couldn't get enough of him, wanted him even more. He imagined his cock sinking into her mouth, hitting the back of her throat, and then he was pumping fast, heart racing. He could see the water hitting her slender back, her long dark hair plastered to her creamy skin, and her cheeks caving in as she sucked him deeply into her mouth.

He came quickly, but it fell short. It didn't satisfy. Because, ultimately, he was alone in a grimy shower stall in the bowels of an arena somewhere in San Francisco. And Emmie was alone in their house in Austin.

He'd left his clothes and shaving kit in the bathroom that held a long line of sinks and toilets. So he stepped out of the shower and walked naked to get his towel.

Piper stood there, standing in front of the mirror, dressed and made up for her show.

"What the hell're you doing here?" She should be with her band. He reached for his towel, quickly scrubbed his face and hair before wrapping it around his waist.

"I have a few minutes. It's insane back there. Roger's from San Francisco, so he literally invited everyone he's ever known in his life. I've never seen it so crazy in the greenroom." She caught his gaze in the mirror. "I don't think he's going to work out."

"Why are you here?" He couldn't keep the irritation out of his voice. She had her own bathroom. There were eleven guys on the bus, and one woman. She had the whole women's shower room to herself. He stood behind her, just to the side, talking to her reflection in the mirror.

"Look at us." She took them in with a look of awe. "We're fucking perfect."

We? What the fuck was she talking about? He hadn't given her a hint of interest because *he had none*. "Look, Piper, I—"

She reached for his arm—making it look like a friendly gesture. But then her warm hand slid down his skin slowly, ending in a squeeze. "Hey, I've got an idea for you."

He narrowed his eyes. She had to share her idea with him now? When he was alone in the men's room? Buck naked?

"You know that bridge you're having such a hard time with?"

His pulse quickened. How did she know about the song he'd struggled with for weeks?

She had his attention now.

Her mouth curled into a seductive smile. "I hear you in the back lounge. Everyone else has their headphones on, but I'm listening to you. I like your music. I like your process. Mine's different, so I'm fascinated by yours."

"How's it different?" He didn't like talking to her without his clothes on. She'd get the wrong impression. Yet, he wanted to hear what she had to say about the bridge. She was a damn good songwriter. Maybe she had a suggestion.

"You're, like, an artist. You work on your craft. And it's really cool. You take it so serious."

"What do you do?"

She shrugged. "I don't sweat it. It just comes. I keep a notebook and a digital voice recorder with me all the time. So, like, I'm in the grocery store and I'm deciding between the Slim Jims or the spray cheese and crackers, and all of a sudden these lyrics hit me. Like, just a line or two. And then I'm out. I can't even think about meat sticks anymore. I have to abandon my cart and go to my car and let it come."

"You're lucky."

"I know. I'm not tortured like you are." She squeezed his biceps. "I've got a stadium to rock, but let's meet in the back lounge when I'm done, and I'll play you my idea."

"They're already signed," Arturo shouted in her ear. The club was packed, the instrumentation so loud it drowned out the vocals.

Emmie's shoulders sagged. This band was the first she'd really liked in all this time.

Seated at a table with several of Amoeba's promotions guys from around the country, she leaned into him and shouted back, "Are you sure?"

He nodded. "Brian McKesslar, Star Records." He tapped the manila envelope on the table in front of her. "But don't worry. We've got some good ones for you. Check 'em out."

The guys were in town for a multi-band show at the Three-Sixty, and she'd spent the last several days with them talking about up-and-coming bands. She'd gotten over a dozen possibilities from them—thankfully.

A woman who'd been eyeing Arturo for half the night

finally got up the nerve to saunter over. She leaned down and whispered in his ear.

Emmie watched his lips curl into a smile, and then his jaw dropped and his eyes went wide. He threw his head back and laughed. Bumping shoulders with her, Arturo leaned in and said, "Just got an offer I can't refuse. You gonna hang around awhile?"

"Sure." Either that or go home to an empty house. And the thought of being in that house without Slater made her ache.

She missed him. Missed him so hard sometimes she couldn't catch her breath. How was that possible? Absence was making her heart grow *acutely* fonder.

Arturo scraped his chair back. "Well, if you don't, it was great seein' you, Em. Let me know what you think of those bands." He pressed a soft kiss to her cheek and took off with his, uh, date.

Emmie turned her attention to the other guys, tuning back in to the conversation about the grossest things they'd seen artists do on tour. Her phone buzzed in her lap, and she discreetly checked it.

She smiled as the video loaded. In the six days since the boys had left, Slater had sent her photos and videos, texts and Facebook messages. Just as he'd promised.

Excusing herself, she threaded her way through the crowd to the exit. Once outside on the busy boulevard, she pushed play.

The guys sat around a table in the lounge of the bus holding up the care package she'd sent them. Thanks to all her years in the music industry, she had promotions guys all over the country that would pass along the packages in exchange for extra tickets to the shows. She wanted to make sure her guys had a touch of home throughout their time away.

"Nom, nom, nom," Derek said. "You make the best chocolate chip cookies on the planet."

"Fuckin' A," Pete said. "We miss you, Em."

Cooper reached into the box and grabbed a handful. Derek yanked the box away. "Don't be greedy, asswipe."

When Ben tried to wrestle the box away, Pete leaned over to stick his hand in the box, causing Derek to leap up in the too-small space. As the guys fought for possession of the cookies, Slater's hand entered the screen, whacking their heads, trying to get them to pay attention to the camera. It resulted in a slap-fest among the guys that had them laughing their heads off.

"We're supposed to talk to Emmie, you jerk-offs," Derek said.

"Guys, shut the fuck up," Slater said. "I'm recording."

Slater turned the camera toward himself, shaking his head as if to say, *Forget it.* "Anyhow, we all wanted to thank you for the cookies. Obviously, we love them." He looked uncomfortable, bringing the camera a little closer to his beautiful face. "I know you're at a show right now. I hope it's a good one." He swallowed. "I miss you." The video ended.

She brought the phone to her heart, closed her eyes, and let the emotions wash over her. What they had—it overwhelmed her. Needing to talk to him right away, she hit his speed dial.

He answered on the first ring. "Emmie?"

Oh, God, she missed him. She wanted him. She wanted him so much. "Jonny," she breathed.

He didn't say anything, and she worried she'd caught him at a bad time. The low rumble of music and laughter filled the background.

"Are you there? Jonny?" She felt a little embarrassed. "Do you want to call me back?"

"No. I'm here. I was just . . . letting it sink in."

"Sink in?"

"You called me Jonny. I like that."

She smiled, stepping aside as a group of rowdy teenagers walked by. "I miss you."

"Yeah." Such heaviness weighed down the single word. "Where are you right now?"

"The Whiskey."

"Still hanging out with the guys?"

"Yeah. This is their last night. They're all leaving tomorrow."

"Did they give you any good leads?"

"I hope so. I've got a list of bands to check out."

"Of course you do."

She smiled. And it all came rushing back—their stunning connection, their voracious need for one another. "How'd the show go tonight?"

"Great. It's been crazy because of all the press—I swear Piper's a fuckin' media whore—but it's all good."

"Who's hungry?" a woman's voice called out in the background. *Piper.* Emmie's body tightened.

"Holy shit," someone said—maybe Pete? "What is all that?"

"Damn, that smells good." Ben. The guys started talking over each other—strange voices mixed in, too.

"What's going on?" Emmie asked Slater.

"Hey, hey," Piper shouted. "What the hell is that? Are you eating *cookies*?"

"Give 'em back," Cooper said. "Emmie made 'em."

"Yeah?" Piper said. "Fuck the cookies. I've got trays of manicotti."

Voices shouted over each other. The guys seemed excited.

"Slater, what's going on?"

"Looks like Piper brought dinner."

"What does that mean, she *brought* dinner? Don't you guys have catering?"

"Em, I should go." She could barely hear him over the excited chatter on the bus.

"Just answer. Don't you have catering?"

"Yeah, of course. I don't know. She said something about getting us home-cooked meals whenever possible."

A knot of anxiety pulsed in her chest. Piper got them *home-cooked meals*?

"What the fuck—hey, don't throw them out," she could hear Derek shout.

"Is she throwing out my cookies?" Emmie asked, one hand pressing into her stomach.

"No, of course not." He must've taken the phone away because she could hear his muffled voice—angry now. "Give it to me." And then he came back to her. "I have to go. Let me call you back later." He hung up.

Emmie stood on the sidewalk, aware of the thump of bass from a car passing by, a couple making out against the plate glass window of the office building next door.

For the sake of her sanity, she tried hard not to think of Piper on that bus. Her familiarity with the guys. Like, did she walk around naked? Did she try to be one of the guys—swearing and pranking? Or did she play up her femininity? Did she sit on the guys' laps—on *Slater's* lap?

But Emmie'd never imagined Piper playing the maternal

role. Taking care of the guys. Flirting, seducing, sure. But trying to *replace* Emmie? They weren't in competition. They had different roles in the guys' lives.

Oh, my God, had she actually tried to *throw out* the cookies Emmie'd made?

Okay, you know what? This is ridiculous. She called Slater back. She wouldn't let Piper get to her like this.

"Hey," he said. The vibrant conversation and laughter in the background made Emmie sick to her stomach. "Let me go upstairs."

"Wait, if you're eating, we can talk later." She realized just then he usually only called when he had time alone. Which meant she'd never had this insight into their time as a group before. And it sounded like they were having a blast.

"No, I want to talk to you now. I hate that . . . Well, let me just get upstairs." A few seconds later he came back on the line. "Okay."

She didn't know what to say. Where to begin. She hardly wanted to spew her insecurities all over him. But then again, what chance did they have if she didn't voice her fears? "I guess I'm a little rattled by all that. I mean, home-cooked meals?"

"Yeah." He sighed. "She likes to 'take care of her boys.' "

"I just . . . wow." She blew out a breath. *Just ask.* "Okay, I have to know . . . How, um, how it's going with her? You know." The screech of metal jarred her as a car scraped along the curb. Doors opened and club-goers spilled out. The car sped off.

"I'm going to translate that into, 'Am I developing feelings for her?' "

She felt a pop of release, and all the anxiety drained away. *Slater.* "It's good you speak Emmie. Makes it so much easier to communicate." He made everything better.

"No, no feelings. And I won't. I want you, Emmie. Only you."

She bit down on her bottom lip, her hand covering her heart. She believed him.

He was quiet for a moment. And then, "We're not stupid, Em. We know what she's doing."

"Okay. I'm sorry, I just . . . She freaks me out. The things she does."

"Yeah, I know. But I don't care about her. I care about you. Us." His voice went all gentle.

Piper squealed. Feet trampled. "Slater!"

Slater released a huff of breath, as though someone had slammed into him. "I gotta go, Em. Talk later?"

But he didn't wait for her response.

SEVENTEEN

Her cell phone chirped. Tossing her toothbrush into the cup she shared with Slater, Emmie spit out the toothpaste and ran into her bedroom. Diving onto the bed, she snatched the phone from her nightstand, rolled onto her back, and said, "Hey, baby. Shouldn't you be onstage right now?"

"Hello, this is Val Johnson calling from Amoeba Records for Emily Valencia."

"Oh. Oh, my God. I'm so sorry, Val. I thought it was someone else."

"Mr. Ledger has asked me to call on his behalf."

She rolled her eyes at the receptionist's bizarre formality. "Okay."

"He'd like to know the current status of your employment."

Now why would Val call her for Irwin? "He knows what I'm doing, Val. What's this about?"

"He'd like to know if you'd consider coming back to work for him temporarily, until he finds your replacement."

She'd already *found* her replacement. "Please don't tell me he drove off Roxanne?" Everyone loved Roxanne. The woman ran the office like a pro.

"Miss Taylor no longer works for Amoeba Records. May I give him an answer?"

"Why are you talking to me like this?" And then it struck her why a twenty-two-year-old girl with blue hair and five-inch wedged combat boots would talk like a robot. "He's right there, isn't he?"

Val let out a strange murmur.

"Put him on the phone." Emmie waited as sounds filled the receiver. What sounded like a hand covering it, a scuffle of some sort, and then the clearing of a male throat.

"What?" Irwin. Sounding like a petulant boy.

"Why didn't you call me yourself, you knucklehead? You probably made poor Val pee in her pants."

"She's not wearing pants. She's wearing a rubber band. And why would I call you? You left me."

"After finding the perfect replacement for you."

"Perfect? That woman was *old*. And disgusting. She ate ham sandwiches with her mouth open. I still have nightmares of that horrible ball of mush, white bread, pink ham, and little bits of lettuce. Disgusting."

"Irwin, she's been with Amoeba for years. Everyone likes her. And she met all your needs."

"No, she didn't. She didn't turn down my sheets and put a chocolate on my pillow."

Emmie pulled the phone away from her ear, wanting to bang it on the kitchen counter. "She's not a hotel maid. She's not even supposed to be in your house."

"That was a metaphor. I thought you went to NYU? The point is she isn't you. She didn't give turndown service. You make me feel how I do when I come back to my room after a long, awful day of insanity and find my bed turned down with a chocolate on the pillow. A really fine chocolate. That's what I want. I want you back."

"Well, I can't come back just yet, now can I? I haven't found a band you're willing to sign. Of course, I *have* found a great band—a freaking sensational band—but you're too stubborn to sign them."

"Bollocks. I'm not stubborn at all. And I *am* interested."

Emmie straightened, her breath catching in her throat. "You are?"

"I'm also interested in Piper, but if you say one word about it to anyone, I'll fire you."

She smiled. She really did love her boss. "I'm so excited."

"And I'm in hell. Come back."

"When I discover *another* band."

"You can do that here."

"Not when I work for you, I can't. That's an all-consuming job. Besides, I'm not going to be your personal assistant. If I come back, it's in a different role."

"You don't want to work with me?" He sounded hurt, and her heart squeezed.

"Of course I want to work with you. Just not jumping into a cab so I can run to Dylan's Candy Store and fill a bag of red M&Ms for you." She blew out a breath. "Look, the truth is, you don't need turndown service. You're an incredibly competent guy. You need someone as efficient and professional as Roxanne. Why don't you hire Val in the meantime? Until you've found someone who doesn't chew with her mouth open?"

"Bloody hell, she'll blow anything that walks into the office. God, no. Look, I won't make you work so many hours."

"It's not just the hours." Although, of course, it was the hours. She'd had neither the time nor the energy for anything else when she'd worked for him. "I want a promotion."

"Come back to me, and we'll discuss possibilities."

"You mean come back to you, and we'll pretend that someday you'll give me more to do than pick out a tie for your new shirt?"

"Stop depreciating yourself. Helping me pick out a tie was one tiny morsel of what you did for me. Managing every aspect of my life, my artist's lives, and anticipating all of our needs is a job only a highly intelligent, competent person can handle. There are very few of you in the world."

Emmie pulled her elbows in tight against her body, resting one hand over her heart. She hadn't realized how badly she'd needed to hear him say that.

"I'll do whatever you want. I'll double your pay."

She appreciated how hard he tried to get her to come back, but come on. Whatever she wanted? She kept *telling* him what she wanted. Did he listen to her at all?

"Why the hell didn't you tell me it was about money? I'd pay you anything to stay."

He'd misunderstood her lack of response. "It's not about

the money. God. It's about the promotion." Seriously, he still didn't get that?

"What if I promote you to something and you keep on doing your work for me?"

"Really? You'd do that for me?" She couldn't believe him. "Gosh, Irwin, you'll really promote me to Something? I've always wanted to be Something!"

"That is the only thing I don't miss about you. I'm not sure, really, why I even hired you in the first place."

"Look, I don't want a fake promotion. I want a real one. I want you to think I'm so good that I'm wasted in my role as your personal assistant. Until then, I'm going to keep looking for a band that'll knock your socks off."

"But you're not wasted. You're irreplaceable. Now, look, Emmie, I do have other things to do than listen to you mock me. But before I go, it's important you don't say a word to anyone, including your brother, about my interest in their band. Or in Piper."

"Of course. You know I've got your back. But Piper's with Flow. She's with Eric. How can you—"

"Her contract's almost up. And Eric's a small-time hack."

"Everyone's a small-time hack compared to you."

"Do you see why I need you here? You don't for one moment believe the Masticator made me preen like that, do you?"

"No, Roxanne's all business. Which I thought you'd like."

"Why on earth would I want all business when I can have you? Having you is like having little smiley-face emoticons pop up all over my life. It's the little touches, Emmie, that make life worth living."

He sounded so sad. It killed her. "We will find you a great replacement, I promise. In the meantime, let Val step in."

"I'd sooner sell shoes for a living. In a suburban mall. While eating fat pretzels dipped in mustard. No. Absolutely not. She'd be worse than the masticating old lady."

She heard the fumbling, muffled sound of the phone being passed again. And then Val came on the line. "Em?" She sounded nervous.

"Well, that went well."

"What did you tell him?" Val asked in a rough whisper.

"That I'm not coming back."

"You're crazy. Who wouldn't work for Irwin Ledger? Why can't you be happy with what you've got? You're only twenty-five. Stick with this job and see where it takes you."

"I've already done that. It's taken me exactly nowhere. Besides, you don't know what it's like working for him. He has no boundaries. He's all-consuming."

"I'd happily consume him."

And that's the problem right there. "Yeah, well, he's going to have to keep searching for someone new."

"He doesn't want anyone new, Em. He wants you."

She couldn't deny that with each passing day temptation grew. It would be so easy to slide back into her old job. She knew she couldn't take it, of course, but how much longer could she hold out? She had no income, yet she had to continue to pay rent on her New York apartment until she found a new tenant.

Of all the job possibilities in her field, the only one that put her inside the music world would be A&R coordinator. Publicity, management, promotions, those jobs would keep her on the outside—doing busywork for the artists. Besides, any other job would be entry level and, after putting in *eight years*, she wasn't willing to start out at the bottom in another field.

No. She had to win that damn promotion.

———

He needed to talk to his girl, but he didn't want to be interrupted when the guys got back on the bus. Two rows of bunks, tiered in threes, mirror images on either side of a narrow aisle, precluded privacy.

Dropping out of his coffin, he moved quietly down the narrow aisle, the rumble of the engine overpowering any sounds he made. He punched her speed dial, brought the phone to his ear as he tread carefully down the steep staircase. A couple of their roadies played a video game in the main section, so he closed himself inside the back lounge, which was strewn with pillows, random instruments, and empty beer bottles.

"Jonny?" she answered sleepily.

He couldn't keep from smiling. "Hey, sorry to wake you." He loved that she used his real name. Settling onto the cushion, he tucked a pillow under his arm. "We had a great show tonight."

"I'm so glad. Is this your first venue that's not in a college town?"

"Not really. University of Las Vegas is here."

"Oh, right. So, they loved you?"

"I don't know about that, but it felt good." If he told her about the song, he'd have to mention Piper. "How about you? What'd you think of Under Cover?"

"I like them a lot. Unfortunately, so does Brian McKesslar from Star Records. So much so, he's going to sign them. Oh, well. But on a happy note, *Rolling Stone* just bought another article from me. Oh, and I pitched them a series."

"Yeah? What kind?"

"Taking a band from the garage to the amphitheater."

"That's awesome. Is the band called Snatch?"

"No band should ever be called Snatch."

"You're not going to use us for the article?"

"Maybe. Not sure the lead singer's got enough appeal."

"Why don't we take a poll?" he said. "Put his picture up on Facebook, and let the fans vote? Hey, we can get them to vote by offering a date with him? One lucky winner."

"Okay, down boy. No one's getting lucky with you but me."

"There's my girl."

"See? This is what I like about you. You make me smile. Every day. You make me happy."

"What else do you like?"

"Oh, gosh, let me see. Actually, this is an easy one. I love how you see beyond what people say. You're really sharp that way, and it turns me on."

"Are you turned on right now?"

"Duh. But I'm not done yet. I love how you appreciate everything I do. You go out of your way to thank me—sometimes you do it in front of everybody to make sure they take a moment to appreciate me, too. That makes me feel . . . Well, that's a pretty incredible thing you do. I love how intense you are. You put on this act of not caring about anything, being this careless playboy, but I get to see another side of you. You think about everything. You consider everything. And it's incredibly hot to watch you compose or write or fix something."

"Well. I'm glad we had this discussion." He loved the

sound of her laughter, so genuine, so true. Nothing fake about her. He knew exactly where he stood with her.

"You, um, you didn't call this morning. Did you go out and see the city?"

He closed his eyes. He'd never lie to her. "A little. We had breakfast with everybody, walked to the Strip, but then we came back to work on a song."

"When you said *we*, I got a little stab in my heart. Because I know you meant Piper. It's okay. You've been with her for three weeks. It's just . . . I really have no idea what your life is like out there."

Piper Lee appeared in his mind, teasing, taunting. She rose like an apparition between them, because Emmie should know the truth of his life on the road, how Piper was gaming him. Sitting in on his interviews, hanging on his arm to be sure she showed up in all the pictures, jamming with him so they could come up with a duet. But he couldn't tell Emmie. Even though he'd made her promise to tell him everything— it was their only hope of working—he now had something he couldn't tell her. Because she'd freak if she knew how hard Piper was working to manipulate him.

"It's just writing songs, Em. Nothing more. I like writing with her. She's intuitive, and it helps me. We work well together." Probably too well. But he'd manage it. "But that's it. There's nothing more." And just like that he knew what he needed to do. "Come out here."

"Where?" He heard a rustling of paper. "You're in Port-land next, then Seattle. That's too far. Oh, you'll be in Denver soon. Hang on. Let me see how far that is."

"I don't care how far it is."

"Well, I do. Plane tickets are expensive."

"I don't care. *I'll* pay. I have to see you."

"I want to see you, too."

No, he *had* to see her. He thought of that night, when Piper had come into the men's restroom. When she'd looked at them in the mirror and said, *We're perfect together.*

She was just like all the others. She saw his face, his body, the reaction he got onstage—and that's all he was to her. She saw what he could do for her.

But Emmie knew him. Knew him and still wanted him. "Book a flight. Tonight. Now."

"I'll look into it."

"Don't look into it. Do it. I'll pay. Put it on my credit card."

"No, I have money. I'm just afraid to spend it when nothing's coming in."

"We need to see each other." End of discussion. He'd purchase the ticket himself if he had to.

"I know. Oh, you know who called today? Irwin. He fired my replacement."

"Already?" His gut tightened.

"Yeah. He wants me to come back."

Oh, Christ. Was it happening already? She'd come running to Austin to get away from her boyfriend's betrayal, her boss's slights. He'd always known she'd go back. But once she did, once she got sucked back into that life, what would happen to *them*?

"He's pretty desperate, said he'd double my pay."

Irwin knew how to hit her where she hurt. He sighed. "What did you tell him?" He had no right to ask her to stay alone in that fucking house in the middle of Happy Familyville.

Likely, after this tour ended, if Piper had her way—and she *would*—they'd get signed by Flow and go out on another, larger tour together. He couldn't quit the band at this point. What kind of asshole bailed on the band he'd worked with all these years? When they'd finally reached this point?

And, dammit, he *had* to see this through. For his dad, yeah, but for himself. He couldn't spend the rest of his life as a fucking failure.

Shit. The situation sucked.

"He sounded so sad. I felt so bad for him."

"You're such a girl."

"What?"

"You feel bad for him. Is this the same man who won't give you the promotion you deserve?"

"That's the one. And I don't think you'd like me quite the same way if I weren't a girl." Her voice got all sexy, which made him go instantly hard.

He rubbed his cock, feeling the surge of desire rush through him. "You're right, Em. I like you just the way you are." He could hear noises outside, a bark of laughter, a squeal, shoes shuffling on pavement.

No hard-ons in the back lounge. He shifted positions, putting his need out of his mind. "Do you want the job? Do you want to go back to New York?" To her old life?

The door opened, and the guys climbed in with half a dozen skanky women giggling and stumbling on high heels. He glared at Ben, the first one on the bus. Rule number two on a tour bus: no girls.

Number one? No shitting. But that one was harder to control.

"Get them off," Slater said.

"What?" a drunk Ben said. "Piper's not even halfway through her set. She'll never know." The bunch of them fell onto the built-in couches, the girls spilling all over the guys.

"Piper won't let them bring groupies on the bus?" Emmie asked, voice pitched high. "She's travelling with eleven guys. What did she think would happen?"

"Piper's tour. Piper's rules."

"I cannot believe her. No one has rules like that." She paused. "This is about you. You realize that, right?"

"You want the bus full of groupies?"

"No."

"Then consider it a rule I can live with. Besides, Em?"

"Yeah?"

He loved when her voice got all soft and sexy like that, making him feel like he was in bed with her, just the two of them, bodies wrapped around each other. "None of this shit matters. The only thing that *does* matter? Us. Now book the flight."

Why hadn't Slater answered his phone all day?

From the moment she'd jumped on the earlier flight, she'd texted and called but hadn't heard back. Why wouldn't he look at his phone when he knew she was coming to visit?

As the cab neared the club, worry bit down and slipped into her bloodstream. What if he'd gone out with the band? It didn't matter. She'd just hang around the bus until he got back—except it wasn't only Snatch on the bus. It was Piper and her guys, too.

"You want me to let you out here?" The cab driver pulled into the club's parking lot.

"I think they park the buses around back. Would you mind going there?" If the buses weren't there, then what would she do? Derek hardly ever used his phone, so she doubted she'd hear back from him.

But, no, there they were. One huge tour bus, a smaller one for the crew, and a tractor-trailer for their instruments and gear. "Great." She pulled some bills from her wallet and thanked the driver, dragging her carry-on out of the car. Her pulse kicked up, knowing she would see Slater soon. God, she hoped he was there and not out with the guys. He didn't expect her for hours. Maybe his old, crappy phone had finally died?

As the cab left, she stood in the parking lot. The gray skies, the cold air, gave her a bad feeling, but she shook it off, shook off the chill.

Would it be the same? In spite of the brittle air, her hands felt clammy. God, she was actually nervous about seeing him. Afraid what they'd shared in Austin had faded with distance.

Just go already. She headed for the bus, anxiety building with each step she took.

Maybe she shouldn't have hopped on the earlier flight. But Tiana could only give her a ride before work, so she'd have been stuck sitting in an airport for hours. No, no, she'd done the right thing. Even if he were out with the guys, someone would know where he was. She'd find him.

She knocked on the bus doors. No one answered. Her anxiety ratcheted up. If no one was on the bus, if he didn't answer his phone—

The doors opened, and a very sleepy and disheveled older man sat up in a driver's seat that was reclined as far back as it could go.

Her hand came to her mouth. "I woke you up. I'm so, so sorry." Of course he slept all day. The poor man drove all night. "I wasn't thinking. I . . ." Her shoulders slumped.

The man smiled. "Don't worry about it. I've been driving thirty years. I'm used to everything. What can I do for you?"

"I'm here to see Slater?"

His features pulled into a scowl.

"No, not like that." God, how many groupies had pulled this stunt? She showed him her carry-on. "I'm his girlfriend."

His *girlfriend*. It sounded so weird saying it as she stood outside a massive tour bus in a parking lot in Seattle.

He smiled. "Emmie?"

All her doubts and fears dropped away. The bus driver knew her name. Now, what did that say about her man? "Yes." He'd talked to the bus driver about her. *Sweet*.

"He'll be glad to see you. Come on in. They're in back."

They? "Thank you." She'd wanted to spend some time alone with him, obviously, but if he was with the guys, she'd have to spend time with them, too. That'd be okay, though, since she'd gotten in so early.

He got up to reach for her bag, but she held up a hand. "I got it. It's nothing." And he settled back in his seat.

As Emmie climbed the stairs into the bus, she took in the black leather couches on either side of the narrow aisle, the flatscreen TV built into the wall. She passed through a kitchen area with coffee grounds spilled all over the counter. The sounds of acoustic guitar, murmuring, and a woman giggling made Emmie's gut tighten. She knew what the band sounded like when they hung out together. These sounds were nothing like that.

She recognized Slater's deep voice singing quietly, happily, like he was messing around. A terrible image formed in her mind.

Setting her bag down, her hands shaking, she drew the accordion-style door open and found Slater and Piper leaning against each other, smiling, relaxed, feet propped on the table in front of them. He strummed his guitar as she tilted her head against his shoulder, giggling softly.

Pain cracked open in Emmie's heart, and she felt a searing sting. Emmie gasped. Slater looked up, an expression of horror hijacking his handsome features. She turned so abruptly, she tripped over her luggage. Hands held out in front of her, she stumbled back down the length of the bus, banging into counters and chairs.

"Emmie," he shouted.

But she didn't stop. God, she had to get out of there. "Could you please let me out?" she asked the driver in a shaky voice. Shudders wracked her spine, and her stomach squeezed into a fist.

He lurched forward, glancing down the aisle behind her.

"Now. Please." She sounded desperate, frantic.

He pushed the button, and the doors opened. Emmie ran down the stairs, but Slater was too quick. He caught her around the waist so roughly her feet lifted off the ground.

"Stop. Just . . . stop. It's not what you think."

"Get off me." She couldn't catch her breath, couldn't stop shaking. Something dark and heavy draped over her mind, making it impossible to think clearly. "Oh, my God, just get the hell away from me."

"Never." He lowered her but didn't remove the arms belted around her waist. "Listen to me. Emmie, give me a chance."

"I did, you jerk. I gave you a chance." Oh, God, the pain, it kept slicing through her, shredding her. She felt a presence, jerked around to find Piper watching from the steps of the bus.

He looked, too. "Piper. *Fuck*. Can you just go?"

But there was something awful in the woman's eyes, something like satisfaction.

Drawing on her deepest well of strength, Emmie stopped struggling. She would never let that woman see her like this. "Get. Off. Me."

His arms relaxed but didn't release. "Not until you talk to me."

"I have talked to you. Every day. Every single day you tell me there's nothing going on between you and Piper." She finally looked into his eyes. "Every day I make the decision to trust you." She paused. "And look what it's gotten me."

He buried his head in her hair. "We're writing songs. That's it. I swear."

"Do you think I'm that stupid? Do you think anything you can say will turn what I saw into something different?"

"Yes, I do. Because you're turning what you saw into what you most fear. And that's not what's happening. We're writing songs. That's it."

"It's more than writing songs, and we both know it."

"No, it's not. I swear." He shook her shoulders. "I don't want her, Emmie. I don't."

"You might not want her, but you're starting to need her. And that's a thousand times worse. Now, let me go. I'm done here."

"You're not done. You're not going anywhere. Because nothing happened, nothing will happen. I want you to look me in the eyes, Em. Right now, turn around and look at me. Because you know me. You know me all the way, deep down. Look the fuck at me."

She drew in a deep breath, not wanting to see his truth. Not ready. She was bleeding, aching. She'd never get the image out of her brain—and not just of him snuggling with Piper, but of the woman's expression. The confidence of knowing she was winning.

"Let me go."

And he did. And that probably scared her more than anything.

"Can you please get my bag from the bus?" The ground turned watery, her peripheral vision narrowing.

"No. I'm not your pussy ex. I didn't fuck around on you."

She swung around to him. "Yeah, I know that, Slater. I'm very clear on the difference between screwing and *snuggling*. Having now lived through both scenarios, I'm kind of an expert. And you know what? What you did is a thousand times worse than walking in on Alex with two nameless, faceless groupies."

He scraped a hand roughly through his hair. "Fuck."

He could go to hell. She headed back to the bus. The last person on this earth she wanted to see was Piper, but she'd rather do that than stand around playing mind games.

He grabbed her arm, yanked her to him. "Guess what, Em? You're not running away from me. Want to know why? I didn't do anything wrong."

She pulled her phone out of her purse, hit the four in 411. She'd call a cab company, head right back to the airport.

But he ripped the phone out of her hand and shoved it deep into his front pocket. Then, he tipped his head back and shouted, "Why does everything have to be so fucked-up?"

"It doesn't." She yanked out of his hold, backed away from him. "You wanted it both ways. You wanted to be Slater and Jonny at the same time. And you just found out you can't."

"Emmie, I didn't do anything with Piper, and I don't want to. I'm crazy about you. You know that."

"And yet . . . look how comfortable you are with her."

"When we're *writing*. I like writing with her. I've only ever written alone. And it's fucking hard work. When I write with her, it's easier. The song isn't completely mine, so I don't like that part. But right now, when I'm on the road—"

"And you're lonely, and there's this really great woman who knows just how to take care of all your needs, it's easy to forget the woman you left back in Austin? The one who *used* to take care of them?"

He shook his head aggressively. "Wrong. You're dead wrong. I know exactly who Piper is. And this isn't about what happens on the road. Not even a little. While your bro—" His jaw clamped shut. He looked down at the ground, lips pressing into each other, one hand on his hip. "I watch them, the other guys, and they're going wild, like nothing I've ever seen before. I stand there and . . . and I don't feel a thing. I don't want it. Not any of it. I want to get back on the bus and talk to you. Obviously, since that's what I always *do*."

"I get that you don't want groupies. I'm clear on that. But I also get that you're lonely on the road and you're turning to *her*. Just like I knew you would."

His breath caught, his eyes widened, and for one moment he looked absolutely tortured. "Emmie, I love you. I fucking *love* you."

Her heart settled down. The shaking subsided. His words hung in the air. She heard them, but they didn't sink in.

"I'm so fucking in love with you I don't know what to do with myself."

The ice cracked, and her blood started flowing again. Warmth suffused her as her heart absorbed his words. He loved her.

She knew he did. She *felt* it. It flowed between them in every conversation. The need to touch him overwhelmed, but just as she reached for him, the horrible image of him with Piper flashed in her mind. So, she stopped, tucked her arms to her sides.

"Nothing's happened between me and Piper."

"Wrong. Something has. You've gotten close. And she's dangerous. You *know* that."

"You don't get close to someone like Piper. She's all about herself."

"The worst thing you could do right now is try to bullshit me. I know what I saw. You *are* getting close to her." Her gaze bore down on him. She needed him to really hear her. "She's playing you brilliantly. She knows how to give you just what you need, and you're falling right into her trap."

She could see he recognized the truth of her words, and so

she continued. "She's working her way in. And each time she breaks down one more barrier, it gets easier to touch her, lean against her, laugh together. Pretty soon you've got private jokes and secret smiles. And then that day when we've had a big fight and too much time has divided us, it's that much easier to turn to her for *all* your needs. She's dangerous, and if you don't recognize that, then we have a serious problem."

"If I hadn't met you, then, yes, everything you're saying would be true. But I have you. I know what *us* feels like. There's no turning back. I want this. I want us."

A cab rolled into the lot. The moment the doors opened, her brother, Ben, Cooper, and Pete spilled out. They strode toward them, a pack of badass rockers, laughing, nudging each other.

"Slater, dude," Pete called. "Let's go." The cab took off behind them.

"Emmie?" her brother called. He jogged over. With a big smile, he pulled her into his arms. "Emmie."

"Derek." She didn't want her brother to see her like this.

He set her down, his smile fading as he took in her expression. "Are you okay?" He narrowed his gaze, looking between her and Slater. Then his eyes widened. "So help me God, if you fucking hurt my sister." He came at Slater with both hands thumping his chest so hard Slater stumbled back. "I knew shit was going down with you two."

Slater shoved her brother back, hard. "No. You're wrong."

Emmie put her hand on her brother's tensed arm. "He's not. Derek, he's not."

"Then why the face?"

"She walked in on me and Piper writing together."

Derek drew in a rough breath. "Yeah, that's a pretty bad idea, bro." Then, he shook his head as though troubled. "But they're writing some really good shit."

Emmie tried to smile. She felt just like she did the first day after the flu, weak, jittery, but no longer ready to die. "So I hear."

"You got in early," her brother said.

"I caught an earlier flight. I tried to reach both of you, but you don't have your phones on."

Slater reached for her hand, just as Derek elbowed him. "We've got an early sound check 'cause there are so many bands playing tonight. Come on. Let's go."

"In a minute," Slater said.

Derek gave her a questioning look, and she appreciated that he was there for her. But he couldn't help, so she nodded, letting him go.

He took off, leaving Emmie and Slater in uncomfortable silence. Honestly, she didn't know what to do. Part of her wanted to leave, get out before he completely destroyed her. She could see the writing on the wall. It was only a matter of time.

She could fill all of Slater's needs but one. His art. And that was the most intimate part of him.

And, dammit all to hell, but Piper could fill *all* of them.

He cupped her face in his hands. "Stop. Turn off all those terrible thoughts. They're wrong. I love you, Emmie. I swear I wouldn't torture you this way if I didn't. I'm not like your pussy ex. If I had feelings for Piper or anyone, I would tell you. I wouldn't put both of us through this fucking hell. You have to believe that."

"I do." She grasped his wrists, pulled his hands away from her face. "But what I walked in on?"

"Won't happen again."

She hadn't expected him to concede so easily, so quickly. Not when writing with someone meant so much to him. She didn't understand.

He smiled. "Em, if I showed up at the house for a surprise visit and found you on the couch *snuggling* with your pussy ex, I'd beat him to a pulp. Do you hear me?" She nodded. "I would pull his balls out his ears." He reached for her hips. "I wouldn't be half as reasonable as you are right now." He drew her to him.

"I don't know what to be."

"But you believe me?"

"Believe what? That you're not going to sleep with her? No, I guess I don't. Because you're allowing her in. And you know where that leads. You're enjoying her company, Slater. Don't deny that."

"I didn't. I told you I like writing with her. It's a *relief*."

Right then she saw him. The lonely man. Even though he filled his home and life with four roommates and hundreds of hangers-on, he was still alone all the time. He ate alone, he wrote alone, and he slept alone. Banging random women had to be the worst kind of loneliness.

He dug his hands into his pockets, looking scared. "I won't write with her anymore. She may not have boundaries, but I do." He blew out a breath. "I know what she's trying to do."

Unease prodded at her, twisting in her gut. "I'm not comfortable holding you back. You like the songs you write with her. That's important. It's important for your career." Of course, it would end their relationship. No way would she sit that one out.

"I don't need her to write songs. I just enjoyed the break from being inside my own head. She's the wrong person to find that outlet with."

"I just—"

"There's no discussion. If it were you and Alex . . ."

"I get it. Balls through ears."

He smiled, his face lighting up. She could almost see the fears and worries tumbling off him. "Can I kiss you now? Please?" His mouth lowered to hers.

She shook her head, even while she got up on her toes, straining to meet him, to close the distance. "No. I don't want you to kiss me."

"Okay. I won't." And then his lips touched hers, so gentle and warm and sweet. But sweet quickly turned hot as he licked into her mouth, pulled her closer, his hands sliding down to her ass and cupping her. He moaned. "Fuck me." Then he deepened the kiss, turning her limbs to liquid heat.

Her blood boiled, her nerves sparked and flashed, and she lost herself in the incredible heat of his mouth, the gruff motion of his hands on her back, her ass. His hips rocked into her, pressing his hard length against her stomach.

"No fucking in the parking lot, Slater," Pete shouted.

Emmie turned to find the guys getting off the bus.

"God, what will people think of us?" Ben said.

"Sound check, asshole, let's go," Cooper said.

Slater pulled away slowly, pressing soft but frantic kisses over her lips. "My Emmie," he moaned into her ear as he clutched her one more time. "I miss you so fucking much." His hands slid down her arms, weaving his fingers through hers. "Come on. Watch me turn into a rock star."

EIGHTEEN

He'd said he loved her. No, he *fucking* loved her. A shiver ran down her spine as she recalled the look in his eyes when he'd told her. Part of her wanted to think he'd pulled out the big words to gloss over the situation she'd found him in, but she knew better. She *knew*.

But was it enough? The odds were against them to begin with, but with Piper so damned determined . . . And distance, as she well knew, did *not* make the heart grow fonder for a guy on the road. The image of the two of them leaning into each other so comfortably tore through her. God, she had to shake it off. She either let it go or she let *him* go.

Emmie stood at the side of the stage, watching. In addition to the usual two songs Snatch did for sound check, they also tried out the new one, making sure they got the harmonies down. Listening to the lyrics and hearing his voice move with the emotion of the song made Emmie's stomach flutter. It was a great song. He sang it with such passion.

She couldn't—wouldn't hold him back. She whipped out her phone, texted him.

The song is amazing. You should write with her.

No matter what it cost her peace of mind, she couldn't hold him back. What was that expression? She texted again.

If you love something, set it free.

She hated that she'd fallen for another musician. Hated how much time she spent alone in the house wondering what he was doing—well, *great*, now she had an image to call up whenever she started wondering. Terrific.

But Slater wasn't just another musician. He was . . . God, he was unbelievable. And their connection? It was too powerful, too special for her to walk away.

So she had no choice but to hang in there. She was crazy about him.

Finished with sound check, the guys headed toward catering. She expected to find the typical spread of subs, sodas, and boxes of grocery store cookies. Typical for smaller venues like this one.

Instead, she found aluminum serving trays of lasagna, garlic bread, and fresh green salad. Homemade brownies heaped on paper plates. She raised her brows at Slater, who just shook his head. "Nice spread," she said.

A hand clamped down on her shoulder, and Emmie got a whiff of Piper's perfume. "I like to make sure my boys get some good food when we're on the road."

"So I've heard." Emmie watched the guys fill their plates high and then settle into the chairs and couches around the room.

"I try to call ahead, find a place near the venue." Edging between her and Slater, Piper rubbed his belly. "Like to give them the feel of home, you know?"

Slater jerked back, holding Piper's gaze in a silent communication that looked too familiar.

Sickeningly familiar. Obviously, he'd had to tell her to knock it off before. Or—God, had he warned her not to do it around Emmie?

Reaching for Emmie's hand, Slater tugged her toward him, forcing her to knock Piper aside.

"Excuse me," Emmie said, quietly.

But Piper smiled serenely. Nothing rattled her. She was in total command.

She clapped her hands. "Eat up, boys." And then she perched

on the arm of Derek's chair, wrapping an arm around his shoulder.

His flash of confusion let Emmie know Piper had never been that familiar with him before. Emmie was being played. And she didn't like it one damn bit.

She stepped away from Slater, stared at the side of his head, watched him spoon lasagna onto his paper plate. For a moment, he concentrated on the food, but then he finally exhaled, his shoulders slumping. "Don't."

She took the word like a body blow. He was angry with *her*? Didn't want *her* to make a scene? Enough of this crap. Maintaining a relationship with a rocker on tour didn't work, period. Add a determined bitch to the mix, and Emmie was *asking* for drama.

Screw it. She'd had enough of this bitch's games.

One step was all she took before Slater slapped his hand around her wrist and towed her to a corner of the room. "Don't let her do this to us. This is what she wants. She wants to drive you away. I see her, Emmie. I see exactly what she's doing."

"Then stop her."

Oh, God, the look in his eyes. She could see the strain, the frustration.

"Emmie, I'm trying to keep her happy. At the same time I'm trying to hold on to you. Can you see how difficult this might be? If I piss her off, I risk the tour, risk the band getting signed. If I don't handle everything just right, I blow up it all up. Can you see that?" She'd never seen him so tense.

Of course he saw through the scheming bitch. He wasn't stupid. "Yes, I can. Of course. I'm just—"

"You're not anything. I don't blame you. I'd react the same way."

She had a decision to make. Give up her boyfriend, her brother, her band—just walk away for some perceived peace of mind. Or ignore the bitch.

It wasn't even a question. No more of this wavering. She'd make a decision and stick with it.

She got up on her toes and pressed a kiss to his mouth. "Okay. I won't let her do this to us."

Leading him to a table, she let him settle in as she went back to spoon some lasagna and salad onto a paper plate for herself. Then, she sat beside him and let it all go. She had a limited time with Slater and the guys, and she didn't want to mar it with anger and jealousy.

Slater loved her. She had to trust in the gift he'd given her. And make no mistake, it was a gift. One he'd never bestowed upon anyone before.

Interestingly, it didn't take long for the guys to make their way over to her table, drawing up chairs, snatching bread off Slater's plate. And the six of them were all laughing and enjoying each other.

It couldn't have been more perfect. Slater gripped her thigh, giving it a squeeze, then kissed her mouth. He was finally relaxed.

She had a natural rapport with them. Piper hustled them. Clearly, they felt the difference.

And then it was show time. And—surprise, surprise—Piper stayed with Snatch. Normally, the headliners didn't hang out with the opening act. Why would they? They had hours before their show. But she, of course, stayed close to Slater.

Before heading backstage, each band member took a black Sharpie and wrote something on the hallway walls. Except Slater. He just kept walking, holding on to her hand.

At the side of the stage, as the guys jumped up and down, did vocal exercises, loosened up, Slater pulled her aside, tucking them inside a thick velvet theater curtain. He ran his hands down her arms, pulling her palms to his mouth and kissing them.

"Are you still upset?"

She wouldn't lie to him. "Yes." Gazing up at him, she cupped his gorgeous face in her hands. "But don't worry about it now. Get out there."

"I can't stand the way I hurt you."

"I know."

"No, you really don't. You're not in my head. You don't know how I feel. I probably chose the wrong time to tell you, but I mean it, Em. I love you. It's only you for me. And what you saw? It just fucked up everything—all the trust I've worked so hard to build."

"It was a really good time to tell me." But she couldn't say it back. She just couldn't do it.

"Emmie, what you saw? I want to delete it from your brain."

"You can't. Just go." She pushed him, but he didn't budge. She knew that look in his eye, though.

"Please don't be angry with me. We only have a few hours together." He pushed her hair away from her ear and whispered, "I need you."

She could feel his desperation in the hands that gripped her arms, through his intense and imploring gaze. He had this way about him. Or maybe it was *them*, their chemistry, their connection. But he always broke through. "It's okay." She pressed her mouth to his cheek. "We're okay. You can go."

His mouth found hers, kissed her greedily. Grabbing her hand, he rubbed it over his erection. "Fuck. What you do to me."

"Jonny. You can't go out there like that." She smiled against his mouth.

"I know. Fuck, Emmie." He fumbled with his jeans, opened the top button.

"Jonny." Her tone sounded like a protest, but her hand reached in and closed over him, so hot, so hard, and she couldn't help but squeeze, feel him shudder and thrust up into her hand.

"I need you. Now." He bent his knees, cupped her ass, and lifted her off the floor.

Her hands scraped through his hair. Of course she should stop him. Of course they couldn't make love right there. The curtain was thick—it was huge—but would it hide them? She could barely think as his fingers pushed her panties aside, stroked into her, and the burn of desire whisked through her, spreading everywhere so fast the soles of her feet tingled. Her hands clutched the back of his neck, and she moaned in his ear at the rush of sensation.

"Jesus, Em, you're so fucking hot." He pushed into her. She could barely make out the announcer's words over the screams of the crowd. Thousands of people waited just on the other side of the wall, his bandmates waited for him, and neither of them could tear themselves away from each other.

He pulled nearly all the way out and then rammed into her again and again, harder and harder, until she lost herself completely as the heat tore across her skin, the searing sensation curling, twisting, tightening between her legs.

He gripped her ass hard, spreading her legs, forcing her to cross her ankles behind his back to hold on. Her fingers dug into his shoulders.

"Ah. Fuck. Oh, Jesus. Yes, Emmie, oh, fucking yes." He dragged his mouth to her ear. "I'm gonna come so fucking hard."

He pounded into her, sweat dampening his back, his muscles bunched tightly underneath his T-shirt. She needed him so much, couldn't get close enough to him no matter how hard she ground into him, how tightly she clenched her inner muscles to feel him deeper, harder inside her.

He grunted in her ear and then slammed into her, crying out with his ferocious release. He pumped in and out a few more times, and then his shoulders fell forward and he eased her to her feet.

Tipping her chin up, he pressed hard, quick kisses to her mouth. "I fucked up, and I'm sorry. Just. . . ."

They heard the riffing of drums, the guitars, a synthesizer. "Go."

He let out a big breath, swiped the perspiration from his brow, and gave her a breathtaking smile. "Be right back."

After the show the band's energy was higher than she'd ever seen it. Slater came right for her, caught her up in his arms. "What did you think?"

She dug her hands into his sweaty hair and brought his mouth to hers. After kissing him long and hard, she said, "You guys get better and better. It's amazing. You were great before, but you're seriously stars now."

"Listen, I have to do press. Will you wait for me in the greenroom?"

"Sure."

"But just . . . wait in the greenroom, okay?"

"Of course." She wondered why he seemed so worried. Did he still think she'd grab her luggage and go?

He took off, and she wandered around backstage looking for the greenroom. She found her way back to catering, where a group of guys huddled together, talking quietly. Given their costumes and styled hair, she figured they were Piper's guys.

And then Cooper and Pete came in—not even noticing her, which was weird. The other guys looked up, and then all of them disappeared into an adjoining room, leaving the door ajar.

Curious, Emmie headed over, listening to their hushed

voices. They seemed frantic, serious. She peered in, stunned to find her guys bent over a table snorting lines.

Drugs? Since when did the guys do drugs?

Two seconds later the door to catering flung open. "Show time," a guy called. "Let's go."

Piper's band dashed out. Emmie wanted to say something to her friends, but not just then. Besides, it wasn't her place. She'd definitely talk to Derek, though. Nothing killed careers quicker than drugs. She'd seen it so many times before.

She wanted to leave before they came out, so she headed back out into the dim hallway, looking for the greenroom. She could hear the crowd roar for Piper Lee, who was just taking the stage. She really hoped Slater didn't expect her to hang around and watch the show. Not gonna happen.

She came upon a door with a piece of paper taped to it. *Artist.* Probably the greenroom. She turned the handle, expecting to find a bunch of hangers-on, people who cared less about the show and more about hanging around backstage with artists.

Instead she saw . . . bodies, humping, thrusting, arching. It took a moment to process, but—oh, God—it was Ben, his pants around his ankles, having sex with two women. Both were topless. One serviced him on her knees, one hand gripping his bottom and the other fisting his erection. He had his mouth on the other girl's breast and his hand between her legs, stroking furiously.

Heart pounding, Emmie quickly shut the door. Drugs, sex . . . God, they were living the life, weren't they? Exactly what they'd dreamed. It almost disgusted her that she'd helped them get to this point.

What did it mean for Slater? Was this, ultimately, who he was, too?

She had to get out, so she made her way to the end of the corridor and pushed out the double doors. The cold night air washed over her. The low, thick cloud cover made it hard to breathe. She practically ran to the bus, knocking on the door.

It opened right away, and she thanked the driver in a rush as she climbed the steps and sat down on one of the couches.

"You all right?" he asked.

"Oh, I just . . ." What could she say? He'd spent thirty years on the road with rock stars. Maybe he liked the lifestyle, too.

Tears burned, and she said the only thing she knew was true. "I'm not sure this is the life for me."

He laughed. "It takes a certain personality."

"I don't have it. I don't understand it." She'd said too much. She didn't know him well enough.

"Well, your guy's different. I've seen it all, I tell you, over the years. Yours is one of the good ones."

She didn't answer, pretty sure she looked as uncertain as she felt.

"Most of the artists ignore me. Sure, some're polite. But it's the rare guy that sits in the passenger seat and takes the time to get to know me. Now, don't get the wrong idea. I'm not complaining. It's no one's job to talk to an old man. But the ones that do? They're special. They're different." He patted his heart. "Yours is a keeper."

"You knew my name."

He smiled, eyes twinkling. "He talks about you all the time. What you did for the band, how you saved him."

"Saved him from what?"

A knowing look took hold of his features. "From everything you just ran from."

Slater tore through the greenroom. He couldn't find Emmie anywhere.

Fuck. She did *not* leave. Christ, when he closed his eyes, he saw her expression, the shock and devastation of seeing him with Piper.

Okay, he had to get his shit together. She wouldn't leave him.

He shouldn't have taken so damn long, but hell, what could he do? After the interviews Piper's manager had pulled him and Derek into a meeting, and time had gotten away.

Think. He knew she wouldn't watch Piper's set. Slater pushed out the doors, stepping into the cool air. He headed for the bus. One hard knock, and Don opened the doors for him. Slater must've looked as freaked out as he felt, because Don just smiled and pointed upstairs.

"I told her which bunk was yours."

"Thanks, Don." He climbed aboard but paused at the top step, clutching the railing. "Is she okay?"

Don shrugged. "A little upset."

"Yeah, okay. Thanks." Shit. What had happened? He hoped like hell Piper hadn't fucked with her. He hurried up the stairs, hunching over on the second floor thanks to the low ceiling. With anxiety driving his every step, he reached his bunk, pulled the curtain, and found her on her side, facing him, hands under his pillow, sleeping.

She looked so sweet and innocent, and his heart expanded at the sight of this pure-hearted woman he'd fallen in love with. He wanted to be worthy of her. He wouldn't do anything to fuck up this relationship. Well, any more than he already had. What the fuck had he been thinking giving Piper any opening at all?

Hopping in, he climbed to her other side. She jolted, her eyes fluttering open. When she saw him, she looked worried. "Oh. I fell asleep."

Drawing the curtain closed, he couldn't help the rush of happiness coursing through him. He had her in his bunk, just as he'd fantasized for weeks. Alone with her in this tiny space, he could breathe in her fresh, sweet scent and press the full length of his body over hers. "Sorry it took so long."

"Don't worry about me. I'm fine." She rolled onto her back, opening her arms for him. "I'm glad you're here now."

"We won't have long. The guys'll be boarding soon. We're having a meeting." He hesitated, not wanting to spoil their time together. "We got some good news tonight." He ran his finger over the furrow between her eyes. "Hey, what's the matter? What happened?"

"I just . . . um."

"Talk to me, Em."

"I saw Cooper and Pete doing lines with Piper's guys, and Ben having a threesome in the greenroom."

"What? Are you sure? About the coke?"

"I've been around this stuff a long time. I know what I saw."

"Shit. I'll talk to them."

"I've seen this too many times before. This is how a band blows up. I've seen it, Slater."

Slater. She'd called him Slater. So, he hadn't won her back all the way. *Fuck.*

"Please talk to Derek. You two have to be on the same

page. And Ben with the girls . . . What's going on? He's not like that."

"I think he's got to find that out on his own. He's living out some fantasy."

"But . . ."

"You're thinking about Tiana. Take her out of the equation, and is there anything wrong with what he's doing? He's a single guy with two willing participants."

"No, you're right. It just surprised me. I didn't think he was like that."

"Come on, you know better than anybody. Most rockers grew up in their bedrooms with a guitar in their hands and a sticky copy of *Playboy* under their beds. They didn't date or go to parties. Suddenly, they're onstage, and girls are dropping their panties. It takes a while—if ever—to get that out of your system."

Thank God, she smiled. "Fortunately for me, you weren't that guy."

"No, I wasn't."

The doors whooshed open, and the bus filled with the sounds of laughter and conversation.

"So, tell me the big news."

He didn't know how she'd take it. It was great for the band but possibly devastating for their relationship. But what could he do? It was happening.

"Eric wants to sign us. We've got a record contract with Flow."

The guys spread out on the two black couches, Emmie tucked in close to Slater's side. She hadn't said a word since he'd told her the news. Both Cooper and Pete kept in constant motion, tapping their fingers, jackhammering their legs, cracking their knuckles. Confirmation of what Emmie had told Slater.

"After we did press," Derek said, his hair messy and stiff-looking from sweat. "Eric and John called us into a meeting." He broke out in a big smile. "Guys, we're getting signed."

"Holy fucking shit," Ben said.

Cooper pumped his fist, jumped out of his seat, and did some weird kind of dance.

"A fucking record contract." Derek shook his head like he

couldn't believe it. His gaze caught Emmie's, and the look of love and respect between them blew Slater away. He wanted that ease with her—that total trust.

Emmie leaned into him. "Your dad would be so proud of you." She smiled and pressed a soft kiss to his cheek. "Congratulations."

Caught in that intense force field that locked them together, he didn't smile, didn't even breathe. She was right. Holy shit.

I made it.

He looked away, his heart pounding thickly. He'd made it. And his dad wouldn't be there to see it. To live it with him. It'd been his dad's dream—all he'd ever wanted.

Fuck, this hurts.

Pulling out his phone, he texted his mom—the closest he'd ever come to sharing this moment with his dad. Got a record deal.

She responded immediately. Gracious! That is wonderful news.

About to put his phone away, it buzzed again. His mom. I'm proud of you.

He'd never heard those words from her, and somehow they filled him in a way that the record contract didn't. Think Dad knows?

Several moments later, she responded. No doubt, by pure force of will, your dad's found a way to keep watch over you. Can you imagine what he's putting the heavenly bodies through to stay close to his son?

He could actually. He smiled at the winking smiley face she'd included. He quickly wrote her back. Didn't know you had such mad texting skillz.

We'll celebrate when you get home.

Sounds good. And, surprisingly, it did.

"Slater?" Derek said.

Slater looked up, pocketing his phone. Emmie gave him a squeeze.

"You still with us?"

"Yep."

"I was saying I'm going to go over all the details with you

guys tomorrow, and then we can all decide together if this is what we want."

"What's to discuss?" Pete said. "We're in."

"Fuck yeah," Ben said.

"Yeah, yeah," Derek said. "But we still have to go over the details. Em, can you get us an attorney? We're going to need someone to look at the contracts."

"Sure." She said it quietly, making Slater wonder what she was thinking.

"I can't believe this is happening," Ben said.

"Em, you're the best thing that ever happened to us." Cooper jumped out of his seat, leapt across the short aisle, and scooped her up in his arms. "We love you, man. Seriously."

"I'm happy for you," she said.

"A record contract?" Pete tipped his head back, hands skimming his hair. "Jesus. It's not Amoeba, but it's sure as fuck something. Hell, yes. I don't need time to think about anything, man. I'm in. We're all in."

"Actually." Slater released Emmie's hand and got up. "I'm not sure if I'm in."

Pete stopped moving. Every one of the guys wore identical expressions of shock. Emmie's eyes went wide.

"What're you talking about?" Derek said with a guarded expression.

He almost couldn't believe what he was about to say. "Before I met Emmie, I wouldn't think twice about any of this." Yeah, scoring the contract meant a lot to him. But Emmie? None of it would matter if he lost her.

"Slater," she began.

He gave her a look, asking her to hear him out. "But I *do* have her, and it's changed the game plan. Don't get me wrong. I want to move forward with this band, but only if we're on the same page."

"What does *that* mean?" Cooper looked pissed.

"It means that as much fun as we're all having here, ultimately, we're talking about our careers. We've worked our asses off to get to this point—and it's finally here. But I think we could fuck it up pretty spectacularly if we don't have a focused, professional approach. And unless we can all agree on that approach, I'm just not willing to risk my relationship with Em."

"What the fuck, Slater." Derek held his gaze, looking in-credulous and confused. "Are you trying to *impress* her?"

"I'm telling you that I can see us fucking up, going a little crazy with all this opportunity that's been handed to us. And I've got a line in the sand I'm willing to draw."

"Like?" Derek sounded hostile.

"Like drugs."

Derek shook his head in disgust. "We don't do that shit. Never have."

Cooper, Pete, and Ben looked away. Slater held his gaze steadily on them, demanding they fess up.

"What's going on?" Derek elbowed Cooper, who sat next to him. "Are you partying?"

The tension thickened in the room. No one spoke. Derek waited, but he looked like he was ready to lose his shit if someone didn't answer pretty damn fast.

Finally, Cooper let a breath. "A little."

"It's not that big a deal," Pete said.

"It is to me," Slater said. "Nothing will kill us quicker than drugs and acting like out-of-control rock stars."

"We're just partying with Piper's guys," Ben said. "It's not a big deal."

"Piper hires session guys," Slater said. "She hires guys to go on tour with her. They're all replaceable. We're a band. We're in this together. And, frankly, we're building a brand. I take this shit seriously. If we're going to take the next step, then I have to know you're all going to take it seriously, too. That means no drugs."

"I agree with that," Derek said to the other guys. "That's fucked-up, you guys."

"U2, R.E.M., they didn't get where they are without a plan," Slater said. "You don't just become a legend. You put your heart and soul into it, you have a goal, and you don't take your eyes off it. And I'm willing to give you guys a hundred percent—you're my brothers—but only if we can agree we're not in it to be rock stars, to fuck groupies, and party. Because that shit's going to burn out fast. I'm not risking Emmie for a situation that'll wind up in failure. And that's what I predict if we continue on this path."

"This is why we have the no-girlfriend rule," Pete said. "You're thinking with your dick."

Slater spun on him. "Wrong, asshole. Do you know what drives me out of bed every day of my life?" He saw Emmie shift, saw her move closer to him. "Failure. Thanks to my dad, that's all I knew growing up. He'd take me to an audition, enter me in a contest, whatever, and I'd come close. Sometimes, I'd even get the gig. And then they'd drop me because no one would work with my dad. He fucked up everything."

"We're not failing, man." Cooper looked at Slater like he couldn't believe this discussion. "We're pure fucking win."

"Not with the shit we're doing right now. My dad failed because he had no discipline. He was all over the place. He thought rock 'n' roll was one big party. And it sure as hell can be. If you want to be a roadie or a wedding band. But I don't. I'd rather make a living publishing my songs than be in some out-of-control party band. You know I'm totally committed— I've never done anything to make you think otherwise. But I'm only willing to go forward if we all decide we want the same thing and are willing to make the same sacrifices to get there."

"Well, I am," Derek said. "And I completely agree. Look at Bon Jovi. He's like a fuckin' CEO. He runs that band like a boss. We can still have fun—hey, it's the nature of this gig. But we have to do it the right way."

The other guys didn't look convinced. Slater understood. They were still teenage boys alone in their bedrooms strumming on guitars and beating off to the memory of the girl who sat in front of them in history class.

"This is bullshit, man," Pete said.

"Fuck you," Derek said. "Are you on drugs right now?"

Pete looked remorseful. Good sign.

Derek shook his head in disgust. "I've waited a long time for this chance. And this is it, guys. How long have we been spinning our fucking wheels? And then Emmie comes along—"

"It's not me," Emmie said. "It's you. It's Slater, who spends every day composing, writing, studying his craft. It's Derek, who handles the business end so well. It's all of you committed to rehearsing as often as you do, making sure your sets are perfect. You got to this point yourselves. All I did was open the door. If you hadn't been ready, you wouldn't have gotten in. Do you understand? You're there. Where you've worked hard to be. Where thousands of bands wish they could be. You're right there."

"But if we want to take it to the next level," Slater said, taking over so no one blamed Emmie for his line in the sand, "we're going to have to agree to stay completely professional and focused."

"Does that mean we can't fuck our headliner?" Pete gave Slater a hard look.

Rage lit him up like a match, and he lunged for his friend.

"Shut the fuck up." Derek said, grabbing Slater's arm and jerking him aside. He towered over Pete. "This is what drugs do, you asshole. All you're doing is proving Slater's point." He shoved Pete's shoulder. "I'm not going forward, either, unless we all agree to cut this shit out right now. We've never been assholes to each other, and you're being an asshole right now."

"Come on," Pete said. "The guy who's stuck his dick in all thirty thousand of our Facebook fans is suddenly telling us we have to be good little soldiers?" He gave a bitter laugh. "So, we have to all become saints now that you've got a girlfriend?"

"I'm not telling you to be anything. I'm telling you that I'm not going to sign any contracts until we have a conversation about the direction of this band. Which is what we should do. This is a career. You can vote me off the island. The four of you can carry on without me, no hard feelings. I want you to make your own choices. I've made mine."

Slater didn't want this conversation to escalate, but he couldn't allow Pete to disrespect his girl. Slater tried to keep himself under control when he put his face in front of Pete's and said, "I know you're high right now, but if you ever disrespect Emmie again, I will fuck you up. Brother or not, you don't ever hurt my girl. Do you understand?"

Pete looked shaken, features stained red.

"There's no band without you, and you know it," Ben said to Slater. "I'm in."

Slater shook his head. *Wrong answer.* "No decisions tonight. I want us to think about it, about what we want and what we're willing to sacrifice to get it. It's an important turning point for us, and I don't want anyone resenting me or going along with anything just to make sure we sign the contracts. Let's talk about it the morning."

NINETEEN

Slater climbed the steep staircase behind her, unable to take his eyes off the gentle sway of her hips. As soon as she hit the second floor, she turned and caught him in her arms. "That was so hot."

"Yeah?" He lifted her, loved that her legs immediately wrapped around him.

"Yeah." The whole walk to his bunk she squirmed against him.

"Em." He breathed into her ear, awash in her scent, the erotic rush of sensation spiraling out along his limbs. "Don't get me started. Cooper's bunk is above mine and Ben's is below. We can't do anything tonight."

"Nothing?" She licked his ear, and desire sizzled along his nerves.

"Nothing." He set her down. "Go downstairs and get ready for bed. There's only one bathroom, so get done what you need to before everyone starts fighting for it."

But she didn't go. She gazed up at him with so much pride and love he wanted to look away. But he didn't. He couldn't.

"You love me." She said it like it was a revelation.

"Yeah, I do."

"No, I mean, you really love me. *Love* me, love me."

He cupped her cheeks, felt the jolt of electricity travel down his spine. "I'm in love with you, Em."

His heart thudded so hard it hurt. She looked at him with awe, with surprise—but that's not what he needed. He needed her to feel the same way about him.

After what she'd seen in the lounge, he doubted she could do it. Or maybe she wasn't all the way in.

"Why do you seem surprised?" he asked.

"I don't know. Because . . . it seems too soon? In three years with Alex, it was never like this."

"Like what?"

"This . . . big. This intense. Because we're still together, even after you've been on the road. We could've fallen apart. The feelings could've faded since we're not together every day. But instead, it just keeps getting better. Stronger. I didn't know it could be like this."

"Me neither." He loved hearing her talk like this—like she really was in it with him.

She swallowed, looked away. Reaching for her toiletry bag, she blinked several times.

"Hey, you okay?"

Shaking her head, she pushed past him.

"Em," he said, reaching for her. "Talk to me."

She curled her hand around the back of his neck, brought him down to her. Pressing her mouth to his ear, she said, "I want . . ." Her fingers curled into his skin. "I want you so much . . ."

He pulled her away.

This morning she'd walked in on him and Piper. He got it.

She wasn't all the way there yet.

With his back against the wall of his coffin, Slater held Emmie close, an arm across her waist, their legs intertwined. The engine rumbled loudly, and while he couldn't hear his eleven bunkmates, he was extremely conscious of their presence.

"Are you worried what they'll say tomorrow?" Emmie whispered, her hand under his T-shirt, stroking his bare chest.

"Not at all."

"I'd be freaking out."

"Yeah, well, I can only control my own actions. If they don't want to stop partying, it'll suck. It'll mean Derek and I will have to start over again. But it's smarter than carrying on with guys who're gonna blow themselves up. It'll be okay."

"Hey." She smiled. "You're here. Your dreams are coming true."

Slater nodded, sinking into those warm brown eyes.

"Are you thinking about your dad?"

"A little." He nuzzled into her neck. "Yeah."

His dad would go nuts. What a disaster to have chased so hard after something and never gotten even a taste. If he'd lived, he would've finally felt the satisfaction of victory.

Yet, another part of Slater, deeper, closer to the bone, knew he might never have gotten this far with his dad in the picture. His dad fucked everything up.

As had Slater. If Emmie hadn't come into his life, would he still be sabotaging himself?

He kissed her, overwhelmed with emotion for her.

Her hands went into his hair. "You're a good man. You're so much better than you let on. Tonight, you let them see you. That's . . . that's huge."

"You make me a better man." He deepened the kiss, loving how she opened up to him so completely, her mouth letting him in, her legs shifting restlessly. But he had to stop it before he got too stirred up. "I want to tell you something, but I don't want you to get upset."

"Okay."

Rubbing his thumb against the furrow that appeared between her eyes, he said, "I was taking a shower not long ago, and Piper came into the bathroom."

Her eyes flared with both anger and tension.

He smiled, stroked his thumb across her smooth cheek. "Don't worry. It doesn't turn me on. It just annoys me. But she looked at us in the mirror and said we made a perfect couple. She tried to pass it off like she meant us as a touring act, but I knew what she was doing." He whispered in her ear, "She's not as clever as you think."

Emmie let out a huff of breath, like she didn't believe him.

He continued. "But in that moment I thought, *this* is it, right here. This is what I want Emmie to understand. It's why you never have to worry about us. Because you see me, and for some reason I'm not going to question, you want to be with me. Piper, the others, they see what they want me to be. And it means nothing. Everyone's just trying to manipulate me, use me for their own purposes. You want me for me." He kissed her again. "And that's what I need."

She let out a shuddery breath, lifted up to meet his mouth, and kissed him.

She kissed him and kissed him and kissed him, the incredible softness of her mouth inciting a dangerous need within him. Desire pulsed through his body as her hands scraped across his scalp and her breasts pushed against his chest.

He shifted between her legs, because he had to feel her, had to press himself against her. Her hips arched, and his dick surged with intense need. Grabbing her hips, he pushed them down.

"We can't." He kissed her some more, losing himself in her sweet scent, the urgent thrust of her hips, the breathy whimpers that told him how desperately she needed him, too. All his edges blurred, and he didn't know how he was going to make it through the night without sinking into her.

As tightly as he held her, she wouldn't stop thrusting up into him. Their mouths fused, and he couldn't stop. He needed her, all of her. Her hands shifted down his back, pushing underneath the waistband of his gym shorts. "Fuck," he breathed into her mouth, trying to pull away, but she caught him to her again, wrapping her legs around him and squeezing, her hips grinding, rubbing. Through her cotton shorts, he could feel the shape of her, the hot indentation that beckoned him to slide inside.

His back bowed, breaking the hold her legs had on him. "We can't."

"I have to." Her hand pulled out of his shorts, came around between them, and rubbed his painfully hard erection. Grasping him and stroking him hungrily, her mouth licked and kissed her way down his chest. "God, I *have* to." She shoved his bottoms down, her hot breath at his navel, skimming lower and lower. Her tongue took a long, sexy swirl around his tattoo before traveling lower.

"No, Em." He shook her shoulder, but she ignored him, shucking his bottoms off his hips and taking his aching cock into her hot, hungry mouth. She sucked him in deep, making his body jerk, and then drew him out slowly, her tongue dancing and licking around him. Christ, liquid heat shot through his veins, and he didn't know how the hell he was supposed to not move.

Her hand gripped him at his base while her mouth sucked him to the back of her throat, her tongue working him madly.

If he didn't thrust, he'd go insane. It was too much, too intense. But if he moved, everyone would know what was happening in his bunk. He couldn't embarrass Emmie that way, but Christ, she felt so good. Her hunger for him, the insane suction, the tightness of her fist, the slick heat of her mouth. He couldn't take it anymore. With as much control as he could muster, he pumped his hips, careful to create as little movement as possible. His fingers curled into her silky hair, and he let himself go, let himself feel everything she did to him. He was close, so fucking close.

And then her hands cupped his ass, pushing him deeper down her throat, so deep his balls pulled in tight, his spine tingled, and then his body went rigid as he exploded into her succulent mouth. He was out of control, pumping his hips, desperate to finish without making a sound, but . . . *Christ.*

She licked him clean, kissed the tip of his cock, then crawled back up to him with those needy, urgent hands running all over his chest. He enfolded her in his arms and crushed her to him.

"You're shaking," she whispered so quietly he barely heard. Or maybe the blood roaring through his veins drowned out her voice.

"Yeah. You do that to me."

"You make me crazy." She moved restlessly against him, her arms sliding over his chest, along his biceps, down his stomach, sweeping around to his back. It was like she wanted to feel his every muscle. Her body trembled, pulled taut with need.

He'd never felt this connection with anyone before. "Don't give up on me, Emmie."

"I'm not."

He couldn't bear to lose her. He loved her. He loved her so much. His hand pushed under her shirt, reveling in all that warm, smooth skin. He slowly moved up her stomach, fingers tracing her ribs, until he cupped her breast, causing her back to bow and a hiss of breath to escape from her lips. His thumb brushed over the sexy little tip, and he thrilled at the feel of it beading at his touch.

And then they were kissing again, wilder than before, as she arched into his hand. He loved her breasts, loved their softness, the weight of them, the hard bead rubbing against his palm.

"Jonny." She whispered his name like a plea.

He slid his hand between her legs, and she spread open for him, her body trembling. He stroked into her curls, and the moment he found her slick, hot center, desire shot through him like a bolt of lightning. One slow stroke across her clit had her gasping, and he covered her mouth with his to quiet her.

But she tore away. "I can't," she whispered in his ear, clutching him to her, writhing against him. "Oh, God, I can't."

His finger made slow swirls around and over the sensitive nub, and she was bucking, grabbing for his hair, clutching fistfuls.

"Oh, my God," she said, giving a tiny little cry that made him smile against her mouth.

"You're so fucking beautiful." He plunged his fingers inside of her, curling them so they rubbed against her spongy wall, and all the while his thumb continued to circle her honey-soaked clit.

She buried her face against his shoulder, biting down into his flesh. Her body jerked, stiffened, then rocked against him for long, sensuous moments as he continued to stroke her until she gasped and collapsed against him.

She blew out a slow breath, hitching her shorts back up and straightening her top. "Do you think anybody heard?" she asked, one hand on his cheek.

She was adorable.

Emmie stood in front of the grimy mirror in the truck stop bathroom and tried to tame her messy hair. While the just-got-laid look made her feel pretty damn hot, she didn't think she should show up for the band meeting flaunting it. So, she pulled her hair back into a ponytail. Zipping her toiletry bag, her teeth feeling clean, her mouth tasting minty, she turned to go. Just then the door opened and in walked Piper Lee.

Jeez. Even without makeup, she was just as pretty, just as glamorous. All that long, straight, shiny hair. Her lean figure in black leggings, expensive black ballet flats, and a tight black tank that accentuated her high, perky breasts. How could any guy resist her?

Funny how Emmie worked with the biggest names in the business, but no one made her as uneasy as this one woman. In New York City, at Amoeba Records, Emmie felt powerful. Respected. But this woman? She sucked the power right out of everyone in the room, drawing it into her own core.

Well, Emmie would take it right back. "Morning." *She'd* slept in Slater's bed. He'd told *her* he loved her. This woman did not have any power over Emmie or her and Slater's relationship unless Emmie gave it away.

A smile bloomed over Piper's elegant features. "Oh, hey. So glad you got to spend some time with the guys. You must really miss them." She gave a pitying expression that said, *Your loss.*

Yeah, Emmie missed the guys. But the way Piper looked at Emmie made her question whether or not the guys missed her. With their crazy schedule, all the press and travel . . .

Emmie wanted to smack her head against the mirror. Score! Piper was so freaking good at this game, making Emmie question whether or not the guys missed her. How did Piper *do* that?

No, no, no. The guys *did* miss Emmie. She remembered how they'd gathered around her table last night, the easy banter, the warm exchange. She had an unquestionable bond with them.

"But don't you worry about a thing. I'm taking good care of them." Piper breezed past, her subtle perfume floating in the air around them, and reached for the handle of a stall.

"That gives me peace of mind." Emmie's voice rang out in the windowless bathroom. "Thank you."

Piper cast a glance over her shoulder, her expression unreadable. Clearly trying to figure out the coded message. *Well, guess what? There is none.*

Not playing.

"Hope the rest of the tour goes great." Emmie strode out of the bathroom. "See you."

Emmie came out of that bathroom and leaned against the rack of potato chips. She could see why Slater found managing her and Piper so exhausting.

*   *   *

When Emmie boarded the bus, she found all the guys but Pete sitting on the couches. The guys talked easily, as though last night's tension hadn't happened. Slater's gaze latched onto her, watching as she sat next to her brother for a moment.

"Do you want me to wait upstairs?" she asked Derek.

"Not at all. You're part of us, Em."

Cooper leaned forward, touching her knee. "Hey. I don't remember much about last night, but I know from Slater's ugly face that we fucked up. You're the best, and I hope I didn't say anything to insult or . . ." He looked away, all sad and regretful. "Hurt you," he said quietly.

"It's okay. We're good."

The toilet flushed, and Pete came right out of the bathroom.

"Wash your fucking hands," Slater said.

"Didn't your mother teach you anything?" Ben called, smiling.

Emmie took that opportunity to cross the aisle and sit beside Slater. His hand wrapped around her waist, pulling her in tight.

Pete came back out, balling up a paper towel. He tossed it at Slater, who easily ducked.

"Okay, let's get this done." Derek stood up, leaned against the wall, his powerful arms crossed over his T-shirt-clad chest. "So, Slater and I talked this morning. We thought we should be more specific about what it means to behave professionally. We've got a list here." He nodded to a piece of paper on one of the small tables. She recognized her brother's messy scrawl.

"Just so we're all on the same page. It's more than just the drug and groupie issues. It's how we conduct ourselves. So far we've been acting like a bunch of teenage—"

"Forget it," Ben said. "I'm in. I agree completely. I feel like an asshole. I thought it would be fun, but it isn't. I mean, it is. In a way. But I don't want to feel like an asshole every day of my life." He looked down at his bare feet. "That said, I reserve the right to fuck groupies. But discreetly and not all the time. I know how I've been acting."

"I agree," Cooper said. "Truth is, dude, I don't even know what we said last night. I remember nearly peeing in my pants when you came at Pete, but I don't remember what we were talking about."

"Pete accused Slater of fucking Piper," Ben said.

Pete's gaze shot right to Emmie, and she let him know with a gentle smile that she forgave him.

"Oh, fuck, Em." Pete scrubbed his face with his hands. "I'm sorry. He hasn't . . ." He looked to Slater, like he was judging what he should or shouldn't say. "He's been good, I swear."

"Leave it alone, Pete," Derek said.

"Fuck." Cooper ran a hand over his unshaved jaw. "I don't remember any of that. And that's fuckin' scary because, well, you know my mom's an addict, and . . . shit, I can't believe I even went there. I mean, growing up with that shit, I swore I'd never . . ." He blew out a breath, looking so sad and lost. Emmie reached across the table and took his hand, gave it a squeeze. He looked so forlorn. "I agree we need to stay focused, have a plan. I'm in."

"Well, I'm not a pussy," Pete said. "I want to get laid and do drugs." Everyone looked at him as though they couldn't believe what he was saying. "But I want to be a fuckin' rock star more. So, yeah, I'm in. But, like Ben, I reserve the right to get laid. I can be discreet, though, like Slater—" His eyes went wide. "Sorry. Shit."

"It's fine," Emmie said. "I know what he did before he met me."

"Yeah, well, I know what I said last night, but the thing is, Slater, you always kept it clean and discreet. You played it right."

Slater's hand curled into a fist on the table, the big muscles in his arms flexing. He looked ready to pounce.

"Besides, you're the talent behind this whole operation. If you go, we've got nothing." Pete shot a look to Derek. "No offense. We couldn't do it without you, either. But I agree we're not going to get where we want to go unless we're focused and professional. So, yeah, I'm in."

Slater sat back in his seat, body tense, hard. Shouldn't he be happy? They'd gotten the coveted prize—the record contract. Something was wrong. She could feel the tension thrumming in him.

She turned to face him. Their gazes caught, held, and the fear she saw in his eyes shot right to her heart.

In that moment, she got it. What this news meant. The guys were signing with a record label. Everything would change now. Once they signed, their lives went into overdrive. Tours, endless studio hours cutting tracks, constant promotion.

He was worried about her. She tried to give him a reassuring smile, wanted him to enjoy the dream he was finally living.

But she knew. He was right to worry.

This new direction? It didn't involve Emmie at all.

In line for security, Emmie's phone rang. She couldn't answer it, though. She had to untie her boots—why had she worn lace-up boots to an airport?—and get her laptop out of her messenger bag. Her phone buzzed. She'd grabbed a bin, set it on the conveyor, and started to load it with her boots, when a second text came in. *Okay, something's up.*

She gave a sheepish grin to the family in line behind her, motioning them to go ahead. Gathering her items into her arms, she set the bin back on the stack. She had to drop her boots, let go of the handle of her carry-on in order to dig her phone out of the inside pocket of her messenger bag. Six new texts.

All from Slater. Don't fucking ignore me.

She checked the one before it.

You have to talk to me. You can't just leave a text
like that.

Like what? What text was he talking about? They'd had a great good-bye in the cab just minutes ago. They'd kissed so passionately, he'd had her laid out on the backseat.

She scrolled back in their conversation, found the one she'd written while watching him onstage the night before. When she'd told him to continue to write with Piper. How could that possibly make him angry?

Well, she couldn't get back to him just then. She'd call him when she got settled at her gate.

The moment she reached for the bin, she heard his voice shouting her name across the airport. Adrenaline shot through her, and she turned to find him racing up the escalator toward the security line, a guard moving in to block him. The last thing she needed was an airport scene. She quickly shot off a text.

Stop. I'll be right there. Don't yell.

The security guard reached him just as he pulled up his phone and read her text. God, what was the matter with him? Towering over the armed guard, Slater's chest heaved as he trained his fiery gaze on her. He'd better control himself. She could just imagine him getting cuffed in the airport.

"Can you excuse me, please?" She smiled apologetically at the people around her as she pushed through them, cutting straight across the zigzagging line. Lugging her boots, carry-on, and messenger bag, she ducked underneath the rope to get to him.

"What the hell, Emmie?"

God, he looked so fearsome, his cheeks enflamed.

"I don't know what your problem is." She stood before him, sweating, arms aching from carrying all her belongings.

"What the fuck was that text?"

"Is there a problem here?" the security guard asked.

Slater never took his fierce gaze off her.

"No," Emmie said. "Sorry. We'll go over here and talk." She gave Slater a stern look and then headed toward the far wall. He snatched the handle of her luggage and strode ahead.

The moment she reached the wall, he grabbed her boots, dropped them on the floor. His anger rolled over her, pressing in on her. "What the fuck, Em? Did you break up with me?"

"What? How did you make the leap from me backing off about the whole Piper thing to me dumping you?"

He played with his phone, bringing up the original text. "If you love something, set it free?" He moved in menacingly. "I don't want you to set me free. I want you to own me. I want you to fucking possess me. How do you not understand what I want? How the fuck did anything I say or do in the past twenty-four hours lead you to believe I wanted my *freedom*?"

Own him? Possess him? Could he make her any hotter? Perspiration beaded over her lip, and sweat trickled between her breasts. "I could seriously have sex with you right here and now."

"What?" He backed off, jamming his phone in his jeans' pocket and scratching the back of his neck. "Are you high? I don't have any idea what's going on here."

Jerking on the strap of her messenger bag, she pushed it behind her so that nothing stood between them. Her fingers curled into his belt loops, and she tugged him forward, making him stumble into her. Heat ignited in his eyes.

"That song you wrote with Piper? That was great. I mean, really great. Jonny, you need to write songs like that, and if that means you write with Piper, then you write with Piper. You're going to be a superstar. I want you to be happy. I don't want to be the person who limits you or makes demands. The only way we can last—the only hope for us to even have a good relationship—is if I let you go. So I was telling you not to worry about my insecurities. If you want to work with Piper, then work with her. If something happens . . . then, I don't know, we deal with it."

"Nothing will ever happen."

"I'm just saying that if it did—theoretically—then I'll have to deal with it. But we're never going to work if I make up a list of things you can and can't do based on my fear of what might happen. That's not healthy. I'm saying do what you need to do and don't worry about me. Because I . . ." She held his gaze, her body heating up, her pulse quickening. "I love you. I want to be with you."

"You love me?" His smile transformed him from badass to little boy.

She nodded, running her hand through his soft, silky hair.

The tension left his body. "You freaked me the fuck out."

"I'm sorry. I meant it in a good way."

"Jesus, Em. I thought you were dumping me."

"I sent it last night. You just saw it now?"

"You were with me all weekend. Why would I look at my phone?"

"You and Derek are so lame. You need smartphones. You're big boys now."

He ran a hand through his hair. "Listen. I'm not *something*. And what's the point of loving someone if your feelings are dull enough to say you're willing to set them free? I want you to want me so completely you'd engage in hand-to-hand combat with a pack of sex-starved groupies to hold on to me. I don't believe in fate. I believe in working hard for the things I want, and I want you more than anything I've ever wanted in my life. So I'm not going to *set you free* in the hope fate means for us to last. We're going to last because we take hold of each other and hang on with all we've got. Jobs come and go, money doesn't bring happiness, and when I die, the only thing I know I get to keep is my love for you. Are we clear?"

She belted her arms around his waist, hugged him tightly. "Very, very clear."

"Say it again."

"I love you."

"Now that's what I'm talking about."

She could feel the tension leave his muscles as he curled around her, burrowing his face into her neck.

TWENTY

The moment Emmie entered the house, she aban-doned her suitcase, tossed her jacket on the couch, and called Irwin.

He answered his private line right away. "Emmie Valencia, please tell me you've changed your mind."

"No, but I'm about to change yours. Eric's offered Snatch a contract."

"I heard every word in that last sentence except the third."

"Irwin."

"Yes, yes, I'm on it."

"Meaning . . ."

"Meaning you win."

"You'll sign them?"

"Yes."

"I can't believe this. I'm so excited. This is amazing. This is the best news ever. What convinced you?"

"The video you sent me."

"That was over a month ago."

"Indeed."

"So, you've known since then?"

"Quite right. So, let's talk about what really matters. When are you coming back?"

"You're promoting me?"

The pause made her spirits deflate.

"Irwin?"

"Emmie, are you still sleeping with the singer?"

She collapsed on the couch. "How did you find out?"

"Those cookies you made were delicious. Why didn't you ever make them for me?"

"I never had time." Of course. Some promotions guy told Irwin all about the care packages she'd been sending the guys. "You went to see Wicked Beast in Albuquerque?"

"That's what I love about you. You're sharp as a tack."

"Irwin. Come on, I didn't introduce you to the band because of the singer or my brother. They're the most talented act I've seen. And I've kept you apprised of everything I've done to get them where they are."

"You have." He mumbled something to someone, then got back on the line. "Em, I have never doubted your capabilities."

"Not that it's any of your business, but I've slept with exactly two guys in my life."

"All the more reason to limit the number of bands you work with."

"I've earned this promotion."

"As long as you're sleeping with Slater Vaughn, you're not going to be their A&R coordinator."

"Irwin, please. I want to be part of this. It means so much to me. And I've *earned* it."

"You will be part of it. Through your brother and your boyfriend. Look, even if you weren't engaging in unspeakable acts with the singer, you simply can't work with your brother. The ties are too sticky."

Oh, dammit, dammit, dammit. "What about Piper? Are you going to sign her?"

"I suspect so."

"Is she . . ." God, she hated how much she wanted an answer to her question. "Do you think she's talented?"

"Janis Joplin."

"What? She doesn't sound anything like Janis Joplin. She certainly doesn't look like her."

"Which makes her even better because she's bloody gorgeous, her voice is sultry and powerful, and she's a superstar onstage. Her musical ability reminds me of Joplin, the way she absorbs a variety of musical influences and mixes them together like an alchemist to create her own style. It's genius. She's fresh. She's ballsy. And not only from an artistic point of view. She's a terror of a businesswoman."

"Why don't you marry her instead of signing her?"

"Well. Isn't this *fascinating*? In all my years with you, I've never seen your claws come out. I never even knew you had them. Where is this coming from?"

"I don't understand why you're hesitating if you think she's all that."

"I haven't met with her yet."

"You haven't met with Snatch yet, either."

"I certainly have."

"You have?"

"You've lived with them. You've worked with them. I know all I need to know."

He trusted her implicitly. That might have been the highest compliment ever paid to her.

And that and $3.50 could buy her a medium decaf latte.

Stepping out of the shower, Emmie heard the distant ring of the phone.

Who would call on the house phone?

She snatched the towel off the rack, wrapped it around her, and tore out of the bathroom. Racing down the stairs, she skidded at the turn into the kitchen. She answered breathlessly. "Hello?"

"Em?" She could hear excited chatter and hollering in the background.

"Jonny?" *Yes.* He'd heard the news. Her heart pounded as she waited for him to share. Nothing had been harder than keeping such important news from him.

"Let me talk to her," she heard Derek say.

"Why the fuck didn't you tell us?" Sounded like Ben.

"Fucking *Irwin Ledger*?" Definitely Pete.

"Love you, Emmie." Cooper.

And then someone started singing "You Light up My Life," and they all started cracking up.

"Okay, okay, back the fuck up," she heard Slater say. Slowly, their voices receded. "Em?"

"Yeah." Her face hurt from smiling so hard. She was so happy for him. For all of them.

"Why didn't you tell me?"

"Irwin made me promise not to. Not until he was sure."

He went quiet. Her fingers curled tightly around the phone, wishing so badly she could be with him. "You okay?" she asked.

He let out a shaky breath.

"This is pretty cool, huh?" she prompted.

Still, he didn't answer.

"It's where you guys belong. Top label, top A&R guy. I promise you, Irwin will take you where you guys should go."

She waited, not quite sure what Slater was feeling or thinking. But she had a sense he was overwhelmed, maybe thinking about his dad. Thinking about his future—Irwin would make them into huge stars.

"I love you," he finally said.

And her breath caught in her throat because he'd been thinking about *her*.

"None of this," he said. "None of it would've happened without you." His voice so low, so gravelly, she had to press the phone to her ear to hear him.

"Let me talk to her," Derek said, right before distortion sounded in her ear. "Emmie?"

"I'm so happy for you, Derek." But her heart, her mind, her whole essence was still with Slater. God, she wanted to be with him so badly. Share this moment in person.

"I can't believe you did this for me. I swear to fucking God, you are gold. Pure gold. Fucking hell. Amoeba. Irwin. This is . . ." He blew out a breath. "It doesn't get better than this."

"I know. But Derek, you have to know, you did this. It's your talent. You're one of the best damn bass guitarists in the business."

He was quiet for a moment. And then, "Fuck," scraped out of his throat. "That means fucking everything to me."

She knew.

He cleared his throat. "So, does this mean you're moving back to the city?"

"He's not promoting me, so, no. I'll stay until I discover a different band."

"What the fuck? You've got to be kidding me? *You* made all this happen."

"Okay, let's not go there right now. Let's just be happy with today's news." She wouldn't ruin their good news by telling them *why* Irwin wouldn't promote her. "So, what's next?"

"Em, I'm going to make it happen for you. Not now. I haven't even signed yet, but after I do, I'm going to make sure you work with us. Only you."

She appreciated his conviction, but he wouldn't have that kind of power for years. Besides, she'd make it for herself. Of course she would. "It's okay, Derek. It'll work out for me, too. Alex has a band for me to see that he's sure I'll love. So, talk to me. What did Irwin say is next for you guys?"

"He's flying us out to New York City the week after next. Wants us out there for the weekend. Wine and dine us—"

Her stomach gave a sharp twist. "I know exactly what he'll do for you." She didn't want to think of her brother—the little boy who'd run out of the room at the first sight of the flying monkeys in the *Wizard of Oz*—doing the disgusting things the Amoeba guys would provide for Snatch. But she *really* couldn't bear to think about Slater surrounded by all that decadence.

"You should come out, too."

"Weekend after this one?"

"Yeah."

"I can't. That's when I'm checking out the band Alex told me about. Plus, Tiana's got something planned for my birthday on Friday night. But, no, believe me, you guys won't want me around for that."

"You know what, Em?"

"What?"

"I'm partying with you on your birthday."

"What? No. You just said you have to be in the city."

"I'll fly to Austin on Friday, then fly to New York City Saturday morning."

"You can't just make those decisions. If Irwin wants you on Friday—"

"He hasn't given us firm plans yet. Besides, let me worry about that."

"That's sweet, but you don't have to come out here."

"Fuck that. Mom and Dad never did anything for you. Everything revolved around Dad and his fucking world. Besides, none of this would be happening without you. None of it. I *want* to be there. I know it hasn't been an easy time for you lately, and the last thing I want is for you to spend your birthday alone in Austin."

"I'm not alone. I'll be with Tiana."

"Can I talk to my girl now?" she heard Slater say.

"Hang on," Derek said to Slater. And then to Emmie, "Listen, the guy who used to be my idol, who's now become this pussywhipped sad sack, wants to talk to you. But, Em, I'm going to see you Friday night. You don't get it. You're the only one who's ever believed in me. And you are single-handedly responsible for today, this moment, when I got the call I never thought I'd get. So, fuck yeah, I'm gonna be with you on your birthday. Oh, and Em?"

"Yeah?"

"Thank you."

"You're welcome, Derek. I'm happy for you."

"And that's the thing. I know you are. That's the most amazing thing. No matter what's going on for you, no matter what *you* want, you're out there thinking about me, making my dreams come true."

"Now who's the sad sack?" Slater said. "Give me the damn phone before she loses all respect for you." She could hear the change of hands, a rustling in the earpiece. "Em?"

"Hey. So happy for you."

"How come you didn't tell me about your birthday?"

"I never make a big deal about it. Tiana's taking me out to dinner, that's all."

"Well, it's a party now. We'll all fly out."

"Fuck yeah," she heard Pete call.

The guys talked about it in the background and seemed pretty insistent.

"You're making it a way bigger deal than it needs to be. The only thing you should be worried about is getting signed. You guys all need to be there."

"We will. We'll just be there on Saturday instead of Friday."

"Slater."

"I'll check with Irwin. But I doubt he'll mind. He kinda digs you. Now, stop arguing and let Tiana know the reservation's just gone from two to seven."

"You're sweet." She wouldn't get her hopes up. "Hey, how come you guys called on the house phone?"

"We got our big-boy phones today."

"Oh, my God, you got a smartphone? So why didn't you call me on it?"

"We don't know your cell number."

She laughed. "Didn't you have them transfer your information onto the new phone?"

"They can do that?"

"Jonny." She dropped into the kitchen chair, tugging the towel over her legs. "Go back to the store tomorrow and have them make the transfer. They should've done it automatically."

"We kind of overwhelmed them."

"I'll bet you did." He was kind of an overwhelming guy. She drew in a sharp breath. "So. Here it comes. The big time. Just like you always wanted."

He didn't say anything.

And neither did she. She was happy for them—truly. But where did it leave her? Even when she'd quit her job, she hadn't felt this scared, this . . . desperate. Like she was running out of time.

Like if she didn't make something happen for herself *right now*, she'd be left behind.

Happy birthday to me.

Seated in a high-backed leather chair in a fancy downtown Austin restaurant, Emmie smiled for Tiana's camera phone.

"You look gorgeous, girl." Tiana looked at the screen. "He's going to love this."

More likely, Slater wouldn't see it until morning, considering how busy Piper would keep him tonight.

The waiter appeared yet again. "Are you ready to order?"

Tiana glanced toward the hostess stand. "Can you just give us five more minutes?"

"Are we waiting for someone?" Emmie had wondered about the extra place setting.

Tiana just smiled. "I'm just not used to eating in places like this. I keep waiting for the bouncer to throw me out."

"We didn't need to go so fancy." Emmie looked around the hushed restaurant, the patrons' features bathed in the yellow glow of candlelight.

"Oh, come on. You deserve the best. Besides, I'm not paying."

Emmie's stomach plummeted. She hadn't found someone to sublet her place in the city because her roommates kept blowing off showings. And, while she didn't have many expenses, she had nothing coming in. The last thing she'd choose to spend money on was a fancy dinner.

"Look at your face. Jeez, girl, I'm not making you pay for your own dinner. Slater is."

"Slater?"

"Yeah, it's on him. He feels bad about not being able to come. That's why he made me promise to send a picture." She lifted her phone.

"That was nice of him." Her voice sounded as flat as she felt.

"Oh, girl. You are bumming so hard. It's breaking my heart."

"No, no. I totally I understand why he can't come." She wasn't angry at Slater, but she couldn't stand Piper Lee.

"That bitch is crazy. She's got serious cojones."

"Yeah, but she's incredibly good at what she does. I just hate the power she has over him." As soon as Slater told Piper the band would be coming to Austin for Emmie's birthday, Piper went and planned a huge signing party for them on the same night. She'd invited everyone—MTV, *Rolling Stone*, even *Beatz*, the music news blog that was *the* source for music news and gossip in the industry. It was the first site everyone in the industry checked when they woke up in the morning.

Even if the idea was brilliant—and she had no doubt it would catapult the band to immediate fame—Emmie still hated that Piper had deliberately planned it to keep Slater away from her.

Whatever. It was done. And it would do great things for the band. Besides, she had momentum of her own. "Hey, I've got great news." She paused. "I've got an interview."

Confusion flashed over Tiana's features. "You're getting a job here? In Austin?"

"No. New York. And it's just one of many I'm setting up."

"You're *leaving* Austin?"

Emmie shrugged, trying hard to ignore the twist in her stomach. "I have to. Come on, Tiana, you know I can't wait around anymore."

"Does Slater know?"

She shook her head. "I'll tell him on Monday. Let him enjoy this weekend. It's such a big deal, getting signed. We can talk about it after." She stuck her nose in her menu, determined to block out her emotions, if just for tonight. "So, what looks good?"

"Emmie?" one of the most familiar voices in the world called.

She looked up, and happiness burst inside her chest at the sight of her big, bad brother striding toward her. In his worn jeans, tight white T-shirt, and leather wristbands, he looked completely out of place in the elegant restaurant. Bolting out of her seat, she threw herself into his arms. "I can't believe you're here."

He rocked her back and forth. "Wouldn't have missed it for the world." They pulled apart, and he handed her a beautiful bouquet of flowers.

She breathed them in. "Thank you."

"That's from me." They sat down, and he handed her a pretty gift box. "And this is from Slater."

She held his gaze, so grateful he'd come for her birthday. If only . . . she wished she could stop the thoughts from coming, but she couldn't help wondering why Derek was here and not her boyfriend. When she saw a hint of pity, she quickly looked away,

"Open it," he said.

She slid the box aside. "Later. So, how come you're here? Shouldn't you be at the party?"

He shrugged, then leaned back as the waiter filled his water glass. "This is where I want to be."

It was that simple. Somehow for Slater, though, it wasn't. No, no. She knew he needed to be at the party.

Derek's hand closed over hers. The cold of his metal rings seeped under her skin. "Believe me, he'd rather be here."

"He has to be at the party. I know that." Her gaze flicked over to Tiana, catching the look of pity in her eyes, too. "Guys, stop. You're the ones making a bigger deal out of this birthday than I am. Of course he has to be at the party. I'm fine."

"Oh, my God, open the present." Tiana pushed the box toward Emmie.

Emmie slid it aside. "I will, but let's order before that poor waiter loses his mind. He's been hovering around us for half an hour."

"Yeah, sorry about that," Derek said. "We sat on the tarmac for, like, six days." He gulped down his water and picked up his menu. His eyes practically popped out of his head. "Are you fucking with me?" He looked between her and Tiana. "Salmon belly? Is that for real?" He read more, and then his head reared back. "Okay, I am not fucking eating some animal's tongue." He looked around the restaurant. "No offense, but whose idea was this place?"

"It was mine, asshole." Tiana smacked him with the menu.

"Tiana, have you met Emmie?" Derek leaned forward, head tilted, as he eyed her incredulously. "She doesn't eat this shit."

Tiana smirked. The three of them burst out laughing.

"We're out of here." Derek pushed his chair back so harshly the jarring sound made the patrons around them turn to look.

"We can't just leave." Tiana looked mortified.

"Why the fuck not?" He pulled his wallet out of his back pocket and tossed a twenty on the table. "It's my sister's birthday. Let's show her some fun."

By the time Emmie got home at three in the morning, her feet ached. But she didn't care because she'd actually managed to spend the last several hours not thinking about any of her problems. She'd had fun.

As Derek locked up the house, she turned to him. "Thank you, Derek. You made it an amazing birthday."

"Nowhere else I'd rather be."

Why didn't Slater feel that way? *Stop it.* Seriously, she had to stop doing that.

His features pinched in concern, and he came right up to her. "Hey, he loves you, Em. He wanted to be with you."

"*You* came home," she said softly.

"Okay, but I'm telling you, Slater tried. He took it to the wall. But when he told Piper he was coming out here tonight, she threatened to cancel the party. He's the hot lead singer— the reason to do a story on our band." Derek shrugged. "She had him by the balls. Now open the present. I want to know what a guy like Slater would get a woman like you."

She'd left it in the car all night as they'd gone from go-kart racing to the batting cage to line dancing. She just . . . wasn't ready to open it. "Later."

His laugh sounded bitter. "I'm the same way. It's because our parents always disappointed us. Did they even pay attention? I remember asking for a Fender one year, and I got a Razor scooter. A fucking *scooter.*"

She smiled, so glad her brother understood her. "I got a box of gift cards one year. I swear Mom must've been at CVS and suddenly remembered it was my birthday. She had to have grabbed one of every kind on the rack because I even had one for Outback Steakhouse." Steak lover she was *not*.

Derek shook his head. "They sucked. What'd they send you this year?"

"Mom gave me a gift card for Amazon."

"Well, she's consistent. And Dad?"

"He sent me an e-card."

"That fucker." He brought Emmie in for a hug. "I have no idea what Slater got you, but I don't think he disappointed you. He digs you, Em. He's never been this way before."

"I know." Given the shape of the box, it wasn't jewelry. And she hoped he hadn't gotten her lingerie—that just seemed too skeezy. What did she want from him? What would make her happy? She honestly didn't know.

She only knew she didn't think she could handle any more disappointment from him.

"Open it."

"I will. When I get upstairs." They hugged good night, and then she went to her room.

Teeth brushed, face washed, Emmie turned off the light and headed for bed. The glow of the computer screen reminded her she'd forgotten to shut it down, so she went to her desk. Hand reaching for the mouse, she brushed against the gift.

Just open it.

Such an odd-size box—like a can of soup could fit in it. She couldn't think of a single thing he'd get her in that shape. Maybe a snow globe? She tore off the paper—a couple of hot pink flyers announcing their show in Chicago—and found a plain white box. Opening it, she found a red lid. She pulled out the can of chocolate fudge frosting and smiled, remembering what she'd told him all those months ago.

At the bottom of the box was a handwritten note.

I want to be your frosting—all good things to you and for you. Slater.

Clutching the can to her chest, she laughed. She'd been so worried he'd disappoint her—but he hadn't. He always shot through her fears and landed right in the center of her heart.

God, of course she understood why he'd chosen the party over coming to Austin. Honestly, she'd never cared about her birthday anyway.

Her fingers brushed the mouse so she could shut down her computer, and the screen came to life. The party photographs were probably up already, so she'd quickly log on to the *Beatz* site before calling him.

Immediately, she saw Slater's face, as gorgeous as a movie star. Emmie's breath caught in her throat at the vision of Piper Lee wrapped around him like a lover. Both of them laughing. Glamorous, gorgeous, sparkling people.

Falling into the chair, her gaze caught on another image.

Oh, my God. Her blood turned sluggish, and she heard a ringing in her ears.

Slater wouldn't do that.

He wouldn't.

She had to squint a little to make sure she was actually seeing what she thought. It didn't make sense on any level, and yet . . .

Feet pounded up the stairs, and her door flung open so hard it hit the wall.

"Fuck." Derek stood in her room, all wild energy. "Tell me that's not Caroline?"

She wanted to turn and acknowledge him, but her neck

wouldn't move. It was like her mind had completely disconnected from her body. She told her fingers to click to the next
image on the screen, but communication had shut down.

"Is it? Is it fucking Caroline Ledger?" Derek stood behind
her. "It can't be what it looks like."

Of course it could. These were pictures. A photograph
simply captured an image. It didn't invent one.

"He wouldn't do that," he said quietly.

Her blood started flowing again as anger crept under her
skin. "Do what, exactly?" She pointed to the picture of a
naked Caroline Ledger draped across Slater Vaughn's chest.
Her face was nuzzled into his neck, her legs wrapped around
his waist. "He wouldn't hold a naked Caroline?" Her brother
was going to defend him?

Like she hadn't seen it happen dozens of times over the
years? Even the nice guys, the ones new to the business, even
they succumbed. With enough liquor in them, they got worked
up from all the wildness around them. Come on, naked women,
hands roaming. Even good guys got carried away in the heat of
the moment. She remembered that first night she'd met Slater.
He'd stood at the bar as the girls gathered around him, touching
him, grabbing him. And he hadn't minded at all. Hadn't been
the least bit uncomfortable when the blonde had actually
stroked him in front of his bandmates, in front of her.

She didn't think Slater had *slept* with Caroline, but so
what? The girl was naked and in his arms. He'd participated
in . . . things.

"We gotta get this down before Irwin sees it." Derek
crouched beside her.

She let out a shaky breath. "Irwin's already seen it." That
she knew for sure.

Derek placed his hand on her shoulder. "Are you okay?"

He thought she was upset about Caroline and Slater. Ha.
He'd missed the point entirely.

He gave her a gentle shake. "Em?"

But her attention remained riveted to the images. One
after another—they just got worse and worse.

"Fuck, Em." He tried to bat her hand away, to stop her from
clicking through the photos, but she nudged him aside. "Shit."

Slater and Piper. Piper and Slater. Hosting a party together.

Arm in arm. Her head resting on his shoulder. Them laughing hard together.

And the quotes? "Slater and I . . ."

"We wrote that one together."

"When the tour ends, we're . . ."

"Piper's talent goes beyond songwriting. She's fucking brilliant. We . . ."

We. We. We. We. Piper and Slater. *We.*

And then the worst one of all. "Jonny and I . . ."

Pain burst in her chest. Jonny? Piper called him *Jonny*? How well did she know him? Had he asked her to call him Jonny? The image flew up into her mind of Piper leaning against him in the lounge, both of them laughing easily together.

Oh, God. He wasn't just hers anymore. He was Piper's, too. That special intimacy was shattered.

About to close the laptop, her gaze snagged on a caption. Underneath the biggest shot of all, the centerpiece of the article, it said: "Piper Lee and Slater Vaughn: The Angelina Jolie and Brad Pitt of the Music Industry."

TWENTY-ONE

Hard raps jerked him awake. Slater's head lifted, and pain exploded in his skull.

"Fuck." His body felt weighted down by sandbags, his stomach roiled. Holy shit, he'd definitely had too much to drink last night. The pounding on the door continued.

"Slater?"

Derek. What was he so pissed about? Slater's heart pounded, thinking he might be late for the big meeting. His gaze shot to the alarm clock—eleven twenty. The meeting didn't start until one. He was fine.

"Goddammit, Slater, so help me God, you better be in there. *Alone.*"

Slater slid his legs out of bed, planting them on the floor. But the head rush knocked him back. "Hang on."

"Open the fucking door, you asshole."

Asshole? How was he an asshole? He'd missed Emmie's birthday to play rock star last night *for the band*. Confused, he got up, threw the locks, and yanked the door open. "What's your problem?"

Derek charged into the room, looking around like he was on the vice squad.

"What the fuck're you looking for?"

"Uh, Caroline Ledger?"

"I took her home hours ago. Why would you think she'd be in my room?"

Derek's hands cupped the sides of his head, and then he drew them back, plastering his hair to his skull. "Did you fuck her?"

Ice water flushed through Slater's veins. "Did I . . . of course I didn't. What kind of question is that?"

After taking several breaths, Derek's head tilted down. "Turn your phone on."

"Let me take a piss first."

"Now."

"Look, man, I don't know what's got you so worked up right now, but I haven't done anything wrong."

"We have a problem. You need to turn on your phone and go to the *Beatz* website."

"What happened?" Slater's mind played through the hundreds of flashes that had gone off last night. The dozens of times Piper had posed with him, grabbed his arm, held him close. "Shit. What did Emmie see?"

"Forget about Emmie. Right now, we have to worry about Irwin."

Slater's heart kicked into overdrive. His stomach plummeted. "No." The memory of him picking up a topless Caroline punched him in the gut. "Caroline?"

"Yes."

"Someone got a shot of it?" Slater dashed to the dresser, turned on his phone. "She was drunk off her ass. She started taking all her clothes off. I grabbed her and got her out of there before anyone could see."

"Wrong."

He'd done it for Emmie. From the moment Caroline had walked into the club, he'd had an eye out for her, remembering what Emmie had said about Irwin's wild daughter. His phone was taking forever to boot up. God, he hated these things. "Come on, come on."

Derek grabbed the phone from him, hit the right buttons, and scrolled down the screen. But before he could get to Caroline, Slater saw image after image of him with Piper. They looked like they were having the time of their lives. Shit, they looked like they were a couple. "I was doing my *job*."

"Congratulations, man. Knocked it out of the park." He kept scrolling.

"Stop." Slater's finger touched the screen, holding one image in place. Piper's arms belted around his waist, her head resting on his chest. They were both laughing, looking like lovers. And then in bold: "Piper Lee and Slater Vaughn: The Angelina Jolie and Brad Pitt of the Music Industry."

The full force of gravity slammed him down to the chair. "Emmie saw this?"

"Of course. Along with the whole fucking world."

"Fuck. Shit." He grabbed his phone out of Derek's hands and punched Emmie's speed dial.

"Forget it," Derek said.

Slater turned away from his friend, mind revving, heart thundering. The line rang.

Derek shook his shoulder. "Dude, not now. You have to handle Irwin."

Slater ignored him. *Come on, Emmie. Answer.*

"Slater." Derek tried to grab the phone back.

Slater nearly punched him. "Get the fuck off."

"Hello?" *Hello?* She answered his call with a stilted *hello*?

"Em, I didn't do anything with Caroline but bring her drunk ass home."

"Okay." She sounded distant, tired. "But I'm not the one you need to be worried about."

"You don't believe me. I hear it in your voice."

"First thing you need to do is get Piper to call her contact at *Beatz* and have them take down that picture of Caroline. The damage is already done, but you need to get it down right away. Then, you need to call Irwin. Don't lie to him. Just tell him straight up. He's used to Caroline's crap."

"Stop talking to me like I'm some business contact. I need you to—"

"You don't have time to worry about me. You have to do damage control."

"Emmie, Jesus, talk to me. You sound like a fucking robot."

Derek shoved him. "Don't talk to my sister like that. You're an asshole if you don't know what you've done to her."

"I was doing my job." He had to block out Derek, focus on Emmie. "You know I wanted to be with you last night. Piper threatened to cancel the party if I didn't show. I know what it looks like in those pictures, but it's not what happened."

"They're *photographs*, Slater. Images capture *what happens*. Therefore, it happened. But none of that matters right now. What matters is fixing this situation with Irwin. You don't want him as an enemy in this industry. Now, hang up with me and talk to Piper. Then get in touch with Irwin. You have to fix this. I have to go now."

"No, wait."

"Slater, stop. Believe it or not, Piper's the best thing that's ever happened to you."

"Bullshit. You're the best thing that ever happened to me."

"I might've helped you get to this point, but Piper will take you the rest of the way. Trust me, what she did—as long as you fix it with Irwin right away—will make you a household name."

Her words hit like a fist to his solar plexus, knocking the wind out of him. "I'm not talking about my fucking career."

"You should be. Come on, it's obvious how great you and Piper are together. I knew it from the start. Go with it, Slater, the whole Brangelina thing. You guys can be Sliper or Plater. You're the wordsmith. Come up with something great."

"Why are you talking like this?" He didn't even recognize her. Is this what she'd done after she'd walked in on Alex banging the twins? Gone on autopilot? "Stop this shit right now. There is no Piper and Slater."

"If you think PR isn't going to want to continue this sham, you're naïve. But, hey, why bother pretending? Why not just go for it? She's great at everything else. I'll bet she's dynamite in bed."

"No. No. No. I'll quit the band before I give you up. I love you, Emmie."

She went quiet. Had he broken through? Was she softening? He had to get through to her. "Em—"

"Good luck, Slater." And with that she disconnected.

Jesus, *good luck*? Like he was some guy she barely knew? She'd given up on him.

"Goddammit."

"Call Piper," Derek said.

Slater grabbed his gym bag, started stuffing his clothing inside.

"What are you doing?"

"I'm going to Austin."

"You're not going anywhere." Derek yanked the bag out of Slater's hands, tossed it across the room. "You're staying here and fixing this."

"I'm fixing things with Emmie first."

"The fuck you are."

"None of this other shit matters."

"You don't get it, do you?"

In the bathroom, he grabbed his toothbrush and razor. "Get what?"

Derek stood behind him in the mirror, holding his gaze. The intense and deadly look in his eye fused Slater's joints.

"You just blew up our record deal."

Derek couldn't have hurt him worse if he'd taken a tire iron to the side of his head.

Jesus Christ. He'd done it again. Gotten so close and then fucked it all up. Only this time it wasn't just his career. It was the guys. His brothers. He'd fucking failed them.

He was just like his dad.

"You're staying until you fix it. You owe us that."

"I'll call Irwin on the way to the airport. I will. But I have to fix things with Emmie first."

Slinging his duffel over his shoulder, he threw open the door and strode down the hall. Derek caught up with him, latching onto his arm and swinging him around.

"Slater."

That tone jerked him back. It wasn't just urgent. It held an undercurrent of pity.

"Listen to me," Derek said. "There's nothing to fix."

"Bullshit." Tearing out of his friend's hold, Slater continued on toward the elevator, hit the call button.

"She's done."

Slater's blood turned to ice, and he turned to face his friend.

"Seriously, man, I know my sister. She's done with you."

Frigid air hit him the minute the revolving door belched him out onto the street. Slater went right to the valet and asked for a cab. Derek was on him like a fucking leech.

"Get off me." Slater said it low, rough.

The cab pulled up, and Slater tossed his duffel onto the seat and slid in. Just as he reached for the door, Derek's arm came out, forcing it open. He climbed in.

"LaGuardia," Slater said.

At the same time Derek said, "Rockefeller Center."

The driver twisted around to give them a confused look.

"I'm going to the fucking airport."

Derek held up a finger to the driver. "We're going to Amoeba Records. We're talking to Irwin. Emmie's already talked to Caroline. She's agreed to meet us there."

"Great. Sounds like you've got it under control." To the cab driver, he said, "LaGuardia."

"No. You're the one who has to talk to Irwin. And you haven't even called Piper yet."

"I'll call her on the way to the airport."

"You'll call her now."

"You sure you want me to do that?" Slater gave Derek a hard look.

"Of course I'm sure."

"After what she's done to me, you want me to talk to her?"

"What did she do, man? Seriously? We couldn't even buy this kind of promo. What she did was pretty brilliant."

Slater had never in his life worked harder to tamp down rage. "She fucked with me. She fucked with my life." She cost him Emmie.

"Yeah, she did. But she's played you from the start. Don't tell me any of this shit comes as a surprise."

"Do you know how hard I've worked to manage the entire situation?" *While you got laid and loaded every night and had a great time?* "The only reason last night happened is because I was trying so hard to not fuck things up. You think it hasn't been killing me to balance that manipulative bitch against my career and my girlfriend? Jesus, fuck, Derek. You have no idea."

Slater blew out a breath, tilting his head back against the seat. He swallowed, pulled himself together. "Everything I've done, I've done for the band. Last night, I should've been with my girl. But I played my part. Because it got us press, just like you all wanted. We're a name now because of those pictures on that fucking blog. And it cost me my girl. Now get out of my cab and let me go work things out with her. You can do damage control here. You don't need me to do it."

"Not sure Irwin's gonna see it that way. Look, man, you're the one in the picture. You gotta make it right."

Reason burned through Slater's panic. The noise in his head settled down. He *was* the one who needed to tell Irwin what had happened last night. And he owed it to the guys to try and fix things. "Fine." He turned to the driver. "Rockefeller Center."

But by the end of this fucked-up day, he'd be in Austin with his girl.

Slater's hand shook as he tried to align the key with the lock. He couldn't get it in. Fuck, fuck, fuck. Pounding on the door, he shouted, "Emmie?" Okay, he had to calm down. He had to have his wits about him when he talked to her.

He got the key in, turned the lock, and pushed the door open. The emptiness hit him right away, and he almost didn't want to step inside.

Never in his life had he felt such a dead, lifeless room. All the air had been sucked out of it. "Emmie?" Dropping his bag, he noticed the raincoat she left on the hook by the door was gone. He tore through the house. Everything was neat and clean, barely lived in.

What the fuck? She'd *left* him? Why hadn't Derek told him that?

Fear spiked into the base of his spine, releasing an electrical current that stung his skin. It was a perfectly sunny day. Two coffee mugs sat on the counter, and the orange light of the coffeemaker was on.

Okay, okay. He was losing it. Maybe she *was* here. "Emmie," he snapped. He reached for the back door, remembering her skinny dipping all those months ago, how completely taken with her he'd been even then. It was locked, so he spun around and raced up the stairs. The door to her room stood wide open.

He felt death. The same cold fear he'd experienced when the police had come to the house with the news that his dad had died in a car crash.

He stepped into the empty room. No computer on the desk,

no framed photos on her dresser, no pink sweater on the back of her chair. A spot of red on the floor under the desk caught his attention. Crouching, he found the can of frosting he'd given her for her birthday.

Shit. He picked it up, then kicked open the closet to find nothing but hangers. On the floor he found a pair of sparkly flip flops, a white tank top, and a single hoop earring. He scooped up the earring, stuffed it in his pocket.

He thought he was going to die. It wasn't possible to live with this pain in his heart. He turned to the bed, noticed the rumpled sheets. Looked like she'd had a restless night.

Because of *him*.

Because of Piper. In all his life he'd never hated anyone. Hadn't cared enough about someone *to* hate them. But he hated Piper Lee. The idea of finishing out the tour with her . . . not going to happen.

He couldn't bear to be in Emmie's room, filled with her fresh, sweet scent, so he headed out into the hall, pushing open the bathroom door with one finger.

Stripped clean of his girl. She'd taken everything. All that was left in the damp shower stall was the small white bar of Dove soap that still held her lather.

Gone. His girl was gone.

Slater came back into the house after a five-mile run. Sweat dripped into his eyes. He lifted his T-shirt to swipe his face but found it soaked through. Wild frustration raged through him, and he slammed the door so hard it knocked a picture off the wall.

He tipped his head back. "Jesus Christ," he shouted.

Anxiety spun in his chest, creating a wall of sound so great he couldn't stand it.

He'd lost her. He'd fucking lost her.

Where had he gone wrong? He'd worked so hard to balance it all—the band, Piper, Emmie. He couldn't take it anymore. Yeah, it was three in the morning, but he couldn't bear her absence. He called her for the hundredth time. *Please, for God's sake, just answer the damn phone.*

"Yes?" She sounded exhausted.

"Emmie." Relief flooded him. "Emmie. Fuck."

She was quiet for too long. And then she took in a breath that sounded pained. "Listen, it's been a long day. I need to sleep."

"You moved out."

"Yes, I did."

"Why?"

"Can we talk tomorrow, please? I'm exhausted."

He hated that she didn't sound like his Emmie. That her voice held no emotion.

"No. I've been out of my mind trying to talk to you. I need to explain what happened."

"No, really, you don't. I know you didn't sleep with Caroline."

Thank God for that. "Of course not. Where are you?"

"Back in the city. My apartment. Good thing I never found someone to replace me."

Shit. Fuck. He had to get her back. He *had* to. "Em, there's nothing between me and Piper."

"Stop. Just . . . stop. I've had a really crappy day and night, and I don't want to get into it. Are you here? In the city?"

"No, I'm in Austin. I came home to talk to you. To be with you." His hand cupped the back of his neck as he stared down at his running shoes. "I need you, Em. Please talk to me."

"What's to talk about? Piper licked off all the frosting on this relationship."

Humor. *Thank God.* "We won't let her, Em. We can't let anyone do that to us."

She didn't respond, and in that moment Slater braced for an impact he knew was coming. His senses were heightened so sharply he could feel the air-conditioning drying the perspiration on his skin, smell a hint of her fragrance in the air, and hear the contraction of muscles in his throat as he swallowed.

"Slater, you know . . ." She exhaled. "Come on. You know we're over."

Heat exploded out of every molecule in his body. "The fuck we are. You're hurt, and it's my fault. I fucked up. I didn't want to screw things up for the band, so I—"

"Slater. Stop. I've already talked to my friends in PR at Amoeba. I know their plan for you, and it's exactly as I suspected. They want you to go with the whole VaughnLee thing. They love it."

"No. No. I won't do it." He wouldn't fake a romance, period.

"Our success will come because we earn it, not because I pretend to date a musician."

"It'll catapult you guys to the top. Best plan ever. Piper's good. *Really* good."

"I won't do it. You come first."

"Yeah, found that out on my birthday."

"Oh, fuck, Em." He strode into the kitchen, wanting to throw both mugs out the window. "You know I wanted to be there." He should've gone to Austin. His gut had told him to go.

"Sorry, sorry. I shouldn't have said that. That was a stupid thing to say. We both know you needed to be at Piper's party. I don't even care about my birthday. Well, intellectually, I can say I don't care about it. But emotionally? When Derek showed up and not you? It hurt. But that's my problem, not yours."

"Please don't do this, Em. I love you."

"Maybe you do. But those pictures showed me you're in so much deeper with Piper than you realize. And you know what? From this point on, she's the one you need. I just don't have anything to offer you anymore."

"*Offer* me? What the fuck? This isn't some business arrangement. I *love* you."

"Oh, cut it out." Finally, she had some emotion in her voice. "God, we knew this was coming. From the moment you went on tour with Piper, we knew this thing between us would end. We just didn't want to let go."

"This *thing* between us?" A billion electrical impulses fired inside him at once, lighting him up in a blinding fury. In a blur of motion he grabbed a mug and hurled it through the kitchen window. Glass shattered, shards glittering in the moonlight.

"What happened?" She sounded anxious. "Slater, are you all right?"

He wasn't all right. He was going out of his mind. His body shook in a cold sweat. "I want you back. I want to fix whatever I've done wrong and get you back."

But he didn't know how.

Dawn poured peach light into the living room. Too wired to sleep, Slater had finally collapsed on the couch an hour ago.

His mind would not slow down. But he didn't want to head to the airport until he'd gotten at least a few hours of sleep. Unfortunately, until he saw her in person, he didn't think sleep would happen.

His phone rang. Slater lunged for his cell, sending it flying off the coffee table. "Shit." He dropped to his knees, snatched it up, and hit Answer. "Em?"

"No, it's Derek."

"What do you want?"

"I want your ass in Minneapolis."

Fuck that.

"Listen, I know it sucks, but you need to finish the tour. We have an obligation—*you* have an obligation to this band."

"I'm going to New York. I have to talk to Em."

"Jesus, Slater, leave her alone."

"Never."

"You want her back?"

He didn't need to answer that.

"Then give her some space. Let her get a handle on her job situation. All you'll do right now is push her further away. I know my sister, man. She needs to get her head on right."

What Derek said cut right through the panic. Slater could feel his shoulders relaxing. It made sense. She needed time. The shit she'd seen on that blog? Yeah, she just needed some time. He didn't know how to give her that, but he would. He had to.

"And you need to finish up this tour."

He sat up. "Performing is the last thing on my mind. And I don't want to be anywhere near Piper Lee."

"I'll keep her away from you. You don't have to talk to her, don't have to be anywhere near the greenroom. I swear I'll keep her away from you."

"You can't. It's a bus. I can't do it, man. I can't be any-where near that calculating bitch."

"Slater. Stop it. Look, *we* didn't do this. Okay? You did it. Remember our rule? No girlfriends? This is why."

"Jesus, Derek. She's not a girlfriend. She's my fucking heart."

Derek blew out a breath into the receiver. "Shit, man. You're killing me here. I'm sorry it went down this way. Dude, I am. But right now you've got a job to do. And you can't let us down."

Everything Slater'd done, he'd done for the band. And look what it'd gotten him.

Still, he knew Derek was right. Irwin's continued radio silence allowed the guys to hang on to a single thread of hope. Slater couldn't do anything to take it all away from them.

He thought of Piper and his stomach clenched. "You keep that bitch away from me."

Every time exhaustion came to pull him under, he'd remember. Adrenaline would spurt into his veins, bringing him fully awake, and then he'd lie there obsessing over her. Why had she given up on them so easily? He understood she'd been upset, but why wasn't she fighting for them?

She couldn't have moved on from this—from them. Not possible.

Okay, show time. Slater rolled out of his bunk, head thick, body sluggish. He knew his performance sucked, but he only had two more nights. His phone buzzed in his pocket. Hope thundered in his chest—Emmie?—but when he pulled it out, he saw a text from Derek.

Just got the word from Amoeba. Irwin's done with us. No contract.

Shit. Fuck. How had he fucked everything up so colossally? He wrote him back. Reason?

He's "turned his attention to pressing issues with other bands."

Hell. But he knows I didn't fuck Caroline.

Yep. Forget it. We'll go to another label. Get ur ass out here. Sound check.

And that was the thing Slater couldn't understand—how cool Derek was being. All of the guys had accepted his unwillingness to play the fake romance card. He didn't think they agreed with him—he was pretty sure they'd go along with it if they were in his situation. But they understood he needed success based on his talent. Not because he was Piper's arm candy.

He hated that he'd let them down so badly.

He headed down the stairs, his body reacting violently to the sight of feminine legs covered in black leggings, the toenails a bright bloodred. True to his word, Derek had kept Piper away from him. Other than passing her backstage a few times, he hadn't come into contact with her at all.

Until now. Their gazes caught, and a shitstorm of anger kicked up inside him. His fingers curled around the handrail, and he squeezed tightly.

She blocked his way, her expression holding a hint of challenge.

"What do you want?" He sounded menacing. Good. He felt menacing. She'd ruined his life and gotten away scot-free.

"I want to know what your fucking problem is." Her lip curled. "We could have had it all."

He ignored her, shifting sideways to get past her.

"Did you know Irwin was going to sign me, too?"

He stopped, eyed her warily. Let the words sink in. "No."

"Bullshit." She shoved him. "Your stupid girlfriend works for him."

"You're with Flow. How could he sign you?"

"My contract's up."

"Wait, you set up that whole fiasco to get Emmie out of the picture and turn us into an overnight sensation—and you used *Irwin Ledger's* daughter? Are you stupid?"

Hard as she tried to hold on to her composure, he could see the fear in her eyes. "Of course not. I didn't set anybody up. I turned the situation to my advantage."

"You sure as fuck did."

She obviously didn't appreciate his sarcasm. "I didn't take any of those pictures, nor did I have anything to do with which ones went to print. I just *arranged* the evening."

He shook his head. "You arranged it brilliantly."

"No, you know what's brilliant? VaughnLee. That's brilliant. And all you had to do was play the part for a couple of months. And then we'd both have gotten signed by Amoeba, our careers would've been directed by Irwin Ledger, and you could've had all the pretty little girlfriends you wanted." She leaned toward him. "It's not too late for you to get your head out of your ass and play along. I can get us back on track. I can still make it happen."

"Yeah, see, that's the difference between you and me. I don't play games." He shoved between her and the wall, relieved when he cleared her.

"Why? How does it hurt anybody?"

"It hurt Emmie."

She rolled her eyes. "There are a million Emmies out there, you moron. And you can have every one of them. Right now, you need me. I can take you all the way."

"But, see, I don't want you." He drew in a breath to force himself to calm down. "And if it's a choice between having you and nothing at all?"

He walked away.

For some reason, the guys were being really nice to him. Even though he'd killed their dreams, they still went out of their way to make him coffee or throw his clothes in with their loads in the washing machine. They still invited him out.

He hated constantly rejecting them, so tonight he'd gone out with them. Not that he'd stay long, but he couldn't keep blowing them off while they kept being so damn patient.

He hadn't written a song in weeks. He felt useless, old, and . . . well, he *ached*.

The guys sat around a table in the club, a girl on each lap, others loitering around them, waiting for an opening. Tiana and Ben had their hands all over each other, and Slater wondered if his friend had learned a lesson from what had happened to him and Emmie. Maybe Ben would finally appreciate what he had in Tiana.

"Hey, handsome," a female voice said, sidling up to him.

The woman looked familiar. Blond, big tits . . . blah, blah, blah. "Not tonight."

She made to sit on his lap, but he blocked her. "So, when are you guys going to play here again? We miss you."

He couldn't do this. Nothing felt right. He got up, taking his glass with him. "Excuse me." Heading to the bar, the press of bodies made him feel claustrophobic. He'd never felt so much unrelenting pain. Where was she? What was she doing right then?

He wondered if Irwin had finally promoted her. If so, had she found the happiness she sought?

"What can I get you?" the bartender asked. A new one. An older guy.

The usual bartender stepped in, set Slater's usual beer on the counter. "I got this. How's it going, Slater?"

"Okay, thanks."

"Hey, you guys gonna play here soon or what? Been a while."

"Takin' a break." Slater glanced back to the table. Derek looked up at him with concern. After a moment, he got up and walked over.

"Glad you came out with us tonight, dude." Derek slapped Slater on the back.

He turned away from the bar, using his body to block the bartender and patrons around them. "Why are you being so cool with me? I fucked everything up. Again."

"You did?" Derek held Slater's gaze, steady, strong. "What'd you do, exactly?"

Irritation sparked the fuse of anger that had smoldered in his chest. "What are you talking about? I lost the record contract." He nodded toward the band's table. "Back to square one. That is completely on me."

"What did you do?"

"Piper—"

"Yeah, I know what Piper did. What did *you* do?"

"Irwin won't even talk to us, man. He'll never get over that goddamn picture."

"Maybe not. But what did you do?"

The fog in his brain cleared a little, giving him some clarity. "I didn't manage Piper well. If I'd . . ."

"Did you fuck her?"

"Of course not."

"Did you fuck Caroline?"

"Obviously not." He looked away. "If I'd managed her better, she wouldn't have gotten so crazy, and I wouldn't have lost Emmie and the record deal."

"Shit, dude, I've never met anyone so caught up in failure. It's like you expect it, man. But you didn't fail. Dude, you got us there. You got us all the way to Irwin fucking Ledger. Do you get that?"

Slater looked away.

"What?" Derek said. "You think Irwin wanted to sign us as a favor to Emmie?"

Slater looked beyond Derek to the table of middle-aged women laughing, their sequined dresses sparkling in the overhead lights, to the waitresses twisting through the crowd with their drink trays.

No. Irwin didn't operate like that.

"You think Irwin's got some time on his hands, so he'll give the fuckups from Austin a go? What, we were some project to him?"

No.

"He wanted to sign us because of your songs. Because of you. I mean, yeah, we're a good band. We've got a great sound. I'm a fucking great-looking guy." His smile quickly faded. "But, dude, no lie, you're the talent. We all know that. Why don't *you* know that?"

Slater could feel himself straighten, could feel energy flowing back into his body.

"You're not your dad. You're nothing like your dad. You gotta stop expecting failure."

Hard to argue with that.

"You know what's on you? You were so fucking worried about failing that you let that crazy bitch manipulate you. You're too smart for that shit. But you had Irwin, you had fucking Emmie, and you didn't think you deserved either of them. *They* knew you did, or they wouldn't have given you the time of day, but you didn't. So you didn't trust your gut. Your instincts are good, man. Your instincts got you Irwin, got you Emmie. So stop worrying about fucking up and just be the good guy you are."

Slater's blood turned cold, his skin prickly. "I don't want to be like my dad."

"And you're not." Derek shrugged. "You're nothing like him." He let out a breath. "Listen, it's not like me and the guys haven't talked it to death. Behind your back, of course." He smiled. "You had a choice to make. You could've played along with the VaughnLee thing, and we'd be signed. We'd be in the studio cutting our first single right now."

Slater closed his eyes, immersing himself in it. How completely he'd let down his friends.

"But the choice was yours to make. And whether or not we agree with it, you stuck to your guns, man. That's pretty badass. And, you know, who're we to judge? None of us had anything to lose, not the way you did, so . . . I'm saying we respect your decision."

"But why? You wanted success more than any of us."

"Ah, fuck it. I wanted it for the wrong reasons. And you know what? I really don't give a shit about proving anything to my dad anymore. What I care about is music. And us." He motioned to the guys. "We talked about it. Decided we're brothers first, a band second."

A painful knot formed in Slater's throat, his body heated with emotion.

Derek shrugged. "Hey, man. We got time. We'll get there."

Slater didn't know what to say. Emotion had a grip on him. He started to speak, but the knot hurt too much.

Derek clapped Slater on the shoulder. "So . . . just sayin', you're talented enough to get Irwin Ledger's interest, you've got some pretty impressive integrity, and you won my sister's heart . . . not seein' you as a failure here."

Slater nodded, his brain focusing, energy rushing in. "Fuck."

"Yeah. Fuck." Derek smiled.

Restless energy had his nerves jumping. "I gotta get out of here."

"Where you going?"

"Home. I've got some shit to do."

And suddenly it seemed absurd that he was sitting around feeling sorry for himself, allowing Irwin to ignore his calls. He'd go to New York, talk to Irwin—like a man, not like some groveling fuckup. And if Irwin still didn't want to work with them, he'd find another A&R guy who did.

And then he'd get his girl back because, *goddammit*, he hadn't failed.

TWENTY-TWO

Emmie sealed up Zuzu's Petals' press kit and stuffed it in the messenger bag she'd take to the post office in the morning. She reached for her to-do list, scanned the many items. As much as she needed to write a few paragraphs for her article, she really ought to blow-dry her hair. She didn't want to be late for her interview, and taking care of her hair now would be one less thing to do in the morning.

Oh, crap. Honestly? The energy it took to keep busy exhausted her. But she pressed on. Every minute of every day. Because if she didn't, she'd curl up in bed and cry her eyes out.

Not going to happen. But how long before she bounced back? When she'd broken up with Alex, she'd been hurt, deeply hurt, but she hadn't dragged like this. Why did nothing feel right? Her clothes didn't fit right, and food tasted funny. She didn't fit in her own skin anymore.

Slater. Oh, damn him. Damn that charming, sexy man who'd turned out to be so much more than she'd ever imagined he could be. No one had ever loved her as unconditionally, as wholeheartedly. As *passionately*. She loved the way he looked at her, his eyes wild with love and want.

God, what was she doing torturing herself like this?

Grabbing the bag, Emmie brought it to the front door. She

pulled out her phone to let the guys know in a group text that their press kits were going out the next day.

Carl, the lead singer, responded right away, good businessman that he was.

Awesome. Thx.

Alex had been right. Zuzu's Petals rocked. Working with them until she found a permanent job would be fun.

The doorbell rang, startling her. She wasn't expecting anyone. Two of her roommates were out, and the other had already gone to bed. She wasn't in the mood to talk to anyone, and she wasn't answering the door in her pajama bottoms and T-shirt, so she ignored it.

When the bell rang again, Emmie wondered if something was wrong. She remained motionless, waiting for whoever it was to go away. They'd give up after ringing twice, right? Anything else would be rude this time of night.

A rapping followed the third ring. Emmie pushed off the wall and peered through the peep hole.

And there stood a big, tall, gorgeous man pacing the hallway like a caged animal. She nearly jumped out of her skin.

Slater.

What was he doing here?

Unlocking the bolt with shaky hands, she closed her hand around the knob. She hadn't wanted to see him because she knew how easily she'd fall back into his arms. Who was she kidding? She wasn't that strong. She craved him. One touch and she'd . . . God.

She shouldn't let him in. Love or not, they were in two different places in life. She couldn't get distracted again. She had to stay focused. Get her career going.

She shouldn't open the door. She should let him walk away.

Oh, come on. He was right there.

She *had* to see him.

She opened the door, heat flooding her body, electrical impulses sparking along her nerves. His eyes went wide when he saw her, and he leaned into her, scooping her off the floor and hugging her tightly.

"Emmie." Relief infused his voice. He squeezed her to him.

And then his cheek crushed hers, his mouth seeking, finding its home, and good God, he kissed her, their mouths melding, fusing, their tongues furiously mating. He set her down, letting his hands loose on her body, pressing hard as they slid down her back, opening wide over her ass, and clutching it as he pulled her to him.

She grabbed fistfuls of his hair. She couldn't get enough of him. His scent made her weep with its familiarity, and his seeking hands made her desperate for more of him, all of him. He kissed her with a ferocity that set her on fire, awakened every cell in her body.

Knees dipping, he cupped her ass and lifted her. Her legs belted around him, her hips rocking against his thick erection, making her limbs turn liquid. He carried her to the couch, then turned and sat down, holding her tightly against him.

Straddling him, knees digging into the cushion, she thrust forward, her breasts at his chin, her hands holding his head in place, so she could slant her mouth over his, take him in deeper. Her tongue stroked wildly, her hips thrust urgently.

His hands cupped her head. "Emmie. I miss you. I miss you so fucking much."

She didn't answer. Couldn't speak. She should push him away, but she was too desperate.

His hand slid under her shirt, stroking her skin. He toppled her onto her back, surging into her, his erection sliding over her stomach through layers of clothing. He let out a shaky breath, and she reached between them, rubbing her palm over him. Rough, erratic breaths escaped his throat as his hand slid to her stomach, swept up to her breast.

"Ah, God," he moaned, his hand closing over her bare flesh, cupping her, fingers running over her nipple. She arched into him, fumbling with the top button of his jeans, struggling to unzip them so she could feel him in her hand.

He scooped her up. "Wrap yourself around me."

Mindlessly, she did as he asked, never breaking the press of mouths, the swirling of tongues.

"Bedroom."

"We shouldn't—"

"Bedroom."

"Down the hall."

He sat up, his hand sliding into her pajama bottoms and gripping her bare ass, stroking down until his fingers reached between her legs.

Brilliant sensation lit her up, and she gasped into his mouth. Her ass lifted off his thighs, pushing her against him. "Oh, God, Slater. Oh."

She thought she saw a flash of surprise then disappointment on his gorgeous, masculine features, but then he was shifting forward, getting to his feet. Her arms wrapped around his neck, and her legs wound tightly around his waist as he headed down the dark and silent hallway.

"Second room on the left."

He kicked the door open, dropped her on the unmade bed, dragged her to the pillow, and kneed her legs open. He positioned himself between them, bearing his weight on his arms and rubbing himself rhythmically over her, each pass igniting a fiery response inside her.

Tugging at her tank top, he yanked it over her head, and his mouth came down over her nipple and sucked it in. His tongue licked and swirled and then gave a long, deep pull. Her hips shot off the bed, and she cried out, the sensations in her clit and nipple aligning into one erotic jolt of desire.

"Pants off."

She shimmied out of the bottoms as his mouth sucked her other breast and his fingers tweaked and rubbed the damp nipple. "Yes, oh, Slater."

And then he sat up, shoved the jeans down his hips, and came back over her. His mouth back on hers, he thrust inside her aching, pulsing core.

She cried out, eyes open wide with the intensity of feeling seizing her body. Every nerve ending responded to his sensual assault. He held nothing back as his hands caressed her breasts, his tongue tangled with hers, and his erection plunged into her with wild force and pure abandon.

His mouth tore away from hers, his neck muscles straining, color saturating his features. "Oh, fuck, Emmie, come. Please come. Oh, motherfucking hell."

Reaching between their bodies, he pressed a finger to her clit, rubbed it, and she bucked hard. He looked like he was having a heart attack, and his hand left her clit to cup her ass and tilt her hips. The angle had him sliding over her nub with each wild, frantic thrust, and her body lit up in flames, tension tightening and coiling, sensation lifting her to unbearable heights.

As she felt her release roaring through her, she planted her feet on the mattress, lifted her hips, and thrust with total abandon against him. Her climax hit with a stunning explosion, and she cried out again and again, shocked at the sensations rocking through her.

She'd never seen Slater so out of control. He slammed into her ferociously, sweat dripping from his face. He reared back, shouting his release. As his punishing rhythm slowed, he locked their bodies together, his hand on her ass, holding her in place.

Exhaling roughly, he collapsed on top of her, still wearing his shirt, his jeans around his thighs, his boots still on. He rolled over, never letting go of her. He drew her to him. "Sleep."

His head sank into the pillow. She started to get up, but he tightened his hold on her.

"Stay."

"I'm just taking your boots off."

"Stay. I need sleep. Just . . . stay."

She settled in beside him, knowing she couldn't possibly sleep. Not after that. She'd wait until he drifted off before undressing him.

It didn't take long. Within seconds his breathing had deepened, evened. Carefully, quietly, she lifted his arm, but he cinched it back around her.

"Stay."

Okay. She'd stay.

Deep into the night, she felt the heat of his body pressed to her back. His erection pulsed hotly between her legs. Her body thrummed with desire as his hand kneaded her breast, his fingers rubbing roughly over her nipple. His mouth sucked and licked her neck, making her squirm and thrust back against him. And then he pulled away, leaving her bereft, but a moment later he thrust up into her, sliding into her slickness and filling her deeply, deliciously. Sensation skidded along her nerves, infusing her every molecule with dazzling, flickering light.

"Oh, yes, Slater, yes." She met his thrusts, ramming back

into him, covering his hand with hers as he cupped and gently squeezed her breasts.

His choppy breath at her ear excited her, but when his hand left her breast to clasp her hip, holding her tighter to him, and his thrusts shortened, grew fiercer, she turned her face into the pillow, allowing herself to fall completely into this moment—quite possibly her last—with him.

He grunted—once, twice, a third and fourth time. He powered into her, releasing himself inside her. His hand opened on her stomach, and he leaned into her, kissing her cheek. "Goddammit, Emmie," he breathed. "*Goddammit.*"

The strong scent of coffee awakened her. She felt strangely light and then realized his arm was no longer cinched around her. Rolling onto her back, she found an indentation in the pillow and a terrible empty space beside her. Her spirits plummeted.

He'd come back into her life, reminded her of everything they'd shared, and now she had to leave him all over again.

What did he think would change by coming here? Making love to her? That they'd get back together and forget about everything that had happened with Piper Lee? He wouldn't want to admit it, but Emmie'd been right. Absence didn't make the heart grow fonder on the road. No, intimacy developed in intense situations, in confined spaces.

And if not Piper, it would be someone else. That was just the nature of the entertainment industry. Relationships couldn't hold together, not with that much exposure to so many beautiful people, *artists*, and lengthy stretches away from home.

Forget it. And, really, did he think she'd go back to Austin and continue to flounder while he pursued his dreams? No. He belonged with his band, and she belonged in the city, where she'd eventually find work as an executive in a record company.

She got out of bed and headed into the bathroom.

Looked like she'd have to skip the post office this morning. She didn't know how long he'd stay, but nothing would make her miss her interview at BellCap Records. She hoped by going in with a Zuzu's Petals demo, they'd think of her as an A&R coordinator.

She found Slater in the kitchen, a mug in hand, his broad

back to her as he gazed out the window to the neighboring brick wall. "Hey."

He startled at the sound of her voice, sloshing hot coffee on his bare chest.

She tore some paper towels off the holder, and a bright spot of red caught her attention on the crowded counter. Next to the sink she found the can of frosting he'd given her for her birthday. He'd brought it all the way out here—why? Without taking her eyes off it, she handed him the towels. "Here." Please. Did she really think *he* could bring her happiness? He was the worst offender of all.

"Thanks." He wiped up the brown liquid trailing down his chest toward his boxers. Nodding toward the window, he said, "Nice view."

"Yeah." Her pulse quickened at the sense something was wrong, off. He just seemed . . . detached.

No, she couldn't go back to him, but come on. He'd always fought for her. "So, um, what're you in New York for?"

"For you, Em." He smiled, but he wasn't happy. "And I talked to Irwin."

"Oh. Is he, uh . . . ?"

"Does he want to sign us? Uh, no. He's not 'interested in the complications surrounding' me and Piper Lee."

Yeah, she could see that. Irwin obsessed over the music, the artists. He wanted nothing to do with drama. "I'm sorry."

He shrugged. "There are other labels. If Irwin Ledger thought we were good enough, others will, too."

"Definitely. You guys are so talented."

"Yeah, well. How important is talent if a label like Amoeba wanted me to fake a romance?"

"No, no. Don't misunderstand. You've already got the talent—no one would bother with you if you didn't. The point is how to get Snatch to stand out when social media sites are inundated with bands. And that's what made Piper's plan so clever. She really did nail it. With your talent, your *GQ* looks, Snatch would've slowly found its way to the top no matter what. But with VaughnLee? Meteoric rise." Emmie shook her head wistfully. "It was pretty brilliant." She hated reliving these horrible feelings—remembering the pictures of Slater and Piper clutching each other, looking so happy together. So she flashed him a big smile to show she'd moved on. "All you had to do was show up at a few events with her, and voilà, fame, money. Mega rock stars."

"I'm not interested in *fame*. I want to make music. I want to go platinum because people *like my music*. Not because I'm in the tabloids. I thought you of all people would get that. And if Irwin can't see that, then he's not the right A&R guy for me."

Turning away from him, she pressed her fingers into the cool tile counter. She *had* lost sight of him. She would never have talked to him about publicity plans like he was some artist on her label, instead of this man she *loved*. She did know what success meant to him—and it wasn't shallow. He needed to know he had actual talent. He needed to know it would last.

But wasn't this distance what she wanted? Needed? If he thought she understood him, if he sought the intimacy they'd once craved, she'd be naked on the couch with him in two seconds flat.

Distance was better. "Irwin doesn't care about marketing stunts. He's got people who take care of that. But the publicists, the marketing staff? That's their job. Every day they've got a list of bands they have to make famous in an oversaturated marketplace. They were just trying to give Snatch a jump start. You can't blame them for working any angle they can."

"Right. And what an angle it was. Just blow up the lead singer's life, force him into a fake romance with a manipulative bitch, and make him give up the girl of his heart." He shook his head bitterly. "Yeah, not for me."

The girl of his heart? Did he really believe that—still? A bud of longing unfurled in her belly. She loved him. She did.

But she couldn't have him. He didn't get it—he couldn't, since he hadn't lived it yet—but she knew what his life was about to become. Touring three hundred days a year, endless hours in the studio, promotional trips. His every second would be consumed with work. And he wouldn't achieve the kind of success he needed if he didn't give it 100 percent.

And neither would she. She loved him, yes. But she couldn't have him. She shifted, took a mug down from the cabinet, and poured herself come coffee. "That's why Irwin's such a good fit for you. He doesn't care about all that noise, either. He'd make sure he surrounded you with the right people so you could focus all your energy on what you do best—writing songs and performing." She busied herself with pulling the milk from the refrigerator, grabbing a spoon from the drawer. Her body tensed, waiting for his response. When none came, she glanced at him.

"You're like a stranger to me right now."

Hurt streaked through her. "Well, I'm not on vacation anymore. This is me, Slater. Me in business mode."

"Bullshit. This is you in hiding. Instead of dealing with it, instead of *fighting*, you become efficient."

"Screw you. I'm *unemployed*, Slater. I have no income. In two months, I won't be able to pay my *rent*. This is life or death. I *have* to get a job. And you know what terrifies me? If I don't get a job, then I'm going to have to go back to Irwin. And if I do, God, what does that mean? That's all I'll ever be? A personal assistant?"

"Stop defining yourself by your job title."

"Are you kidding me? I needed that damn promotion to prove to myself Irwin valued me as more than just the woman who could talk his most temperamental artist off the ledge, and you of all people should understand that." Her voice turned bitchy at that last bit, throwing his words back in his face. She immediately regretted it. She was a stranger to *herself*.

"You don't need Irwin's stamp of approval. He's just a guy, Emmie. He just happens to be good at what he does. He's not better than you. You're brilliant. You can do anything you want." He leaned toward her. "So *do it*. Do what you want and forget about what anyone else thinks. Because that's all the promotion means to you—his confirmation that you're good enough. You don't need him or your goddamn father to tell you anything. Because you're fucking amazing, Emmie. In every way."

"And what did the record contract mean to you?"

His features stilled. He had no response.

"That you made it. Just like the promotion would've meant to me." She waved her hands as if clearing the air of all the misunderstanding. "But even still. When I *do* get another job, I'm going to be working in New York City while you're on the road with Snatch, in the studio with them, touring the world. So where does that leave us?"

"Why are you making up these excuses? It leaves us together, working it out. Just like any other couple. Only we're not any other couple. We're us. And it's fucking killing me to have you standing there like some record executive I once worked with."

"I'm sorry if you don't like that I'm back in work mode right now, but I'm fighting for my life."

"I want you to fight for *us*."

Her hands jerked, the mug lurching, sending coffee sloshing everywhere. "Why can't you just let this go?" Oh, dammit. Damn him. She snatched paper towels off the holder and dropped to her knees to clean up the mess. Perspiration glued her tank top to her back. "You don't need me anymore, Slater. Just let it go."

He crouched beside her, a wad of paper towels in his hand. A frown creased his forehead. "I can't. Because you're in here." He tapped his heart. "I love you—not because you turned Pete's pubes into dreads, but because I *love you*. Because we have this bond, this connection, that I can't fucking explain, but it's there and it's perfect and I want it, and I don't know how I'm supposed to live without it." He stood up, leaning against the counter. "Because it's not going to come around again. This thing we have? It's irreplaceable."

She stood, caught in this whirlwind of emotion. Fear, anger, but also . . . hope.

His gaze searched hers, looking for an answer she couldn't give. "But you're too scared to see it right now. And that makes me so fucked."

She wanted to believe him, of course she did. But love wasn't all they needed. She could see his side, but he didn't know how crazy his life would become once the band got signed. If a two-and-a-half-month tour felled them . . . come on, they didn't stand a chance.

"Em, I'm here." He shrugged. "You know I love you. I'm all in. I'd give all of this up to be with you. Truth is, I was doing this for my dad. Because he worked so damn hard to turn me into a rock star. But I can't live my life for him. Yeah, I'm a musician, a songwriter, but I have to figure out my place in this business. And I want to do it with you."

"Slater—"

"But it's not about me. It's about you. Thanks to your asshole father, you think the minute you're not useful to me I'm going to dump you and not look back. Emmie, Jesus, I don't need your help with my career. I need you to just be you. I need you to love me. I need you to *be with me*. Because no one in my life has ever loved me just for me. Except you. I've never felt as good about myself as I do when I'm with you. I like you. I like being with you. And without you? It's just going through the motions."

He scratched his head absentmindedly. "Thing is, there's nothing I can do. I've told you. I've shown you . . . There's nothing more I can do. It's you. You don't trust that I won't dump you like your dad did to your mom. Like Alex did to you. I think you know if I could do anything—anything at all—I'd do it. I'd do anything to win your love."

"You have my love. All of it. That's never been in doubt."

"Your trust." He said it casually, like he was dismissing her love. "Emmie, I'll wait for you forever because there's no one else for me, but you have to trust yourself. You have to believe that you're enough just as you are. I don't know what it will take for you to trust yourself, but . . . Christ, Em, how *do* people trust?" He waited for her answer, and she had the feeling he expected something meaningful, something profound, something that would fix them right then and there. But she just didn't know.

"I guess we take a leap of faith." Emotion gripped his features. "I'm not your dad. I'm not Alex. I *will* catch you." But then he wiped it away and took his mug to the sink.

Stowing it in the dishwasher, he reached for a kitchen towel, dried his hands. Finally, finally, he approached her, hands reaching again . . . but then settling at his sides. "I should go."

"*Slater . . . ?*" How could he leave her like this? Wait, wait, wait. She couldn't think straight. They couldn't be together. She knew she had to let him go, so why did she feel destroyed all over again hearing it from his mouth?

He'd always fought for her. He'd never wavered. Not once.

"See, I don't know what I did to become Slater in your eyes again."

She sucked in a breath, not even realizing she'd called him that. And then she remembered the blog. *Jonny and I.* "Piper. In the *Beatz* article she said, 'Jonny and I are just in sync.' She called you Jonny."

He looked alarmed, holding her gaze as he seemed to think it through. But then all the energy drained out of him, and he just looked resigned. "She once asked me why you called me Jonny, and I told her. I guess she used it against you. And won."

She felt the horror of those two simple words all the way down to her bones.

He sighed, shook his head. "I can't help what other people do. I can be true to you, and that's all I can do."

Heading out of the kitchen, he stopped at the threshold, tapped his fist against the doorway, and said, "If you can do it, if you can take that leap of faith—and I sure as hell hope you do—I'll be waiting."

TWENTY-THREE

"What do I like?" Irwin asked. He'd brought the wrong glasses, the distance ones, so he'd shoved them down to the tip of his nose and peered at the menu with a ridiculous expression.

Of course they'd been to Basil a hundred times before. Tucked into the side of a rock outcropping under the Highline, Basil was a cool, tiny bistro that catered to wealthy artsy types in the city. The menu listed possibilities, not actual entrees.

The waitress, a woman Emmie didn't recognize—she'd been away that long—gazed out the window at the pedestrian traffic in the funky Greenwich Village neighborhood. She didn't seem bothered in the least by Irwin's inability to order.

Emmie took the menu out of his hand. "I'll have the number two with avocado, Monterey Jack, and please ask him to throw in some jalapeno peppers for me."

"I'm sorry, we don't have any peppers."

"He keeps some for me." Even as the words came out of her mouth, she realized how long it had been since this had been her life. "Well, he used to. If he doesn't have them, that's fine. Maybe he can put some salsa or something in it to give it a little umph."

"Sure." The waitress turned to Irwin, who was now squinting at his iPad.

"He'll have the number seven. Please make it with just fresh vegetables, no meat whatsoever, and ask Chef if he wouldn't mind stuffing a bunch of fresh spinach in there."

"I hate spinach." Irwin peered up at her.

"Cleansing," was all she had to say to make him flinch and go back to his iPad. "Also, instead of the sweet potato fries, can he please have a bowl of fresh fruit?"

"That'll cost extra."

Emmie gave him a private smile. "He's worth it."

"Yes," Irwin said. "And, of course, I'm paying, so you could throw in gold doubloons and she wouldn't care."

"Okay." The waitress gave them an awkward smile. "Be right back with your drinks."

"If you ordered me wheat grass, I'm not going to touch it. I don't eat grass. It's not a vegetable, no matter how hard you try to convince me of it. Besides, I think you're just trying to make fun of me. You think I don't pay attention to you. But I do. And I want you back. I can't live without you."

She had to admit, she appreciated his persistence. "It's not a good idea."

He set his iPad down. "What exactly are your job prospects?"

"I'm exploring some options."

"Do tell."

The second interview with BellCap Records hadn't gone well, so she wouldn't mention it. The place was chaotic, and the A&R staff seemed more interested in partying with the talent than actually developing it. Maybe Irwin had spoiled her, but she'd rather keep looking than take a job with an unstable label.

"I'm working with Zuzu's Petals. I've just sent out their press kit. I'm also writing a series for *Rolling Stone*, taking a band from the garage to the amphitheater."

"Wonderful. Excellent. I sense win. So, currently, the choice is between working for me in the music industry, flying around the world, and eating in famous restaurants, or wandering around your apartment in your pajamas trying to keep busy?"

"No, no. I've gone on interviews. I'm looking to—"

"Be an A&R rep. Yes, I know."

The waitress set down their drinks. Fresh-squeezed lemonade for her, a wheat grass shot for him. He gave her a comically dull look.

"Thank you," Emmie said to the waitress, lifting her glass to Irwin and offering their usual Zulu cheer. "Oogy wawa."

He raised his shot glass. "Oogy wawa." His features squinched up, and he knocked back the shot. His eyelids flew open, and he looked like he'd been Tasered.

"Now that you've cleared the toxins from my body, can I order a real beverage? Preferably one with a high alcohol content?"

"When was the last time you ate healthy food?"

"Since the night you had that rather deceptive meal delivered to my office. Candles, chocolate lava cake . . . I thought you were going to propose to me. Not tell me you'd replaced yourself with the Masticator. I haven't quite recovered. But you could come back to me, and all will be forgiven."

"I could possibly come back temporarily, it's just I . . ."

"What's grossly disturbing to me is your wishy-washiness. This is not my Emmie. Why do you take such command of my life and yet squander your own?"

"What?" Stunned, she felt like he'd tossed a glass of ice water at her.

"Look, you're a sharp girl. I wouldn't have been able to find my own socks each morning if you hadn't laid them out for me the night before. And I mean that completely metaphorically." He rolled his eyes with great exaggeration. "How can someone so clever be so lost in her own life?"

"I'm not lost." She was totally, helplessly lost.

"You're simply not the type of person to *not* know what she wants. To not make happen exactly what she wants."

"I can't have what I want, Irwin."

His head snapped back, eyes widened.

"What?" She was getting exasperated.

"You are not the Emmie Valencia who walked out of my life four months, two weeks, and two days ago."

The waitress set a platter of vegetable dumplings down in front of them. "Compliments of the chef." She flashed a smile at Emmie. "He says to say, 'Hell yeah, I've got her jalapenos.' He wondered where you'd gone."

"Thank you. Tell him, thank you so much." The waitress left, and Emmie sat uncomfortably, not sure what to make of Irwin's words. "I'm not the same person. I know that. I can't even stand to be in my own skin. You know what? I will take my job back." *Yes*. Finally, she'd made a decision. And it felt so . . . so . . . Well, it was the right choice for now.

"You can't have it."

"What?" Her head spun.

"It's no longer available."

"Irwin." She stabbed a dumpling, dunked it in the soy sauce, and brought it to her mouth.

"What happened to discovering a band?"

She shrugged. "I did discover one."

He held her gaze, and the world narrowed to just the two of them. The room grew insufferably warm, and her heart thundered.

Finally, her shoulders gave, and she practically hunched over. "I suck at it. I don't like living in clubs and schmoozing with bands. I'm not cut out for A&R."

"So we agree."

It actually felt good to admit it. "We agree. But where does that leave me? I don't want to do publicity or marketing, and I'm not—"

"The only jobs on God's earth are at a record company?"

"Well, if I want a promotion . . ." She didn't want to go into the whole explanation about starting over somewhere else from the bottom again.

"So the only job of value comes from me? My promoting you?"

"Well, it would have made the most sense. Anything other than A&R will be entry level."

"You've no other talents? Interests? Because I might point out what you did with . . ." He made a sour face.

She waited, but he didn't go on. "Snatch?"

His hand made a quick flicking motion, as if to bat the horrible name away from the table. "You knew exactly what to do to turn them into a real band. You got them the tour with that viper of a woman. So, while you may not be cut out for A&R, you may be cut out for something else. Manager, perhaps?"

He stabbed his fork into a dumpling and stuffed it in his mouth. Chewing, he grimaced. "It has carrot bits in it."

"Yes, it's a *vegetable* dumpling."

"You know, there are other food groups. I'm allowed to partake of the others."

"Vodka is not a food group."

"Alcohol is a cleanser." He exhaled, looking frustrated. "Emmie, you are invaluable to me. I trust you."

She knew exactly the weight of that sentiment. "Thank you. That means a lot to me."

"And you know how important it is to me to have as few annoyances as possible, which is why I pine for you?"

She nodded.

"And one of the biggest annoyances is dealing with pratt managers. You, as a manager, would not annoy me."

Her pulse quickened as the waitress set their plates down.

"Thank you," Emmie said as Irwin stared in horror at his meal.

"They forgot the food. Excuse me, miss?"

The waitress spun around, looking concerned.

"I think someone vomited on my plate."

Emmie waved the waitress off, "Nothing, he's fine. Thank you."

"I do have teeth. I'm able to chew actual food."

"You always complain until you take the first bite. You love Chef Orlando."

"Should I use a straw?" He stabbed his fork into the steaming mass of steamed vegetables on a bed of quinoa and bulgur wheat. "If I close my eyes, I can pretend I'm eating Chef Charlie's confit chicken leg with morel mushrooms and a curry-scented crust." He brought the forkful of food to his mouth, inhaled, winced, and shoved it in. He chewed briskly three or four times, then swallowed, making a childish face of disgust. "Maybe if I pinch my nose?"

"You know you like it. Now eat it all, and if you're good, I'll buy you a perfect little canelé from Balthazar's."

His head popped up like a dog that had just scented raw hamburger meat. "Now you've done it. I can taste the delicate custard on my tongue. Ah, that first crunch of the crystallized caramel. For the love of God, woman, don't tease me. Is that a promise?"

She smiled, and again he closed his eyes and breathed in the steam from his meal. "Mm. Smells better already." He went quiet, keeping his eyes closed. "Emmie. Do as I'm doing right now."

"Act like a baby?"

"One of us has to be the adult. It's always been you, let's not change things now. Close your eyes."

"Then I won't be able to enjoy watching you eat your quinoa."

"Close them."

Reluctantly, she did.

"What does your perfect future look like?"

Her lids flashed open to find him smirking at her.

"You can't see your future while looking at me."

Fine. She closed then again. "How far into the future?"

"Now who's being churlish?"

"I see me in my pajama shorts and tank top in my office with the sun streaming in through the windows as I write articles for *Rolling Stone*."

"I didn't need to know the wardrobe choice. That's not fair. Go on."

"I can have more?"

"You silly girl, you can have anything you want. Don't you know that about yourself by now?"

"My boyfriend—okay, my husband, the love of my life, is in the other room working on a song." Her heart clutched at the vision of Slater in the other room. Jonny. Her love.

Her *heart*.

"And what's *he* wearing?"

"Nothing but black boxer briefs." And, oh, the sight of Slater's bare chest, the hard, defined muscles, had her hands itching to reach out and touch him.

Oh, my God. Surely a piece of her soul was missing. Surely that explained this constant pain, this throbbing ache that lived inside her.

That *wouldn't go away*.

"I'd hoped to keep this PG, but apparently that's not possible."

She burst out laughing. "Okay, fine. I just put him in pajama pants. But nothing else. What's your point?"

"Tell me what's stopping you from having that life?"

"Oh, well, I mean, come on. I have to have a job. I have to work for somebody." Even as the words came out of her mouth, she felt her cheeks burn.

"I can see we're getting somewhere on the job front. And the fellow in boxers in the next room? Why can't we have him?"

"Because he's a singer, Irwin. He's a gorgeous, hot singer in a rock band. Once he gets signed, he's going to be on the road . . ." Her chest hurt, and she didn't have the energy to go on and on with the same crap. "He doesn't need me anymore."

He shoved a forkful of steaming food into his mouth and swallowed it whole. "I didn't go to university, but I'm fairly sure one's usefulness is not in direct proportion to one's lovability. I mean, for fuck's sake, you're Emmie Valencia. Who wouldn't fall madly and wildly in love with you? And not because you offer turndown service, but because you're you. You're delightful. I can count on you, and that, my love, is a rarity. A gift. You are indispensable to me not because you're efficient—the Masticator was certainly efficient. But because I *like* you. I like your company, your humor, your spirit, and your integrity. You're honest and true. And lovely. And dear God, how many people on this earth possess those qualities? Not enough. I wanted you back for those qualities. Not for your ability to book a tour bus. I'm sorry if I didn't make that clear."

"I'm not sure what to say."

"You don't need to say anything. You need to do something. I don't believe you'll make a good A&R coordinator because I don't believe you're all about the music. You, my love, are all about the people. Your gift is in knowing people, reading them, and that combined with your extensive knowledge of the music industry equals managerial success. That's an equation I made up all on my own, no degree required." He set down his fork, lifted his napkin off his lap, and dabbed the corners of his mouth. "Now, have I eaten enough to earn my canelé?"

"Sure." Still a little dazed by his good opinion of her, she motioned to the waitress, who came over right away. "Can we please get the check?"

"You got it. How was everything?"

"Astonishingly delicious." Irwin wowed her with a dazzling smile.

The woman's cheeks turned pink, and she backed away with their plates.

"So, my love. If you had no fear, you'd be writing your articles, possibly managing bands, which, let's be honest, is your calling in life, and living happily ever after with your rock god in a little valley by a stream on a ranch in the heart of Texas."

Her calling in life? Had Irwin just said managing bands

was her *calling in life*? He thought she was great at something. She let that knowledge sink deep, warming her to her bones. "It's not fear that holds me back. I'm just being realistic."

"And are you enjoying this realism? Is it quite fulfilling?"

A smile spread slowly and surely across her entire body, opening her. It was like uncurling a fist after clenching it too long. "It sucks."

"Then stop making decisions based on fear. Live the life you dream about, not the one you settle on because you're too afraid to reach for more, and never, ever make me eat baby mush again." He stood up, digging into his pocket and dropping a hundred dollar bill on the table, more than twice the bill, she was certain. "Shall we?"

The limo eased to the curb.

"Well, this should be interesting," Bax said. And the Texas jokes began. Big hair, shitkicker boots, belt buckles . . . blah, blah, blah.

Emmie tuned it out. All her energy, all her thoughts were fixed on the man inside the club. The driver came around and opened the door. She slid out of the leather seat, her chest tight with excitement.

She'd never seen more cars parked outside the club before. Music pounded through the walls, a familiar song. "Get it, Boy." She smiled, imagining Slater holding the mic, tendons in his neck straining, perspiration glistening on his skin. Bax opened the door to the club for her, and she entered.

The place was packed, standing room only, and the noise was deafening. She stepped aside so the guys could get in. They headed straight for the bar. Emmie skimmed the edge of the crowd, trying to get closer without drawing attention to herself. Not that he'd see her in this throng, but still. She wanted to watch him for a while, let him finish his set.

The crowd loved this song, with its hard-driving guitars and walloping drums. These guys were meant for stadiums. She knew they'd go all the way.

And Slater? God, his presence—no one in the club could take her eyes off him. Gorgeous, muscled, and radiating a command and stage presence that utterly captivated.

She threw a quick glance over her shoulder to make sure the guys were as captivated as she expected. Every one of them stood transfixed, staring at Slater.

All of a sudden, the music stopped. She whipped around to find him jumping off the stage. The crowd lunged toward him, everyone wanting to lay hands on him, but he plowed through, his gaze trained on hers with an intensity that made her heart leap into her throat. Heat flooded her body.

How had he seen her? He couldn't possibly—with the lights, the crowd, the way he concentrated up there. And yet, there he was, emerging from the throng, heading right toward her with a smile filled with pure happiness.

Oh, my God. Jonny. Her Jonny. She could scarcely breathe. And then she was moving, picking up speed, her heart beating with the strength of great, powerful wings, and she took off, leaping into his arms. He caught her, holding her tightly to him. She was home.

"Emmie," he whispered in her ear. "Oh, *fuck.*" Tremors rocked his body. "You came back."

She turned her face into his neck, wanting to block out everyone, wanting him, only him. "I'm sorry, Jonny. I'm so sorry." What had she been thinking to let this man go? She couldn't hold him tightly enough—couldn't believe she'd walked away from him, from her heart. It only made her squeeze him harder—and then harder again. She had him back in her arms—and fear seized her, literally had her in a chokehold, because she'd actually let this man go.

"You're here now, Emmie. It's all right. Everything's all right." His body trembled, head to toe, and it rattled her, what she'd done to them. But, God, she'd snapped out of it. She had him back.

The screech of reverb cut through the club. "Uh, Slater, dude?" Derek called out into the mic. "Think we could finish the set?"

The crowd erupted into shouts and whistles, but Slater ignored them, never taking his eyes off her.

"I love you," she said, trembling. "I love you so much."

He kissed her sweetly, chastely at first, but need roared through her. She could feel his body heating up. Her mouth opened to taste more of him, and then the tips of their tongues touched, and electricity shot through her. His mouth slanted, deepening the kiss, and his hands slid to her ass, squeezing, pulling her tighter against him. One hand held her in place while the other went under her knee, hitching her leg up, and he ground against her. He let out a shuddery breath in her ear. "Thank you for coming back to me."

They kissed, oh, they kissed, and heat and love flooded her, filling all the aching spots. When his hand fisted in her skirt, hiking it up, she heard a familiar voice.

"Would now be a good time to speak with your fellow?"

Emmie's mouth pulled away as she lowered her leg. Her hands cupped Slater's jaw, her forehead pressed to his. She laughed, her body throbbing, little tremors pulsing through her. "Um, Jonny?" Her skin cooled a little, and she took a step back from him, to include Irwin and the others.

"Irwin," Slater said warily, shaking hands firmly, his mouth still wet from their kiss. He reached for her, his arm wrapping around her waist. His eyes were glazed with lust, but she continued the introductions.

"And, of course, you remember Bax, James, and Connor. The Amoeba Records team."

"Of course." He shook their hands, still wary and hesitant.

"Good to see you, man," Bax said.

Slater gave him a firm nod, then looked back to Emmie. "What's going on?"

"Well, a couple of things. Irwin and I have been talking. He'd really like to sign you guys, but he wants to make sure you have a good manager."

"The best, actually," Irwin said with a big grin.

Slater focused on her. "You want to manage us?"

She nodded. "Would that be good?"

"Yes." He *still* seemed wary. He turned to Irwin. "And you want to sign us?"

"I do."

Slater cocked his head at her. "You want me to sign with a record label?"

She nodded.

"You want me to have all of it? Tours, gigs, records, rock videos . . . everything that comes with it?"

"Everything."

"So, we can do this?"

"We can. We will."

He kissed her full on the mouth. Then, he reached for her hand and brought it to his lips. He turned toward the executives. "Thanks, guys, for giving us this opportunity. I, uh, should probably finish my set. And then I need to spend a few minutes with my girl, but after that, I'd like to sit down with you."

Irwin nodded. "Take your time. Your girlfriend here has cleansed me to the point where I squeak when I move. Must grease the gears." He turned to the guys. "Shall we?" And they headed back to the bar.

"Dude?" Derek called into the mic. The crowd started clapping, stomping.

"One second." The noise of the crowd drowned his voice, so he held up a finger. He drew Emmie in close, shutting out the rest of the world. "I love you, Emmie. Thanks for taking the leap. You won't be sorry."

With Ben in his bunk talking to Tiana on his cell phone, and Cooper and Pete thrashing around on the couch and shouting at each other as they played some violent video game, Emmie found herself wandering around the bus. Even though the driver handled cleanup, Emmie couldn't stand the filth that accumulated in the small kitchen. She dumped all the beer bottles in the recycling bin.

"Hey," Cooper called, not taking his eyes off the TV screen. "I'm not finished with that."

"I only threw away the empty ones." As she dumped last night's take-out containers into the garbage bin, she noticed the empty can of chocolate fudge frosting. Heat rushed up her neck, burning to the tips of her ears as she recalled how she and Slater had used it the night before. Her nipples tingled at the reminder of how he'd licked them clean. And then she smiled because he truly had become the frosting in her life— all good things to her and for her.

Glancing at the clock, she wondered how it was going with his mom. He and Derek had stayed after the show for the interviews and press she'd set up. Afterward, they'd taken Elizabeth to the hotel, and Emmie assumed they'd stay to have a drink. Flying her out here for the tribute song to his dad had meant a lot to Elizabeth, and Emmie figured they'd want to reminisce.

She missed him. Even though they spent most of every day together—her writing articles and taking care of band business, him writing songs—she always missed him when they were apart.

Nothing left to clean, she sank down on the couch, drawing her knees to her chest and gazing out the window. It was dark, so she saw only her own reflection. What a difference a few months made. She loved her life. Wouldn't trade it for anything.

She picked up the book she'd been trying to read, but couldn't concentrate because she knew he'd be home any minute. He had to, since the bus was leaving at midnight to reach Pittsburgh in the morning.

Tires crunching over gravel alerted her, and while her body lit up, she remained placid on the outside. She tried hard not to make the other guys uncomfortable, limiting public displays of affection as much as possible. With Slater that wasn't possible nearly as much as she'd have liked. He didn't care what anyone thought. He just wanted his hands on her.

Car doors slammed, and her heart pounded at the sound of his voice. She pulled her legs in tighter, trying to contain the buzz of anticipation running along her limbs. Her man. God, she loved him.

And then he appeared, his dark hair a little longer now, more relaxed, and shiny-clean from the shower he'd taken after the show. His gaze landed on her the moment he hit the landing. He looked hungry, intense. Desire washed through her in a slow burn.

"How'd it go, man?" Cooper asked the guys.

"Great." Derek rubbed his hand over his buzz cut. "I think we might get the cover of *Rolling Stone*."

"Are you kidding me?" She couldn't believe it. What a coup. Pete stuttered out a laugh. "Fuckin' A."

"Yeah." Derek looked to Emmie, shaking his head. "You are gold."

"Hey, I had nothing to do with scoring a cover."

"No," Derek said. "But you're the one who suggested the article to them."

She'd pitched the article on breakout bands mostly to

promote Blue Fire—a marketing tactic Slater had much preferred over fake romances. And if they got a cover out of it . . . bonus. She didn't need to point out that they wouldn't have had a shot at the cover if they hadn't changed the band's name.

"I tell you," Derek said. "A cover sure as hell wasn't on the menu, but they took one look at GQ over here, and I guess he's the best looking of anyone in the breakout bands they're featuring."

She smiled at Slater, but his gaze remained intensely focused on her, muscles strung tight, ready to pounce. If it were up to him, they'd be alone already.

"Dude, grab me a beer," Derek asked Slater.

Slater, coiled and moving like a panther, pulled open the fridge and tossed a cold one to Derek then handed a water bottle to Emmie.

Cooper spun around, arm shooting out as he pointed to them. "Four minutes."

Derek scowled. "Didn't count. He didn't touch her."

"Totally counts," Cooper said. "Their fingers touched."

"Nope," Derek said. "I watched. No contact."

"What are you talking about?" She finally looked away from Slater, who'd sat down on the couch across the aisle from her.

Pete motioned to the white board they'd hung on the wall over the couch. "Longest he's made it before touching you is seven minutes."

"What?" She noticed the number seven in the far right corner. Flecks of various colors around it told her the number had been corrected many times. "You time how soon before he touches me?"

The three guys burst out laughing.

"We're trying to be discreet, you idiots." She stretched out her legs. "We don't want you to be uncomfortable."

Slater sprang. He scooped her off the couch and into his arms. "Good. No more games."

"It's not a game." She latched onto his neck as he lifted her off the couch and then turned to carry her down the narrow corridor. "I was trying to be nice," she called to the guys. "For your sake."

"What do we care?" Pete said.

"Like we can't hear you?" Cooper said.

Mortified, she tucked her head into Slater's neck. "They can hear us?"

"You're right there," Cooper shouted. "And you're not exactly quiet."

"I am so quiet," she shouted over Slater's shoulder.

"No, you're not," Slater said, and she tugged his hair. "Hey, I don't want you to be. What did you think they thought we were doing in here?" He kicked open the door and gently set her on her feet.

"Five minutes, by the way," Pete shouted.

"Disgusting," Derek said.

Slater closed the door to their small bedroom. The guys slept in the four bunks that lined the hallway just beyond the kitchen. So, yeah, she guessed they could hear.

"I'm so embarrassed."

Slater threw off his black T-shirt, and her pulse quickened at the sight of his gorgeous chest, the cut lines of his muscles, his taut stomach, and oh, the tip of that sexy tattoo. He unbuttoned his jeans, shrugging them off and then kicking them aside.

"You're still dressed." He reached behind her to unzip her sundress, quickly flicking off the straps and letting it fall to the floor. He took her hand so she could step out of it.

He cupped her breasts in the bra, lowering his face into the mounds of flesh, licking her cleavage and dipping one cup so he could tease her nipple with his teeth. She ran her hands through his hair, holding him close.

Lifting her, he knelt on the bed and hauled her to the pillows, pulling her in tight to his hot, hard body. One hand pulled down her plain cotton panties, while he licked the shell of her ear. "I missed you."

"I missed *you*." She turned in his embrace, wrapping her arms around his back, and hugging him. "How'd it go with your mom?"

He pulled back a little so they could see each other. "It was good. Thank you for arranging it."

"You're welcome."

His hand rested on the curve of her waist. Slowly, lightly, he stroked over her hip and along her thigh. "She thinks it's pretty cool that you sent her a video of me performing the song, but she said it was nothing like hearing it live. And she loved that you framed the lyrics for her."

"I'm glad." She scraped the hair off his face. "Did you talk about it? The song?" Slater hadn't been able to find a song his dad had written that he could work with. Yeah, his dad had been that bad. So he'd written a song of his own.

He nodded, fingers brushing the hair off her shoulders, behind her ears. Soothing, sensual, sexy. "Yeah. She said it's a much better way to see him." He pressed the softest, sweetest kisses across her cheek, the bridge of her nose, the corner of her mouth, while his hand sifted through the hair at the back of her neck. "Thinks it rings true."

"Which means?"

His mouth fluttered down her chin, along her neck, and then he licked her collarbone. "Which means you made me see him differently. Turned him from a selfish bastard to a guy who just wanted his son to have a better life than he did." Slater glanced up at her. "She said it was just a shift in the way we saw him, but that it changed everything. You did that for me."

"That's because I'm an outsider."

He smiled, eyes half-lidded, as he brushed a thumb over her lips. "I never let anyone in before you. And it's made all the difference."

Everything in her softened as love suffused her. "Your dad would be so proud of you, Jonny." She squirmed against him.

His big hand gripped her ass and drew her closer, no space between them. "I thought he didn't see me, that he didn't give a shit. But I was wrong. I think he did see me. He saw me play those instruments, learn them too quickly. Pick up chords, notes, all that stuff. And if he'd left it to my mom, I might be third violinist for the Austin symphony right now. I think he wanted me to see what I was capable of, how far I could go." His tongue licked down her stomach. "I think he thought maybe I deserved more."

This man deserved everything. She'd never met anyone like him. His hand glided over her ass to the back of her thigh, fingers swirling lightly over her skin. Reaching the back of her knee, he lifted it, hitching her leg over his.

"I don't think my dad could help himself, you know? He probably had ADD and all kinds of undiagnosed issues, so I'm pretty sure he lived in hell every day of his life. I see him in a whole new light." His fingers touched her chin, lifted her. "Thank you."

"I love you." Her body trembled with need, with so much love she didn't know how to hold it all in. She ran her hand down his stomach, fingers running slow circles around his tattoo. "I *love* you love you."

"I *love* you love you, too." His hand wrapped around her wrist, stopping her. "How's the article coming? Did you finish it?" He brought her hand to his mouth and kissed her fingers. She loved how they shared this time every night, going over all the details of their day. It made her feel so close to him. For all the craziness of life on the road, he always made sure they had this special time together.

"I did."

"You happy with it?"

She nodded as his fingers intertwined with hers, and he rolled on top of her. He nuzzled her neck, and she squirmed when she felt his tongue on her skin.

"You get back to Irwin?"

"Not yet. If I take on his band, I'll have less time with you and less time to write. I don't want to let him down, but I'm really happy with what I'm doing right now. It's enough, you know?"

"Mm," he said, his hips surged into her, his erection pressing between her legs.

She gasped. "I'm happy right where I am."

"Good. Now, get up on me." He kissed her, cupping the back of her head. His tongue teased her mouth open, swept inside.

She pulled away. "No. They can hear us."

He was on top of her in a flash, arms at either side of her head, knees nudging her legs apart. "Emmie? You're my girl. I'm going to love you every chance I get for the rest of my life. If you don't want to do that around other people, then we won't be around other people." His tongue licked her nipple, sending a jolt of desire ripping through her.

"What does that mean?"

"That means if you're going to become even more *discreet* because of what those assholes just said, then I'll retire right now and buy us that house on the lake." His tongue pulled her nipple deep into his mouth. Her hips arched off the bed. "Someone once told me I can make more money publishing my songs than fronting a band."

"You wouldn't do that to the guys. They're counting on you."

"The fuck I wouldn't." He gripped his erection, stroking it along her seam, making her writhe. Heat flooded her, and desire churned, spinning out in hot waves. And then he circled the head around her clit, and her whole body shot up in flames.

She cried out. She couldn't help it. Under his assault she had no choice. "You don't play fair."

Derek groaned, and the guys burst out laughing. Someone flipped on the stereo, and loud music filled the bus.

Slater smiled at her in the most delicious way. And then he pushed her legs wider and plunged inside of her. "Hang on tight, baby."

Oh, she would. She *would*. And she would never let go.

Turn the page for a peek at the
next Rock Star Romance

I WANT YOU TO WANT ME

Coming in July from Berkley Sensation!

So . . . this is awkward.

Violet Davis stood at the back of the restaurant watching her former client tap his knife against his wineglass, quieting his friends, family, and colleagues.

He rose, resting a hand on the back of his fiancée's chair, and addressed the room. "Thank you all for coming tonight."

In his six-thousand-dollar custom-made Brioni suit, Joe looked nothing like the man she'd known three months ago. Back then, he'd worn soiled clothes, a greasy beard, and bruises. He'd also smelled like a man who'd been locked up in a hotel room with prostitutes on a three-day binge.

Probably because he had been.

This man? The one lifting a champagne flute, smiling with warmth and humility? This man was healthy, clean, and reunited with his former fiancée.

"I cannot begin to express to you what it means to stand here before all of you and announce my engagement to the love of my life," he continued. "Yes, for the second time." Some in the audience laughed. "But this time, I'm not letting her go."

His future bride, a stunning blonde in a sparkling pale blue chiffon cocktail dress, wiped tears from her eyes, careful to not smear her makeup. She reached a hand up to his. He clasped it, brought it to his mouth, and pressed a kiss on her palm.

The dissolute partier had regained his life, his company, and his soul mate. Violet could not have been more him proud of him.

And now it was time for her to go and leave him to the people in his life who mattered.

"Am I the only one who thinks this is freakishly awkward?"

At the sound of the familiar male voice, Violet quickly shoved her foot back into the stiletto she'd kicked off.

Breathing in Randall Oppenheimer's very masculine and expensive scent, she laughed. "Oh, no. Believe me, by the looks I've been getting all night, you could start a whole Facebook group."

Besides board members and Joe himself, of course, everyone in the room thought she was his ex-girlfriend. They'd "broken up" less than a week ago. All night long people had given her furtive and pitying glances. But she didn't mind. She'd likely never see any of them again.

Randall tipped his champagne flute back, looking effortlessly sophisticated and well-bred. With his khakis and light blue button-down, his short-cropped hair and boyish features, he could've been the poster boy for Yale fraternity life.

"You want to get the hell out of here?"

I'd love to. Fortunately, she caught the words before they flew out of her mouth. "I'd better not."

"Oh, come on. You don't seriously want to watch your former boyfriend sexing up his back-on-again fiancée, do you? Come on, we'll get on my hog and ride like the wind."

One eyebrow rose in disbelief. "You have a motorcycle?"

He looked away, half his mouth curling. "Nope. But it sounded pretty badass."

More likely he'd come in his family's limo. With his mom and dad. The Oppenheimers' law firm did a lot of work for Joe's company, so she'd run into them often during the course of her "relationship" with Joe.

"Can't really see myself straddling a hog in this dress anyways." She'd chosen the sleek Armani sheath dress to fit in with the wealthy crowd but not stand out. In her line of work, invisibility worked in everyone's favor.

"Oh, I can." Still looking away, the other half of his mouth joined the first.

"Someone's frisky tonight." The worst part of her job? The lies. "You better go easy on me. I just got my heart broken." But, after tonight, she'd never see Randall again. They didn't exactly move in the same circles.

"Come on." He leaned in, so close she could see the ghost of his beard. "You don't really think I'm buying the whole you-and-Joe thing."

A jolt of fear shot down her spine. Did he know? Nothing mattered more to her business than client confidentiality. Her reputation was her bond. "Now, why would you say that?" She tried to play it cool, but his answer mattered.

"Because he's old. And you're . . ." He eyed her from her mouth to the stiletto she was glad she'd put back on. "You're . . . *you.*"

Oh, thank God. He didn't know anything about her job. He just couldn't picture her with Joe. Well, he was right about that. At forty-eight, nearly twice her age, Joe Capriano was definitely not her type.

"Well, thank you. But Joe's a great guy, and I enjoyed my time with him very much." Once he'd stopped fighting her anyway.

"You *enjoyed your time* with the guy? Doesn't sound like he got anywhere near your heart." He said it with a cute smile, but she couldn't tell if he knew the truth or not.

He was a lawyer, worked closely with the board of Joe's company. He could have found out. "Your point?"

"Date me."

"Date *you*?"

He nearly spit out his champagne. "So, you'll date a man twice your age with a comb-over, but not me?"

What did she say to that? She couldn't date anyone she met through clients. "That's not a *comb-over.* That's a side part. Just ask Donald Trump." She smiled, hoping he'd drop it. Because he certainly wouldn't be asking her out if he knew her real identity.

But then his gaze sharpened, the teasing tone gone. "I really would like to date you. I've watched you for three months, waiting for this moment."

Her heart skipped, sending her pulse skittering. She almost

lost her composure. *Randall Oppenheimer* had waited three months for *her*?

Well, of course, he didn't know the real her. Her pulse settled down at the realization he thought she was a twenty-five year old "consultant" who'd graduated from Williams, came from an "important" family, wore designer clothes, and had tamed major partier Joe Capriano back into a polished and sober CEO of a billion-dollar company.

That was the woman he'd waited three months to ask out. Not her.

"Well, thank you, Randall. That's lovely of you to say, but I'm not really looking to date at the moment." No way could she start a relationship based on a lie. And she couldn't tell him the truth about her identity until she knew him long enough to be able to trust him. By that point, he'd feel duped. And the complications with the board and Joe? Forget it. Wasn't possible.

"I'll tell you a secret." He shoved a hand deep into his pocket, his cheeks turning rosy, and she could not believe how vulnerable this sophisticated, confident man had become. "I knew the moment I laid eyes on you that . . ." He blew out a breath. "Well, that you were special. And that I wanted to go out with you. And, come on, anyone could see there wasn't any fire between you and Joe. So, I'm not going to give up."

Her inner teenage girl gave a little sigh. That was about the sweetest thing a guy had ever said to her.

And he wasn't just some guy. He was a really good one. Not just his education, but his family. Sure, his dad ran the biggest law firm in the city and they had unbelievable wealth, but they were known for their down-to-earth kindness and generosity.

Okay, just stop it.

"Remember that night I dropped you at your apartment?"

She barely nodded. Of course she remembered that night. In the back of a town car with a gorgeous man she couldn't have. Yeah, she remembered.

"I wanted to kiss you."

She did *not* need to hear this. She couldn't date a guy like Randall. And not just because of client confidentiality, but because she just wasn't anything like what he thought she was.

First off, he knew her as Scarlet. Not Violet Davis. But worse?

She didn't live in a Fifth Avenue penthouse. She lived on a farm. And this outfit? All the others he'd seen her in? Purchased for jobs, thanks to a lucrative salary.

If he saw her on the farm, dressed in her shorts and tank top, wearing no makeup, would he still get all shy about asking her out? She didn't think so. "I should get going."

His look turned intense. "Let me give you a ride home. Please?"

Gazing into those intelligent blue eyes, she allowed herself just a moment to imagine going with him. Tossing aside everything—her job, her responsibilities, her history, and just letting herself be a *woman*. A reckless, fun-loving woman who threw herself into passionate relationships.

But then the memory of the social worker's words stabbed into her.

She'll likely never be able to trust or fully experience love.

Well, hell. So much for giving her imagination the run of the place. She simply wasn't that woman.

And yet . . . this tiny ember glowed deep inside her, the hint of hope that the woman could've been wrong. What if she *could* love? She'd had her grandma for four years, so maybe a seed had been planted. No, she hadn't loved anyone yet, but maybe she hadn't met the right man. She got that she'd never love like a normal person. But maybe she could feel *something*.

She'd never know unless she gave someone a chance. She looked at Randall. What if she gave him a chance?

Her phone chimed in her clutch. "I'm so sorry. It's my work phone." She gave him an apologetic smile. "It's the nature of my business." Well, no, it wasn't, but she needed a reprieve from considering what she couldn't have.

"Sure," he said, giving her a warm smile.

Pulling out her cell, she saw Emmie Valencia's name on the caller ID. "Please excuse me, I have to take this." She strode around the periphery of the room, looking for the bathrooms. "Emmie?"

"Hey, V, how's it going?"

"I'm all right." She wound her way behind the tables, evading waiters, and found her way to a long hallway. "How about you?"

"Not so great. I've got a problem."

Seeing that no one was waiting for the bathroom, she stepped inside, locked the door. "What's up?

"Are you interested in a job?"

"I am, actually." Violet took in the dark red wallpaper, crystal faucet handles, and gold accents of the spacious bathroom. The rich scent of roses made her wonder at the source, and she noticed the bowl of potpourri on the counter. Ah— potpourri. What a great idea for her wildflowers. As soon as she got off the phone, she'd text herself a reminder.

"Oh, good. You did such an amazing job with Caroline, you're the first person I thought of."

Uh-oh. "Go on." Emmie managed a rock band. Violet hoped very much she wasn't offering her a job in *that* industry.

"Yeah, so, this one's pretty important to me. It involves my brother."

"I thought your brother was in a band."

She hesitated. "He is."

Now she understood why Emmie seemed wary. Violet had made it clear she didn't work with rock stars. Businessmen could be decadent enough, but people in the music industry? She'd only gotten a glimpse of that world when she'd worked with Irwin Ledger's daughter, Caroline, but it had been enough for her to tell Emmie to lose her number when it came to rockers.

"You still there?" Emmie asked.

What should she do? "Yes. I hate to disappoint you, but I think you know I don't want to work with a rocker."

"My brother's not a bad guy. He's not an addict or anything."

"Okay, but he *is* in that world. And it's just not for me." Although, she shouldn't be so dismissive. She *did* need a job now that this one had ended.

"I know, I know. Believe me, no one knows better than I do. But my brother's not like that." She exhaled. "Okay, bottom line. The guys are partying too hard, getting too much attention in the media for their behavior and not their music, so Irwin's losing interest. They're good, V. And I'm not saying that because of my boyfriend and brother."

"Then again it *is* your boyfriend and your brother." She kept her tone light.

Fortunately, Emmie laughed. "I know. I know how it sounds.

Look, this is so important. And I know I can find someone else, obviously, but I saw what you did with Caroline. It's the way you do it, you know? My brother's really . . . stubborn." She sighed. "That's not the right word. God, I'm so worried you won't take the job that I can't even think. Okay, listen, our dad's always been really hard on him. Always putting him down and criticizing him. So, Derek has a hard time taking suggestions. It has to be delivered in just the right way and, V, you do it just right."

"Emmie, I want to help you out. I do. But I really don't want to work in the music industry." Did she need the money? Of course. Who didn't? But not at the cost of her sanity. Besides, she'd looked forward to spending some time this summer on the farm, developing new products. She closed her eyes, picturing acres of brightly colored flowers, the ocean and clear blue sky creating a stunning backdrop. She lived on the most beautiful parcel of land in the world. And she so rarely got to be there.

"I'm touring with them right now," Emmie said. "So you know if I can handle it, you can, too. Derek keeps the groupies off the bus. He's really respectful of me being there."

Leaning against the wall, she kicked off her shoe and rubbed her foot. "If Derek doesn't have a substance abuse problem, what exactly do you need me to do?"

"I need you to do just what you did with Caroline—give the guys something to do other than partying."

"So, I'm working with four guys?"

Emmie hesitated. "Yes. But, of course, we'll pay you for all four."

Holy cow. Four times her usual pay per month. "How long would you need me?"

"I don't know exactly, but it's a summer tour, so they'll be on the road for three months. Well, two and a half now. Are you free?"

"Yes." She'd hoped to push off choosing the next job for a little while, but she couldn't turn down this kind of money. She had to at least consider it.

But four rockers . . . oh, boy.

"V, I know this is last minute, and I know you said no musicians, but I wouldn't ask you if it wasn't really important. Please. I'll be here the whole time to help you."

"Why don't you give me some information, and I'll do the

research. Get back to you in a few days." When Emmie didn't respond immediately, she said, "Okay?"

"I kind of need you sooner than later."

"Which means?"

"Tonight."

Violet wheeled her suitcase to the elevator, listening as Francesca filled her in on the day's events.

"Cutler's can't seem to keep the ice cubes in stock," Francesca said in her throaty voice. "Customers are raving about them."

A gush of satisfaction flowed through her. Luckily for her, tea had become trendy, and people loved the idea of loose leaf. But the leaves lost their flavor pretty quickly, and some people didn't like the messiness of an infuser, so she'd had the idea to freeze the leaves—wrapped in pretty pink mesh—in ice cubes. Dropping one ice cube in six ounces of boiling water made a perfect cup of tea.

She pushed the button for the elevator. Glancing down at her outfit, she wondered if the super short shorts and thigh-high boots made her look more like a hooker than a groupie.

"Other than that . . ." Violet could hear her friend shuffling through papers. "Other than that, we've got a new order from Barefoot Contessa for the tins. They'd like to try ten tins of each flavor."

"Are you serious? Barefoot Contessa in East Hampton contacted us?"

The doors opened and she wheeled her suitcase inside, then pressed the button for the lobby.

"Yes. I got a call this afternoon."

"Way to bury the lede." Violet smiled. "Francesca, that's huge. I can't believe you didn't call me as soon as you got off the phone with them. That's fantastic. Oh, my God."

"You were at Joe's engagement party. Oh, and if it sells well, they might include us in their catalog."

"Are you freaking kidding me? This is amazing. This could change our lives completely." She could close her company, live on the farm full-time.

Well, if nobody contested her contract. Doubt worked its way back into her consciousness. She tried hard not to worry about things out of her control, but come on. Hard not to worry when all she had to prove ownership was a paper napkin contract. She'd fight, of course, but the more money she earned, the sooner she could own the land outright and put her fears to rest.

"Okay, anything you need me to do before I go?" Violet asked.

"You'll need to transfer funds into the business account, but other than that we're all set."

"I can do that electronically once I'm in the car."

"V, with all we've got going on, what about skipping this job? This is a great time for you to spend some time on the farm."

Her heart practically flipped over. She would love nothing more than to spend the summer out there. They'd gotten a firm handle on the wildflower tea products and were ready to launch the soap. She'd planned on developing stationery and honey next. Oh, and potpourri. She'd have to remember that one. Easy, simple to package.

"That sounds amazing, but I need the money."

"The sooner we get the products into the marketplace, the sooner you won't need to take jobs."

True. But she wanted to own the farm outright, so she needed the income. "You could ask Mimi to come out and help you. Just until she finds a job." Francesca's twenty-three-year-old daughter had recently completed her MBA at Columbia University and hadn't found a job she wanted yet. "Would she like to work on the stationery this summer?"

"I think she'd love it more than anything. But you know she's not going to give up her search for a corporate job. So, no, I don't see her coming out here. Even if we both know it's where her heart is."

The elevator rocked to a stop. "Okay, I have to go."

"So, you're going to take the job?"

She had to. Ever since Jedediah Walker had died, Violet had waited for someone to show up and kick her off the land. She knew he had two adult children. One lived overseas—Tokyo, she thought. The other, in the city. Neither one had ever visited him on the farm in all the years she'd known him, so she clung to the possibility they simply didn't care about the little bit of land at the tip of Long Island.

But another part of her knew better. They—or their lawyer—would show up—any day now—wanting to put it on the market. Would they accept her handwritten contract?

Even so, at the rate she was going in the lease-to-own plan they'd agreed on, it'd take twenty years to finally own the land. So any chance at earning a big chunk of cash . . . ?

"Probably. I have to meet them first."

The elevator doors parted.

"Okay, be in touch. Let me know how it goes."

"Thanks, Francesca. Talk soon." She tucked the phone into her leather messenger bag, hitched the laptop case higher on her shoulder, and reached for the handle of her luggage. Moving forward, she walked smack into the hard wall of a body. "Oh, my God, I'm *so* sorry."

Randall stood before her, eyeing her oddly. He clearly didn't recognize her.

"Randall?"

He cocked his head, gaze narrowing. Once recognition hit, his eyes widened comically. "Scarlet?"

Violet's gaze shot to Louis, the doorman. He gave her a barely noticeable shake of his head and hint of a look that said *You're in trouble now.*

Well, hell. Should she tell him her real name?

No, of course not. Then she'd have to explain why her boyfriend of three months had called her Scarlet. Oh, brother. She turned back to Randall. "What're you doing here?"

And just like that his features shuttered, his eyes went dark. "You left so quickly, I was worried." Gone was the earnest man she'd left in the restaurant.

"I have to work."

"So you said." He gave her a long look, and she hated that he was seeing her in this outfit. "On a Saturday night?"

She couldn't even imagine what he was thinking about her, standing in her Upper East Side lobby, wearing thigh-high boots and super short shorts. Oh, dear God. How did she get out of this one?

"What kind of consulting do you do, exactly?"

She gave an uncomfortable laugh. Normally, she had an easy, professional answer for everything. But it was *Randall*. And an hour ago he'd surprised the heck out of her by wanting to date her. Now . . . God, now she stood before him in thigh-highs.

"I'm afraid I don't have time to explain, Randall. I'm heading to the airport."

Giving him a warm smile, she stepped around him, continuing across the marble-floored lobby. "Maybe when I'm back in town we can grab a coffee and catch up."

"Scarlet," he said in such a commanding tone, she stopped to face him. "Can you please tell me where you're going? I don't understand."

She flashed a look to Louis, but he just rocked back on his heels and pressed his lips together in an expression of, *Hey, don't look at me.* "God. I hate what you're thinking right now." She blew out a breath. "I really am sorry, but I have to go."

His nostrils flared, and she could see him fighting for self-control. "Go where, exactly?" He strode over to her, leaning down to her ear. "Please tell me right now what kind of consulting job requires you to dress like . . . like . . ."

"Like what? What do I look like?"

"Well, frankly, like a hooker."

"I look like a hooker?" Oh, hell. She *had* gotten it wrong. Did she have time to change? She'd Googled groupies and had seen a lot of them in jeans. Plain—but tight—jeans. She turned to Louis for help.

The fifty-eight-year-old father of two tipped his head, giving a jerk, indicating she should come closer. "What're you supposed to look like?" he asked quietly.

"A groupie."

Mouth in a tight line, he assessed her thoughtfully. "The boots."

"Too much? Okay." Resting a hand on his desk for support, she pulled the boots off.

"Scarlet," Randall snapped. "What the *hell* are you doing?"

"I don't want to look like a hooker."

"You . . . What are you talking about? What do you want to look like? None of this makes any sense."

Ignoring him, she laid her suitcase on the floor and dug

through it until she pulled out a pair of wedges. She held them up to the doorman, who nodded with confidence.

"Okay." She slid her foot into the other sandal. "Great. Is my car here?"

"Waiting out front."

She stuffed the thigh-highs into the suitcase, zipped it up, and gave Louis an appreciative smile. "Thanks so much." Swinging the messenger bag over her head, she turned to Randall.

He looked a mixture of worried, angry, and confused. "Wait. Tell me what kind of job requires you to dress like that. Can you just give me that?"

"Give the kid a break," Louis murmured.

He probably thought she'd been Joe's *escort* for three months. *God.* How humiliating.

Louis relieved her of the suitcase, holding the door open for her, while Randall followed them out. It was fairly chilly for June, and she wished she'd brought a wrap. She'd only thought of summer and outdoor concerts.

Louis loaded the suitcase in the trunk as the driver set her laptop case and messenger bag on the backseat. Just before she slid in, Randall appeared at her side.

"I'm sorry for saying you're dressed like a hooker. That was uncalled for." Frustration pulled on his features. "I just . . . I don't understand. Did you bail on the engagement party to go to a concert, is that it?"

"No, of course not. I really do have a job to get to. I wish I could explain it to you, I do. But it's the nature of my work . . ." No, she couldn't talk to him about client confidentiality. He might put the pieces together and figure out the truth. That would be devastating for Joe.

"Go on."

"I don't want to leave you with terrible thoughts, but there's not much I can tell you. I really am dressed like this for a job." She smiled, because she knew that comment made it sound like she *was* a hooker. "But trust me when I say I don't do anything illegal, unethical, or immoral."

"I know that. Of course I know that. I'm sorry."

"No, *I'm* sorry, Randall."

"Can we talk later?"

"I'm not sure how long I'll be gone." She moved to get into the car, but he reached for her.

"Wait. Just . . . wait." He stood there confused. "I knew it didn't make sense for you to be invited to his engagement party. That's all kinds of fucked-up. And you just stood there, smiling, like you were proud of him or something."

"I *am* happy for him. She's the right woman for him."

"I just don't understand . . . *nothing* rattles you. The whole time I've known you, you've never shown an ounce of emotion."

Way to hit a girl where she hurts. "Joe and I had a nice time together, but it wasn't a love affair. Not like what he has with Judy. I'm happy for him."

"Is that what you want out of a relationship? Something *nice*?" He jammed a hand through his short, blond hair. "Do you remember that closing dinner? When you first started dating him? I was there, Scarlet, right behind you when he came out of the bathroom with another woman. You didn't yell or cry or anything. You just handled it so calmly. You didn't even look upset."

Well, of course she'd been upset. But jumping into the drama with her coked-out clients accomplished nothing. Her handling of each situation built the foundation of trust, cultivated an attitude of willingness with them. "Joe and I worked out our issues."

"Jesus, listen to you. Are you always this flat emotionally?"

He was really twisting the knife, wasn't he? No, she wasn't a passionate person—and she hated that about herself—but she certainly couldn't show emotion on a *job*.

But she couldn't explain any of this to him. "No, Randall, I'm not the most emotional person. So, maybe it's best we don't date, after all."

He shook his head, looking frustrated. "But I want to get to the woman underneath."

Oh. Oh, that was so nice. Okay, enough. She really couldn't take any more of this. "I'm sorry, Randall. I have to go now."

"Jesus, do you feel anything? *Is* there a woman underneath?"

And just like that she flashed back to the social worker talking to her grandma.

I'm afraid children without touch or nurturing lose the ability to form attachments for the rest of their lives.

She'll likely never be able to trust or fully experience love.

I wish I could be more encouraging, but it's unlikely she'll ever have normal relationships.

Sadness weighed heavy on her heart. "I sure hope so. Good-bye, Randall."